T0196523

AND
THE DEVIL
WILL
LAUGH

Also by Mima

Fire
A Spark before the Fire
The Rock Star of Vampires
Her Name is Mariah
Different Shades of the Same Color
We're All Animals
Always be a Wolf
The Devil is Smooth Like Honey
A Devil Named Hernandez

Learn more at www.mimaonfire.com
Follow on Twitter, Instagram and Facebook @mimaonfire

AND
THE DEVIL
WILL
LAUGH

Mima

iUniverse®

AND THE DEVIL WILL LAUGH

iUniverse books may be ordered through booksellers or by contacting:

iUniverse
1663 Liberty Drive
Bloomington, IN 47403
www.iuniverse.com
1-800-Authors (1-800-288-4677)

Because of the dynamic nature of the Internet, any web addresses or links contained in
this book may have changed since publication and may no longer be valid. The views
expressed in this work are solely those of the author and do not necessarily reflect the
views of the publisher, and the publisher hereby disclaims any responsibility for them.

Any people depicted in stock imagery provided by Getty Images are models,
and such images are being used for illustrative purposes only.
Certain stock imagery © Getty Images.

ISBN: 978-1-5320-5559-1 (sc)
ISBN: 978-1-5320-5560-7 (e)

Library of Congress Control Number: 2018909703

Print information available on the last page.

iUniverse rev. date: 08/14/2018

Acknowledgements

Special thanks to Jean Arsenault for her help with the gruelling editing process. Thanks also to Jim Brown for helping with the back cover synopsis, handing out booksmarks and everything you do to support my writing.

Last but not least, Rita Hustler, this one's for you!

CHAPTER

1

We all need passion in our lives. It's what makes us feel alive. It's what makes us want to get out of bed in the morning. It's a little spark that sends a shot of excitement through our bodies, through our souls. It's the little voice in our head that says the adventure has only just begun and the world has limitless possibilities. Without passion, we die. We may still be here in a physical sense but are we truly living?

Jorge Hernandez knew all about passion. It had been his life's focus. Whether it be from running one of the world's largest drug cartels during his youth or marrying the love of his life within weeks of meeting her; he was nothing without passion and to him there was no other way to exist.

Of course, it was this impulsive and passionate nature that could've easily thrown him off track. As a child growing up in Mexico, it was the same lust for adventure that caused him to grab his cousin's dirt bike, encouraging his younger brother Miguel to hop on the back. His enthusiasm didn't make up for his inability to properly handle the bike, causing a terrible accident that took Miguels's life. However, even as a child of 12, he knew that fear and guilt shouldn't hold him captive. This was an error many people made and perhaps that is why they punished themselves by turning out the flame of passion. For Jorge, this was not an option.

Now a man in his forties, Jorge Hernandez was always ready to take on anything and anyone. Many had tried to take him down but never succeeded and if they had, Jorge would've died screaming, his hand reaching for his enemies throat as he took his last breath. Giving into death with tears in your eyes was a sign of weakness; the expected response, but then again, isn't that what society wanted? Didn't they prefer people who were spineless minions, mindlessly following the rules?

Jorge's friend of 20 years and in many ways his *hermano,* Diego Silva, insisted that the world was full of sheep. The Colombian had long decided that, if given a choice, he would rather be the wolf. This was a stellar quality to have in a friend as well as a business associate, knowing that regardless of the situation, Jorge could always rely on Diego to rise to the top. He was a man who never backed down and took on a challenge with the same savagery as Jorge would've himself.

This particular morning was no different, as the two men walked through the hallway of a modest apartment building, where they were about to have a meeting with Tom Makerson, the assistant editor of one of Toronto's largest newspapers, *Toronto AM.*

"Fuck, what do they pay editors?" Jorge commented under his breath as they made their way through the dingy hallway.

Beside him, Diego let out a grunt while he twisted his face into the usual sour pose. "What you know about what people make? You're rich."

"I know that being an assistant editor to one of the largest papers in the country should pay enough to live in a decent fucking place," Jorge countered as they approached the man's door. Diego knocked. "Wouldn't you say?"

"It's a dying market," Diego insisted, as he continued to twist his face into an arrogant pose. "They just haven't admitted it yet."

"It's a dying market that's trying to kill me and Athas," Jorge referred to the politician he was backing in the upcoming federal election, a man who had become the disgruntled focus of *Toronto AM.* This was a problem that Jorge Hernandez planned to fix.

The door opened and a pale man in his 30s stood on the other side. While his eyes scanned over the two Latino men in expensive suits, he silently moved aside and let them into the studio apartment.

"What, you don't got a separate room to sleep in?" Jorge immediately pointed toward the bedroom/living room combo that sat within clear view of the tiny kitchen area. "Do they not pay you at this job? I do not understand."

"I'm a minimalist," Tom Makerson spoke bluntly and pointed toward a small table in the kitchen area as he closed the door. "Could I get you a cup of coffee?"

"No," Diego shook his head but glanced at Jorge as if looking for reassurance.

"No, none for me," Jorge replied and continued his original thought as they followed Makerson. "What the fuck is a minimalist?"

"It's ah," Tom started to reply while heading toward the coffee maker on the miniature kitchen counter. "It's like, someone who lives on as little as possible."

"Does that include *space*," Jorge glanced toward the next room. "Is that something to do with religion? Like a vow of poverty or some shit?"

"No, it's like," Tom poured the coffee and appeared nervous while doing so, spilling some on the counter. "It's a lifestyle choice."

"Being poor is a lifestyle choice?" Jorge shrugged as his Mexican accent seemed more prevalent than when they first arrived. "I do not understand."

"No, it's about living a more freeing lifestyle," Tom finished pouring his coffee and turned while nervously running a hand through his strawberry blond hair before gesturing for the two men to sit down. "Rather than feeling tied down with possessions we don't need, minimalist *choose* to live on as little as possible. Plus, you save a shitload of money. I might soon have a down-payment for a condo."

"Well, I hope it's bigger than this place," Jorge boldly commented as he sat at the table and Diego did the same, his brooding, brown eyes carefully watching Makerson. "So, we gotta talk about your boss. I don't got any more patience for that fat fuck, Sturk."

"Tell me about it," Tom sighed and looked down at the cup of coffee in his hand. "Try working for him. He's right and the rest of us are wrong. Even if we have proof, he won't listen."

"Oh yeah…" Jorge spoke with fake compassion in his voice.

"Well, he didn't have to work to get where he is," Tom replied as he appeared to relax and took a drink of his coffee before approaching the table to sit between the two men. "His father, Robert Sturk Senior, gave him the paper before he died, made him editor even though he doesn't know what the fuck he's doing, so the rest of us have to fix his messes. The only reason why he loves this job is because he's power hungry and with a paper, he has a lot of power."

"Even though he has a tendency of printing incorrect facts," Jorge calmly replied as he observed Makerson; this was a man he could own. With nervous body language, his pale eyes jumped between Jorge's face and his coffee. It was clear he knew who he was dealing with and wasn't about to retaliate. Robert Sturk Jr. wasn't as smart.

"That's what I mean," Tom insisted with sincerity. "How do you think I feel? This is my career and name on the line too. These stories about you and Alec Athas is a perfect example."

"So your paper," Jorge started as he reached into his pocket for a pack of gum but he noted the fear in Makerson's eyes and he couldn't help but grin. Perhaps he expected a gun. Jorge instead pointed a green packet toward the nervous man who quickly shook his head and looked away. Popping a piece of peppermint gum in his mouth, Jorge continued. "Has made some *really* disturbing accusations about me and my connection to Athas. It appears he is trying to disqualify his campaign. It's almost like they couldn't find anything wrong with Alec, so they come at me instead, the man who's advising him."

"That wasn't me," Tom insisted and shook his head. "I told him that he was out of line but he won't listen."

"I understand," Jorge attempted to calm him. "But tell me something, Mr. Makerson, if you ran the paper, how would you do so differently? I'm just curious."

"I would run it on the truth," Tom spoke with innocent eyes that jumped between Jorge and Diego, then back again.

"Which is?" Diego encouraged.

"Mr. Hernandez," Tom Makerson's eyes widened and he hesitated for a moment. "You're a successful Mexican businessman who decided to invest here, in Canada. I assume because your wife is from here? Now, you're the owner of many pot stores in Ontario."

"Close," Jorge quickly corrected him. "I was investing here before I met my wife, however, she is the reason I left Mexico to become a Canadian citizen. As for the pot stores, I have managed to take over many across the country. Unfortunately, some people, they wish to run these stores but do not always have the business expertise to do so efficiently and for this reason, we take it off their hands."

Tom nodded. He understood.

"And when you someday take over *Toronto AM*, you will recall this conversation and start reporting the news correctly," Jorge said as he moved forward in his seat, his eyes piercing through Makerson. "I would also, of course, appreciate an apology for reporting the *fake news* that suggests I have connections to organized crime."

"Of course," Tom quickly nodded. "Unfortunately, I don't see me taking over anytime soon. Mr. Sturk is pretty insistent that he will be the editor until he dies."

Jorge exchanged looks with Diego, who arched one eyebrow, a smug grin on his face.

"Humor me," Jorge said with a smile on his handsome face as his dark eyes danced around in delight. "Let us say you have an opportunity to take over in the near future. Wouldn't it be nice to know that you have people you can rely on for help when you need it? People you can call when you have a problem? As we were talking about previously, I like to invest in various businesses. Maybe a newspaper wouldn't be so bad. It keeps jobs in the city and it allows the public to know the truth. Wouldn't you agree?"

"I definitely agree," Tom nodded enthusiastically. "I understand."

"I am sure you do, *amigo,* I'm sure you do," Jorge grinned and glanced toward Diego. "We must go. We have other business to attend to and us," He stood up and gestured toward Makerson. "We will be talking again soon."

It wasn't until him and Diego were back in the hallway and walking toward the elevator that either of them spoke again.

"And Paige?" Diego asked as he hit the elevator button.

"Well," Jorge reached for his phone and glanced at the time. "I would expect that right about now, my wife is making sure that Tom Makerson is the new editor to *Toronto AM.*"

He wasn't wrong.

In a hotel room in east end Toronto, Paige Noël-Hernandez wore a black bob wig while dancing around for the fat, old man who was lying on the bed, wearing only his underwear and a T-shirt that barely covered his bulging stomach.

She played the seductress role to perfection. Wearing a 20's style red flapper dress and long white gloves, she slowly danced to 'Keep Pushin', a 90s dance song that carried a dark undertone.

Although the old man was clearly enjoying the show, it was when Paige eased onto the bed and crawled toward him that he seemed particularly excited, his pupils dilating as she moved closer and reached for her purse; a cheap bag she bought at some crappy kiosk in the mall.

"Now, I want you to close your eyes," She spoke softly, her voice as smooth as honey, causing him to automatically appear at ease. "I have a big surprise for you."

"I like surprises," The old man confided as if they were secret lovers. He was revealing his vulnerabilities to a woman who appeared understanding, her head tilted slightly, her blue eyes expanding in size. He followed her instructions and closed his eyes.

Reaching into her bag, Paige pulled out a knife, and with one quick movement stabbed the old man in the throat. His eyes suddenly flew wide open as he gasped and struggled, but they both knew it was too late. Paige Noël-Hernandez leaned forward, her voice a mixture of assertiveness and softness, and said, "Surprise!"

As he continued to struggle, his life disappearing before her eyes, Paige rose from the bed and grabbed her bag.

"Mr. Sturk," Her voice returned to its original, sweet disposition. "You've made it a sick game of ripping people apart in your paper. You made the fatal assumption that you were invincible and there wouldn't be consequences but then, one day, you picked the wrong person to fuck with. And that person, was Jorge Hernandez."

There was a look of knowing in his eyes as his struggle ended, his body limp on the bed. It was only after she watched him die that Paige Noël-Hernandez, one of the best assassin's in the world, walked into the bathroom and changed her clothes.

CHAPTER

2

"I told you it would've been faster for Jesús to get a cab from the airport," Jorge was quick to point out as he glanced around his kitchen letting out an exasperated sigh. Biting his bottom lip, he heard a beep and moved his phone away to see a text message from his daughter, Maria. Returning the phone to his ear, he continued. "I don't got all day."

"I know I know," Diego snapped on the other end of the phone. "But I didn't think traffic would be this bad when I dropped you off."

"Tell him there is an accident ahead," Jesús Garcia López could be heard in the background while the song *Enter Sandman* suddenly came on the radio.

"Oh fuck!" Jorge shook his head and let out a loud sigh. "Ok, well, do what you can."

He ended the call and glanced at his text message from Maria.

Papa, my drama teacher said I should take voice lessons this fall! She said that I'm a natural actress and having vocal training will increase my chances of becoming a star!

Jorge cringed. The last thing he wanted was for his 11-year-old daughter to become a fucking actress. He had dealt with many starlets while working in California during his 20s and 30s and having been privy to the seedy side of Hollywood, he didn't want his daughter to be part of it. Unfortunately, his assumption that she would grow bored of this acting shit had been wrong.

We will discuss it when you get home.

Suddenly recalling the last time he said these words, only to have his daughter wander the streets of Toronto alone in attempts of finding an acting school, he quickly sent another message.

I promise.

Giving an exasperated sigh, Jorge tossed his phone on the counter just as his wife walked downstairs. Glancing in her direction, a smile lit up his face when noticing that Paige had changed back into the dress she had wore earlier when meeting with Robert Sturk. Thin spaghetti straps held the smooth, red fabric over her lean body. Her blonde hair gently bounced on her bare shoulders as she walked across the floor. He thought the dress resembled something worn to bed and not modeled for some old fuck; however, his wife was more than capable of looking after herself.

"What do you think?" She asked in her soft, smooth voice as she twirled around to show off the outfit. "I was also wearing a black wig, tights, and long gloves....all of which have since been disposed of but I did save the dress to show you before destroying it."

Jorge's eyes drifting over her body as his desires stirred. All previous concerns over a postponed meeting and his daughter's Hollywood dream quickly slipping away as he stared at his wife. Reaching out, his fingers glided over the silky dress causing a warm sensation to roll through his body.

"I do not see any blood," Jorge commented as his breathe grew labored and she moved closer. He continued to caress the material while he stared at Paige in a trance-like state, barely blinking, his eyes fixated on her face. "Do not tell me you were gentle with our victim, *mi amor.*"

"Not unless you consider stabbing him in the throat....*gentle...*" She spoke this last word slowly, dragging it out as if to emphasize the intensity.

"And again," Jorge looked down at his hand trailing down her dress to touch her naked thigh. "Not even a single drop of blood on you. Your expertise, *mi amor,* they astound me."

"He was disrespecting my husband," Paige quietly replied as their eyes met again. "That was his first mistake but regardless of personal feelings, I'm *always* a professional."

Feeling his desire mounting, Jorge couldn't take it any longer. Pulling Paige's body tightly against his, his lips quickly met with hers as his hands slid under the dress to grasp her naked hips. Squeezing her against his body, Jorge felt his heart race with excitement while a soft moan escaped from the back of Paige's throat. His hands worked rapidly; caressing, exploring, while his lips slid down her long, thin neck, his tongue drifting over her collarbone and down the front of the flimsy dress. Finding her nipple, she gasped loudly as his fingers continued to roughly explore her body.

Suddenly pushing her against the wall, his lips again covering hers as their kisses grew aggressive, her hands roughly ran through his hair, greatly increasing Jorge's desires as he let out an involuntary moan.

Pulling away from his wife, his eyes drifted toward the nearby table and as if reading his mind, Paige began to walk in that direction and he followed, his fingertips gently touching her back as his hand drifted down her spine. He gave her a gentle push forward, forcing her upper body to come down against the smooth table as he unbuttoned his pants and pulled down his zipper. Spreading her legs, he slid inside, causing her to gasp. Immediately he felt waves of pleasure fill his body as Paige began to moan loudly, ordering him to move faster as she grabbed the edge of the table.

Following her instructions, his hand slid over her back and grabbed her shoulder as animal-like sound escaped from deep inside of him as he thrust. Paige tilted her head and he roughly moved one hand up, his fingers sliding through her blonde hair, over her scalp, allowing his fingers to gently slide over her face as her tongue reached out and softly licked the tip of his middle finger causing him to lose his mind. Thrusting harder, he was on the edge as she made loud, animal-like noises that automatically sent him into ecstasy, releasing his body into a state of inner peace that flowed through him when he finally stopped and moved away. His hand gently ran over his wife's back as she slowly stood up, still breathing heavily.

"Oh, *mi amor,* that was perfect," Jorge felt his heart continue to pound in excitement as he leaned forward and pulled up his boxers and pants. She turned around and their eyes met as he fastened his pants before leaning in to kiss her.

"I'm shaking," She quietly revealed.

"This is what I want," He replied and gave her another gentle kiss. "To rock your fucking world as much as possible."

"I think you might've rocked more than my world," Paige said with a grin as she leaned in and kissed him back. "I'm going to go take a quick shower before the others arrive."

"That sounds like a beautiful idea, *mi amor,*" He replied as his fingers reached out and grasped the strap of her dress. "And as much as I love this, I do think we should probably safely dispose of it."

"I was planning on it," Paige spoke in her usual, quiet tone as if in a deep state of relaxation. "But first I'm going to throw it in the laundry with super hot water before tossing it in the dyer. I think that should take care of anything incriminating."

Paige was a professional and completely thorough. She knew how to leave no evidence and destroy the bit that she had. He was in awe of her abilities.

"Whatever you wish, my love," Jorge replied. "And me, I think I might change before Diego and Jesús arrive. Assuming that ever happens with this traffic jam they are in."

"They'll get here," She assured him. "You have to relax. You can't control everything."

"Ah, but it is so much easier when I do," He teased as she started to walk away. Turning briefly, she winked at him before heading up the stairs. He reached for his phone. No updates.

Diego, are you any closer?

After a brief pause.

Honestly, not much.

Jorge tossed his phone back on the counter and slowly made his way upstairs. The shower off the master bedroom was already running and although he was tempted to join his wife, he changed his mind.

Glancing in a mirror, Jorge noted that a few more grey hairs sprung up around his ears causing his dark eyes to quickly look away. He tried to pretend aging didn't bother him but how couldn't it? He wanted to be young and powerful forever and yet, his health issues over the last year had proven that he was vulnerable; a word that made him cringe. A minor heart attack had left him feeling powerless. He was much healthier than he had ever been but there was always some concern. Life suddenly seemed much more fragile than it had in his carefree twenties, back when he smoked, drank and snorted coke.

How stupid we are in our youth!

Of course, he knew his wife was planning something for his upcoming birthday, which would take place at the end of August. He preferred to act as if it were just another day but when you have a family that loves you, that was impossible.

The bathroom door opened and Paige wandered out wearing a red robe, brushing her hair. Her eyes observed him.

"Are you ok, Jorge?"

"Yes, *mi amor,* I am perfect," He quickly answered as he sat on the edge of their bed. "This indeed has been a beautiful day."

"You don't have to worry about Sturk being a problem anymore and you're sure that this Tom Makerson will do as you ask?"

"Absolutely," Jorge insisted as he watched his wife place the brush on the dresser and walk toward him. She joined him on the bed. "He knows his place, unlike the other, he will work for me. There will be a retraction in the paper. Alec Athas, he also does not need to worry. Makerson will be…favorable toward him once the election is *finally* called."

"Should be the second or third week of September," Paige replied with a sigh. "It feels like we've been preparing for months."

"This is because, we have," Jorge reminded her with a smooth grin. "Opening a warehouse in Athas neighborhood, creating jobs in his district has made him king so having him voted in shouldn't be a problem, as long as the media doesn't get in my fucking way."

"I somehow doubt they will now," Paige spoke thoughtfully and the two shared a smile.

"Yes, *mi amor,* I somehow doubt anyone else will take that chance now that Sturk is dead."

"Let us hope not."

"And the police, they will put on a show," Jorge shook his head. "Just as they always do but as usual, they will be fucking useless and wait for it to blow over before they throw the file aside and forget about it."

"Have you spoken to someone to do so?" Paige asked as she turned toward him.

"Of course not, *mi amor,*" Jorge replied seductively. "But I do know the police. Most are burnt out and just want to get through the day without being shot, hoping for an early retirement and a fat pension."

Paige giggled. "I somehow doubt that's always true."

"People, they watch crime dramas and they believe what they see," Jorge insisted. "But I know people. Cops know they're powerless against the crime world and once they discover this, life is easier for everybody."

"From your lips to God's ears," Paige teased as she reached out and touched his hand.

"Ah, God!" Jorge laughed. "He has long ago given up on me, has he not? Now the devil, that might be another story."

Winking at his wife, Jorge leaned forward and gave her another quick kiss.

"Now, I must go downstairs," Jorge insisted as he stood up. "I do hope that Diego and Jesús are able to join us at some point today, preferably before Maria is finished of drama school for the day. Would you believe she now wants to take singing lessons?"

"Nothing surprises me with Maria," Paige replied with a smile, love in her eyes.

"This is true," Jorge agreed as he walked toward the bedroom door. "She is a wild child, that is for certain."

"Just like her father."

"Let's hope not, *mi amor,* let's hope not."

CHAPTER

3

"What kind of man would I be if I let my wife shovel snow?" Jorge automatically countered in a debate with Diego. This somehow occurred between giving his associates a hard time about being late and the actual business at hand. The Colombian had a way of always getting their conversations completely off track.

"A man of the 21st century?" Diego smugly replied as he reached for his coffee on the kitchen table, where Jorge was attempting to hold the meeting.

"Maybe even the 20th century, sir," Jesús teased. Jorge's longtime business associate ran a hand over his almost bald head as a lazy grin took over his lips. He then reached for his coffee with a chuckle while beside him, Diego showed less restraint as he broke out in laughter.

"Hey, you two, you say what you wish but I'm a gentleman and a good husband and I do not allow my wife to shovel snow," Jorge automatically halted upon realizing what he had suggested.

"Allow?" Paige gently asked with no judgment in her voice but a smirk on her face. Leaning toward his wife who sat beside him, he quickly pleaded his case.

"*Mi amor*, it is not to say you couldn't do it," Jorge quickly backtracked with a gentle reply as he reached out and touched her arm. "I mean that I would not be much of a man if I had my wife outside shoveling snow on a cold day. What next? I ask you to change the oil in my car? Maybe a tire? I think not!"

"Do *you* know how to change the oil in your car or a tire, for that matter?" Diego continued to tease and waved his hand flamboyantly in the air. Jorge shot him a dirty look.

"Can we now get back to the discussion at hand, please?" He asked while giving both Diego and Jesús a frustrated glance followed by a pleading look to his wife. "These two are holding up our meeting. We must pick up Maria soon."

"What about Chase?" Diego referred to another business associate who managed *Princessa Maria,* an upscale bar for the socially élite. "Can he get away to pick her up?"

"I think his hands are tied with your sister," Jorge countered and watched Diego automatically deflate in front of him. Jolene Silva was a sore spot for them all. "That is fine, this will not take too long. We just need to get off this stupid topic of shoveling snow and move on to what happened today."

"Very well," Diego replied and seemed to grow serious again.

"Now today, we took care of a problem," Jorge reminded them and glanced toward Paige. "Thanks to my lovely wife, we no longer have to worry about this fat fuck, Robert Sturk, since his newspaper seemed to want to bring us down. That will not be happening."

"So this man, sir, that you and Diego went to visit today," Jesús opened up his laptop. "He will not be a problem?"

"No, he is more manageable than Sturk," Jorge insisted, his eyes briefly met with Diego's. "He is a man who can create the image we need in this city. We have already discussed writing a more flattering piece on me and my association with Alec Athas which is, of course, perfect timing since an election could be called in the next couple of weeks."

"Sir, I do not understand why it matters because he will only win for his riding," Jesús inquired, tilting his head slightly. "Perhaps it is new to me, I've only been in Canada for a year, but how will he be helpful?"

"It depends on his role in the government," Jorge replied while reaching for his coffee. "My hope is that he gets voted in and ideally becomes a minister and even if not, he will have power and connections with people who can help us. And of course, my long-term goal is to groom him into a future prime minister for this country. With that, we can do much."

"First, his party must get voted in and even then, I think that's a long shot," Paige added while shaking her head. "I'm just not sure."

"Ah! But my love," Jorge insisted with a smile. "Always open your eyes to the possibilities. Anything is possible. Just look at our own lives."

"I'm surprised *you're* not running for prime minister," Diego commented with a smooth grin, followed by scrunching up his face while he shrugged. "You know, since you already think you are God, I figured it would be the next step for you."

"Ah, but Diego, I do not think I'm God," Jorge quickly corrected him. "But I did think of running for *presidente* while living in Mexico however, I decided against it. I felt that it would take too much of my time. Besides, you have to deal with other leaders and there are some, as you can imagine, I would not have much agreement with…"

"I can think of a few you'd probably have whacked," Diego cut in with laughter in his voice.

"Well, yes, but this is beside the point," Jorge insisted. "Back to the topic at hand. We have taken care of the problem at *Toronto AM* and so now, I believe everything will get back on track. I'm confident that Makerson will write a flattering article that will create respect for me and Athas while apologizing for the terrible things said by the former editor."

"Are we sure he will become the new editor?" Jesús inquired while glancing up from his laptop.

"Yes, this has been looked after," Jorge replied.

"Sir, the comments Sturk has here in this article, they are quite terrible," Jesús shook his head. "He talks about your connections to the cartel in Mexico, how you only came here to take over the drug industry in Canada, specifically marijuana and how you're a dangerous man."

"So, the truth?" Diego asked while twisting his lips together.

"That's a very extremist version of the truth," Jorge insisted although he knew everything the paper said was correct. "I will make sure that in the apology article Makerson writes, he will also comment on how my 11-year-old daughter found this paper and read the article. What a horrible thing for a child to see!"

Of course, Maria had already knew of his role in the cartel, something that sent a sharp pain through his heart when he recalled her breaking the news earlier that year. This was thanks to her *puta* of a mother, a woman who was now deceased. However, the article added extra information that managed to make his otherwise strong, feisty daughter to cry; that was the day Robert Sturk signed his own death certificate.

Diego's face became serious and he nodded.

"At any rate," Jorge glanced toward Jesús who appeared the most concerned. "This matter will be sorted out and meanwhile, Marco has created fake accounts and made multiple remarks under the story, suggesting it is false. People who supposedly worked for us that claim it is lies and an offensive stereotype of Mexican-Canadians. Also, we created suggestions that Mr. Sturk was a member of a white supremacist group, here in Toronto."

Beside him, Paige cringed and they shared a look. It wasn't that long ago that they took on some of these very people. Although things were quiet in recent months, Jorge doubted it would last. He had a bad feeling that the worse was yet to come.

"Do you think this will work?" Jesús inquired. "Do people read these comments?"

"Marco has had many good ideas," Jorge referred to the company's IT professional. Together the two had created a series of unflattering memes suggesting that Sturk was racist and was attempting to sway his readers toward his white nationalist point of view. They located an image of the editor holding a Toronto Maple Leafs baseball cap in his hand with a dismal expression on his face. Above the image were the words, '*When you were hoping for a pointy white hat but are stuck wearing something embarrassing instead.*'

"Ah, very good, sir," Jesús replied and nodded. "I feel like I am never in Toronto lately, so I miss a lot."

"This will be changing," Jorge insisted. "Once I take over everything, I would prefer to hire someone else to take care of the details and you stay here as a...problem solver"

"What about Sylvana?" Diego asked referring to Jorge's brazen cousin. "Look, she's been around since day one and I feel she can do more."

Jorge considered the idea for the first time. Originally he hired her to spy on his office staff, back when his main focus was moving cocaine through Canadian clubs. However, Jorge's Mexican associate now preferred he take over the Canadian pot industry. It was legal, meaning there were no limits to the money they could make. Someone else was taking care of the cocaine side of things which made Syvana's presence at the office less necessary.

"You know, this could work," Jorge nodded and fell silent for a moment. "Jesús I will leave this up to you. This is your area of expertise. Maybe we need to have a conversation and see what she thinks."

"I suspect that Sylvana could do anything she puts her mind to," Paige quietly insisted and Jorge merely nodded. "She's smart and knows how to deal with people."

"Yeah and she's got a mouth," Diego abruptly added. "I don't think anyone wants to go up against her."

"And she's beautiful," Jesús added. "This could also help. People often find beautiful women quite intimidating. Especially, if they are also strong."

"Whatever you think," Jorge shrugged and ran a hand over his face. "I do not care. I can't keep track of who does what anymore, however, it is only a few key people at the top that know the truth about this company. This is our inner circle and we must be careful who we have in it. This is something we've learned the hard way."

Everyone glanced toward Diego, whose sister had given them a great deal of trouble in previous months. Although she had calmed since that time, Jorge wasn't sure he would ever trust the beautiful Colombian again. There would always be a whisper in the back of his head suggesting he watch her carefully, which was more effort than it was worth. If she had not been like family, there was no way that Jolene would still be alive.

"I think, maybe she has a little more perspective now," Diego calmly replied, his usual vigour disappeared; Jolene was like a poison to the group. "You know, after the pregnancy…and everything."

No one commented. It was a touchy subject.

"Yes, well, some things are not meant to be," Jorge offered with a sigh and glanced at his wife. Knowing that his level of sensitivity was often questionable at best, he noted that Paige seemed to approve of this remark. "Unfortunately, this was one such case and perhaps it was for the best."

"She's not taking it well," Diego quietly commented and shook his head. Looking toward the table, everyone fell silent.

"That's normal," Paige calmly offered, her voice immediately infusing hope in Diego's face. "Any woman who has lost a baby would feel the same. It's not easy."

"But the drugs," Diego replied, his attention was on Paige as if they were the only two talking. "Jolene did cocaine during the early part of her pregnancy and although it may not have been for that reason, she still blames herself."

"Maybe she is right," Jorge couldn't help but comment. "But on the other hand, I do believe that Maria's mother, she may have done the same before knowing she was pregnant. This is not something she ever admitted but it's a feeling I have. In the end, does it matter who or what is to blame? Does it change anything?"

"Maybe *you* should tell her that," Diego commented with a certain boldness in his eyes that was unmistakable. "She might listen to you."

"I am not getting involved in your sister's drama," Jorge shook his head. "This is not my place and I'm not interested in bonding with Jolene. No, this is for you. This is for Chase. This is not for me."

Although they thought Chase was the father, no one was certain. Being a naïve man in his 20s, he hadn't pushed the subject.

"Chase, he's not doing so well either," Diego continued and Jorge felt like he was being pulled into something again. "I guess cause losing this baby brought up everything with.."

"Diego, again, this is something that I must put aside," Jorge commented. "You and him are close, so this is something you need to talk to him about. It is not for me to get involved."

The table fell silent and although they had gathered together on a high note, it was quickly sinking in that problems never ended.

CHAPTER

4

"Diego, do you not have your own home?" Jorge's voice was full of humor as he entered the living room on the following Saturday morning. Having a quiet conversation with Paige, the Colombian appeared quite comfortable with both his legs pulled up on the couch and a cup of coffee in hand. They were clearly discussing something of an important nature. "Or did you recently move in when I wasn't looking?"

"We have a meeting later, remember?" Diego abruptly asked, immediately changing his tone. "I'm just early."

"You were here when I left to run errands this morning and two hours later, I'm back and you're *still* here," Jorge continued to tease him while glancing at his wife.

"We went to the Farmers Market for a bit and now we're just hanging out and talking," Paige replied with a smile lighting up here face.

"Oh yeah, about what?" Jorge asked as he sat on a nearby chair, his gaze boldly on Diego. "New boyfriend or what?"

Jorge had a vague interest in Diego's personal life. For a man who was so strong and defiant in the professional world, he was surprisingly weak when it came to matters of the heart. This was most clear when he fell in love with their mutual work associate, Chase Jacobs. The two had been roommates for a couple of years after first moving to Toronto and although Diego had pined over his heterosexual friend, in the end, he accepted that the feelings wouldn't be reciprocated.

"Are you kidding?" Diego asked as he dramatically swung his arms in the air while making a face. "I've been too busy looking after Jolene since her miscarriage. At some point, she took over my entire life. Always at my condo and then Chase would come over and I'd practically be held hostage in my own fucking bedroom while they talked about everything."

Diego's original strength appeared to suddenly melt into a pile of slush as he emphasized his last words, turning his attention back to Paige, he shook his head. His brown eyes full with disappointment. Not that it was a surprise. Jolene brought misery wherever she went. Diego's sister had certainly made Jorge's own life more difficult in the previous months when she became involved with men who wanted him dead. Although she claimed to have been on his side attempting to defuse the situation, he didn't trust her.

"It's like adding insult to injury," Paige gently replied as she reached out and touched Diego's arm. "But at a certain point, you have every right to ask them to leave."

"Tell them to move their fucking pity party somewhere else," Jorge spoke abruptly. Although he had compassion for Jolene when she first lost her baby, he now felt she was using this to manipulate everyone around her. It was a cynical point of view but her many deceptions made him apathetic.

Paige attempted to hide her laughter but was unsuccessful while Diego looked slightly stunned.

"Look, Diego, you were there for her during this whole ordeal and that's a beautiful thing. You are family, after all, and that is what family does during tragic times," Jorge spoke frankly as he moved to the edge of his seat. "However, that was months ago and at a certain point, what more can you do? She needs to get her life back together and Chase…I do not understand that man's need to feel controlled and manipulated by women but then again, who am I? I am not a psychologist. The point is that there is nothing more you can do. She needs to get her life back on track."

"I know and she isn't at my place as often but," Diego shook his head and let out a sigh. "The calls! The calls, they never end. I do not know what else to do."

"Recommend a psychiatrist and move on," Jorge spoke bluntly. "You are a busy man and when your workday has finished, you must enjoy your life and not deal with Jolene's ongoing drama. And Diego, if you have not already noticed, it never ends. It is like the *telenovelas* my mother used to watch."

"Her life is definitely a soap opera," Diego agreed and glanced down at his hands. "I can't even sort out my life, how can I help her?"

"This is a challenge we all have," Jorge replied as he jumped up from his chair while glancing at his iPhone. "Ah, I see that Alec is almost here. *Perfecto.*"

Twenty minutes later, the four of them sat in Jorge's cluttered office. Although the couple had lived in the house for months, he still hadn't unpacked most of his belongings he had shipped from Mexico. In part, this was because Jorge wasn't even sure he liked the house enough to stay. However, they were desperate to get out of a dingy apartment and possibly jumped at the house a little too fast.

"So the election," Jorge started right away, knowing that he soon had to pick up Maria from a friend's house. "It will be called in the next week or two, is this correct?"

Across the desk from him sat Alec Athas, dressed as if he was heading to the office rather than a Saturday afternoon meeting. Of course, he was a politician so it was important to always present himself in a professional manner. The Greek man was groomed to perfection.

"I believe so," His answer was non-committal but encouraging, in a typical politician style as he nodded and took a deep breath. "So, are we going to talk about what took place this week? Or are we going to pretend that the man who was trying to ruin my reputation isn't suddenly dead?"

Jorge didn't like how Alec's eyes automatically shifted to Paige, who was sitting beside him. Not that his assumption about the murder mattered; Alec Athas had a complicated history with Jorge's wife and for that reason, would never stir the pot. The two dated many years ago and although the love was long gone, it was clear that a bond still existed. Although this was a benefit in situations such as this one, it still didn't sit well with Jorge. The man was only part of their lives at Paige's insistence along with the fact that he was a politician; one could never have too many in their pocket.

"There's nothing to talk about," Jorge insisted with a shrug while on the other side of his wife, Diego grinned and looked away. "The man had an unfortunate encounter at a hotel, probably with a prostitute and was murdered. These things, they happen if you hang around with the wrong people. Of course, this is fortunate for us. The assistant editor will take over and unlike Sturk, this man has a favorable impression of both of us. Athas, this will be helpful with the election so soon."

"So you had nothing to do with this murder?" Alec pushed a little further than he would've when they first met. "It's just a coincidence?"

"Ah, but there are no such things as coincidences, that is what Paige always tells me," He grinned and winked at his wife. "My feeling is that this man created many enemies in Toronto and karma, it has a way of catching up."

"I'm not sure any of us should feel reassured by that," Alec replied and bit his bottom lip. "Look, I do appreciate everything you've done for me, Jorge but…sometimes it feels like things are getting out of control."

"Ah, see this is where you and I differ," Jorge moved ahead in his chair and leaned on his desk, his eyes fixated on Alec. "To me, things are more in control. We have a man who looks at both of us more favorably and this could only mean good things for all of us."

Alec hesitated for a moment before glancing at Paige then back at Jorge. "Ok, so, can we be up front. Remember, I was *there* when you shot that man at the dispensary earlier this year. Are we going to brush that under the rug too?"

"There is no one brushing anything under the rug," Jorge commented with a shrug but at the same time, his voice carried the strength of someone who one should never challenge. "As I told you then, this man, he was a white supremacist who decided to target my businesses because he was unhappy that the white man doesn't own everything, including most of the marijuana business in the area. He was going to shoot my employee and possibly all of us, so of course, we must defend ourselves."

"We didn't go to the police," Alec reminded him, once again glancing toward a calm Paige, who appeared unfazed by this conversation. "Where did his body go?"

"I do not think you really want the answer to that question," Jorge replied with a shrug and gave him a cold stare. "The police, they have this way of making situations far more complicated than necessary and at the end of the day, how many crimes do they actually solve? Had we called, what would happen? The police would blame me for protecting my business and everyone's life in that store. They would've been more concerned about the dead white boy on the floor and put us on trial as if we were making up everything. *You,* my friend, would've been deemed too controversial by association and kicked out of your party. Do you not see that the police, they do not want people to defend themselves because it makes their job too complicated."

Alec didn't reply but took a deep breath but Jorge quickly cut him off at the heels.

"Me, I know how things work and I'm not willing to play games with the police," Jorge's words were strong now, while his eyes stared through Alec. "As for what happened earlier this week, I tell you not to worry and that is what you should do. Concentrate on your campaign."

"I think," Paige finally spoke, her eyes meeting with Jorge's as they silently communicated. She was calm, as usual, her voice soothing as a mother's touch. "We have to leave the past in the past. As for this week, it's clear that Mr. Sturk was an arrogant and obnoxious man and whatever happened to him was probably brought on by himself. It was simply a matter of fate."

Alec Athas quickly glanced at Paige and seemed to accept her words with a hopeless shrug. "As long as I don't get put on the spot by either the police or reporters."

"There is no blood on your hands, Athas," Jorge assured him. "What would you know? You, of course, being a religious man, will send your *thoughts and prayers* to his family and if pushed, simply state that you enjoyed how he *challenged* you but felt his facts, they were often confused. Considering he was found in a dirty hotel room half-naked, it kind of speaks of his character, wouldn't you say?"

"I can't deny that fact."

"Now, can we move on from this depressing topic," Diego suddenly spoke up, his words abrupt and sharp. "What's this meeting for? I don't got all day."

"Oh *now* you're suddenly in a rush to leave, are you?" Jorge teased with a slight grin on his face. "Well, we wanted to go over a few things before the election is called. Alec," He turned his attention back to the politician. "Do you have a girlfriend?"

"What?" Alec looked slightly stunned by the question.

"Ok, then *boyfriend*? I don't particularly care," Jorge pushed further. "I am thinking that maybe this would be a good time to prance someone around in front of cameras, to show your romantic side. It seems that a lot of women respond to this kind of thing and since they are probably more likely to vote with their heart than men, perhaps we should use this?"

"I'm single…*and* straight, for the record," Alec looked slightly perturbed by Jorge's comment. "What does that have to do with anything?"

"Women appreciate a committed man," Jorge insisted with an innocent shrug. "You know, it's not too late to pull some woman out in the public eye and make sure you're seen together. I would suggest a white woman, everyone loves white women."

"Oh yes, *everyone* loves white women," Paige quipped.

"Look," Alec appeared frustrated, moving to the edge of his chair. "I don't have to pretend to be in a relationship to appease voters. This isn't how it works."

"Oh, isn't it?" Jorge said with laughter in his voice. "Look at your opponents, they are all married so, they will seem more stable than you."

"That's ridiculous," Alec complained. "Married people aren't necessarily more stable."

"But people, they want to believe this," Jorge commented while across from him, Paige shrugged and made a face.

"But the single card," She gently butted in. "That could also work. There are a lot of single women voters too. Didn't I hear statistics stating that many people in Canada are living alone? Possibly single too? We have to remember that demographic. Maybe he should speak to them and not, you know, the working, middle-class families. Don't they get enough attention?"

Alec raised his eyebrows and nodded. "She's right. As a single man, I know *my* demographic is often overlooked."

"And disrespected," Diego jumped in once again. "Everyone acts like single people only live for the next party and aren't responsible. That's not fucking right."

"You make good points," Jorge nodded while Alec watched him with skeptical eyes. "You appeal to the singles for many reasons. Ok, forget what I said, try to avoid being seen with any women throughout the campaign because you will seem 'getable' and maybe, perhaps that will win you some voters. Maybe some women will see this *Greek God* and decided to work for free on your campaign, I don't know. This is good. I like it."

Although Diego was nodding enthusiastically, both Paige and Alec appeared unsettled by the idea. Not that Jorge cared. It was important that at least one of them thought like a politician.

"Look, I'll listen to what people want and take it from there," Alec attempted to reason but Jorge was already rising from his chair, indicating the meeting was over. "I don't think we have to play any kind of games."

"Oh, quite the contrary," Jorge commented as he reached for his phone. "As I have told you all along, people, they do not know what they want. It is your job to *tell* them what they want and make it seem as if it is their idea."

"And what?" Alec spoke hesitantly. "Flirt with women to get their vote?"

"I don't care," Jorge grew tired of the topic as he rushed across the room. "Flirt, take selfies, do whatever you want. Just get voted in."

Everyone looked as if they wanted to speak all at once but Jorge was already halfway to the door.

"Now, if you will excuse me, I gotta pick up my daughter."

And with that, he left the office.

CHAPTER

5

"This is not the birthday surprise I was hoping for this morning, but ok," Jorge teased Paige as he leaned across their bed to give her a quick kiss. The smell of bacon cooking filled their bedroom. Downstairs, dishes were rattling, cupboard doors closing and Maria was singing along to the radio. This made him smile.

"It means a lot to her," Paige whispered while his eyes scanned her body. There was something about a woman who just woke up, a certain vulnerability that was incredibly sensual and beautiful. Wearing a thin red robe over her nightdress, her hair pulled back in a ponytail, she pointed downstairs. "Maria suggested that I take a shower and 'get pretty' for our breakfast but I'm more concerned that the house will burn down, so I'm going back downstairs."

Jorge grinned but didn't reply as his wife left the room. He watched her until she disappeared from his sight. Dismal thoughts of growing older filled his head and yet, he felt the need to play along with the celebration. Of course, his family and friends loved him and he appreciated these beautiful gestures but it would've been his preference to forget his birthday.

In truth, Jorge never thought he would make it to 45. For a man who had taken a lot of risks in his day, he was lucky to be alive. The life he knew wasn't what he would've predicted during his youth, once assuming he'd always be a lone wolf with no emotional ties. In many ways, it was easier but it certainly wasn't an incentive to get out of bed in the morning. Paige and Maria filled his heart.

Reaching for his phone, he immediately scanned through his text messages. Ignoring a Happy Birthday wish from his estranged mother, he moved on to a message that was from Jesús. Although his longtime associate sent birthday wishes, he also included an article that talked about the murder of Robert Sturk. It was the usual dog and pony show from the police; they were investigating every angle, talking to people, spending endless hours on the scene, all the usual bullshit that added up to nothing. Jorge grinned when he recalled a conversation with someone high up in law enforcement that told him that they had no leads, no evidence and weren't sure how to handle the matter.

The sound of feet pounding on the stairs pulled his attention away from the phone, as his 11-year-old daughter flew into the room and pounced on his bed with excitement in her eyes.

"*Feliz cumpleaños, Papa!*" She lurched forward and planted a wet kiss on both his cheeks and he quickly pulled her into a hug.

"Ah!! What a beautiful way to start the day!" Jorge gave her a quick kiss before she pulled away and sat back on the bed, watching him with adoring eyes. "I heard you were cooking me breakfast. How lucky am I?"

"I was," She shyly shrugged and looked away. "I wasn't doing very well though so Paige took over."

"Ah, do you think maybe you should be downstairs helping her?" Jorge asked and raised an eyebrow. "You must not expect Paige to do everything if it was your idea."

"I know, I am," Maria insisted as she reluctantly stood up. "I just wanted to come see you for a minute while she…fixes things."

"Ah, and what things would that be, *niñita?*" Jorge teased while his daughter started to giggle.

"I may have some eggs mixed in with the bacon…and maybe, some egg shells too," She gave him an innocent look as she made her way toward the door. "*Papa*, I am not a very good cook, I am afraid."

"But you will learn…"

"Maybe," She shrugged. "But Papa, when I'm a world-famous movie star someday, I will have my own people hired to do things like cook for me, so I won't need to know."

With that, she rushed out of the room and Jorge grimaced at the thought. Of course, he wanted his daughter to have a successful life but he felt his stomach tense every time she suggested becoming an actress. Such a terrible profession, full of morally bankrupt people! Of course, he was perhaps throwing rocks from his own glass house.

The smell of delicious food continued to reach him, pulling Jorge out of bed. Rather than go downstairs, he decided to first take a shower. Something told him it would be a long day.

A couple of hours later, he found himself walking through the door of *Princesa Maria,* a bar that was part of Hernandez-Silva company. The upscale club was well-known throughout the city as the place where social elitists gathered for meetings, dates, and celebrations. They had even made it to a few 'top ten night spots' lists. Of course, Jorge made sure of this fact but regardless, it gave bragging rights to the club's manager, Chase Jacobs.

Not yet open for the day, Jorge locked the door on the way in and headed to the office. Nestled behind the bar, Chase had left his office door open. He sat behind the desk, his laptop opened and a cell phone pressed against his ear. Glancing at Jorge, he nodded, a grin attempted to take over his lips but quickly disappeared.

"I have to go," He spoke bluntly into the phone as he loosened his tie. "One of the delivery drivers is here."

After a slight pause, Chase took a long, frustrated breath. He frowned and finally said an abrupt "Yup" before ending the call and tossing his phone on the desk.

"Do I ever have to ask?" Jorge asked.

"No," Chase replied. "I can't deal with this anymore."

"Nobody, my friend, can deal with Jolene," Jorge shook his head and bluntly continued. "See, this is the thing we learn in our 20s. Be careful what you put your dick into because sometimes, these women have a way of haunting your life. Look at me, I didn't learn until my 30s and Maria's dead mother still haunts me from her grave."

"You would've thought I had learned by now," Chase shook his head and Jorge couldn't help but laugh. His friend was incredibly naïve. Not only had he managed to impregnate a woman he didn't even like at the tender age of 18, he later went on to have two more babies with her before they divorced. His choices in women since had been less than spectacular.

And then there was Jolene and her honey pot.

"My friend, you must follow your passions but when your passions entice you to women who eat your soul, it is time to step back and reevaluate why your dick hates you," Jorge spoke bluntly, causing Chase to laugh and nod.

"I think you have a point," He replied as he stretched, displaying his massive frame. Although he was soft-hearted by nature, Chase Jacobs was a large man who made him very valuable on more than one occasion. Half indigenous, he was originally from small-town Alberta, a place where his two remaining children still resided.

"You are what? Twenty-five, twenty-six years old?" Jorge asked with a shrug. "There aren't many years left where you can blame such mistakes on youthful ignorance. This is the time, my friend, to reconsider the women you invite into your life."

"I know but with Jolene, it was different," Chase said with a frown on his face. "We had worked together for years before anything happened and at the time...I guess I wanted to believe it was real. In the end, it was a fucking mess."

"Everything, my friend, with Jolene, is a fucking mess," Jorge commented gruffly. "She is poison and me, I would rather keep her away from everything."

"She wants to return," Chase warned him. "She flips from being super vulnerable, to very fiery, wanting to jump back in with both feet. It's almost as if she wants to be in danger. Its like she has two personalities."

"Well, I don't think this is news," Jorge grinned and grabbed his beeping phone, glanced at it and slid it back into his pocket. His mother was attempting to call him. He would not answer. "We can only learn."

"It's hard though," Chase confessed with a shrug. "When Jolene first told me about the baby, I was furious. I didn't want to have another child but then, when she had the miscarriage, it brought up everything with.... just *everything*."

He, of course, was referring to the death of his oldest son, Leland. It had happened a few years earlier and Jorge was aware that the anniversary of that terrible day was quickly approaching. It was something that he couldn't fathom and had it been Maria, Jorge would've lost his fucking mind.

"The two experiences, they are not the same," Jorge gently insisted and hesitated briefly before continuing. "But in many ways, they are the same. It is a loss, either way."

"I felt *gutted* all over again," Chase commented with an intensity in his eyes. "It was a rough time but you know, I kind of resented having to experience it with Jolene. I mean, when Leland died and I had to deal with my ex, it was different. In a way, it almost healed our relationship but with Jolene, I felt like I didn't even want to deal with her but yet, I had to...."

"As I've said, she is poison," Jorge insisted with a shrug, growing tired of this discussion. "There are no other words."

"I think she's going to your party tonight," Chase warned.

"Who the hell invited her?" Jorge immediately began to complain. "Me, I do not even want a party but why would anyone invite her?"

"I think she invited herself."

"Really?" Jorge made a face. "How did she know?"

"I think she overheard Diego on the phone," Chase replied. "That's what he told me. I can't see him inviting her under any circumstances."

"Yes, there is a lot of bad blood between Jolene and all of us," Jorge said and recalled how the woman who was once a huge part of their organization was now ostracized. "It is not good, you know? And yet, what can we do with her?"

Chase answered with a shrug and then changed topics.

"By the way, Happy Birthday!"

"Ah, birthdays," Jorge shook his head. "Like most holidays, they are meaningless, however, my family, they love me and want to celebrate, so what can I do?"

"I think Diego is more excited than anyone."

"Diego, he likes to organize parties," Jorge grinned. "But it is nice. I cannot say it's not kind of him. And it is the first birthday I am celebrating with my wife."

"That's right, you didn't meet her until after your birthday last year," Chase said with a grin on his face.

"Yes, I keep telling her, she was my late birthday gift," Jorge said. "This morning, her and Maria made me breakfast. Originally, it was Maria's idea but it didn't work out so well so Paige took over. It was nice."

"Yes, Maria texted me that she was planning to cook you breakfast this morning," Chase laughed. "It's pretty bad when I hear from your kid more than my own."

"Ah! Your children are young," Jorge commented but deep down, they both knew that their step-father had taken over Chase's role as soon as he left Alberta. "To Maria, you are family, she considers you one of her favorite people and to me, this is good. I want my daughter to have people looking out for her, as you often do."

"Will she be here tonight?" Chase asked as he pointed toward the wall, indicating the VIP section where Jorge's party was to take place.

"Unfortunately, no" Jorge insisted. "And although you know I'm not a man who follows the rules, I would prefer she not be in a bar. I will be having dinner with my family before we come here to meet the others for a few drinks. That is my plan for this evening."

"I look forward to it,"

Jorge didn't reply but instead glanced again at his beeping phone.

CHAPTER

6

"*Excelente!*" Jorge commented triumphantly as he tossed his phone back on the table while Paige reached out and gently touched his arm. They were alone in the private VIP area of *Princesa Maria,* where his birthday party was to start in 20 minutes. It was rare for the couple to be early but on this occasion, Jorge's day had gone unusually smooth and they decided to have a quiet drink before the others arrived.

"What was that about?" Paige grinned as Jorge reached for the bottle of red wine and poured them each a hearty glass. "You usually aren't this excited to see anything on your phone."

"Ah, but this time, *mi amor,* it is good news for a change," Jorge commented as he leaned in to kiss her. "Makerson wrote a brilliant article that erases most of the damage Sturk created. Just another beautiful event in my day! If I get laid tonight, then this will be the perfect birthday!"

"There's a good chance of that happening," Paige quietly commented as the door slid open and Diego hurriedly walked in carrying a large gift bag, his eyes fixated on Jorge.

"The world, it must be coming to an end!" Diego remarked abruptly as he dropped the gift bag on the table beside Jorge's glass of wine before sitting on the other side of him. "You two, you are never early."

"What can I say, my friend, the day went rather smoothly for me," Jorge reached out to peek into the gift bag but it was full of colorful paper and resembled a giant Easter decoration, "This is for me?"

"Of course! It's your birthday!" Diego insisted with a playful grin as he glanced at Paige.

"I told everyone, no gifts, I need for nothing."

"It's not about that," Diego insisted. "Come on! Open it!"

Jorge reluctantly picked up the gift bag and began to remove the colorful paper and then he suddenly hesitated. Reaching inside, he pulled out an autographed copy of The Beatles *Abbey Road* LP. In stunned disbelief, he stared at it, slowly turned it around and then back to the front. "Oh my God! Diego! Where did you get this?"

"Online, of course!" Diego insisted. "You can find anything on there. I thought it would look nice in your office."

"Oh, *mi amigo*, this is the nicest gift I ever received!" Jorge placed the album on the table and looked over at his friend. Rising from his chair, Diego did the same as the two embraced. "Diego, this is so incredibly thoughtful. You know how I love The Beatles."

"No big deal," Diego shrugged in response as Jorge moved away and returned to his chair, only to pick up the record again and stare at it some more. Beside him, Paige reached out and touched his arm as he slowly eased back into his seat.

"I had it checked by an expert, to make sure it was real," Diego continued and Jorge glanced up to see him and Paige exchange looks. "I can't take full credit for it, it was actually Paige's idea."

"Well," She quickly started to shake her head. "I just suggested something Beatles related but I figured you would buy him a t-shirt or something like that…"

"Nah," Diego shrugged and twisted his lips into an arrogant scowl. "Anyone can do that, it had to be special."

"This, Diego, this is definitely special to me," Jorge replied, carefully placed the LP back into the bag. "I feel as if I must put it somewhere safe."

"You could put it in the SUV," Paige suggested with a shrug. "But I'm sure it is fine here. It's just us."

"I would feel better if it was locked away," Jorge insisted and began to stand up. "This here, it is too valuable to have just sitting around."

Diego beamed with pride as Jorge picked up the bag and headed for the door. "I will be right back."

Once outside, he felt a sense of glee as he made his way to his vehicle, quickly putting the bag safely inside. He turned around to see Jesús arrive and hesitated. Although tempted to show him the album, he decided against it. Jorge had been very clear to his associates that they were to bring no gifts. Of course, Diego was like his *hermano,* the gesture was much more special.

Locking the SUV and walking toward his associate's car, Jesús slowly got out and immediately broke into a smile.

"I received the article you sent to me," He referred to Makerson's attempt to redeem Jorge Hernandez, painting a picture of him as a charming, distinguished businessman and not the ruthless criminal that Sturk had suggested in his article a week earlier. Of course, in Jorge's mind, both stories had some truth but the media had a way of never getting it right. There was usually missing or incorrect information and more times than not, an exaggeration that misleads audiences. Unfortunately, they were a necessary evil.

"Much better than the last one," Jorge commented as the two walked toward the club. Jesús was nodding as he continued. "He, of course, ran it by me before adding it to their website and sharing it on social media. Athas should be happy, Makerson made him look like a fucking God in the editorial."

"Sir, you have a way of always smoothing everything over," Jesús commented as they entered the club. Hesitating just inside the door, his eyes immediately jumped to the other side of the room. "Jolene is here. Was she invited to your party?"

"Nope," Jorge swiftly replied. "But, it appears, she has invited herself. If there is one thing Jolene is good at, it's showing up where she's not wanted."

Jesús didn't comment but scowled as they both watched her head in their direction. All around the Colombian beauty, men watched as the curvaceous Latina crossed the floor, her eyes fixated on Jorge, seemingly unaware that he was not pleased to see her.

"Jorge, I must talk to you in private," Jolene slurred her words and beside him, Jesús sniffed in disgust before he glanced at his boss. Giving him a brief, exasperated nod, Jorge returned his attention to Jolene as Jesús walked toward the VIP room.

"What do you want, Jolene," Jorge snapped, "I don't got all day."

"We must talk in private," She purred and leaned in, the smell of alcohol on her breath, Jorge didn't reply but gestured to a quiet corner beside the VIP room. It was off to the side, out of sight, so they had some privacy.

"What you want?" He repeated his question as soon as they were away from the crowd.

"I want to make it up to you, everything," Jolene commented in her usual broken English. "I wish to make you forget all of this badness between us."

"Very unlikely," Jorge insisted as she leaned in.

"But I, I must," She spoke with flirtation in her voice, her eyes fixed on him as she moved closer, her breast brushing up against his arm as if it were simply an accident. Her hot breath was on his face as she continued to move toward him as the song "Africa" filled the room, it suddenly grew louder as Jolene placed her hand on his crotch. "And I think, I know how to do this.."

"Jolene, this here," Jorge abruptly moved back, suddenly realizing that she had him literally backed into a corner. "This is *not* happening. You must leave."

"But I know you want me," Jolene continued to ease closer, her hot breath touched his face and although he had no doubt that another man would've quickly given into her aggressive advance, he instead grew furious. This was the same woman who was almost responsible for his death and yet, she thought that seducing him would somehow even everything out?

"Jolene," Jorge turned his head trying to avoid her lips that were moving awkwardly close to his face. Unfortunately, if he were to cause too much of a disruption, it might alert everyone in the VIP room. The last thing he wanted was for his wife to see Jolene making such an aggressive sexual advance on him. What if she thought he had instigated it? What if Jolene made it seem that way? He simply didn't trust her.

"I will make it better," She whispered in his ear as he attempted to squirm away, completely stunned to find himself in such a bizarre situation. Again, she reached out and boldly grabbed him but suddenly she moved away. However, upon turning his head, Jorge quickly recognized the look of quiet fury in his wife's eyes, as she stood behind a nervous Jolene.

"First, you try to have my husband killed and yet, I let you live," Paige spoke in her usual smooth tone as if she was making a gentle observation that had no implications behind it. Her eyes jumped briefly toward Jorge and back at Jolene. "Now, you're what? Trying to seduce him? How exactly did you think this was going to play out?"

"I….I just…I'm sorry, I have much to drink and…" Jolene stuttered and suddenly appeared more intoxicated than she had been earlier. Finally stepping away from Jorge and apparently trying to ease around Paige, she moved to the right. "I must…"

Before she could finish her sentence, Jorge watched in disbelief as Paige lurched forward and punched Jolene in the face. Stumbling back in stunned shock, Jolene's eyes turned furious as she staggered forward toward Paige, her fist mid-air when Jorge grabbed her arm, attempting to pull her back while his wife's furious eyes expanded in rage as she jumped forward and punched Jolene a second time, this time knocking the Colombian off-balance, causing her to fall against Jorge, who also lost his balance and fell back on the floor with Jolene colliding on top. Paige was wasting no time jumping forward when an alarmed Chase suddenly ran in their direction and grabbed Paige around the waist from behind, pulling her away.

Jolene slowly started to move while Jorge abruptly pushed her, fearful that his wife had the wrong idea, his first priority was to explain what happened but that was when Jesús and Diego rushed out of the VIP room, both stunned to see Chase pulling Paige away.

"What the fuck?" Diego rushed ahead, grabbing Jolene's arm and hastily pulling her up from the floor. "What did you do, Jolene? Paige is ready to kill you!"

"Yes, well it's my birthday and that," Jorge jumped up from the floor. "Sounds fucking perfect right about now."

Rushing past Diego, Jolene and a stunned Jesús, Jorge returned to the VIP room to find Paige drinking a glass of water. Chase was heading toward the door.

"I'll get you some ice for that but please," He put his hand up in the air and glanced toward Jorge. "Stay in here."

Chase wasn't even out the door and Jorge rushed toward his wife. "Paige! You must know, I nothing..did…I did nothing wrong." His throat felt dry and suddenly English words were jumbled in his head. "*Ella intentó seducirme. No hice nada malo!*"

Tears formed in Paige's eyes but they quickly disappeared and she appeared skeptical, although silent.

"Please, Paige! Come on!" Jorge insisted. "Ask Jesús. She came up to speak to me. I did not approach her."

"She was all over you," Paige calmly remarked. "I could see from in here. What if I hadn't come along?"

"She had me fucking cornered," Jorge pleaded his case. "What? Was I supposed to shove her? A room full of people nearby, you do not think this would've made me the bad guy? The rules, you do not understand, the rules are very different for men and women. Had no one been there, I would've pushed her aside."

"That's not what I mean," Paige spoke gently. "If the situation were different….if you hadn't been here but somewhere else, like her apartment or our house and you were alone…"

"Paige! No!" Jorge insisted, stunned that his wife would think he would do such a thing. "I do not want Jolene."

"But she's very beautiful and we've been together for a year now… it's just…"

"Just what? You think I'm growing bored?" Jorge asked in disbelief. "What? You think all men, we are dogs? We fuck anything that comes along cause we can?"

"That's not what I said," Paige shook her head.

"I do not have an attraction for Jolene," Jorge moved closer and touched her arm. "Paige, I married you because I want to be with you. Regardless of what people say, not all Latino men cheat."

"I wasn't trying to say that…"

"*Mi amor*, I do not like to do this but I must point out," Jorge spoke in a gentle voice as he moved closer to his wife. "You spend a lot of time with Athas and unlike Jolene, you had him as a lover once."

"Twenty years ago!" Paige spoke sharply while her eyes filled with tears.

"Exactly, but it did happen and sometimes, yes, I am jealous but if you say to me that nothing will happen, I trust you," Jorge insisted. "Even if he were cornering you like Jolene just did with me. I would believe you," He hesitated for a moment. "I would *kill* him but, I would believe you."

A smile appeared on her face, despite the fact that she was trying to hide it.

"I'm sorry," She suddenly appeared defeated. "I know that. I know what I saw and she did have you backed in a corner but what I mean is…"

"Jolene, she is poison and you are letting her poison you now," Jorge spoke in a soft voice and leaned in to kiss his wife on the face. "That is what she wants. You do not think this was on purpose?

Paige's eyes were full of sadness and Jorge merely smiled and moved away.

"Now, let us forget this," He reached out and inspected his wife's hand, which was now swelling. "This is what we need to take care of....I'm so flattered you were willing to fight for my honor."

Paige laughed and looked away.

"And on my birthday at that," Jorge continued to tease her. "How lucky am I?"

CHAPTER

7

"We will not talk business tonight," Jorge remarked as he glanced at his phone before leaning in to kiss Paige. Although Jolene's bizarre interruption had created some tension, he would get the party back on track. His original disinterest in having a birthday celebration had diminished. Now that they were all together with a bottle of wine in the VIP section, it suddenly felt like exactly where he should be. "We are here from this point on to have a beautiful night."

"Now that Jolene is gone, you mean," Diego spoke up, his face twisted into a frustrated expression.

Noting the tense look on his wife's face, Jorge leaned back to where she couldn't see him and shook his head 'no' indicating for Diego to change the topic.

"But, you know, whatever," He immediately took Jorge's cue and shook his head and turned his attention to Chase. "Maybe what we all need is a shot of tequila to get this party started."

"Ah! You're reading my mind, Diego," Jorge smirked and watched Paige turn and smile. Winking at her, he grabbed her leg under the table before moving his chair closer to the table.

"I'll go get it," Chase jumped up and headed toward the door while a silent Jesús merely nodded and took another drink of his red wine.

"She's not going to come back is she," Paige asked as she leaned in close to her husband.

Jorge didn't answer but stared into his wife's blue eyes while on his other side, Jesús quickly replied.

"No, Chase, he threw her in a cab earlier," His answer directed at Jorge even though it was Paige asking the question. "She will not be returning."

"Maybe she will go back to hell," Jorge commented and looked away with an exasperated sigh.

"Colombia," Diego jumped in with wide eyes. "Now that would be hell for her. You piss off the wrong people in our country, it might be the last fucking thing you do."

Jorge thought about his words but didn't comment. He preferred to kill this conversation. Unfortunately, Chase returned just in time to catch the end and quickly picked it up again.

"I think that's why she was so desperate tonight," Chase remarked as he sat down a tray of shot glasses, a salt shaker, slices of lime and a bottle of expensive tequila. As if on cue, everyone grabbed a piece of lime as he poured them each a shot, passing them around the table. "She's scared."

"If Jolene was scared before, imagine how she feels now that my wife punched her in the face twice," Jorge laughed heartily just as a shadow caught his attention and he turned to see Alec Athas quietly enter the room.

"Sorry I'm late," He hesitated while Jorge gestured for him to join them at the table. "I got caught in a meeting. Did I hear you say Paige punched somebody?"

"Oh God," Paige shook her head and sighed heavily.

"Yes," Jorge leaned forward as Alec sat across the table from him and Chase rushed out of the room. Jorge put an arm protectively over Paige's shoulder. "My wife, she punched another woman in my honor, what a beautiful birthday gift!"

"Wow," Alec's eyes grew in size as a smile crept across his face. "I can't say I'm surprised but did I hear Jolene's name when I came in? Isn't that your sister, Diego?"

"Unfortunately," Diego scowled and shook his head just as Chase returned with another shot glass. "She had it coming."

"Ok, may I ask why?" Alec glanced at Chase placing a shot of tequila and lime in front of him. "Oh, none for me."

"No is not an answer tonight, *amigo*," Jorge insisted and glanced at Alec's shot of tequila.

"Unfortunately, Jolene apparently thought the same!" Diego complained.

"I don't understand," Alec replied as he moved his chair forward. "So, what happened?"

"Does it matter?" Jorge once again attempted to change the topic.

"Jolene was hitting on my husband," Paige calmly replied and then added. "*Very aggressively* hitting on my husband."

"She had him backed against a wall," Diego's eyes expanded as he told the story. "Like, in a very rapey sort of way."

"What?" Alec appeared confused.

"It was pretty aggressive," Chase agreed. "I saw, she literally had him backed against the wall."

"And if I had tried to shove her or something, guess who would've been the asshole?" Jorge attempted to explain himself, perhaps to save some pride. "She was…you know…"

"She was grabbing his junk," Diego spoke in excited fury, much to Jorge's frustration.

"Ok, can we not talk about Jolene anymore," Jorge spoke up, briefly glancing at his wife, who appeared upset. "Can we drink our shots and have a pleasant evening?"

"You know, that's sexual assault," Alec commented in a matter-of-fact voice. "It's no different than if I went out in the bar now and backed a woman into a corner."

"Oh come on!" Diego said with a laugh. "That's not the same!"

"It *is* the same," Alec insisted.

"Come on," Diego continued to laugh. "So, if I backed *you* in the corner now, that's me sexually assaulting you?"

"Ah, if you were not allowing me to leave and touching me inappropriately without my consent," Alec replied with a grin. "Yes, that's actually sexual assault."

"No," Diego said and continued to shake his head. "You have to actually *do* something, you know….like…"

"Ok, can we not talk about this any longer?" Jorge cut in and leaned forward. "This is getting out of hand."

"Just wait a second," Diego continued and appeared to ignore Jorge, his attention on Alec Athas. "So, you're telling me women can sexually assault men? So, Jolene assaulted Jorge? A man, who is physically stronger than a woman, larger than a woman. I mean…. not in Jorge's case, but most men."

"Hey! I'm not that short," Jorge intervened. "I can look after myself just fine."

"Well, sir," Jesús finally spoke. "With Jolene in heels, she will tower over all of us. She is also very aggressive, so when you look at it that way...I think Mr. Athas is correct."

"It wouldn't matter if she didn't tower over him," Alec replied. "What was he supposed to do? Shove her? Hit her?"

"Well, in fairness," Jesús replied. "If that were a woman, and say, I had her backed in the corner, she could realistically hit me to protect herself."

"Ah, but do you really think a man could do the same in that situation?" Alec asked. "He would be in the wrong. I guarantee it."

"It is a double standard," Jesús nodded.

"It is," Alec agreed. "Unfortunately, this is one of the areas where a woman kind of has an advantage. Regardless of what the law says, there is no way he could've touched her to get her to back off without him being in the wrong."

"Unbelievable!" Jesús nodded.

"I still can't believe that men can be assaulted," Diego returned to the original topic. "It just, it don't make sense."

"Come on, Diego," Jorge sighed. "You go on a date with a guy and he fucks you up the ass after you say no, that's not rape?"

"That's different," Diego insisted. "That's two men. It's not the same."

"And in fairness," Jesús reached for the bottle of wine. "Do you really think Diego would ever refuse getting fucked up the ass?"

Jorge laughed while Alec attempted to hide a grin and Diego twisted his face into a scowl.

"Very funny, Jesús, very funny," Diego replied even though he was fighting a smile.

"Can we all stop talking about assault and rape and have a shot of tequila already," Jorge decided it was time to put this topic to rest. "Come on, everyone, grab your glasses."

Everyone followed his instructions. Jorge noted his wife seemed slightly relaxed compared to earlier in the conversation.

"Let me do the toast," Diego insisted, standing up and turning his attention to Jorge. "To one of my best friends, to my business associate and to my *hermano*. Jorge Hernandez, you definitely make life a lot more interesting for everyone at the table. What would we do without you?"

Jorge laughed as Paige leaned in and gave him a kiss. Staring into her eyes for a long moment, he finally turned his attention back to Diego.

"I toast you, *mi amigo*, Happy Birthday and with many more to come."

Everyone took a shot, followed by their slice of lime.

"Ah fuck, that was good!" Jorge commented and pulled Paige close to kiss her on the side of the face. "That shot of tequila was almost as strong as my wife when she is angry."

Everyone around that table laughed and Paige joined in as she glanced at her hand, which she returned to the bag of ice.

"Ah, but the swelling, it is not bad," Diego commented as he leaned over the table and inspected it. "I suspect Jolene can't say the same about her face"

Jorge didn't comment but grinned and rose an eyebrow.

"Yeah, you really popped her!" Diego continued. "What are you, taking boxing lessons from Chase?"

"I was actually thinking about taking lessons from her," Chase joked and everyone laughed again.

"A woman must always know how to defend herself," Paige quietly commented. "That's something I realized a long time ago. It has been helpful along the way."

"Me, I prefer a baseball bat," Diego commented with a serious expression and Jorge grinned. Having seen his friend in action more than once, he knew these words weren't an exaggeration. "I find, it sends a message."

"If you happen to have a baseball bat on hand," Jesús commented as he finished his glass of wine. "Fortunately, for Jolene, there was none available tonight."

Paige laughed and didn't reply.

"Let us, please, talk about something else," Jorge attempted to change the conversation again.

"Let's take some pictures," Diego jumped up and grabbed his phone. "We need pictures of all of us together. A selfie, something to remember tonight."

"That sounds beautiful," Jorge commented as he reached out and squeezed his wife's arm. "Can you take one of just me and Paige as well?"

"Yes, we have almost no pictures of us together."

"Of course!" Diego commented. "I plan to take lots and Jorge, you should take one of me and Paige. You can finally change the picture of me in your phone directory. I hate the one you have now."

"You mean, this one," Jorge grabbed his phone and held it up for everyone to see. It was a photo of an angry Diego pointing toward the camera just as the picture was took. Everyone laughed.

"Yes, that one, we can do better!" Diego insisted.

"I don't know, Diego," Jorge insisted. "I'm kind of fond of this one. I feel it really captures who you are..."

"Nah, get a picture of me and Paige or...anything but that."

"I think, I will keep this one," Jorge slid the phone back into his pocket. "It makes me laugh every time you call me."

Diego rolled his eyes while everyone gathered together for a selfie. It would always be a reminder of a perfect night with his family.

CHAPTER

8

"**W**hy does your hand look funny?" Maria piped up at breakfast the following morning. Picking at her bowl of cereal as if skeptical whether or not to eat it, Jorge's daughter was observing her step-mother's bruised hand with interest. Leaning in closer, she studied it carefully before her eyes sprang back to Paige. "Its kind of swelled. Did you get it caught in the door or something?"

"Ah, no…it was…I just hit it against something," Paige spoke hesitantly as her eyes glanced toward Jorge, who merely grinned.

"Is that true?" Maria asked suspiciously. "You guys are acting funny. Was this sex thing?"

"Maria!" Jorge snapped as the smile slid off his face. "What have I told you, *again and again,* you do not ask such things! This is rude."

"I'm sorry, *Papa,* but you guys are acting weird," Maria insisted with no shame as she sat up straighter in her chair. "Why do you treat me like a child?"

"Because you are a child," Jorge replied with frustration in his voice. "This, this here has to stop. You might think you sound older by saying such rude things but it just makes you seem like an obnoxious teenager."

"I am almost a teenager, *Papa,*" Maria replied defiantly. "I'm 11, that is practically 12 and 12 is a teenager."

"I disagree," Jorge said as his eyes challenged his daughter's until she finally looked away. "And this, this is beside the point. No matter what the age, that is a rude question and is not acceptable."

"I'm sorry," Maria muttered and looked down at her cereal.

"Now, eat your food," Jorge continued in hopes she would forget about Paige's bruised hand. The last thing he wanted was for her to think that hitting other people was acceptable. His daughter was daring enough without having some justification for getting into a fight at school if the mood struck her. As much as he hated to admit it, Maria was very much his daughter in temperament and boldness. "You are not eating well lately and this concerns me. I hope you don't have some ideas about going on a starvation diet like all these moronic actresses and models that you admire so much!"

"Of course not, *Papa!*" Maria sharply replied and Jorge noted that Paige was doing her best to hide the injured hand, while his job was simply to distract his daughter. "I eat all my meals. I just do not overeat. I don't want to get sick like you."

"Ok, first of all," Jorge replied, feeling his anger creeping up. "My health, it is fine. Now, when I did have some issues it was because of stress, eating too much fatty food and smoking. These, they are not good things but I still eat. You pick. You barely eat anything and you're very thin. This concerns me."

"I don't want to be too thin, *Papa*," Maria said as her brown eyes shamefully looked down at the table. "That's not my goal. I just am not hungry."

"You must eat," Jorge said as he calmed down. "And hurry up, you'll be late for drama school."

It was after she rushed back upstairs to get her backpack that Paige raised an eyebrow as she stood up from her seat.

"Nice diversion," She spoke smoothly and reached for Maria's empty bowl.

"No no!" Jorge said and put his hand up. "Maria will put that in the dishwasher. I may have my daughter in a private school but she will not be a spoiled, entitled brat. She will clean up after herself."

"Ok," Paige replied with a grin as she picked up her coffee cup and headed toward the sink with Jorge in tow.

"But *mi amor,* your hand, it doesn't look as bad as I expected it would," Jorge muttered as his daughter ran down the stairs. "This may surprise you but I've never had a woman fight for me before…it's very sexy."

"I believe you got that point across last night when we got home," Paige whispered and Jorge grinned, with his eyebrow raised, he leaned in and kissed her. "I do have some regrets today, however."

"Go sit on your meditation pillow and sort it out," Jorge insisted. "Me, I think you did the right thing."

He turned to see his daughter standing defiantly by the table, watching them.

"Miss Maria, your dishes," Jorge's tone suddenly changed as he pointed toward her. "We are not here to wait on you."

"I forgot," She complained and picked up her breakfast dishes.

The drive to Maria's class was interesting. She chatted on about her drama lessons, the teachers she liked, the teachers she didn't like and of course, the vocal lessons she wanted to take.

"Maria, it is not that I don't want you to take the lessons," Jorge replied calmly as they sat at a light. Rain started to tap against the windshield. "It is just that school will be starting next week. You're already taking self-defense and you'll also be involved in drama at school. You do not have to do everything at once."

"But *Papa*, it is very competitive out there," Maria spoke with concern in her voice. "In order to be an actress, I must have an advantage. The more I can do, the better my chances of getting work."

"Maria, you're *11*," Jorge felt his frustration creeping up again. "Your focus should be school. You are going to exhaust yourself."

"Do you think any successful person has made it by being lazy?" Maria countered and glanced at her father. "You, you were a very successful man in a cartel for a number of years, I shouldn't have to tell *you* this."

Jorge felt his anger turn to guilt. He hated that his daughter knew about his illegal connections. One of the greatest heartbreaks of his life was the day Maria confided that she knew of his criminal past. It was his enormous shame and at first, he didn't reply. Glancing at his daughter, he then realized that she was attempting to manipulate him.

"Look, Maria, this here," Jorge replied with regained strength. "This is *not* going to work. I did not start with the cartel when I was 11 years old and *niñita,* as I have told you, again and again, it was a terrible mistake that I did at all."

"I am sorry, *Papa*, I just meant you must understand hard work," Maria spoke sorrowfully.

"I did, however, Maria, not when I was 11," Jorge countered. "I enjoyed my childhood."

"But what about the accident?"

Fuck! His daughter had this way of hitting his sore spots. She was, of course, referring to the terrible dirt bike accident that took place when he was 12. It was because of his own careless actions that Miguel had died.

"Maria," Jorge snapped. "This manipulation, it has to stop."

"I'm not trying to manipulate you," Maria started. "I just.."

"That is it, Maria," Jorge spoke sharply this time. "I'm finished talking about this for now. When school starts and I have a better idea of your schedule, we will talk about the voice lessons but I am not promising anything."

"That is all I ask," Maria replied to the attempted negotiation.

"And you," Jorge continued as they drove into the parking lot of her summer acting classes. "If you defy me and take off one day looking for the place these classes take place, as you did earlier this year, I will say no."

Maria nodded with tears in her eyes. It was during a particularly stressful time that Jorge's daughter had brazenly left school to visit a drama school. Without telling anyone or answering her phone, she wandered the streets of Toronto on her own. At the time, Paige's life had been in danger and the white supremacists were attacking his businesses, so he had feared the worst.

"Now, I know we are no longer in Mexico," Jorge continued as he put the SUV into park and turned toward his daughter. "But here in Canada, bad things happen too. Never let your defenses down."

Maria nodded. "I know, *Papa*." She leaned in and gave him a quick hug and kiss before getting out of the SUV.

Heading to the offices of Hernandez–Silva Inc, Jorge thought about the fact that his daughter was growing up too fast. He had to keep a close eye on her because she was at a vulnerable age and it was up to him to make up for Verónic's terrible care during the child's early years. How stupid had he been to think that she would've been a good mother? Instead, the *puta* snorted coke in front of their daughter and had various men in the house while he was away on business. It was a terrible, dysfunctional relationship and so different from what he had with Paige.

Eventually making it through traffic and to the office, Diego met him at the door.

"Ah, look who bothered to show up!" He teased with his usual abruptness. "Did you oversleep after too much tequila last night?

"No, I had to drive Maria to drama school," Jorge replied casually as the two walked toward the boardroom. "It's her last day and she's already asking about fucking voice lessons."

"She's ambitious, that niñita," Diego commented as they entered the empty room and closed the glass door behind them. On the long table, there was already a pot of coffee along with two empty cups and cream and sugar. "She is very much like you."

Jorge grunted. "Maybe a little too much."

"So, Paige," Diego spoke with affection in his voice. "How is her hand? I texted her but she hasn't replied."

"She's heading to Alec's office to help him with some stupid video for Facebook," Jorge replied and rolled his eyes. "It's not bad, actually."

"I'm assuming better than my sister's face this morning."

"Your sister's got a lot of problems," Jorge commented with a shrug. "What's one more?"

Diego didn't reply as the two sat down and Jorge glanced around. "Clara?"

"She was in already," Diego replied, referring to the woman who regularly checked their homes and offices for listening devices. Although few had shown up over the years, it was important to keep on top of things.

"*Perfecto!*"

"She's monitoring everything closely," Diego continued as he poured them each a cup of coffee. "And she's mentioned a few suspicious characters around the warehouse recently."

"Oh yeah?" Jorge spoke casually as he reached for the cream.

"Let's hope that it's not more problems like we had earlier this year," Diego commented, referring to the white supremacists that had targeted their businesses in the latter part of the winter. Jorge had sent a very strong message that this was not to continue but he didn't fully trust that they would listen.

"She's keeping a close eye on it," Diego continued, taking a drink of his coffee. "Too bad she still wasn't living in your basement apartment. At least you would have her close at hand."

"It's ok," Jorge replied with a shrug. "She is back with her husband, who is immigrating to Canada."

"So, Sylvana agreed to take the job," Diego mentioned the woman he often bitterly referred to as 'The Italian' even though she was half Latina. "This means that I can stay in the office more, she can do the traveling and Jesús of course, will continue setting up and take over other shops across the country."

"Beautiful!" Jorge nodded with enthusiasm. "Some good news!"

"We are doing it," Diego continued and leaned toward Jorge. "When you said we would take over the pot industry in Canada, I wasn't sure because of the various rules in each province but yet, here we are."

"Yes, one store at a time," Jorge insisted with a smirk. "Ontario was easy, I took it over in one swoop but I have more power here. The rest of the country has been slightly more prickly but everything is possible if you have the right attitude. I never doubted for a second that this industry would be mine."

"I gotta tell you," Diego replied with a shrug. "I don't know how you did it. In a matter of, what? A year? Look at everything you've done."

"I'm not a patient man, *amigo,* I do not like to waste time," Jorge replied and leaned back in his chair. "This country, it will eventually be mine. I'm running one of the largest industries. Pot, it is the new oil."

"Ah, let us hope so!"

"Diego, my friend, I know so," Jorge insisted as he drank his coffee. "Nothing is going to stop me now."

CHAPTER

9

"Things have been quiet lately," Jorge commented a few days later. He sat at the boardroom table at Hernandez-Silva with Jesús, a man he had worked with for many years. "The silence makes me nervous. It is rare for things to be so quiet."

"I agree, sir," Jesús replied and shook his head. "Compared to the early half of this year, it's been an unusually quiet summer. Then again, perhaps we were so busy that it was not for us to see anything beyond expanding the business."

"Let us hope," Jorge raised his eyebrows and reached for his coffee just as Marco Rodel Cruz walked into the room with his usual, bright smile and pleasant disposition. The Filipino nodded to the men and headed toward the table, laptop in his hand.

"Good morning, Mr. Hernandez, Mr. López," Marco said as he sat in the chair beside Jesús and placed his MacBook on the table. "Beautiful day today?"

"Yes," Jorge quickly nodded and glanced toward the window. "Tell me, how are things in the world of IT, Marco? The websites look fantastic. I like how you have added a section to work with us and I noticed some other changes."

"I cannot take all the credit, sir," Marco insisted. "My assistant, she has been helpful. I am now able to relay instructions on to her while working on other things myself, it's been an enormous help."

"Very good," Jorge replied with a nod, as he glanced at his laptop and clicked on the main page for Our House of Pot locations. "You're doing a tremendous job but this morning, I would like to ask you about something else, Marco. When I was in Mexico, I know that we often had some business taken care of through, what you might refer to as, The Dark Web. Are you familiar with this?"

"Yes sir," Marco nodded as his eyes grew in size. "It was not something I learned in school but yes, I do know of such things."

"I assume much of the expertise you have used for me aren't taught in school," Jorge grinned and reached for his coffee. Marco had hacked emails and even companies in the past. It was often the skills that people didn't have on their resume that was more valuable than those taught in a class. "Tell me, Marco, is this something you can access, maybe look around a bit for me?"

"Of course, sir!"

"What I want is you to let me know what is going on," Jorge said as he leaned back in his chair. "I want to know if you can find any talk of me or this company on The Dark Web, maybe look around and see what specifically is going on with our enemies especially here in the Toronto area, if you can find such information."

"I can look, sir," Marco agreed with an enthusiastic nod. "Whatever you wish."

"I don't know exactly what I want to find but something tells me we should look more closely at this world. It is not the same for me here as in Mexico. I find Canadian culture, you hide so much. After all, we have men like Fulton Harley as a politician and yet, he's a man secretively active in the white supremacy movement. I am not saying that in Mexico everything is out in the open but for some reason, I had a much easier time finding out what I had to know when I lived there."

"Oh yes," Jesús nodded. "This is good, sir, we must keep an eye. This is very important."

"Unfortunately, much of what you will find will either be quite offensive to possibly ridiculous," Jorge commented as he closed his laptop and glanced toward an unfamiliar female employee approaching the glass door and knocking. "Who is she?"

Marco turned and sprang from his chair. "Oh, sir, this is one of our new employees that works in Marketing, Amanda."

The young white woman opened the door and gestured toward Jorge. "Excuse me, I don't mean to interrupt but there's a woman here to see you," Her dark eyes quickly glanced toward the main entrance. "She used to work here?"

Before Amanda could go into more detail, Jolene rushed ahead and pushed her way into the room. Although she clearly was wearing a great deal of makeup, evidence of Paige punching her was still quite obvious, causing Jorge to wonder how terrible it had looked the morning after their fight.

"Jolene!" Jorge snapped and jumped up from his chair while Marco and Jesús looked equally alarmed. Amanda appeared stunned by everyone's reaction and carefully slid out the door. "What the hell are you doing here? Why are you interrupting our meeting? You were not invited."

"Why must I buzz in now as if I am nobody?" Jolene snapped, her voice carrying a sense of vulnerability despite her prominent stance. "I do not work for this company any longer? I told you I would like to come back."

"Are you not forgetting?" Jorge shook his head and began to laugh. "Let's see, you went to rehab but that was after you attempted to have me killed and of course, before going on the run. Why is it, exactly, that you thought you *would* be coming back? This is what I must know, Jolene."

"I tell you, again and again," She inched toward the table and glanced briefly at Marco, who was doing everything he could to avoid eye contact with the Colombian woman. "I did *not* try to kill you. I save your life. I save you from that man who wanted you dead and the drugs, this is a problem, it is a disease."

"Oh fuck off!" Jorge snapped, his eyes blazing. "You can twist this around any way you want, Jolene, it does not matter. I don't trust you. No one trusts you. We cannot have you a part of this company when we never know what you will do next to destroy us. You are lucky to even be on this side of the ground right now, so Jolene, do not push your luck."

"Then what am I supposed to do?" She attempted to hold back her tears, something that Jorge suspected was an attempt to win their sympathies. Jolene was desperate. "I have money saved but it will run out."

"I don't know, Jolene," Jorge snapped and waved his hand in the air. "Maybe go out, get a job."

"Doing what?"

"This, this is not my problem," Jorge replied while fire blasted in his eyes. "If I were you, I would leave Toronto. Go somewhere else. Get an apartment. Find a man. Grab *his* junk instead of mine and see if you can manipulate him into your dark world. I do not care what you do, Jolene, just so long as you don't do it here and you don't do it with me."

His last remarks seemed to catch Marco's attention, as he glanced toward Jesús who gave a slight nod.

"I was drinking that night, I did not think straight," Jolene attempted to explain herself as she took a step forward. "I should not do but I thought maybe, this was what you want, you know?"

"You thought I wanted you to grab my crotch at my birthday party, while my wife watched?" Jorge asked with a ring of frustration in his voice. "How fucking dumb are you, Jolene? I do not want you or anything you have to offer. You are fortunate that we pulled Paige off of you because my wife, she does not react well in these situations."

"I will apologize to Paige," Jolene spoke sorrowfully.

"You will not go near my wife," Jorge replied defiantly. "And this, this is good advice and not a demand because it is to your benefit to keep far away from her. She will not forgive and forget but she might tear the eyes out of your head."

"Can I….could I talk to you alone?" Jolene asked in a soft, wimpy voice as she glanced toward Jesús and then Marco. "Please."

Jorge was about to say no but hesitantly said yes.

"We will continue this meeting later," He glanced at Marco, who picked up his laptop and walked out of the office.

"Sir, I will not leave without checking her," Jesús was insistent and Jorge nodded. Approaching Jolene, he patted down the pathetic Colombian woman and then checked her purse. "She is clear sir."

"I do not want to harm," Jolene said as humility swept over her face and she suddenly looked older than she had only moments earlier. "Please, I just want to talk."

"Very well," Jorge replied and gestured to the chair across from him. "Sit but make it fast. I don't got all day."

Jesús gave Jorge a look as he headed out of the office while Jolene sat down and he did the same. Placing her handbag on the table, she suddenly appeared quite nervous as she spun a ring around on her finger.

"Jorge, I make a lot of mistakes," She spoke without looking into his eyes. "I cannot believe what a mess I have made of my life but I do want to do better. I want to be part of this company again and I am willing to do anything to prove this to you."

"Is that right?" Jorge said, slightly humored by her suggestion.

"Yes, I do," Jolene replied and looked into his eyes. "It was not always like this. I was good once, remember, I do good work. Everything, it got off track with the drugs and my own fears, when that man approached me.."

"Jolene, I don't need to skip down memory lane with you," Jorge said and shook his head. "I know what happened. That is why I cannot trust you."

"But if I were a man, would you not give me another chance?"

"If you were a man," Jorge pointed toward her breasts. "You would be dead now."

Jolene took in his words and nodded.

"Jolene, why do you want this?" Jorge asked. "Why do you want to stay so much? Why not do what I say? Go away, start new? We recently started to look at shops in Nova Scotia. Why not go there? It's quiet. Peaceful. No one knows about your past. You can start fresh."

"Alone," Jolene added as she looked down at her hands. "Diego, he is my only family. I want to be close to him."

"You're going about it the wrong way," Jorge commented. "Pulling this shit with me, having an affair with the man you *knew* he was obsessed with for years….these are not smart choices if you are trying to bond with your brother and still, what does that have to do with the rest of us?"

"I want to be a part of something," Jolene attempted to explain. "To belong to something. I have no friends outside this group. I need people in my life otherwise, what is the point?"

Jorge knew he had a choice. He could've easily pushed her away into a world of despair and then, perhaps her own misery would take care of his ongoing problem with her; but then he thought of Diego. Although he had no use for Jolene, Diego was like a brother to him and for that reason, he bit his bottom lip and nodded.

"Ok, Jolene, I cannot make any promises," Jorge replied and saw the hope in her eyes. "But I will give it some thought and talk to Paige."

"I would like to apologize to her," Jolene spoke nervously. "If even in a card or maybe an email but I must. I did not learn much in rehab but I know that it is important to claim your mistakes and try to amend."

Jorge merely nodded and said nothing.

"Please, you will see," Jolene continued as she slowly rose from the chair. "I will do better. This is important to me. Whatever you ask. If you want me to kill, I will kill. If you want me to seduce, I will seduce. I will do what you need but please, do not push me out."

Jorge slowly nodded and stood up, slightly impressed with her attempts to fix the situation.

"Very well," He replied and looked into her eyes. "I would like you to email my wife and tell her the truth about everything. What you did the night of my birthday, be clear that it was your idea and not mine."

"Yes," Jolene said with a nod, her eyes growing in size. "I would prefer to speak to her in person."

"I wouldn't bombard her as you have with me today," Jorge suggested. "You can ask her but maybe its better in this case to not do it in person. Meanwhile, I will give this some thought."

"This is all I can ask," Jolene said in a soft voice before picking up her purse and heading toward the door. Before opening it, she turned for a second and nodded. "Thank you."

After she was gone, Jorge exhaled and glanced at his beeping phone. It was Paige.

There was a bit of a situation with Maria at drama school today.....

Fuck.

10

"**Y**ou were WHAT?" Jorge didn't attempt to hold his temper, especially when faced with a daughter who appeared to have no guilt or regret over her most recent actions. "You were kissing a boy at drama school?"

"*Papa*, I cannot believe the instructor is making such a big deal about it," Maria spoke with defiance in her voice. "I was merely kissing him goodbye since it was our last class."

Stunned by his daughter's tone, Jorge glanced at Paige who was already shaking her head.

"It wasn't *that* kind of kiss," She spoke evenly while giving her stepdaughter a stern look.

"Papa, I don't understand why this is such a big deal," Maria spoke with a sense of arrogance in her voice and shrugged it off. "I'm practically a teenager and teenagers kiss. What did you expect me to do, play with dolls?"

Jorge stared at his daughter in stunned disbelief. He knew that she was testing him and it was necessary that he passed.

"So, what is this, your boyfriend or something?" Jorge decided to push the topic further and shook his head. "Was this going on all summer? Maria, please tell me that you have not....done anything else with this boy."

"No, *Papa*," Maria rolled her eyes and appeared frustrated as if he was wasting her time. "We just kissed a few times and that is all."

"Ok, that is good," Jorge felt slightly relieved until he shared a look with Paige.

"You might want to ask her how old the boy was that she was kissing?"

"Ughh! What difference does it make?" Maria spoke defiantly. "Boys my own age are immature and smell funny."

"Maria!" Jorge's voice boomed through the room as he moved closer to her. "How old is this boy?"

"Josh is 14."

"*Josh* is 14!" Jorge repeated her answer. "Does *Josh* realize he was kissing a child."

"I am *not* a child," Maria countered, her dark eyes blazing as she stood her ground with a strength that would've made him proud of under almost any other circumstance.

"You, little girl, are most certainly still a child," Jorge shot back. "Whether you want to believe this or not, I do not care. You are *not* to go anywhere near this boy again!"

"What are you going to do?" Maria yelled as she jumped up and placed both hands on her hips. "Lock me in my room until I'm 25."

"Well, this does sound like a good idea," Jorge countered with a tone that matched his daughter's. "And you, you can forget about those voice lessons you asked for earlier today. Apparently, when you are off at these lessons, you cannot be trusted to behave."

"I was *kissing* a boy not *killing* him," Maria yelled the words that sent a shudder through Jorge's heart. His daughter had read the editorial wrote by Sturk suggesting that he was not only involved in cocaine but also unofficially linked to some deaths in Mexico, if not Canada.

"That is *enough*," Jorge said in a tone that demonstrated great restraint yet something in his voice appeared to alarm his daughter as she stepped back. Maria knew that she had crossed a line. "Now, you're going to your room because I cannot look at you anymore."

"*Papa*, I'm sorry…" She started but he quickly cut her off.

"Go to your room, Maria!" Jorge jumped up and pointed toward the stairs. "I will not be disrespected in my home by anyone including my own *hija*. I do *not* want to look at you."

Now biting back tears, Maria suddenly looked more like the little girl and not the defiant teenager as she turned and ran upstairs.

Looking at Paige, he shook his head.

"This is fucking unbelievable!"

"You have to calm down," Paige spoke in her usual soft voice as she stood up and gently touched his arm. "We can't do anything about what happened and you know she's just bringing up what was in Sturk's article to hurt you because you won't let her get her way. This is Maria, she always does this."

"Yes and she knows how to hit a nerve," Jorge replied as he reached out to his wife and gently pulled her close. "Do you think maybe we are kissing in front of her too much or something like that? I do not understand what would inspire a child her age to be this way. What were you like at 11?"

"I don't recall, we're talking like 30 years," Paige said and smiled while shaking her head. "I know for a fact, I wasn't kissing boys."

"I am quite disturbed by the fact that he was 14!" Jorge said with a grimace as he moved away from his wife. "Do you know what boys are like at 14? Believe me, I do not want my daughter being around 14-year-old boys when *she's* 14 let alone now."

"Well, that's why the instructor called me," Paige replied. "Thankfully."

"I am surprised, she did not call me?"

"I think Maria was hoping I would let this go," Paige replied in a whisper. "I don't know why. She knows I tell you everything. Perhaps to soften the blow?"

"I do not think that is possible," Jorge frowned. "Why would a 14-year-old boy want to have anything to do with an 11-year-old? That is fucking sick."

"I think she might've told him she was 12 or 13."

"Ughh!" Jorge sighed and frowned. "This here, this is not good. I do not know what to do, Paige. Other than locking her in the house until she's an adult."

"All you can do is talk to her and be brutally honest about the consequences of her actions," Paige suggested and shook her head. "Look, this is new to me too. I can do some research online?"

"You do, whatever you feel you should do," Jorge said as he pulled her into another hug. "This here is going to give me my next heart attack."

"Don't even joke about that," Paige replied as she pulled him tighter against her body. "There was one point I was about to break things up because I was worried about you."

"Oh, *mi amor,* you know I've been in much more stressful situations than this one," Jorge laughed and gave her a quick kiss as he moved away. "You are right, this here will be fine. If Maria wants extra lessons, then she must be good or they simply will not happen."

"Yes, that's true," Paige nodded. "Her acting and voice lessons are important to her."

"Does this drama school, does it not have a performance or evaluation at the end of classes?" Jorge attempted to find his words but his phone was already buzzing. "I mean, isn't that how these things work."

"Good questions," Paige replied as he glanced at his phone. "What?"

"Diego, he tells me to go to the warehouse," Jorge said and took a deep breath. "You know, I was just saying that things were quiet lately. I guess I spoke too soon."

"What is it?" Paige asked.

"I don't know but apparently there is a problem and he feels that I should get there ASAP," Jorge said as he shoved the phone back in his pocket and leaned in to give her a quick kiss. "I will text you later."

"Do you need me to do anything?" She asked as Jorge started to walk away.

"Make sure my daughter doesn't escape her room," Jorge said with a shrug as he reached the door. "That, alone, would be beautiful."

Paige merely grinned in response as he slipped out the door.

Jumping in his SUV, Jorge pulled out of the driveway and made his way down the residential street, quickly picking up speed as soon as he got out of sight of his neighbors. He tore down a series of streets that finally took him to the grow-op and distribution centre that opened in Athas' neighborhood earlier that summer, making sure that word got out that the Greek politician had approached Hernandez for help in providing well-paying jobs in his district. It was a sneaky way of winning over potential voters before the election call and it was this very move that caused Sturk to retaliate with the provocative and unpleasant article about both the politician and the Mexican businessman.

Arriving at the warehouse, Jorge pulled into the parking lot and found a VIP spot before slamming on the breaks, putting his SUV in park and turning off the ignition. Tossing his sunglasses aside, he jumped out of the vehicle and headed toward the side entrance, using his security pass to get inside. Wandering through the dark hallway, the scent of pot filled his lungs as he headed toward the secret passage that enabled him to escape employees and cameras. The office was in the back.

Walking into the dark room, his eyes automatically landed on a young, scrawny, white man on the floor. Noting the blood dripping from his face, he turned his attention to the side as he closed the door. Both Diego and Jesús were standing nearby while a security guard held a gun on the *gringo's* head.

"What the fuck is this?" Jorge bluntly asked as he looked at his associates. "Who the fuck is he and why was I called in?"

"Doesn't he look familiar?" Diego asked as he pointed toward the young man.

"Some fucking *gringo*," Jorge guessed with a shrug. "I dunno."

"Remember the building we bought that was burned to the ground," Diego asked as he tilted his head toward the young man and twisted his lips while he waited for Jorge to take another look. "That fucker that was holding out on it when we tried to buy."

"Ah yes!" Jorge replied as he took a closer look. "Did you not break his hand, Diego?"

"Yes, that is the one."

"Oh, I see!" Jorge nodded in understanding. "And he thought he would come back to see us, did he?"

"He was caught, sir," Jesús spoke up while crossing his arms. "He waited for an employee to get in and held a knife to her to force his way inside the building. As you can see, that did not fair well for him."

"I see that," Jorge said with a casual shrug. "What I don't understand is why he's still alive? Is this, something you want me to do?"

"Sir, we are afraid he might be working for someone," Jesús replied with some reluctance. "Perhaps he knows about the property burning down? Maybe even more, I do not know but I thought maybe we should find some creative ways to make him talk."

"Well, you know, I do *like* it when you're creative," Jorge directed his remark toward Jesús before turning his attention back to the frightened man on the floor. "But you, my friend, you may not be so impressed with his creativity."

"See, in Mexico," Jorge continued and walked toward the young man, who was shaking. "We like to express our emotions with more passion than here in Canada. Have you noticed that, Jesús?"

"Yes sir," He replied slowly as he nodded. "Canadians tend to be more…diplomatic? Is that the word?"

"Yes, see, *amigo*, in Mexico," Jorge continued as he watched the fear in the white boy's pale eyes. "We tend to be a bit, old school. Some would say, barbaric. But you know, it does seem to work. Few people refuse to talk when you're cutting off fingers or toes. Jesús over here, he tends to like using razor blades to ever so delicately shave off pieces of people's eyeballs. It's really quite clever. You know, a man will let you do a lot of cruel things to him but you touch his eyes or his testicles, for some reasons, this seems to be a breaking point."

"It is true, sir," Jesús calmly directed his comment to Jorge. "These are things that I find most men value beyond anything."

"Well, it does make sense," Jorge spoke calmly. There was something about seeing the fear in another that relaxed him. Perhaps torture and murder were the antidotes to his anxiety. "You know, take a man's eyes, he is defenseless without sight and if you take his balls, he is no longer a man. Really, when you think about it, it makes sense. You can live a pretty normal life without fingers, toes….ears…"

Glancing at the man on the floor, tears and snot were now flowing freely down his face as if he was a four-year-old child; it repulsed Jorge but at the same time, it demonstrated that he was spineless.

"But then again, do you think it will matter if we cut his balls off," Jorge directed his question at Diego this time. "Is it possible to make this *gringo* less of a man?"

A smile lit up Diego's smug face as he nodded in agreement. "It does not appear so."

"Sir, for this man, I would like to try something I have not done before," Jesús started in his usual calm manner. "You see, he tried to bully his way in here with this rusty old knife…"

"Oh?" Jorge asked.

"Please, I will talk!" The man on the floor sobbed. "Please! Whatever you want to know."

"I am glad you are willing to talk," Jorge spoke in a matter of fact tone. "Cause us here, we got a lot of questions."

"I will tell you anything."

"You better believe you will," Jorge replied and suddenly had an idea. "Diego, call you sister. She said earlier today that she wanted to prove herself to me. Tell her to come here now. I think I have an idea."

CHAPTER

11

Much to Jorge's surprise, Jolene didn't take long to arrive at the warehouse. It was almost as if she was waiting for his call even though she had no reason to think he would ever contact her again. However, she showed up with an unmistakable look of appreciation in her eyes before quickly noticing the bleeding man on the floor.

The *gringo* appeared completely awestruck by the Colombian woman. Her beauty was undeniable, with long, dark hair, huge eyes and large pouty lips, she matched the profile of a beauty queen not one of a potential killer, which perhaps made her even more dangerous. She wore a basic pair of jeans and t-shirt, however, both clung to her body exhibiting her every curve and that was exactly what the kid on the floor was taking in with lust in his eyes. It humored Jorge but it appeared to piss off Jolene.

"What is this here?" She pointed toward the young man as if he were a sack of garbage. Any looks of admiration she received from the young man were met with disgust, as Jolene quickly glanced at both Diego and Jesús. The security guard had returned to his duties allowing the others to take care of the intruder as they saw fit. Except, of course, there was nothing 'fit' about what they could potentially do to this man.

"This here," Jorge calmly responded, his voice slow as he picked his words with ease. "This *gringo,* he has a bit of history with us. I am not sure if you recall the shop we bought that later burned to the ground?"

At the time, Jolene had been on the outs with the rest of the group but couldn't have missed the story on the news.

"Yes, I do recall hearing of such, yes," She nodded and pointed in the man's direction while turning slightly in Jorge's direction. "It was he?"

"Well, we aren't sure," Jorge replied and grimaced. "Unfortunately, the camera footage wasn't clear but he is the man who we originally bought it from. We had some differences of opinion about how business deals run. Diego, Jesús and me, of course, we believe that an agreement is a promise and at the last minute, he put up the price. It did not go so very well for him however, you see he is still alive, so it could've been much worse."

"Ah," Jolene nodded in understanding and turned to catch the man on the floor staring at her ass. Anger spread across her face as she turned slightly as if to make the view less assessable.

"This here," She pointed to her body. "This is not for you, so do not look as if you have a hope in hell."

Jorge snickered but didn't comment.

"This piece of shit," Diego moved closer to them while Jesús continued to watch the man on the floor. "He tried to substantially increase the price. However, we were able to negotiate to our satisfaction."

"One broken hand and phone later," Jorge muttered.

"Hey, he's lucky that's all I broke," Diego countered and returned his attention to Jolene. "He apparently did not get the message. Chances are that he also set the place on fire but we were unable to find him after the fact. Until now, when he decided to pay us a visit."

"Yes, he tried to threaten one of our staff to get inside the building," Jesús added. "But he will not tell us why or who he is working for...I do not think he got the message last time, that we are not people who you keep information from."

"We here," Jorge pointed toward his associates as his eyes watched the man on the floor. "We believe in honesty and integrity in business. Unfortunately, I do not see you displaying either of these things. This is a problem."

"One chance, *amigo*," Diego spoke with his usual arrogance as he twisted his mouth into an odd expression. "You can talk and make this easy or you can make us torture it out of you."

"I wanted to get in to steal some weed to sell," He spoke hurriedly.

"That there," Jorge pointed at the man on the floor. "Sounds like a rehearsed story."

"I figured I could slip in behind the employee, grab some weed and leave," The shaking young man replied as he attempted to slide away from them. "I didn't think I would run into you two crazy fucks again."

"Surprise!" Jorge mocked him and turned his attention back to Jolene.

"So, you did say earlier today that you would do anything to prove your loyalty," His comment was abrupt as he reached into his pocket and took out a piece of gum. Opening the wrapper, he casually slid it into his mouth. "You need to get the answers out of this piece of shit by any means possible."

Staring at her breasts, the man sat up a little straighter. "I would talk if you…"

"*Oye!*" Jolene's voice was loud and sharp this time, her eyes blazing as she glared at the man on the floor. "I do not think so! Why do you men think that us women, we are only here to seduce you and what? Make you dinner afterward?"

The loud click of her shoes could be heard as she lurched forward and with an abrupt, unexpected move, Jolene drove her long heel into the man's groin. All the men in the room flinched as the kid on the floor let out a loud yelp as he reached protectively toward his crotch to block her from doing any more damage.

"See, I was going to ask you if you knew how to torture someone into talking," Jorge commented as he shook his head. "But I guess, this is not necessary. Apparently, you came prepared."

"I am, what you say? Resourceful?" Jolene replied as she looked away from the man on the floor, her eyes full of disgust. "Back in Colombia, I did not hang out with what you call, the 'good crowd'. A girl, she must always know how to protect herself, her dignity because so often, men, they do like to take it away."

"Yes, well," Jorge started to laugh as the man looked terrified. "I do believe it is not your dignity that is broken."

The two exchanged a look that brought a sense of relief to her eyes while Diego and Jesús appeared surprised by Jolene's sudden demonstration of strength. It had been a long time since she had given any of them a reason to respect her but clearly, she was determined to prove herself and to regain her place within their organization.

"Now, if he do not talk," Jolene turned her attention back to the man on the floor. "I will do more until he tells us truth."

"Do you hear that, *amigo?*" Jorge directed his attention to the squirming man on the floor who almost seemed to shrink before their eyes, his presence growing smaller by the moment. "We will get the answers out of you one way or another and this time, I can promise you that you will not leave here with just a broken hand. This time, it will be much worse."

"Will you let me go if I tell you what you wanna know?" The man seemed willing to negotiate, his face full of vulnerability. "Are you going to kill me?"

"Did we not let you go last time?" Jorge asked with a shrug. "All we want to know is why you are here and if anyone sent you because this is too much of a coincidence and I don't believe in coincidences."

"This guy that hired me," His voice was nervous this time as he focused on Jorge. "He wanted me to see how things were set up, to learn from you. He said that the mob owned this place so they aren't likely to call the cops on me and just toss me out."

"Oh really?" Jorge said and showed signs of intrigue. "So he thought that we what? Let you in for a friendly tour of the facilities? Maybe give you some free samples?"

"Hey asshole," Diego suddenly spoke up. "This ain't no chocolate factory. We're not in the business of showing you nothing."

"The mob?" Jolene suddenly jumped in. "You thought the mob owned this place but yet, there would be no consequences if you snoop around. No no, this story, this does not make sense."

"And who is this man who hired you," Jesús said as he walked closer to the man on the floor. "I do not hear a name. Maybe we start with this, then tell the truth."

"Yes, all these stories," Jorge shook his head. "They have to stop. Jolene? I think it's time you try something else."

"No no!!" The young man put his hands over his crotch. "I will tell you everything."

"The truth, maybe?" Jorge asked. "It would be nice. You know, we all have lives here. Personally, I'm getting kind of hungry, so could we move this along?"

The young man awkwardly sat up and looked down at his feet. After a moment's thought, he began to speak.

"The time you were going to buy my property," He started slowly, his voice barely audible. "I didn't know who you were. I didn't care. I just wanted to sell the place and then my uncle came along and said, you know you're selling to the Mexican mob. They're trying to take over the pot business in Canada. I said, 'I don't care', I just want their money."

Jorge showed no expression but glanced at Diego, who raised an eyebrow. He believed him.

"My uncle, he started to talk about white nationalism and all this stupid racist shit," He continued. "At the time, I was in a bad place, my girlfriend had just…."

"Can we skip the daytime drama and get to the rest of the story," Jorge cut him off while beside him, Jolene appeared skeptical.

"Anyway, I guess I just jumped on the bandwagon, that's why I asked for more money," He continued. "It was stupid and afterward, I told my uncle what happened and he just shrugged it off. He didn't give a fuck about me so we went our separate ways until this week when he basically threatened me if I didn't try to get in here….he wanted me to set a fire."

"The last fire, was that you?" Jorge pushed as his eyes zeroed in on the man.

"No, no way, man," The kid shook his head. "That was my dad's business for over 20 years, there's no way I would burn it down. Are you kidding?"

"Then who did?"

"Someone my uncle hired, I guess," He replied. "Look the guy is powerful, he can get away with whatever he does cause of his status. That's why I'm here today. I was trying to keep out of trouble but he told me that if I didn't come here, that he would go to the police and say that I confessed to burning down the shop you bought. I thought, whatever…I will sneak in, set a fire, your alarms will go off and you'll put it out….whatever, it would get him off my back."

"Why didn't you tell us this before?" Diego pressed. "It's not like we haven't been here forever, waiting for some fucking truth."

"Because my uncle will send me to jail if he knows I told you anything," He insisted. "The guy is super connected and I have a record. The police would love to throw me in jail."

"This uncle, who is it?"

"Fulton Harley."

"Oh, no fucking way!" Diego snapped. "Not *that* guy again?"

"Apparently, he did not get the message last time," Jorge replied and exchanged looks with Diego and then, Jesús.

"Who is he?" Jolene asked.

"He's a fucking politician," Jorge replied and Jolene groaned and made a face. "And he's a white supremacist. We had to send him a strong warning last time he was fucking with us but apparently, we weren't clear enough."

"He thought enough time passed that it didn't matter," The kid replied, appearing helpless on the floor. "This guy is invincible. He's got people in places, you know, people who believe the same shit as him."

"Do you?" Jesús asked. "Do you believe this too?"

"No, man, I don't care," He put his hands up in defense. "Hey, my ex-girlfriend was black. I'm not racist."

"Do not use 'I used to date a black lady so I'm not a racist' excuse with us," Jolene snapped. "That does not mean anything."

"It's true, though," The *gringo* insisted, his eyes widened as he stared at Jolene. "She cheated on me so my uncle used that somehow to make me feel like, I don't know, I guess that we should 'stick to our own color'. I know its stupid but…"

"Again, enough with the soap opera drama," Jorge cut in and shook his head. "So Fulton Harley, he is behind this, that is all we need from you."

"Are you going to kill me," The kid shrunk back with fear in his eyes. "I will do anything, just tell me. I will go to the police and tell them about his…"

"No!" Diego cut in this time. "NO *POLICIA*!"

"OK, let's calm down," Jorge spoke evenly and took a deep breath and everyone looked in his direction. "I'm not going to lie, when I first walked in here today, I was going to kill you."

The boy blanched.

"But now, I do not know," Jorge glanced at Diego and Jesús. "What does everyone think?"

"I think" Jolene cut in. "That maybe you should also ask me. I am still in the room."

Jorge turned and gave her a look. "Yes, Jolene, what do *you* think?

"I think, I should kill him," Jolene replied and reached into her handbag and pulled out a gun. "It will be easy. We cannot trust him."

"Nah," Diego said and twisted his lips, shaking his head. "Too much work. Then we gotta get rid of the body and I don't think he's gonna talk."

"He won't talk sir if we cut out his tongue," Jesús added.

"Hey, I told you the truth." The kid started to cry. "I did what you asked. *Please*!"

"Not quickly, you didn't," Jesús replied.

"You all raise good points," Jorge replied and sighed. "Tell me something though, what is your uncle's issue with us because it is clear he's not exactly a law-abiding citizen either."

"Are you kidding?" The kid replied. "It's all about power with these guys. All his rich friends, you don't think most of them are white? We're talking the 1%. They want to own this city and then you come along and in like, no time, you're taking over one of the biggest industries in this country. People are using cannabis and not taking overpriced pills. Do you know how many of his friends and supporters are in the pharmaceutical industry? Are you kidding me? You're fucking them over, big time."

"Is this true?"

"They want you out of the picture," The kid continued and appeared to relax, despite the threat that loomed over him. A peacefulness filled his face. "But you keep cutting them off at every turn. My uncle is pissed."

"What is your name?" Jorge asked.

The kid once again looked guarded but finally answered. "Andrew."

"Andrew what?"

"Collin," His voice was small, nervous as if he were a child.

"Well, Andrew Collin, you now work for us," Jorge commented. "And trust me, you would rather be working *for* us than against us."

CHAPTER

12

"Wait, what?" Paige cut into his story and raised one hand in the air while the other held a coffee cup close to her mouth, almost as if it were a barrier. Leaning against the cupboard while Jorge opened the dishwasher and proceeded to put his plate inside as if nothing was out of the ordinary. "Did I hear you correctly? Did you just say that Jolene helped? The same Jolene who was working with people who wanted you dead? The same Jolene that grabbed you at your birthday party?"

Although his wife was usually calm, she prided herself on being centered in most situations, there was something in her voice this time that suggested frustration. Taking a deep breath, her eyes fixated on him as he closed the dishwasher. At the time, everything had made sense but now that he explained it to his wife, Jorge wasn't so sure.

"She came to the office to talk to me," He slowly began to explain to his wife in a hushed voice. "She wants to be back with us and I told her, you know what? Move away. Start somewhere new, a new life and pretend you do not know us but she said no. She said she would do whatever we needed to prove herself and I said I would think about it. Then, this situation came along so I had the idea of calling her in. I was planning to kill this…Andrew guy and figured I would leave the dirty work to her."

"This still doesn't make sense to me," Paige shook her head and sat her cup on the counter. "All along, you wanted her dead. All along, you wanted her out. All along, you didn't trust her but now, you have her working with us again? How do you know she's not working with the police? How do you know that we can trust her? Just cause she kicked some guy in the groin? Now she's suddenly ok?"

Jorge hesitated and thought for a moment.

"Ok, I see how this looks," He started as he touched her arm. "I follow my instincts. I feel we should give her a chance and if she fails, then that is fine but maybe, maybe she can help."

"Your instincts?" Paige spoke in a low tone. "Are you sure it's your *instincts* that you're following?"

"What?" Jorge said, shocked by her suggestion and for a moment, didn't know what to say. "I cannot believe you are saying this! You know how much I love you, I do not….I do not wander away…and…*Yo nunca haría trampa.*" He felt his heart racing, his hand reached for the counter. "Paige, this is not me! You know this…Jolene, we had a long talk. No one was more skeptical of her than me but…."

A knock on the door interrupted his ramblings, as Jorge attempted to explain his side. He had somehow forgotten that Alec Athas was stopping in on his way home from dinner. This couldn't be worse timing. He should've waited to tell her everything later.

While Paige headed toward the door to let him in, Jorge felt a wave of anxiety sweep over him as he leaned against the counter and controlled his breathing. It was rare for them to argue but this was the first time he saw that look in her eyes. He felt desperate to make her understand but how could he do that with Alec in the room; of all people, her ex-lover from years earlier?

Jorge pushed back his frustration as Alec's voice could be heard at the entrance and Paige returned to her usual, calm demeanor, almost as if nothing had just taken place moments earlier. Standing up straight, he took a deep breath and headed toward his office, where they would meet. As expected, he found both Paige and Alec already there, engrossed in a conversation. While Paige didn't look his way when he walked in the room, Alec gave an enthusiastic nod as Jorge headed to his chair on the other side of the desk.

Glancing at his wife, he noted she was avoiding eye contact with him and it made his heart sink. They had to get through this meeting quickly so Alec would leave and they could continue their discussion. He had to make her see that his intentions were pure.

"Ok, we do not have a lot of time," He spoke hastily, surprised to hear his voice shake slightly, something that appeared to grab Paige's attention, causing her to look in his eyes. Helplessly, he held back no vulnerability before continuing to speak. "Alec, I wanted to discuss Fulton Harley with you. Once again, his name came up today. It seems that he has a nephew, an Andrew Collin, the same man I bought a shop from some time ago, the same one that burned down. He showed up at the warehouse today, snuck in and was caught. After....a bit of coaxing, we found out that he was there in hopes of setting a fire."

"What?" Alec appeared shocked even though he was hardly new to these kinds of situations but his naïvety continued to shine through. He was so much like Chase when it came to these matters but with Alec, it was almost like he was playing the role of 'shocked' rather than actually feeling it. "So this guy was the person who burned down that shop?"

"No, it seems that particular fire was set by someone else but it was Fulton Harley who ordered it," Jorge rushed to explain as he leaned against the desk. "But this Andrew man, he told us that Fulton has some issue with us taking over so much of the pot business here in Canada and that some of his rich friends, they also have an issue, especially those in the pharmaceutical industry."

"Well, yeah," Alec nodded and leaned against his hand. "I mean, people are starting to see the medicinal purposes of it and are moving away from prescription drugs. It makes sense that they wouldn't be too happy with you. I heard that one of the major players has taken a hit in their shares."

Jorge nodded but didn't say anything.

"It's not as if we didn't see this happening," Paige quietly added and even though her comment had nothing to do with their argument, the softening of her voice somehow relaxed Jorge, as they shared a brief minute of eye contact.

"Yes," Alec cut in, appearing to not notice or sense anything going on in the room. "But I think Big Pharma would scare people into thinking otherwise. They've spent months investing in propaganda suggesting that kids would get addicted to pot and turn to hard drugs, that it would permanently affect their brain, which is interesting because they have no problem putting 5 years olds on pills for ADD even though it's a chemical."

"Yes, but that is our world," Jorge said with laughter in his voice. "This whole 'war against drugs' must always rise up when people aren't fearful to remind them that they should be. That is what Big Pharma wants, to create fear. So they were behind those ads in the newspaper and such?"

"Well, that and the 'scientific evidence' of course, they sponsored," Alec spoke with a grin on his face and shrugged. "It would be like *you* having a scientific study proving that cannabis has many positive health benefits."

"But it *does,* my friend!"

"It does," Alec agreed with a hesitant nod. "But if it didn't, do you think a study that you're paying for is going to say the opposite and if it did, do you think that it would ever see the light of day?"

"This is a good point," Jorge agreed with a nod, briefly glancing at Paige again. "Well, this is not a fight that they will win. I am not playing around with these Big Pharma people."

"I wouldn't underestimate them either," Paige quickly added with a look of warning on her face. "These people have a lot of money to lose and they won't go down quietly. Trust me, there are people who've disrupted their world who have ended up in jail or worse. I know this for a fact."

Both Alec and Jorge fell silent. Paige had spent many years as an assassin and contrary to popular belief, most of her clients weren't in the cartel or any form of organized crime, but often the so-called law-abiding citizens who had money to lose. Oddly, it was rarely money that caused Jorge to kill: disloyalty, threats, there were many things that caused him to kill but rarely was money a reason to end someone's life. Then again, a man who was truly successful knew how to win the game without going to such means.

"Ok, well, all we can do is be vigilant," Jorge thought quickly but unfortunately, his mind was still on his argument with Paige. "I have Marco examining The Dark Web. I also hired this Andrew guy from today, he will now work for me. Fulton Harley, of course, will not know but his nephew will be our source of information."

"What? You didn't tell me that part," Paige immediately jumped in. "I don't understand. First, you start trusting Jolene again and now you trust this Andrew guy, who probably would've said anything so you wouldn't kill him."

"Jolene?" Alec asked, his eyes widening as he glanced at Paige and Jorge. "Isn't that the lady from the party…"

"Yes," Jorge replied. "But there is a long, complicated history…"

Paige shook her head in defiance.

"I…I guess I just don't understand," Alec calmly replied. "And Paige is right, this Andrew guy, we don't know if we can trust him."

"I got a feeling..." Jorge attempted to explain but suddenly felt vulnerable as Paige and Alec stared at him in silence. Maybe it didn't make sense. Maybe he had been wrong.

"Look, I don't know what to tell you," Jorge finally continued. "Jolene, she's Diego's sister. I can't kill her. She made a fair argument. I see that she's being direct and honest with me and wanted a shot to prove herself and I will be fair. This Andrew guy, I was going to kill him. Actually, I was going to get Jolene to torture and kill him to learn the truth but he spilled the entire story and it made sense. I felt like he could be our inside track to whatever Fulton has planned."

"Well, maybe," Alec appeared uncertain but showed his fairness. "I mean, that could be true."

"I don't trust either," Paige quietly replied. "I especially don't trust Jolene and I don't understand how, after everything that happened, especially on the night of your birthday party, that you would suddenly think that I would be ok with all of this."

"Paige, she wanted to apologize to you," Jorge said but immediately felt as though his argument was falling flat. "I do not know how to explain it. I feel that she is sincere. Today, as soon as I called, she was there and she did whatever I asked to get the answers from this *gringo*. She was going to kill him. You have to understand, there is something different about her since she lost her baby. She is not the same."

"I saw that the night of your birthday party," Paige muttered.

Taking a deep breath, Jorge noted that Alec appeared concerned and although he hated to admit it, he was now feeling some of the same jealousy that Paige was clearly feeling toward Jolene.

"Paige, this has nothing to do with it," He insisted. "I swear. I do not want Jolene. Other than misleading Diego as a joke at one time, there has never been anything with me and her. As opposed to you two, I might add, and you notice that I have no issue with you two working together."

"I wouldn't exactly say that's completely true," Paige reminded him in a calm tone while Alec appeared uncomfortable. "It's different though because you haven't caught Alec feeling me up lately. So, clearly, it's not the same."

"It would be the last thing he would ever do if that were the case," Jorge spoke frankly, unconcerned with Alec's continued discomfort. "We both know that."

"Exactly and that's how I feel about Jolene," Paige replied as her eyes grew in size and she tilted her head down and slightly to the side. "But you decided to bring her back instead."

"Ok, Paige, you have made your point," Jorge sunk back in his chair and suddenly stared at the ceiling. "Whatever you want me to do then… that is fine. Do you want me to kill her? To exile her? I do not care. I do not want to have this argument with you anymore. Whatever will make you happy, I will do. Whatever. Anything."

"Ok, I have to cut in here," Alec interrupted their conversation, his hand in the air as if indicating for them to stop. "I don't want to get into this but first of all, you're talking about murdering people in front of me again. As I've said before, I don't want to know or hear anything about that. It's bad enough what I saw last winter."

He was, of course, referring to the day that Jorge murdered a white supremacist that was attempting to hold up one of their stores.

"What was I supposed to do?" Jorge asked bluntly. "Let him shoot all of us?"

"Call the police?"

"Once again, let's not be funny, ok?" Jorge shook his head in disgust. "The police, they would do what? Throw him in jail for a day? Close down the shop since it would be on the news? Close down all my shops? Charge us for murder? You would've been pulled through the mud through association and your political career, do you think you would still have one? We've been *over this before*, Athas. You're a smart man, I do not have to tell you this."

He didn't reply at first but finally nodded.

"Ok, so that part, fine, I get it," He spoke gently as if to show his peaceful side. "But can we please not talk about potential murders in front of me. I don't need to know this."

"Ok," Jorge hesitated before answering. "This is fair."

"And also," Alec glanced toward Paige. "Any concerns you have about me and Paige, are unfounded. Our relationship happened many years ago. We've been friends since that time and that's it. Even if I felt differently, I would never do anything to hurt someone's marriage. That goes against everything I believe."

Jorge nodded and didn't say anything. He was clearly telling the truth.

"Even if I were to approach you and grab…" Paige started.

"Ok, that is fine," Jorge jumped in before his wife could finish her sentence. "We do not need to play the 'what if' game."

"I wouldn't," Alec turned his attention toward Paige and shook his head. Jorge noted that her defenses fell slightly. "I really wouldn't."

"Look, you guys, I'm a counselor," Alec continued and turned his attention back to Jorge. "This isn't about me or Jolene, there's something else going on here and you guys have to figure it out. Maybe it's because your marriage happened so fast before you could build a strong enough foundation. Maybe there are some old insecurities that are showing up in this relationship. I don't know but it's not really about me or Jolene."

Neither Paige or Jorge spoke but shared a look.

"If there's nothing else, I'm going to take off," Alec continued and after Jorge nodded, he stood up. "This may be none of my business but I'm trying to help."

"Thank you," Jorge replied and nodded while Paige merely smiled at Alec as he rose from the chair and headed toward the door. "We will talk more later."

It was after he was gone that they shared a long, silent look.

CHAPTER

13

Alec's words would haunt him for the rest of the evening. Immediately after his departure, Maria rushed downstairs and asked that Paige take her to the mall to start shopping for back to school. The list seemed endless compared to what he, himself needed when growing up but Jorge simply shrugged and looked at his wife. Her eyes were soft, apologetic in return, all the frustration replaced by warmth and although that should've given him comfort, he was edgy until they were finally able to speak later that evening.

"So, the shopping," Jorge asked as he climbed into bed wearing only a pair of boxers, the day too humid to think about wearing a T-shirt. On the other side of the room, Paige was pulling her hair back in a loose ponytail. Wearing a delicate, pink and white nightdress, she crossed the floor while nodding.

"Some of it," She replied in a quiet voice as she slowly got into bed and looked into his eyes. After a brief hesitation, Paige shrugged. "There's more and the mall was so busy. I wish she hadn't left this to the last minute."

"What does she need?" Jorge asked with a shrug. "Some notebooks? Pencils? Why clothes when she wears a uniform?"

"She's grown so much over the summer that a lot of her winter clothes no longer fit. Plus there's a whole list of stuff her school wants her to have," She replied absently moving closer to him. "To me, it's ridiculous. We got most of it but we still have a few more things. I dread going back."

"Well, let me, I will take her," Jorge insisted with confidence while beside him, Paige turned with a skeptical look in her eyes. "You know, it's not fair for me to put this on you. Plus, she is getting out of control, I want her to know she cannot have the world. I think it would be good."

"You hate the mall," Paige gently reminded him. "And it's really busy."

"It is ok," Jorge said with a shrug. "I will be ok. We will go sometime tomorrow and you can relax, have a day to yourself, do something fun."

Glancing toward his wife, he noted a skeptical look on her face that turned into a grin.

"You know, maybe the problem here with the boys," Jorge considered and turned toward Paige. "Maybe she needs more time with her father. We will go shop, have some lunch and it will be good."

"Ok," She hesitantly agreed. "Yes, I mean, that might be right."

"You know me, Paige, I try to do the right thing by my family."

She quietly nodded.

"You could come with us too," He hurriedly added. "That would be nice. We could all spend time together."

"Maybe," Paige considered and looked away as if she was attempting to pick the right words. "I think we need to talk about everything that happened today."

Jorge reluctantly nodded.

"I've thought about what you said, what Alec said," Paige began to speak slowly, as she moved closer to him. "I'm sorry, I shouldn't have….I shouldn't have suggested that you brought Jolene back for the wrong reasons and I definitely shouldn't have brought this up in front of Alec. This was a personal matter. I don't know why I reacted that way."

"It is because Jolene," Jorge shook his head as he reached for her hand. "She is poison. I've said it many times."

"Then why are we working with her again?" Paige asked as she tilted her head to the side. "I don't understand."

"In truth, neither do I," Jorge replied and squeezed her hand. "*Mi amor*, I feel that we need to do this for Diego's sake. This is the only true family he has and I believe he will feel the need to pick sides. Diego acts strong but in fact, he is quite fragile. He needs family."

"Can we trust her?" Paige asked as she moved closer to him.

"I think, for now, that remains to be seen," Jorge answered honestly. "Do not worry, I will be watching her closely. As for what happened at the party, that is nothing for you to worry about. I would never cheat on you with anyone, certainly not Jolene."

Paige appeared saddened by his words, as if they triggered a whole new series of thoughts and for a moment, Jorge regretted bringing it up. However, it would've been unnatural to avoid the obvious elephant in the room.

"About what Alec said today…"

"Paige, the man is divorced, he is hardly an expert on marriage," Jorge spoke with confidence, unsure of how to tackle the subject. "I understand that he is a counselor and has studied these topics but still, Paige, what would possibly be the underlining issue here? It is natural to be jealous. We are humans, after all. It is our nature."

"True," She nodded and shared a gentle smile with him. "But I do think that there may be some truth to it too. We did get married quickly. Everything *did* happen fast. Maybe we needed more time to build a foundation."

"How does time help such things?" Jorge asked with a shrug. "I don't understand. We met, we fell in love, why would we wait to marry and even if we did, would it matter? If we were just living together now, would I be less jealous of Alec Athas? Would it not bother you seeing Jolene grabbing me? As I said, these are normal, human emotions. They are natural."

"But if we both know the other wouldn't cheat, then why are we upset?"

"As a reminder of our love and maybe, to a degree, our fear," Jorge responded quickly, feeling it was important to always answer fast to show conviction. "This is not about distrust or a shaky relationship, it is about fear. We worry that our happiness can't last because it happened so quickly, so beautifully, it only makes sense that we fear that one day it might all disappear."

Paige's eyes widened as she listened with interest.

"When I was a child, we did not have much money," Jorge began and moved closer to her. "My father, he starts this coffee business with a friend and eventually, he took over. However, it was a long time gaining in popularity and so for that reason, we did not always enjoy much in the way of luxury."

"Of course, me, I got involved with the cartel," He continued as he looked into his wife's eyes. "I made a lot of money and I made it quickly. As soon as I started to build up my life, I immediately begin to worry; what if something takes this away from me? That is the fear of every rich man and that's why people, they do terrible things over money because the biggest fear of those who have everything is to lose it all. I went through this and it took me many years to see that I would be fine. I have money stored away in so many places, *mi amor*, I will forever be rich."

She grinned and leaned closer to him.

"But of course, love, it is not the same," He continued, staring into her eyes. "I cannot clone you and make a million Paiges to hide all over the world, there is only one you and that makes you beyond value to me. It is a scary thing, the possibility of someone or something could take you away. You do recall what I did to the man who threatened your life?"

He was talking about a man named Urban Thomas who had planned to kidnap, torture and kill Paige Noël-Hernandez. In the end, it was his own barbaric murder that would prove that threatening someone Jorge Hernandez loved was like creating a suicide pact with the devil.

"I recall," Paige replied with tears in her eyes.

"So, you see," Jorge snuggled closer to her. "It is a love like this one that no one can break through. You need not worry about such a thing. Jolene, she is a poison, as I said but unfortunately, she is family even though we may often wish her dead."

"Yes, you're right," Paige agreed. "I know you didn't do anything wrong the night of the party. You handled it perfectly, I guess...I guess a part of me sees her and thinks, you have more in common with her than me."

"You think I have something in common with a *loco* lady who has addiction issues and has fucked up her life?" Jorge laughed.

"No, I mean, cause she's Latino," Paige quietly replied. "Maybe that's the underlining issue for me. I mean, I know you don't always trust white people but you married a white woman."

"I know, it is quite ironic but so what?" Jorge replied with a shrug as she looked away. "I have some distrust for white people, yes, but I think that comes from doing what I've done for the last 20 years. I do not think that being Latino makes me close to someone like Jolene. Really, other than that fact and her connection to Diego, we have nothing else in common. You know, it's not important to me."

She nodded in silence.

"And me, worrying about Alec Athas," Jorge continued and she looked back into his eyes. "I know you would never do anything wrong. In fact, I also know he wouldn't either. I think if you were single, I am not so sure but as a married woman, I know he would never do anything. I just...I guess I get jealous because you had that connection. This is not something I experienced before meeting you. My relationships were fleeting and unimportant to me. Even Maria's mother, that was a fling and nothing more to me."

"But you must've had some kind of commitment when you lived together?" Paige whispered.

"No," Jorge replied and shook his head. "I kept her around because of my child. That was it. I was with many women when we lived together, I was honest with you, as I was with her. That is why you must believe me when I say, I have not always been a man with morals but I have always been honest with you. I would not cheat. I know you wouldn't either but I guess….you know, with Alec, it is kind of how you look at me and Jolene and think about how different she is from you. Your ex, he is a good man. I, however, have not been such a good man."

"I was an assassin for several years," She gently reminded him.

"I know," Jorge teased her. "Do you not remember how we met? You were going to kill me."

"It was a mistake, my first and only mistake," Paige replied with a smile. "And I obviously saw that something was amiss."

"Good thing or my brains would've been splattered on a hotel room wall," Jorge continued to joke. "But hey, who can beat that story? It turned into the best night of my life and here we are….and jealousy, it is kind of nice too. I mean, it was flattering when you got angry and punched Jolene in the face. I thought it was sexy."

Their eyes met and he immediately saw something change in hers; a fire rose from behind the beautiful shade of blue, as her pupils dilated.

"You must admit, it is nice that I am jealous of other men sometimes," He teased her with an evil grin on his face. "I mean, at least I don't punch them so you must admit, *mi amor*, you might have more serious jealousy issues than me."

"Oh please!" Paige started to laugh. "Are you kidding? If you walked into a room and a man, *any* man was touching me inappropriately, you would lose your shit."

Jorge answered with a laugh and pulled her close.

"You would kill him." She giggled.

"Yes, my love, you are right," Jorge agreed and kissed her on the top of her head. "I most likely wouldn't start with any kind of warning shot."

"But I get what you're saying," She seemed to get serious for a moment, tilting her head, Paige looked into his eyes. "It *is* scary sometimes. It does make you feel like you're on shaky ground especially with the lifestyles we have chosen."

"Yes, *mi amor*, but the other side of it, I guess is that we *all* live on shaky ground," He reminded her. "It don't matter who you are or what you do for a living, all of the time, we are on unstable ground. We never know when our time will be up."

It was a reality they had faced the previous year when Jorge confessed to Paige that he had a 'mini heart attack' without her knowledge. It was something he hadn't even known about himself until his doctor noticed something in a test. The life he had taken for granted in his youth only now had meaning because of family and although he tried to not fixate, it was a reality that stared him in the face every time he looked in the mirror. It put everything into perspective and for that reason, issues with people like Jolene seemed quite minor in comparison.

They were family. There would be good days. There would be bad days. However, in the end, you knew that they had your back when faced with an uncertain world and things were about to get very uncertain.

CHAPTER

14

"You don't exactly gotta have a tea party with her," Jorge commented as he and Paige got out of the elevator and walked toward the office of Hernandez-Silva on the following Tuesday morning. Pausing before entering the door, he reached into his pant pocket for the security pass card to scan but hesitated. "She's probably going to apologize for the birthday party incident and that will be all."

Paige didn't respond but had a scowl on her face which she attempted to smile through. Standing tall in her heels, wearing a peach-colored summer dress, his wife had a way of looking lady-like yet assertive at the same time. Jorge responded by giving her a wink and smile, as he leaned in to kiss her before smoothing out his tie and scanning the card.

Once inside, he could hear people moving about and talking. Where they once had a skeleton staff, the past few months required them to hire more people, filling the one-time empty offices, bringing new life to the company. He reached for Paige's hand and they walked together toward the boardroom. They found Jolene and Diego already there, clearly involved in a tense conversation, which immediately halted as soon as Jorge opened the door.

"Looks like we are interrupting," Jorge commented and headed for his usual seat while Paige did the same. "Perhaps a family squabble of some kind?"

"Just the usual," Diego replied and made a face. "Jesús is coming here from the airport and Chase is somewhere talking on the phone to his kids in Alberta. They called before their first day of school. You know, the time difference and all."

Jorge merely nodded in silence while watching Jolene squirm in her chair. She finally made eye contact with Paige, took a deep breath and began to speak.

"Paige, before the others, they arrive, I want to say I am sorry," She stumbled over her broken English and although Jorge had moments when his own wasn't great, he sometimes wondered how hers never improved. "I was very drunk the night of Jorge's party and I do not know what I think but it was stupid of me. I am very regretful of my action as well as what happen last year. I promise I did not want Jorge killed."

Paige took her words in with ease and merely nodded in silence. Although it seemed as though she wasn't going to respond, she finally did.

"Very well," Paige quietly replied, her voice calm, soothing in tone despite the words that were about to follow. "However, if anything ever happens to Jorge and I find out you're in any way responsible, it will be the last thing you do. I promise you that."

Jolene pulled back slightly and immediately started to shake her head.

"No! I promise, no, this will not happen," Her voice cracked and the fear in her eyes was unmistakable while the strength in Paige's face was strong. "I will not. I promise."

"And if anyone approaches you again," Diego immediately cut in with a heightened energy as his eyes widened in excitement. "You *don't* hold back from telling us, right? No more secrets, Jolene. I don't care if it's an enemy or the *policia,* you fucking tell us!"

"I will!" Jolene insisted, almost in anger this time. "I tell you that last time…"

"Ok, let's not go back through all this again," Jorge cut in and shook his head, taking a deep breath. "Everyone, let us cool our heels, as they say. Can we move on?"

"I said what I had to say," Paige calmly replied, her eyes fixated on Jolene as she shuffled uncomfortably in her chair. "The only other thing is that if I ever see you attempt to seduce my husband again…" Her words drifted off and she continued to stare into Jolene's eyes without even blinking. "You know what? Let it be a surprise."

Jolene nervously nodded in understanding. She quickly looked down at her hands in shame. Paige was expressionless as this tense conversation ended. From outside the glass doors, Chase could be seen walking toward the conference room with the phone to his ear and a smile on his face as he ended the call. Entering the room, he appeared unaware of the tension and Jorge pushed forward as if nothing had taken place.

"Chase! I hear you had a conversation with your children," Jorge commented as the indigenous man sat across from them with a grin on his face. "They are also going to school today? I hope you didn't have to buy them as much school supplies as we bought Maria."

"I dunno, they seemed to need a lot," Chase replied and laughed. "Both of them looked to have heavy backpacks. I don't remember having that much as a kid."

"Me neither but it was a different time, place…"

"Century," Diego added with a grin.

"Ah! But we are close to the same age, my friend," Jorge grinned at the comment. "You are in no position to throw rocks from that glass house."

Twisting his lips into a grin he shrugged.

"Coffee?" Jorge asked and continued to ignore the tension in the room. "Do we have coffee this morning?"

"Yes!" Diego jumped up and headed for the door as Jesús arrived. "I will go get it."

"Good morning," Jesús greeted everyone as he walked through the door wearing a shirt and tie, with a laptop bag swung over his shoulder.

Everyone exchanged pleasantries when Diego arrived back with a small cart carrying a coffee pot and 6 cups, along with cream, sugar, and milk.

"A cart? Really, Diego, you need a cart?" Jorge asked. "You know maybe we can get a coffee maker for this room? It might be easier since we have so many meetings here."

"Nah, cause then we still have to drag the cups back to the staff room to the dishwasher," Diego insisted. "This is better. And actually, we can use this cart for many things. I thought it was a clever purchase."

Jorge grinned as Diego placed a cup in front of each of them and proceeded to pour a coffee, saying each of their names in a tone that indicated his relationship to that specific person. While Paige received an affection tone, Jolene not so much. It was as expected.

"Ok, I don't got all day," Jorge piped up as Diego finished and moved the cart aside while everyone eagerly prepared their coffee. "Let's get right to business and get the hell out of here."

"Clara was in earlier," Diego commented, referring to the 'cleaning lady' for the company. "Office is good."

"*Perfecto*," Jorge replied and took a sip of his coffee. "So let's begin. Chase, how's the club?"

"Great!" He answered with a shrug. "Business as usual."

"The numbers, still good?"

"Yup, all is running smoothly."

"Perfect," Jorge nodded, thinking how Chase was originally intimidated when they decided to switch the club to a more classy, upscale environment to attract a wealthier clientele, however, he managed to take on the role with ease. "Very good. The election should be called any day now and once it is, we will start to work on having some events for Athas at the club."

"Great," Chase replied and reached for his coffee.

"Do I know the Atheist?" Jolene asked and it took a minute for Jorge to catch on to what she meant.

"Athas, Jolene, *not* Atheist," Diego spat out from the end of the table as his eyes bulged out and he pointed toward the side of his head. "Put on your listening ears, Jolene!"

"I did hear," She snapped back at Diego. "I thought he say 'Atheist'?"

"No, Athas," Jorge impatiently corrected her and moved on. "Maybe the election, it will be called today? Alec will let us know when."

"Who is Alec?" Jolene cut in again and received a warning look from Jorge. "You get mad but I do not know. I was not here for all of this..."

"Alec Athas is a politician," Jorge replied and noticed that Chase silently focused on his coffee, ignoring Jolene while Jesús appeared humored. Paige remained stoic while Diego rolled his eyes. "We're...supporting him in his campaign. That is where our newest warehouse was opened, in his district and we gotta make sure he wins this election."

"Oh, ok," Jolene spoke with compliance in her husky voice. "I do see."

"All the way to the top, is that right sir?" Jesús asked with a pensive look in his eyes. "Do you think we can do this?"

"Yes, we gotta get him in and make a name for himself and in the future, we will back him for prime minister. This is when he will be most helpful to us."

"Have you actually talked to Alec about this?" Paige asked uncertainly. "Are you sure he even wants to go that far?"

"There is only one way to go, Paige," Jorge said with a shrug. "Of course, he will agree once he gets a bit of power. It is, what they call, an aphrodisiac."

Paige didn't respond but grinned and nodded.

"I think, you're talking about you," Diego piped up. "It's an aphrodisiac to *you*."

"Is an aphrodisiac, is it not suppose to be a sexy thing?" Jolene piped up again. "You know, to get you in the mood?"

"Jolene!" Diego snapped at her. "Your English, it is terrible! How long have you been here in Canada! This is pathetic."

"OK, let us not fight," Jorge cut in immediately. "We will be here all day. Let's move on from here."

"So, the election, it will be called soon," Jesús took over and nodded. "At that time, will you need anything from me."

"It is possible," Jorge didn't expand on that thought. "We will see how things play out, however, now that we have a new editor for *Toronto AM*, I don't foresee any issues."

Diego grinned and raised an eyebrow.

"Is that, the newspaper?" Jolene sheepishly asked. "Did you not have a bad article about you in that, Jorge?"

"Yes," He replied. "The editor has since passed away so…we don't anticipate any issues."

"Oh," Jolene nodded in understanding and fell silent.

"So, staff?" Jorge looked around the table. "We need more people?"

"Not right now," Diego answered. "We got lots and every time we take over a shop anywhere, we keep the same staff."

"Makes sense," Jorge replied and took another drink of his coffee. "There is something extra good about this coffee today, Diego."

"Ah! I added a little extra spice," He spoke excitedly. "I was reading about on the Internet. It is good, isn't it?"

"Always is," Jorge replied and took another drink before turning his attention toward the others. "So, we got this new Andrew guy helping us out. I think everyone but Paige and Chase has met him."

"What will he do, sir?" Jesús asked.

"I'm not sure," Jorge replied. "Right now, I'm gonna keep him hanging. I want him to be my eyes and ears and once he proves himself, we will see. He won't be in our inner circle but if he wants to stay alive, he will keep us informed."

No one replied.

"We are taking over more stores in the East?" Jorge asked Jesús. "Is that right?"

"Yes, sir," Jesús replied with a nod. "I am working closely with the politicians in various Maritime cities."

"Any issues?"

"Nothing I can't handle, sir," Jesús replied without elaborating. "I have some boys up from Mexico helping me."

Jorge grinned and nodded in understanding.

"That should take care of any problems we might have." Jesús continued.

"And Sylvana, she is helpful?"

"Yes, sir, she's good with these people," Jesús replied and shrugged. "Sometimes, her mouth, it can be a little too big."

"Yeah, that girl's got a mouth on her," Diego spoke with frustration and shook his head.

"Must be the Italian in her," Jorge insisted with a grin. "Can't be the Latina."

Everyone laughed and any remaining tension in the room seemed to disappear.

"Anything else?

"The dark web, sir?" Jesús inquired. "You had Marco looking on it?"

"So far, we are seeing the usual stuff, nothing that relates or affects us."

"I have question," Jolene piped up. "You say I can come back but, what do I do? My office, it is someone else there now, I do not know what to do."

She seemed pathetic at the moment and Jorge wasn't even sure how to reply.

"Maybe she should learn the stores with us," Diego suggested with a shrug. "I can take her around, show her how we do things now."

Jorge was satisfied with this answer. "That would be perfect. We will see from there. Jolene, consider this your orientation week."

She smiled and nodded in appreciation.

"You know, sir," Jesús spoke up again. "Perhaps she would be a good fit for the warehouse. It would be nice to have someone keep an eye on things especially in light of the most recent incident."

"What incident?" Chase asked and glanced around.

"Ahh! We had a small incident with this *gringo* Andrew, that I mentioned earlier," He pointed toward Diego. "I will have Diego fill you in more later and give Jolene the background information this week. If that is good?"

Diego nodded with enthusiasm. "No problem."

"Very good, then if that is all," Jorge stood up from his chair and glanced around the table. "Me and Paige, we must go."

He watched his wife hesitantly stand up.

Once in the hallway and out of earshot, Paige quietly commented. "We could've stayed longer."

"Paige, we would be there all day," Jorge insisted. "Jolene would have a million questions and they can be answered by Diego. I don't want to go over all this again and again."

"Sir! Mr. Hernandez?"

Jorge turned around to see Marco rushing down the hallway with a laptop in hand. "Oh sir, I am so glad I caught up with you. Would you have a moment, please? There is something I must talk to you about. It is urgent."

Exchanging looks with his wife, the two didn't hesitate to follow Marco back toward the boardroom.

CHAPTER

15

"What you got?" Jorge asked bluntly after Diego, Chase, and Jolene left the room. It wasn't that he didn't trust his associates but sensed that this information might be highly sensitive and the less people involved in the conversation, the better. "Was this from the dark web?"

"No, sir, it actually was not," Marco replied, his brown eyes expanding while the three of them stood around the conference room table, anxiously awaiting whatever news he was about to share. Noting that he was leaning against the table, clearly frazzled, Jorge glanced at Paige in hopes that she would know what to do. She did.

"Marco, what happened? You look upset," Paige spoke calmly as the company's IT specialist opened his laptop and hit some keys before turning it around for them to see. It was someone's private email. She leaned in to read it while Jorge decided to cut to the chase.

"What's going on?" He asked as anxiety filled the room. "What are you looking at?"

"OH MY GOD!" Paige suddenly gasped in horror, her eyes met with Marco's as she covered her mouth. "We have to let someone know right away!"

"What is it?" Jorge asked as he watched tears form in his wife's eyes, both he and Jesús moved closer to read the screen while Marco hurriedly rushed to explain.

"I hacked this man's Facebook," He spoke with emotion in his voice. "He appeared to have some connection to this far-right group associated with Fulton Harley and I see…I see this….I do not know what to do. I want to contact authorities…but…I don't understand who they are…"

"They're a group of involuntarily celibate men called incel that became radicalized," Paige rushed to explain while reaching for her phone. "They want to attack an all-girl school."

"Your daughter, Mr. Hernandez, is this her school?" Marco spoke with fear in his eyes while Jorge attempted to register what they were saying. "Does she go here?"

"No," Paige answered for him but suddenly was speaking into the phone. "Chase, can you pick up Maria? Right away!"

Meanwhile, Marco was on the phone and speaking to his wife in Tagalog.

"What?" Jorge was stunned by the news. In disbelief, he glanced at Jesús then back at the screen. Feeling helpless as his heart pounded in fear, his body weak, Jorge grasped the table and watched everything happen around him.

"Alec!" Paige was almost screaming into the phone. "We have an emergency! We're sending an email to you but it's hacked, so you can't let anyone know where it came from. It arrived anonymously to your inbox and you must act on it right away!"

As Paige instructed Alec on the phone, Jorge felt powerless as Marco grabbed the computer and started to type vigorously while beside him, Jesús was tapping on his phone and began to read. A look of alarm was on his face.

"Yes!" Paige continued to speak. "Please, you don't know where it came from but you must call the police immediately. Thank you."

She ended the call and Jorge reached out to touch her arm, he felt unable to speak. Was his daughter in danger? Every mistake he ever made seemed to lead up to this moment as waves of guilt flowed through him.

Paige was about to say something as her phone rang and she answered it.

"Chase?" She appeared to calm slightly, although not much. "Like, run! Get in there fast. Call me when you do."

She ended the call and turned toward Jorge and was about to speak when she halted, instead and turned her attention to Marco.

"Your kids, are they…"

"Paige, thank you, they are with my wife," He replied even though his eyes were full of fear. "I knew they had dentist appointments but I was not sure if she had picked them up yet."

"Ok, good," She took a deep breath and turned toward Jorge.

"This group," Jesús started to speak. "These people? What is wrong with them? I do not understand."

"It's a group called incel," Paige slowly began to explain, her voice seemed slightly calmer than it had been. "They're involuntarily celibate."

Her phone rang and Jorge let out a quick laugh as Paige answered.

"This here, is it a joke or something?"

"Ok, she's fine?" Paige was speaking into the phone. "Thanks, just bring her by the office, if you don't mind? I will explain when you get here. Thanks."

She ended her call and turned toward Jorge.

"No, I'm afraid, this is not a joke," She shook her head and reached out to touch Jorge's arm. "This is a group of misogynistic men, who essentially blame women for not having romantic or sexual relationships."

"What's that got to do with my daughter? With these schools?" Jorge pointed toward the laptop that Marco was once again typing vigorously on while Jesús read over his shoulder. "She is safe?"

"Yes, Chase is bringing her here," Paige replied with concern in her eyes. "Her school wasn't threatened but I had her taken out just as a precaution."

Jorge shook his head, still attempting to make sense of everything.

"This man," Paige pointed toward the laptop and Marco looked up and shook his head in dismay. "This crazy asshole was going to attack an all-girls school in the north end because he feels that these girls, these *children* are going to someday be the kind of women that reject him."

"You gotta be fucking kidding me?" Jorge felt anger rise up inside of him. "He wanted to, what, kill a bunch of kids because the miserable fuck can't get laid? What the fuck is wrong with people?"

"White boy drama," Jesús said as he shook his head then turned his attention toward Paige. "I'm sorry, but this here, it says it is usually white men. This was never something in Mexico, I am just saying."

"Let us hope not," Jorge fumed as everything started to sink in. "So now, I have to worry about my daughter more because of men like this?" He gestured toward Marco's laptop while their IT expert looked up and nodded in agreement. "Like we don't have enough to worry about when we have daughters? Now we must worry that some misogynistic fuck is going to threaten or kill her because she's a female?"

"Well, you aren't going to have to worry about this guy," Paige said as she pulled out her phone and touched the screen briefly before holding it up against her face. "Because if the police are too fucking stupid to get him, I'm going to!"

Her eyes darkened with anger as she turned and began speaking in a low voice as she walked across the room. Although he couldn't hear the conversation, he felt pride in the fact that he married someone with such passion, with such fire and who held the same values as him. She was perfect.

"Well, I think it's obvious that the police," Jorge directed his abrupt comment toward Marco and Jesús. "They will fuck it up. They always do. They won't be able to find him and if they do, they will hold his fucking hand and probably rub his dick while they ask him questions in a politically correct way."

"Well, at least sir," Jesús said with a grin. "He will be getting some action."

Behind his laptop, Marco let out a groan and shook his head.

Jesús shrugged. "Here in Canada, I hear some really odd things but this, sir, is the strangest yet."

"You're fucking telling me," Jorge agreed while he watched Marco pointing toward his screen.

"The schools, they are all on lockdown now," Marco glanced down and turned the laptop around to show the breaking story. "Thank God, my children, they aren't there. Thank you and Paige, sir, I didn't know what to do about this situation."

"Thank you for finding out about it," Jorge insisted and took a deep breath. "This is some scary shit."

"Shouldn't they be taking kids from the schools?" Jesús appeared confused. "Not locking them down?"

"They are sending RCMP to the school," Marco replied. "It is safer than having everyone out, I guess?"

"What was this dumb fuck going to do?" Jorge asked just as Paige finished her call and walked back to join them.

"He was going to go in shooting," Paige replied and took a deep breath. "He had an AK-15 and other guns."

"Fuck!" Jorge snapped. "Did I close my eyes and wake up in the US today? I thought these problems, these were the kind we heard about on American news?"

With a pensive look in her eyes, Paige shook her head.

"The world, it gets a bit crazier every day," Marco replied as he crossed his arms over his chest. "I just do not know anymore."

"Were you serious, what you said?" Jesús directed his question at Paige. "About the man? He is this kind of crazy?"

She nodded.

"Can you find him?"

"I already have," Paige calmly replied. "The only reason I'm not going after him now is that I don't want to get in the police crosshairs. But if I can find him, they should be able to."

"But in prison, will that make him a hero to his kind?" Jorge asked skeptically.

"Do you seriously think he's going to ever make it to prison?" Paige calmly replied. "He'll be lucky to make it to his trial."

With that, she glanced at her phone. "Maria is downstairs, I'm going to go meet her."

"Thank you," Jorge's comment was heartfelt as he leaned in and gave her a quick kiss and they shared a silent look before she headed for the door.

"This man, he should have his balls cut off," Jesús complained. "Can you imagine, wanting to hurt innocent children because women reject him? Why not just kill himself?"

"Well, he may as well cause it looks like," Jorge gestured toward the door his wife had just walked out of moments earlier. "Someone else will anyway."

"The other point, sir," Marco spoke up as he squinted his eyes. "He could go to prison and there, he may get all the romantic interests he wishes to have, you know?"

Jorge couldn't help but laugh. "Ah! As they say, be careful what you wish for?"

The three of them laughed just as his own phone rang. It was Alec.

"Schools are on lockdown," He said as soon as Jorge answered. "Everyone is asking who told me about this and I said it was an anonymous tip."

"This is good," Jorge nodded toward Marco. "Because although we would like credit to the person who found this, it was not exactly in the most...how do you say, honest way?"

"I gathered that from Paige," Alec replied. "Would you believe that I already have reporters outside my practically clawing their way in the door?"

"This is good," Jorge replied and felt a grin lift his lips. "We must use this to our advantage. Of course, we must give *Toronto AM* and specifically, Tom Makerson the story since he's been so helpful to us."

"I already thought of that," Alec replied. "He's on his way to speak to me shortly."

"Play it," Jorge commented abruptly as he saw both his wife and daughter heading toward the boardroom. "You know what to do."

"I do."

He ended the call just as his daughter flew in the door.

"Oh, *Papa!*" She rushed towards him, although briefly glancing toward the Jesús and Marco "There was a bad man, he wanted to hurt girls at our sister school!"

"I know, *dulce niña*, I know," He pulled her into a tight hug and kissed the top of her head. "This is why I tell you to always be careful. It does not matter that we are in Canada now, there are scary people here too."

"I know," She let go of him and stood back. "Chase got me just in time. He's my hero."

Jorge grinned as did Paige on the other side of the room.

"Well, Maria, he was simply nearby and Paige called him," Jorge briefly considered telling her that it was actually Marco who learned the truth but decided against it. His daughter might talk. "Someone learned about this potential threat and contacted Alec Athas and he, in turn, let us know."

Everyone agreed with a smile and Jorge looked at his wife.

"The world, it is not a safe place."

"No," She agreed and shook her head and quietly replied. "It is not."

16

I'm proud to live in a city where people care about one another and do the right thing.

Whoever sent this email to my office has shown courage and I feel humbled by the fact that they entrusted me to handle it.

Jorge turned toward his wife and mockingly rolled his eyes as the live stream on the computer continued to play.

We must show them that Toronto is a strong city and we will not be intimidated nor will we stand for this radicalization, these misogynistic, these terrorists. We will not allow them to threaten our children and we will not allow fear to prevail. We are Toronto Strong and nothing is going to take that away from us.

Jorge opened his mouth to comment but before he could, Maria ran downstairs swinging her iPad around. Still wearing her school uniform from earlier in the day, her eyes wide with excitement as she spoke excitedly.

"Did you see Alec Athas speaking?" She squealed and shifted her attention toward Paige. "That is *so* cool, he's like a superhero!"

Jorge forced a smile on his face even though he was cringing inside; not because he had an issue with anything Athas said in his speech – his words were carefully picked – but by the fact that it was his wife's ex-boyfriend that was looking like the hero, when in fact he had done nothing to help this situation other than forwarding some information to the police. If anyone was a hero in this event, it was Marco for discovering the incriminating email and his wife for handling the situation quickly and efficiently.

"Yes, *niñita*, you are correct," Jorge replied with a strained smile as he glanced at Paige, who merely appeared humored by Maria's comments. "In some ways, he's a real superhero. Of course, you do realize that he merely passed the information on to the authorities. He didn't find and arrest the bad man, so his part was quite small."

"But did you hear him speak?" Maria pointed toward the iPad and tilted her head to the side. "He sounded so cool and smart."

To that Jorge didn't reply, feeling in part that he created a monster. He merely nodded and took a deep breath.

"Maria, do you have some homework or anything you need to do?" Jorge asked trying to change the subject. "You must keep up with your studies."

"I know, I know!" She dramatically swung her hand in the air. "I had to see Alec Athas speak. I can't wait to tell everyone at school that he's a friend of our family."

With that, she swung around and ran back upstairs.

Giving his wife a perturbed look, he rolled his eyes.

"What? She's 11 and watching the news," Paige reminded him as she got off the kitchen stool and walked toward Jorge. "Let her have it. Kids need positive heroes and role models, this isn't a bad thing."

"I prefer for the words 'hero' and 'Athas' to not be in the same sentence," Jorge complained as Paige ran her hand up his arm. She looked like she wanted to laugh. "It was you and Marco who acted fast not Athas."

"True, but does it matter?" Paige asked and shook her head, the smile falling from her lips. "At the end of the day, we couldn't exactly go to the police so he helped us out. Let him have it."

"He doesn't deserve it," Jorge muttered.

"Let's not let our egos get into this," Paige spoke calmly as she looked into his eyes. "It is what it is. Let's just be happy it's done and the police caught this guy. With all the media attention, they have to do something constructive because everyone is watching. It also might make them more aware and watch schools more carefully now."

"It would be the only thing," Jorge grunted as Paige moved closer to him. "The fucking police, could they be more useless? And as for ego, when have I ever allowed my ego to get in the way?"

"Do you really want me to answer that?" Paige asked as she leaned in and kissed him.

"Well, at least, this will work out good for Alec," Jorge considered as he pulled his wife closer. "However, I will not lie, this insane man who threatened an all-girl school scares and infuriates me. That could've been Maria's school and he could've not been caught in time."

"Maria's school is highly protected," Paige reminded him. "*We* can barely get in without passes."

"But what if he were a parent? What if he was to take someone else's passes?" Jorge whispered, glancing over his shoulder. The last thing he wanted was for his daughter to know how frightened he was over this situation. "This here, this is like an American problem brought to Canada. We hear of school shootings and this insanity there and yet, their government is the first country to criticize Mexico and now, this insanity is coming to Canada. It is wrong. It is *very* wrong."

"I think we might handle it better here," Paige considered. "Let's hope so. Things are out of control with guns in the states."

He decided to let the topic go. It would only drive him insane if he thought about the terrible things that could happen to Maria. The reality that his daughter's school had already taught them what to do in a case of a school shooting was hard enough to digest. He was certainly happy they were proactive but on the other side, horrified that these measures had to be taken. She was a child. How could anyone want to hurt children? Even he, being the maniac he was, had never killed a child. There had been threats, although most veiled but they were only words to intimidate.

It wasn't until they all gathered for a meeting the next day that it hit home. Everyone's fears, thoughts, and views were quickly placed on the table, giving him little control over the meeting, Jorge watched as they all became hysterical. He found it ironic since he and Paige were the only people with a child in a Toronto school and yet, they spoke the least, observing the others.

While Jolene asked her usual million questions to understand the situation, Diego ranted like a lunatic and Chase spoke in a voice of fear, having two young children of his own. Jesús made various comments on how he would like to brutally 'take out' the man involved in the situation and Alec Athas attempted being the voice of reason, even though no such voice would be heard in a hysterical environment.

"Ok," Jorge spoke up and put a hand in the air. "Can we calm the fuck down and get this meeting in order, please? Cause this here, it is not working."

Everyone fell silent, all eyes on him. Each was sitting in their usual spot with Alec on the other side of Paige, something that hadn't gone unnoticed by Jorge. He felt exhausted and frustrated by the meeting that went from calm to insanity.

"What the hell happened?" Diego asked with an erratic nervousness in his voice. "We ended our meeting yesterday and then everything went to shit. Was this why you told us to get out of the boardroom yesterday?"

"Yesterday," Jorge began and spoke calmly toward Diego. "In my defense, I did not know what Marco was approaching me about, so I wanted as few people in on it at the time. He simply said it was urgent and I figured it was something much different from what it turned out to be and things happened quickly. We weren't exactly able to get everyone back and discuss it. We had to act fast."

"So what the hell happened?" Chase asked in an unusually anxious voice. "I rushed to get Maria and the next thing I know, the radio was saying every school was on lockdown?"

"Yes, well.."

"OH my God!" Jolene jumped in and took over. "The children, they must have been so frightened."

"Ok, we got to calm down," Paige repeated Jorge's earlier words. "Everything happened fast and it's just now hitting us how serious this could've been. It was scary but we got through it."

"But why?" Jolene continued. "This email. Why do we have?"

"Ok, first of all," Jorge said and glanced at Diego. "The room? This was checked by Clara?"

"Yup, just before the meeting started," Diego confirmed.

"Very well," Jorge glanced toward Jolene and then Alec.

Everyone fell silent.

"Am I going to want to hear this?" Alec asked. "I would rather not know too much."

"You will know, what you *know*," Jorge sternly insisted then turned his head to look at each of them. "I have Marco watching things for me. There was a specific man connected to Fulton Harley that we were suspicious of and it was while investigating…he found this email from yesterday."

"It seems strange that someone planning something of this magnitude," Alec spoke up with confidence. "Would put it in an email, so blatantly."

"This man," Jorge pointed toward his laptop. "Is no different from most. Think of the criminals like this one who post what they plan or some cryptic message on Facebook before they attack others. It is not so unusual. They are hardly rocket scientists but the point is that this man was bragging in the email about what he was about to do. We were lucky that Marco caught it on time."

"Who was he bragging to?" Jolene piped up again, leaning forward against the table.

"Does it matter?" Diego shot back at his sister.

"It could," She replied defensively.

"In this case, it was another bum in this incel group," Jorge replied."All that matters is that this lunatic was caught."

"Thank God for that," Chase commented and nodded.

"The sad part is that they will most likely not connect this man and Fulton Harley," Jorge replied and sigh. "Paige did right away and yet, the police will take months if at all. They have a tendency to only look at the most obvious clues."

"Yes," Paige spoke up in her quiet voice. "This man made frequent visits to Harley's office, however, the police won't make the connection."

"Cause he's white and educated," Jorge abruptly commented and ignored Alec's eyes. "That is all you need and everyone assumes the best of you."

"White privilege," Diego shot out, his eyes bulging as he did. "They don't know how good they got it."

"I don't know if that's always the case," Alec was now commenting; not that Jorge cared or acknowledged him.

"At any rate," Jorge cut in and took over once again. "The point is that we learned this information thanks to Marco and Paige's quick thinking, the situation was taken care of and now we must move on. The man was arrested so the police can feel like they've done something productive for a change."

"I wish I could tie this to Fulton Harley," Alec spoke with frustration in his voice. "Why would he want any association with this lunatic?"

"In fairness," Paige replied. "He may not have had any idea about this school situation."

"Does he not," Jesús suddenly spoke up. "Does he not have a child in that school?"

Everyone fell silent.

"It says here," Jesús commented pointing at his laptop. "On his Facebook page that he was quite horrified by the events of yesterday because his youngest daughter goes to the targeted school."

"Well, then obviously," Chase started to speak. "He had nothing to do with it."

"It does seem unlikely," Jorge thought for a moment. "We must get in touch with Andrew, see what he knows about this."

"Ah yes!" Diego agreed. "He must know something."

"My belief, sir," Jesús continued. "Is that he will cover his tracks so the connection between them will not be made. Perhaps we must find a way to link the two and get it to Makerson? Maybe this would make a nice story for his paper."

Jorge grinned and exchanged looks with Alec, who quickly looked away.

"That cannot be too difficult," Jesús continued. "I will speak with Tom this morning and we will find a way to connect the two quickly. The faster we can and get it online, the better."

"We couldn't connect the white supremacists to him," Jorge reminded them all. "Unfortunately, he covers his tracks well. Other than seeing him leave the office, we do not know what he was there for or what work he has done with this man."

"Andrew, if he values his mobility, he will talk," Jesús commented with a stern look on his face.

"If he values his fucking life, he will talk," Diego abruptly added. "We gotta grab him this morning."

"Ok, you know what?" Alec calmly said as he stood up at the table. "This is the part of the conversation that I don't need to know about so, I'm going to head out."

He pointed at the door and the others silently watched him leave.

CHAPTER

17

"What? You don't answer your phone?" Jorge asked Andrew Collin a few days later at a small coffee shop in downtown Toronto. It was midmorning as customers slipped in and out but no one seemed to notice the Mexican sitting with the young, pale man at the back of the room.

"I was sleeping," Andrew quickly jumped to his own defence, his voice a mixture of irritation and nervousness. Slumped over, he looked into his cup of coffee as if he didn't know what to do with it. "Where's your friend? The crazy one?"

"Diego?" Jorge casually answered with a shrug. "Ah! I couldn't bring him. He's with Jolene"

"Is that the hot one who kicked me?" Andrew grunted. "You know, she might've done some damage. Ever since…"

"You know what?" Jorge quickly cut him off and put a hand up in the air. "I don't wanna hear about your junk. I didn't dig through the sewer for the last few days to make fucking small talk about your well-being. I'm here cause I want to know what the connection is between your uncle and that maniac that was going to shoot up the girl's school."

"Ok, I had nothing to do with that one," Andrew's pale blue eyes expanded in size and he sat back in the chair as if he expected Jorge to attack him. "Trust me!"

"I never said you did, *amigo*," Jorge joked, humored to see the fear in his eyes. "I just asked a question. Do you know him? Did you know about this? Was your uncle involved in any way?"

"I don't know anything other than what was on the news," Andrew insisted. "Not that I would anyway, I've been avoiding my uncle like the plague since I tried to break into your warehouse."

"What you tell him about that?"

"I said I couldn't get in," Andrew insisted. "That it was locked down tight. That's why you had a hard time finding me. I changed my number."

"Yes, well if Jesús hadn't tracked you down, I wouldn't have found you."

"How the fuck did he find me, anyway?"

"He can find anyone," Jorge answered. "So this incel scumbag? Johnson?"

"Yeah, I can't remember his first name," Andrew said and took a deep breath. "Look, I don't know the guy. I just know he was at my uncle's office once, a long time ago, when I stopped by and I mean, I dunno but my girlfriend back then was creeped out by him."

"Why is that?"

"I dunno, women's intuition or whatever," Andrew replied with a shrug. "She said something about how his eyes or how he looked at her."

Jorge didn't respond.

"But I don't know him," Andrew replied. "I just recognized him from the news."

"So you got nothing to do with this?"

"Are you kidding?" Andrew shook his head. "My niece goes to that school, Fulton's daughter. In fact, that's pretty solid proof that he had nothing to do with it either. He's not going to put his child in danger. Say what you want about him, he's not going to hurt his own kid."

"This is true," Jorge said and took a deep breath and looked outside. "So, he's a lone wolf on a mission?"

"I guess, I dunno," Andrew replied. "Unless he picked that school on purpose? You know? Maybe he had a beef with my uncle?"

"Do you think that's possible?" Jorge asked, remembering something Paige had said a few days earlier. "Something up with that?"

"Maybe," Andrew said and reached for his coffee. "It did cross my mind but honestly, I don't know much about what he even does for my uncle. He kind of keeps me out of things."

"It is probably better for you that he does," Jorge observed.

"You know something though," Andrew seemed to relax. "He has a huge problem with that Athas guy. I guess that's probably because you're backing him in the election. He was talking about switching districts."

"Switching districts?" Jorge asked. "You mean, he wants to switch to Alec's district?"

"Yup, he's talking about it," Andrew insisted. "He said he's getting too popular and that they need to put someone in to bring him down. But that's gonna be hard. Everyone loves Athas since he stopped that attack and the election will be called any day."

"Well, you know, bring it on," Jorge spoke confidently. "He can't compete with Athas."

"But he hates you too, so it could be for that reason."

"Oh yeah?"

"Well, yeah, a Mexican coming to our country and taking over the pot industry," Andrew said with a shrug. "My uncle, you know, he's a racist."

"Really? I hadn't figured that out?" Jorge spoke sarcastically.

"I'm just saying, he's like *really* racist," Andrew said in a lower voice this time.

"I know about the white supremacist thing," Jorge replied. "I've had a situation with another one of his people a few months ago"

"I heard, you know, something about him receiving an ear in the mail?" Andrew asked with some reluctance. "Did that...did that really happen?"

"I don't know, did it?" Jorge asked with a shrug.

"He didn't go to the police."

"I bet he didn't since everything led back to him."

"You Mexicans, he says you're all crazy as shit."

"Well, I got a pretty solid case against some of you white people too," Jorge replied flippantly. "Reminding you, of course, it was a white man who wanted to shoot up a school of little girls this week."

"Yeah," Andrew said with a nod. "You got that right. Seriously, what is with this fucking incel group?"

"You tell me, white boy."

Andrew shrugged. "Truth. Its pretty messed up."

"The world, *amigo*, is pretty messed up," Jorge insisted. "It don't matter what color you are or where you live. There are fucked up people everywhere."

"So you don't hate all white people, do you?"

"My wife's white," Jorge answered his question.

"No shit?" Andrew replied. "See we have something in common. I like women who are a different ethnicity than me too."

"Yup, kid, we got everything in common," Jorge shook his head. "Now, you gotta do something for me. Talk to your uncle, sound him out about this guy. Play dumb. Say you remember seeing him at his office. Show some concern for the school. Do whatever, but I want you to find some answers for me."

"Why am I doing this again?" Andrew asked as he shrugged. "Why am I working for you?"

"Cause you enjoy being on this side of the ground, that's why the fuck," Jorge shot him a look. "You're one of the privileged few to get in my crosshairs and got lucky."

Andrew merely looked down at his coffee.

"So, if I don't find this out, are you going to kill me?"

Jorge didn't answer but stood up. "I gotta go. You got my number."

"Yes," Andrew awkwardly stood up and followed him to the door. "Can I get a drive from you?"

"What?" Jorge asked as they walked out the door. "Do I look like an Uber driver?"

"I gotta get to the mall to meet my girlfriend, can I get a drive?" He rushed to keep up with Jorge.

"What are you, my daughter? I gotta take you to the mall now?"

"Your daughter works at the mall?" Andrew asked with interest. "Which store?"

"My daughter is 11," Jorge commented as they reached the exit. "She *shops* at the mall."

Once outside, he located his SUV and reluctantly told the kid to get in.

"You better not be pulling anything here," Jorge commented. "My wife's expecting me and if I don't show up, she'll find you and cut your fucking throat."

"No," Andrew nervously insisted as Jorge pointed toward the door. "I swear, I just need a drive."

"I'm just fucking with you," Jorge laughed as he walked toward the driver's side. "Get in."

"Oh," Andrew said and followed his instructions.

Once inside the SUV, Jorge pointed toward the road. "Eaton Centre?"

"Yes, thanks."

They drove in silence for a few brief moments before Andrew spoke again.

"You know SUVs are bad for the environment," He insisted.

"So's burning down businesses," Jorge reminded him. "That's not also bad for the environment?"

"Ok, I was only going to start a small fire," Andrew replied. "I told you, my uncle was putting on the pressure. I had to make it look like I tried."

"Why? What's he got on you?"

"He's got control over my money."

"What?"

"My dad, he left me a lot of money but he didn't trust me," Andrew replied. "So my uncle has control over it until I'm like 25."

"How old are you?"

"23."

Jorge nodded. "Kid, you gotta get out of that deal."

"Tell me about it," Andrew said. "I know I'm a fuck up but that's my problem. If I burn through the money, that's not his problem, he doesn't lose anything."

Jorge didn't reply.

"Anyway, that's the only reason why I do anything for him."

"So the time that we were buying your dad's shop from you," Jorge thought back to the previous winter. "You wanted to raise the price cause of your uncle, right?"

"Well, I had massive bills," Andrew shook his head. "Turns out I wasn't very good at running a business."

"Yeah."

"My uncle said I was a moron to not ask for more in the first place."

Jorge nodded.

"Whatever, I guess I didn't know."

"What are you doing now?"

"With what?"

"Your *life*," Jorge asked as they neared the mall.

"Not much," Andrew shrugged. "Gotta get a job, I dunno what I want."

"Well maybe you gotta figure that out," Jorge commented. "If you go back to school, can't you get the money sooner?"

"I think so but I don't know if I want to."

"Well, my friend, then maybe it is time you *did* know," Jorge commented. "Do you know what I was doing at your age?"

"What?"

"Making more money a week then your fucking coffee shop was worth."

"Oh."

"Yeah."

"Is it true you were part of the cartel?" Andrew asked. "Like, you know, that show *Narco* or *Weeds?*"

"You know, Andrew, like most things in life," Jorge commented as they got close to the mall. "The television version is slightly altered but there's always some truth to it."

He nodded in silence.

"Now, *amigo*," Jorge commented as he put the SUV into park. "You've arrived at your destination. Get the fuck out of my environmentally unfriendly SUV."

Andrew smirked and followed instructions.

"And get me my fucking information."

"Will do," Andrew insisted as he got out and headed toward the mall.

Grabbing his phone, Jorge called Diego.

"We gotta meet," He said as soon as he answered. "No Jolene."

"That won't be a problem," Diego said on the other end. "I'm at the club now."

"Stay there," Jorge replied. "I'll meet you."

CHAPTER

18

"I dropped him off at the mall before I came here," Jorge informed Diego later that morning as they sat with Chase in his office. The bar wouldn't open until after lunch, therefore giving them privacy. "He doesn't know much."

"You dropped him off at the mall?" Diego asked as his eyes expanded in size and grew dark. "We talking about the same kid? The one who tried to break into *our* warehouse and start a fire? Now you're driving him around?"

Jorge shot him a dirty look.

"I'm just saying," Diego continued, his voice slightly toned down. "It's weird."

"Maybe *I'm* weird, Diego," Jorge commented with a shrug. "The more I talk to him, the more I just see a kid. This guy, Harley, he's got him by the balls. His father died, left him money and he controls it."

"Why would he control it?" Chase piped up as he leaned forward on his desk.

"He's his uncle," Jorge replied then turned his attention back to Diego. "He's going to find out what's the deal with Harley and this fuckhead Johnson and get back to me."

"I still can't believe you drove him to the mall," Diego said and shook his head.

"Let it go, Diego," Jorge commented with a grin. "Besides, he shit on me for driving an environmentally unfriendly vehicle on the way there."

"It is," Diego said with a wide-eyed expression. "Why do you have an SUV anyway?"

"I always have an SUV," Jorge commented as he glanced toward Chase. "In Mexico, there are places that don't even have roads. You gotta be ready."

"But you're in Canada now," Diego quickly pointed out. "We got roads here."

"Did you not experience the winter we just had, *amigo*?" Jorge reminded him. "I seem to remember someone's prissy little Lexus getting stuck one day."

Diego twisted his lips together and looked away while Chase grinned.

"So you didn't find out much from this Andrew guy?" Chase asked. "Are you sure we can trust him."

"I think so," Jorge replied. "I let him live not once but twice so I think he knows where things stand with us."

Jorge's phone beeped and he glanced at the message.

"Athas is here."

"I'll let him in," Chase said as he jumped up and headed out of the office.

"I still don't know about this kid," Diego said with a shrug. "Maybe he's playing us."

"I think we are good," Jorge insisted. "You know, he's not the brightest bulb on the tree but he's all right."

"Put the fear of God in him," Diego suggested as Chase returned to the office with Athas.

"Alec, nice of you to come by on such short notice," Jorge said as the Greek man sat on the other side of Diego, while Chase returned to his seat behind the desk.

"You said it was important," Alec replied. "I had a break in my schedule."

"*Perfecto.*"

"So you were talking to this Andrew guy?" Alec asked as he turned his attention to Jorge. From a certain angle, Alec and Diego could've been twins; neither had a hair out-of-place and always wore a shirt and tie regardless of the occasion.

"Yes, I did," Jorge said with a nod. "He gave me some information that might interest you."

"Really?"

"He tells me that Harley is thinking about switching districts to go up against you when they call the election."

"What?" Alec's voice rose as he turned in his chair. "Are you fucking kidding me? That's all I need!"

"What? You don't think you can win against him?" Jorge asked with humor in his voice. "You're like a superstar since you stopped that potential school attack. How's he going to win against you? Tell me that. He's got nothing."

"He's going to drag me through the mud," Alec answered in a calmer voice this time. "You know that."

"Let him try," Jorge said with a shrug. "He's got nothing on you and you know how this will play out if he tries to fuck with us again."

"Yeah, I guess," Alec said and took a deep breath but didn't look fully convinced. "I would rather not deal with him than have to watch my back."

"You got us to watch your back," Diego spoke earnestly and Jorge grinned and raised his eyebrows, glancing at Chase, who merely looked down at his desk and smirked. "We will take care of you. Don't worry about him."

"Yes, *amigo*, Diego has your *back*," Jorge said in a sincere tone although there was a sense of mocking underneath. "You will be fine. This means the greater the fall for him and finally, he might get the fuck out of the way after the election."

"I somehow doubt he will ever be out of the picture," Alec said and took another deep breath. "And the election, I think it's going to be called tomorrow."

"Tomorrow?" Jorge asked and nodded. "About fucking time. I feel like we've been preparing for this election for months."

"That's because we kind of has been," Diego replied. "We've built Alec up for months and this latest thing with the school too. I mean, how can Harley go up against that and seriously think he can win?"

"He obviously does or he wouldn't do it," Alec spoke, his eyes pensive. "It makes me nervous."

"You got nothing to be nervous about," Jorge insisted. "Him, however, he might have lots of reasons to be nervous."

"Maybe this Andrew guy is wrong," Chase volunteered. "He might have played around with the idea before this whole school incident but it might be too risky now."

"Let us not worry about such things," Jorge suggested. "I think we're inventing problems that don't yet exist. That is what I heard and I thought I would share it with you, Athas. It might be wrong. It might just be a story, you know?"

"I could see him do it," Alec replied.

"He could or he could not," Jorge said and shook his head. "He don't got a lot of time to think about it especially if the election is called tomorrow."

"And what do you care?" Diego piped up. "With all the favorable press you are getting these days, especially with Tom Makerson at *Toronto AM,* you got this." He rose his hand in the air and shrugged. "I don't see a problem."

Alec opened his mouth as if he was about to say something but then halted.

"But the other thing," Chase wondered out loud. "Isn't this guy supposed to be a white supremacist? How exactly is that going to work in a city as diverse as Toronto?"

"He hides it," Jorge replied. "Like they all do, that's why they hide under pointy, white hoods, remember. They're fucking pussies who aren't gonna show their faces. He's no different."

"But if it got out there that he was one?" Chase asked as his eyes glanced between the three men. "There must be a way we can do that?"

"Proof, my friend, we need proof," Jorge said as he leaned back in his chair. "We know it cause some fucker told us before he suddenly *disappeared.* Now, the challenge would be to have someone else come forward."

"Can't we arrange that?" Chase wondered.

"Makerson said that he heard that too," Diego added as he crossed his legs and leaned back in the chair. "But he got no proof connecting him to this group. People aren't talking."

"We connected….the guy at the paper to white supremacy, why not this guy too?" Chase reminded them. "In fact, it might be easier."

"Not really cause with that situation, there," Jorge answered. "We had some previous editorials that ran far right and were anti-immigration, so it wasn't much of a stretch, we just took it to the television and internet. But now, this time, it's a bit harder cause Harley's a politician. We can always start a rumbling though."

"That we can," Diego agreed. "That we can."

"He must've made some enemies along the way," Alec suggested. "Someone must know something."

"Another question for Andrew?" Chase asked.

"I'll add it to my list," Jorge replied with a grin.

"So now what?" Diego asked.

"We keep it business as usual," Jorge said and thought for a moment. "I suspect that we will know more in the next couple of days. Meanwhile, I will get Jesús on it. He has a lot of contacts in this area."

"He's good at making friends," Diego said and twisted his lips into a smug grin.

"Yeah, he was here the other night with three women," Chase commented and pointed toward the door. "Three *attractive* women, buying them drinks."

"He ain't much to look at," Jorge said and let out a laugh. "But women, they like the money and he's got that."

"He left with all three," Chase added. "Now, I don't know if that means anything but that's what I saw."

"I'm sure he was just escorting them home," Jorge replied and moved to the edge of his chair as if he was about to stand. "Jesús isn't a skinny or spry man, he cannot handle three women at once. Fuck, I don't know if I could handle three women at once these days."

"You better not even think about it with Paige," Diego warned him with dark eyes.

"I was speaking theoretically," Jorge said and gave Diego a dirty look. "I do not plan to cheat on my wife with anyone...not three women from a bar, not your fucked up sister, no one."

"Speaking of which," Diego picked up on the cue as Jorge was about to stand. "That's why I was here today, to talk to Chase about my sister. She's acting fucking weird."

"As opposed to what?" Jorge inquired with a sniff.

"Like totally *loco*, talking about shooting people and stuff," Diego replied with wide eyes. "It's almost like after she lost the baby, something snapped. She's different. Maybe she's bipolar."

"Maybe *you're* bipolar," Jorge teased as he stood up. "Look, as long as we can trust her and can find something productive for her to do every day, keep her out of my hair, I don't care. Maybe having her a little unhinged might be helpful someday, I dunno."

"As long as she doesn't shoot one of us," Diego replied and stood up too.

"I do not think that will happen," Jorge said with a heavy sigh. "Is that it?"

"I think so," Diego replied as the others stood up. "Oh, Jolene is going to start at the warehouse this week. She will oversee it."

"Jolene is used to running things," Chase reminded them. "This should be a piece of cake for her once she catches on and if she's there, we don't have to deal with her often. She can do her job, get a paycheque and hopefully, get on with her life."

"And you," Jorge said as his curiosity peaked. "What about you? Do you not talk to her no more?"

"I would rather keep my distance," Chase replied. "Things were very….emotional after she lost the baby but, I have to be honest, I always wondered if it was even mine."

"I told you, you needed a test," Jorge remarked and shook his head. "I told you that it was important to make sure. It could've been anyone's kid, you know."

"Maybe it wasn't mine but at the time, I didn't think it was right to push for a test," Chase answered hesitantly while beside Jorge, Diego looked away as if he didn't want to be part of this conversation and Alec glanced at his phone. "I'm not trying to be cruel but I'm kind of glad its over."

"It was for the best," Jorge offered and glanced at the others. "So, if that's all? I gotta go."

No one replied.

"Athas, let me know if you hear anything," Jorge instructed as he headed toward the door.

"I will," He replied earnestly. "I think tomorrow is the day."

"Let the races begin," Jorge remarked. "And Fulton Harley, he won't even make it past the first round."

CHAPTER

19

As predicted, the Prime Minister called the election the following morning. Fulton Harley announced that he was changing districts a few days later.

"Its kind of ridiculous that you must announce an election considering it's a fixed date," Jorge observed as he shared a leisurely breakfast with Paige. He was rarely encouraged to eat bacon and eggs unless his wife made them, perhaps because she cooked them in a slightly healthy way. "I find such things to be redundant."

"I guess its to officially start of the race," Paige commented as she pushed a strand of blonde hair behind her ear. "Everyone knows what time its scheduled for but it's important that all participants know when they can start their official campaign."

"Again, ridiculous," Jorge insisted and reached for another slice of bacon. "We started this race months ago and we're gonna finish it on top, even though Harley Fulton, for some bizarre reason, seems to think otherwise."

"Its personal with him," Paige insisted while she picked at her toast. "It's clearly not about serving his people but serving his ego."

"He claims that switching districts was his party's choice," Jorge remarked and took a drink of coffee. "But obviously, we know this is not true."

"He's obviously not going to admit it," Paige reminded him. "He claims Alec is too inexperienced to properly serve the constituents, therefore he wants to be a more viable candidate in that area. He's suddenly concerned about the people."

"This *inexperienced* candidate brought jobs to the area," Jorge sniffed. "People go to him before the current MLA for that district. Does that not say something?"

"He wants to create doubt in their minds," Paige replied with a small grin on her face. "It's a game. Politics, it's just one big Chess game."

"Trust me," Jorge said with a seductive grin. "My life has been a Chess game so he got nothing on me and in the end, he's going against me as much as Athas."

"You have a meeting with him this morning?"

"Yes, in about an hour," Jorge lazily pointed toward the door. "Diego, Jesús and Athas."

"And Jolene, have you heard anything?"

"She's working at the warehouse and out of our hair unless we need her," He replied and finished his coffee. "Diego was saying recently that she has become, how do you say, a little *loco*. He seems worried but me, I think that might become useful."

"Losing the baby has definitely changed her personality."

"In fairness, if I lost a child, perhaps I would be the same way?"

"*Perhaps?*" Paige raised her eyebrows.

"Well, I do not know. I don't see it the same before the baby is born," Jorge replied. "I guess that makes me insensitive but I'm a man. I suppose she was far along when the miscarriage happened."

Paige didn't reply.

Two hours later, Diego was early for the meeting. He brought a box of pastries from a new French bakery in the downtown area. When Jorge attempted to reach for one right away, Diego waved his hand to discourage him.

"Not until the others arrive," He insisted and obnoxiously twisted his lips together. "You can wait."

"Why should I? Last time I checked, this is my house," Jorge reminded him. "You got tons of them in that box."

"Trust me," Diego rolled up his sleeves and headed toward the kitchen. "You're going to want these with coffee. Where's Paige?"

"Upstairs on the phone," Jorge replied. "Some family thing."

"Paige don't like her family." Diego sang out as he went to work preparing the coffee.

"I know."

"Have you met them?"

"Not yet," Jorge replied. "I don't think we can put it off much longer. Her father is ill."

"And your mother?"

"I don't talk to her," Jorge replied as Diego turned around and gave him a skeptical look. "What? We got no relationship for a reason. I let Maria talk to her and she's lucky I even allow that."

The doorbell rang and Jorge rushed to answer it to find Jesús and Alec.

"I found him out there in his car," Jesús gestured toward Alec. "On his phone."

"I swear since this election was called," Alec commented as the two men walked in. "I haven't had a second to myself. I'm so busy."

"Nature of the beast," Jorge commented as they all headed toward the kitchen, where Diego was already reaching for coffee mugs in the cupboard. Paige was on her way downstairs with a neutral expression on her face.

"Everything all right?" Jorge asked in a lower voice as his wife approached.

She merely nodded and smiled without giving any further explanation.

"Very good," Jorge redirected his attention toward the others. "Diego brought us pastries and made us coffee. Let's grab a cup and head to the dining room."

Everyone followed his instructions and gathered around the table, quickly reaching for the French delicacies. Jorge grabbed one with chocolate drizzle and sunk his teeth in, his taste buds immediately on alert as the sweet, smooth chocolate melted in his mouth.

"Oh my God, Diego, these are delicious," Jorge said and immediately took a second bite while his friend nodded with a smile on his face.

"I told you."

Everyone else quickly commented, distracted by the food, it took a few minutes for the meeting to get underway. It was while Jorge reached for a second pastry that he managed to get everyone's attention.

"Ok, we gotta few things to discuss," He spoke with his mouthful of pastry. "So, Athas, what you got?"

"Harley's saying he thinks I'm not qualified to serve the constituents but isn't saying why," Alec commented. "That's about it."

"He's waiting for the last minute to drop a bombshell," Jorge predicted as he slipped the last of the rich treat into his mouth. "But we gotta beat him to it."

"How we do that?" Diego asked as he took a drink of coffee.

"We're going to get Tom Makerson on it," Jorge replied. "I got a meeting with him on Monday. We can't sit around and wait to see what happens."

"Did Andrew tell you anything?" Alec asked. "About Harley or this Johnson guy?"

"Ah, get this," Jorge grabbed a napkin and wiped his hand, glancing briefly at his wife but her expression was still neutral. "He talked to Fulton, you know, showing compassion since his daughter is in the school that was to be attacked."

"Fulton told him the police searched Johnson's apartment," Jorge continued. "He had fucked up shit like Nazi flags, framed pictures of some sicko from the Montreal massacre years ago. The man who killed all the women? That was like his hero or something and that's nothing compared to what he had on his computer. There was literature on white supremacy, plus he was in some far-right online group that recruits people, like a cult, supposedly looking for 'soldiers' for their army. The man hated everyone who wasn't a white, straight male. I guess it goes to show that you never know what kind of sick fucks are out there."

"I'd say," Diego responded calmly as he ate a pastry. Beside him, Alec appeared completely stunned.

"Sir, I do think that a lot of them are out there," Jesús wiped his fingers on a napkin as he chewed the last of his pastry. "They are just to various degrees. This one here apparently was quite extreme compared to most."

"Yeah, the crazies always shine through," Jorge replied. "This one, he's locked up and it don't look like he will get out anytime soon."

"I would hope not," Alec finally spoke. "What was his justification? Why hurt children?"

"Female children," Jorge reminded him. "This guy, far right, white supremacist *and* apparently, hated women. It was a girl's school, so in his fucked up head, he thought it was ok to attack a school since it was only girls. He thought he was sending a message or some stupid shit like that."

"Harley must've been furious since his kid goes there," Diego commented as he took another drink of coffee. "Was Johnson out to get him?"

"Nah, apparently this guy ain't that smart," Jorge replied and glanced at his silent wife. "He didn't realize Fulton's kid was there so it clearly wasn't an attempt to 'get' him. Fulton's trying to separate himself from the dumb fuck now that he's under the spotlight."

"Is there any proof that he was talking to this psychopath?" Alec asked Jorge. "Like, that we can connect them."

"No, but be assured," Jorge commented. "The ax *will* fall on his neck." Everyone silently nodded.

"So, Athas," Jorge decided to switch gears. "What's the deal? You got speeches, baby kissing, that kind of thing lined up."

"My schedule is full to the brim," Alec assured him. "Like I said earlier, I don't have a second to myself and I was actually hoping that Paige could jump in and help some more with social media?"

"Absolutely," She spoke for the first time in the meeting. "Whatever you need."

Jorge cringed and put his hand up in the air. "Within reason, Athas."

"I know, I know," Alec sat back in his chair and redirected his attention to Paige. "I will give you the passwords and authorization for my accounts before I leave in a minute."

"Where you going to?" Jorge casually asked.

"I have an interview with one of the news channels about Johnson, what I've already done for my area," He drifted off.

"Make sure you mention your surprise that Fulton is suddenly running against you," Jorge commented. "Maybe get that out there."

"I will try but this interviewer is quite aggressive," Alec said as he finished his coffee. "Plus they edit it down."

"I bet they do," Jorge remarked and noted that Jesús raised an eyebrow. "Do you need one of us with you? You know, to keep an eye on things?"

"I'm fine," Alec quietly responded.

"You know, throw in one of those Maya Angelou quotes," Jorge advised. "People, they eat that shit up."

"Do you even know who Maya Angelou is?" Paige gently asked.

"Nah, but I see a lot of her quotes all over the place and people saying they love her," Jorge insisted. "That's all I need to know."

"You think that will work?" Jesús asked skeptically.

"Yeah, the white people especially, they're into that," Jorge responded. "They love spiritual and inspirational quotes."

"Hey its better than a quote from him," Diego laughed, glancing at Jesús than gesturing toward Jorge. "They don't exactly make Hallmark cards about Jorge Hernandez."

Everyone started to laugh. Jorge couldn't resist but to join them.

"Maybe they should," He finally responded to Diego's dig.

"Inspirational Cards for Gangsters," Paige calmly added. "I don't think that's been done yet."

"Its best we keep out secrets quiet," Jorge smirked and gave his wife a quick kiss. "Not everyone should be privy to my brilliant thoughts."

Diego groaned and rolled his eyes.

"Hey, you never say what Fulton said when Andrew tell him that he wasn't able to get into the warehouse," Jesús spoke gently. "Should we be watching for someone else?"

"Nah, he wants to keep his nose clean now cause of the election," Jorge replied and shook his head. "He thinks it's too risky but he's still out to get us. He thinks he's going to get into Alec's district and have some control over us once he does, try to push us out so some of his rich, *white* friends can take over the pot stores."

"I don't get how someone who grew up in Toronto could be racist," Alec remarked. "It seems strange to me."

"Sometimes, its cause they live in a diverse city that they *are* racist," Jorge reminded him. "In the end, it don't matter. Somewhere along the way, he got these fucked up ideas. Some people, they are brought up that way."

Alec shrugged. "I don't understand."

"People who aren't racists usually don't," Jorge answered. "And those who never dealt with people being racist toward them, don't either."

Everyone was silent for a moment.

"Now, I gotta pick up my daughter at her friend's house," Jorge finally commented and stood up, reaching for one more pastry but upon seeing his wife's expression, changed his mind. "Anything else?"

They all shook their heads and the meeting ended. Everything felt good. Everything felt light. Little did they know what they would wake up to the next morning.

CHAPTER

20

P olice raided the unidentified teen's house early this morning after they received a tip that he was planning to 'take over' for Johnson....

Jorge swallowed back his anger, instead, reaching out to touch his daughter's arm as she quietly watched television. Unusually silent, he wasn't sure if this was from fear or lack of understanding of the scope of this situation but regardless, he chose his words carefully.

"*Niñita,* perhaps it would be a good idea for you to stay home from school today," Jorge said in the calmest voice he could find, glancing toward Paige who stood nearby, with a coffee in hand. They shared a look of concern. "You know, just until they have this mess sorted out."

"But *Papa,* I have to be in school today, we have a Math test," Maria said while shaking her head in defiance. "Plus, this wasn't my school it was somewhere else."

"I know, but Maria, what if someone attacks your school? Did you ever think of that?" He heard some anger creep into his voice. "We cannot be too careful."

"But *Papa,* lots of bad things could happen today," Maria spoke logically. "But we can't hide in the house forever. They do not let just anyone get in my school plus, there's a metal detector."

Her words were powerful for a child, causing Jorge to take pause. Usually, the last person accused of being overly cautious, he was also the first person who knew how easy it was to get into supposedly secure places. He shared a knowing glance with Paige.

"I do realize this but my concern is that there are others out there doing the same thing," Jorge admitted with some hesitation. He didn't want to scare his daughter but on the other hand, he had to make her aware of the seriousness of this situation. "We must be smart."

"*Papa,* I cannot leave school forever."

"I wasn't suggesting that Maria," Jorge spoke sternly this time. "I'm just saying, for today, maybe we should keep you home."

"Jorge, they'll probably have added security today," Paige calmly reminded him, "I can take Maria to school and talk to the principal if you wish? If I don't feel it is safe enough, I'll bring her back home."

Jorge reluctantly agreed, just as his phone beeped. It was a message from Diego.

Did you see the television? Wow!

Diego, have Marco do some extra research.

Will do.

Fortunately, he was certain that Diego knew what he was referring to; research would be done on this fucked up Incel group to see if there were any other loose wires about to snap. Although the authorities would be looking for the same, Jorge had much more confidence in Marco than the so-called police. It appeared they had only caught this dumb fuck copycat because of a tip, not because of their own investigation.

It was after Paige took Maria to school that Jorge felt a hot vibration take over his body. Sitting on the closest chair, he recognized that it was a panic attack. For all the years he worked in dangerous situations, most of which were right on the front line, it was now that Jorge experienced the most overwhelming stress. Perhaps it was his age. Maybe a man in his 40s was less able to deal with life or maybe he was losing his edge. When he was young, his only worries was work. Now, he had a family, his one vulnerability.

As the anxiety moved through him, Jorge reached for a glass of water on the nearby table and took a sip. His daughter was right. They couldn't hide from life but yet, the world, it was a scarier place every day. At one time, most dangers were underground, carefully hidden from the public, who were mostly ignorant of the crimes that often took place right under their noses. Now, it almost seemed like everything was rising to the top; the prejudices that so many had gone to great lengths to hide or deny for years, the crimes that were once concealed through intimidation and hatred, that most would've preferred to ignore. Everyone had to face the truth and as usual, the truth was inconvenient.

His legs were heavy as he stood up. On days such as this one, Jorge would've preferred to go back to bed but unfortunately, his calendar was full. Glancing at his phone, he grabbed the keys for the SUV and headed toward the door.

Forty minutes later, he sat across from Jesús and Diego in the office boardroom. The dismal morning was weighing on the group, as they drank coffee and waited for Marco to join them.

"It is bad, sir," Jesús finally commented. "The police, I fear they are not doing their job in this matter."

"They don't got a choice," Diego spoke up with fire in his voice. "The whole fucking city is falling apart and they're doing the minimum. You would think schools, of all places, would be top priority."

"Look at America," Jesús commented and reached for his coffee. "School shootings all the time. So clearly, it is not that much of a concern or something would be done."

"You know, that's my fear for Canada too," Jorge abruptly commented as Marco walked into the room, his usual upbeat demeanor deflated. "What if that attitude spreads here? I am feeling as though many of the negative attitudes are starting to show in this culture as well. I hope that this disregard for schools and children will not be one of them."

"Sir, I looked," Marco jumped right into the conversation as he sat his laptop on the table before slowly easing into the chair. "I was not able to find anything new this time. It looks like the account that I located information on was deactivated and if this group incel is still online, they are carefully hidden."

"Fuck," Jorge said and shook his head.

"I know, sir, it worries me a great deal," Marco admitted as he opened his laptop. "I have children in school and I fear the police will show less attention to public schools than the private ones."

"I'm not even very confident about the private schools," Jorge replied and pointed toward his phone on the table. "Paige took my daughter to school and not a cop to be seen, nothing. The school insists it is fine, that they have cameras everywhere, that no one without a special pass can get in but to me, that's not good enough. People lose passes, steal passes, I don't know anymore what to do about this situation."

"It is hard to know, sir, I agree," Marco quietly replied. "It is quite frightening to me."

"See, this is one reason why we need Athas at the top," Jorge abruptly commented. "He would have the power to find real solutions. There is something wrong with any society that claims children are top priority but yet, does nothing to protect them. That is what I say."

Everyone fell silent until Jesús finally spoke.

"I am heading out later today to take over some more stores in the east," He spoke slowly and rubbed a hand over his face. "They are being hesitant in some of these Atlantic provinces, however, I will find a way to convince them it is in their best interest to step aside."

"It's not been a problem before," Diego said as he pulled his chair forward. "The farther we go, the less tightly the government seems to hold on."

"That is because they don't care," Jorge replied. "As long as they get their taxes, as long as the public isn't shitting on them, they don't care. We make good business partners and in the end, we know that money talks with these politicians. Many are learning that there is much more to this then they originally thought. I've done this for over 20 years, I know what I'm fucking doing."

"What about more warehouses, sir?" Jesús asked casually, the mood of the room relaxing from only moments earlier. "Do you feel we should look into more in the East?"

"We can barely keep up with demand here, so yes, we must find more warehouses willing to sell."

"Of course, sir, I will get on it."

"We will one day monopolize this industry," Jorge spoke dreamily.

"It's happening faster than I ever thought it would," Diego admitted.

"Ah! Diego! You underestimate me," Jorge said with a grin on his face. "I don't fuck around."

"And sir, Athas has his interview running later today," Jesús picked up the conversation. "Didn't you say?"

"Yes," Jorge nodded. "Apparently, he was able to get a comment in about Harley and said the reporter asked some questions, so this will help us."

"I don't got a good feeling about them running against each other," Diego said as he lifted one eyebrow. "I just don't."

"The other day you weren't too concerned," Jorge pointed out. "You seemed to think he could win."

"But to go against Alec when he knows how strong he is in his district," Diego reminded him. "He must be pretty confident that he *can* win to take the chance."

"Then we," Jorge spoke abruptly. "We will get something on Harley. In fact, we're already working on it. I got a meeting with Makerson next."

Twenty minutes later, the editor for *Toronto AM* sat across from Jorge in a small coffee shop near the newspaper's office. The sun was shining through the window, hitting his face, which appeared lifeless and tired.

"Tough week already," Jorge commented as he leaned back in the booth while Tom bit into a hearty sandwich. "It's only Monday and you've already got a crazy news week."

After quickly chewing his sandwich, he nodded and finally spoke. "Last week was pretty insane too, with the school thing. I figured this one would be a little less stressful, but I was up half the night getting ready for today."

"Don't you got people to do that for you?" Jorge asked, completely unaware of how the newspaper industry works.

"I do but at the same time, I have to think about what our lead story will be, what we should focus on, what our competitors will do..." He said while staring down at his sandwich as if contemplating another bite. "I'm still new as the editor. I have to prove to our shareholders that I can do the job."

"Sounds stressful," Jorge spoke compassionately.

"That's an understatement," Tom commented and took a smaller bite of his sandwich and continued to speak. "And trying to get answers from anyone is like pulling teeth. No one wants to talk. The police are saying as little as possible, especially today."

"Probably cause they got nothing, as usual," Jorge sniffed. "They don't know their ass from their elbow unless someone tells them."

"They aren't all that bad."

Jorge shrugged.

"Anyway, I've done some investigating on Harley," Tom said in a low voice, glancing around him. "I have people saying that this Johnson guy has been around the office but see, the problem with that, he's in politics so it's not strange that people would go talk to him. It's tricky to prove that they are connected."

"Plus, he obviously didn't have anything to do with this attack since his daughter's in that school."

"I think," Tom said and waited for a moment. "I think we're going about this the wrong way. Why focus on the connection between the two of them? If he has that skeleton in his closet, be assured, there's lots more."

"That's what I'm counting on."

"Word on the street is that he's highly connected to the white supremacists," Tom spoke quietly. "*That's* what we got to get him on."

"I know," Jorge agreed. "I've been hearing that one for months but he keeps his hands clean."

"He's in politics to impose laws that suit him and his group," Tom commented and took another bite of his sandwich. "These guys filter through the system so that they can manipulate what they want. They usually start with creating fear among the people, slowing down immigration, that kind of thing. They know the average person isn't paying attention because they're too busy living, paying bills, looking after their kids to even notice what's going on around them."

Jorge merely nodded.

"Rumor has it, they meet somewhere outside the city," Tom continued. "Somewhere off the radar. We're talking some people pretty high up in politics and business, people who go to church every Sunday and give the impression that they are pillars in their community."

"This here, this is not news to me," Jorge insisted a little more abrupt than he intended. "This, to me, is always the case. There are no saints among us so I am suspicious of those who act like they are, you know?"

"Oh, believe me, no one is more aware of this than me," Tom commented. "But I have to be careful. If I don't have my facts straight, it can be a lawsuit."

"Well, *amigo*, I would suggest you get your facts straight," Jorge smirked. "As for me, I must work on finding a way to get Harley out of the picture. The last thing I need is for him to be making trouble for Athas."

"He will. That's his goal," Makerson insisted as he picked up his sandwich again. "Oh, I do have some information but once again, it's nothing I can print cause I can't prove it."

"Oh yeah?"

"Cops knew about this kid who was going to attack the girl's school already, they just didn't do anything about it," Tom said before biting into the sandwich. "They didn't feel they had enough to do anything but once there was a tip, they had to."

"You know what that tells me?" Jorge asked.

"They don't always do their job?" Tom spoke bitterly as he chewed.

"That, unfortunately, is a given," Jorge replied and leaned forward on the table. "But perhaps it says that there should be more tips. Perhaps there is a paper trail that forces them to investigate. You and me, we can work this to our advantage, don't you see?"

Tom stopped chewing for a moment as a grin formed on his lips. He began to nod.

"Look, my friend, the biggest lesson I have ever learned from this life," Jorge continued. "Is we must take what we are given and work with it. Perhaps we cannot work the Johnson angle but you know, I'm thinking that the white supremacists must be having a meeting soon to discuss this nasty business in the news lately...."

CHAPTER

21

"So thanks a lot, Diego, I'm addicted to your French bakery," Jorge said sarcastically as he entered the empty club on Friday morning. Walking past tables with chairs on top and a stack of boxes with empty beer bottles, he made his way toward the bar. The familiar aroma of Diego's coffee filled the air, as the smug Colombian shot him a wicked grin and merely nodded. "I stopped in on my way here, bought 3 pastries and ate them all."

"I told you they were good," Diego nodded with a mixture of humor and arrogance in his voice. "They're the best in the city."

"You weren't joking," Jorge commented as he jumped up on a bar stool and nodded toward the nearby office. "Chase in yet?"

"Nah, not yet," Diego shook his head. "He was working last night so he's probably moving slow today."

"I thought….does he not have a night manager?" Jorge asked as Diego poured them each a coffee. "You know, to work the night shift, so he can take care of things during the day."

"He does," Diego said as he turned with a white mug in each hand. He placed them on the bar. "But sometimes, he pops in to make sure everything is going smoothly."

Jorge merely nodded as he reached for his cup. He didn't speak again until after pouring some cream into his coffee and grabbing a straw from behind the bar to stir it.

"So…ah…you two, do you still talk," Jorge asked, unsure of how to bring up the awkward topic. Diego had been infatuated with Chase for a substantial amount of time. It was only in recent months that he finally accepted that he wouldn't have a romantic relationship with the straight, indigenous man. Although Jorge didn't really understand, he attempted to show some compassion toward his longtime friend and in many ways, his brother. "Outside of work, I mean?"

"Sometimes," Diego shrugged and made a face as he stirred his coffee. "You know, it's not like it used to be when he lived at my place but I guess that's life. Things change and you have to adapt."

Jorge merely nodded and didn't reply.

"So, ah...don't you got an anniversary coming up?" Diego swiftly changed the topic. "You and Paige."

"Diego, I didn't marry Paige until later in the autumn," Jorge corrected him. "I met her around this time last year. I worked fast but not that fast, *amigo.*"

"That's what I mean," Diego was quick to jump in. "Like, you know, the anniversary of when you met."

"Look, Diego, how many fucking anniversaries can people have, you know?" Jorge commented and laughed. "I do good to remember our real anniversary."

"So when we planning that second wedding?" Diego asked and made a face. "You told me I could plan it as a way for us all to get together and see you sharing your vows."

Jorge sighed and shook his head. Many months ago, he *had* made this promise but things had gotten so busy that it was not a top priority. Although he did like the idea of sharing a ceremony with friends, somewhere along the line, the idea had lost some of its original fire.

"Diego, look, me, I do not know what to tell you," Jorge explained. "Everything, it has been so busy that I haven't had time to consider it."

"Ah, I see," Diego nodded while scrunching up his lips. "The honeymoon's over."

"What?" Jorge shook his head. "What does that mean? The honeymoon's over?"

"It's an expression," Diego informed him. "It means the exciting time after your wedding has worn off, you're getting bored with one another."

"We're not getting bored with one another," Jorge snapped and then backtracked. "Why? Is that...is that what Paige said?"

"Nah," Diego shook his head. "I meant for *you.*"

"I assure you, Diego, my *honeymoon* is *not* over, "Jorge said with frustration in his voice. "We are as madly in love as we were a year ago. It has been a…what you say? Very hectic year."

"Yes, well, this is true," Diego said as he calmed slightly. "Your life, it never stops."

"When it does," Jorge replied as he reached for his coffee. "Then I got something to worry about."

The door opened and Chase walked in wearing a suit minus the tie, which he was holding in his hand. He appeared disheveled and exhausted as he made his way across the floor.

"Chase, you look as if you had a rough night," Jorge grinned. "Please tell me that is a good sign?"

"Not really," He replied as he approached the bar while on the other side, Diego poured another cup of coffee. "We had a little problem last night with one of the staff but its fine now. I resolved it."

Jorge merely nodded and didn't ask questions. He knew that if Chase had any major concern, he would let him know.

"I see, well we could've met a bit later," Jorge commented as he took another drink of his coffee. "It is maybe too early?"

"Nah, its fine," Chase replied as he sat his tie down and reached for his coffee. Diego merely stood back in silence.

"Ok, so we must talk about a few things," Jorge decided to get right to business. "I trust Athas was by to organize a party for rich people? To sign up more people to the party? Whatever you Canadians do during an election?"

"Yes," Chase said with a nod. "I sent a message to Marco to post it on our website and Paige is taking care of the social media and contacting the press. We'll close the bar for a private party. Anyone with a ticket can come. We're ironing out the details later today. I booked off the days in advance for that and election night too."

"Good idea," Jorge nodded in approval. "This is good. So, he will be by later today."

"Yes, I think mid-afternoon," Chase pointed toward his office. "I have it wrote down somewhere on my desk."

"Very good," Jorge commented with a nod.

"We had an interesting conversation," Chase continued as he took a drink of his coffee and shared a look with Jorge. "You really scare the shit out of him, you know that right?"

"He say this?"

"He doesn't have to," Chase grinned. "Its pretty obvious."

"Me?" Jorge asked innocently and shared a look with Diego, who shrugged. "I'm harmless. I never hurt the man."

Diego snickered while Chase merely raised an eyebrow.

"He seems concerned about," Chase started and paused for a moment before continuing as if searching for the correct words. "You know, the violence. He's worried about how much he knows about you, about some specific situations…"

"Ah! This," Jorge pointed toward the coffee cup. "This here is nothing new. Athas, he worries too much."

"I told him," Chase continued while Diego listened with interest. "I said, look if you had a choice between the cops or Hernandez on your side, you're gonna want this guy. The police, even if they did want to help you, then you got the lawyers, the judges all mixed in, everything gets watered down till it's nothing. The legal system is a joke. I've seen that first hand when my son died. The truth is most cops pay lip service and that's all. Even a couple of times I had fights here, they were little more than bouncers in ugly uniforms. I could've tossed people out myself."

"You're preaching to the choir," Jorge said with a shrug. "The police, they got no love from me. I got no use for them and never will."

"What did he say?" Diego asked as he leaned toward Chase, his eyes growing in size. "When you told him this?"

"He had to agree," Chase replied as he leaned against the bar. "Although, he did the typical politician thing and tried to show me the balanced side of everything, but you could tell he wasn't believing it."

"You Canadians," Jorge said with laughter in his voice. "Wanting to believe in the law, the government, these things, as if they're in place to help you as opposed to just giving false security. That is all they are about, no?"

Chase nodded. "Hey, as I said to him, I'm Indigenous. I may as well be pissing up a tree then expecting the police, the courts or anyone in government to give a fuck about my people."

"I thought you were only half," Diego asked skeptically as he leaned a little too close to Chase.

"It don't matter," Jorge replied for him. "He's not white, that's all it really comes down to in the end. It would be like if Paige and I, we were to have a baby and he looked like me. That *nino*, he will forever be judged in this country."

"If the baby looked like you, he already got problems," Diego teased with an arrogant grin.

"What are you saying?" Jorge jumped in. "That I am not handsome? With me and Paige, there is no way he wouldn't be a beautiful child."

"How do you know it would be a boy?" Chase asked with a grin on his face.

"Real men make boys," Jorge insisted.

"But you, you got a girl!" Diego quickly pointed out, as his eyes grew in size and he began to laugh.

"I was out of my mind the night she was conceived," Jorge reminded him. "Tequila and *cocaína*, so this was different."

Diego rolled his eyes and looked at Chase who merely shrugged.

"I had three boys."

"See?" Jorge replied and finished his coffee. "This, also, it reminds me of another terrible conversation I recently had with Maria. She asked me if the sexual position made a difference on whether you had a girl or boy baby. I thought I would have another heart attack."

"What did ya say?" Diego began to laugh. "Knowing you, you agreed with her."

"I said, it does not matter if you are top or bottom, it is up to God," Jorge spoke seriously and upon seeing Diego open his mouth to say something, he quickly cut him off. "Different kind of 'top' and 'bottom', Diego."

Chase grinned while Diego attempted to hide a smile behind a veil of annoyance.

"The point is that my daughter, she is giving me problems," Jorge complained. "She recently was caught kissing a 14-year-old boy at her drama program during the summertime. She's 11 going on 35 and this concerns me."

Both men made a face.

"Exactly," Jorge replied as he stood up. "It is too much for me."

"Hey, before you go," Diego stepped forward. "What's going on with Jesús?"

"He's in eastern Canada, trying to shake some things up," Jorge replied. "We gotta get those pot shops and we must get another warehouse or take over where others are growing the product. He's looking into it and should be back by the weekend with some answers."

"So, when Athas comes by today," Chase picked up the conversation as Jorge glanced at his phone. "Anything I gotta know?"

"Plan his parties, continue to put the fear of God in him," Jorge replied as he looked back up. "This can never be a bad thing, especially now that my wife is working on the campaign. It is good if he is a little scared."

Diego grinned and didn't reply.

"Jolene, she's still working out ok at the warehouse?" Jorge asked as he started to turn. "Everything, it is fine?"

"Yup," Diego grew serious again. "She's fine."

"Good, now me, I gotta go," Jorge pointed toward his phone. "Marco and I must talk. We're trying to make a connection between Harley and his white supremacists and I got an idea. We gotta catch them together and get rid of that fucker once and for all."

"Hey, you know, there are other ways," Diego reminded him. "You just say the word."

"Not yet, Diego, not yet," Jorge responded as he made his way to the door. "But Diego, I love your enthusiasm."

He smiled before slipping out the door.

CHAPTER

22

"I didn't think you'd be around now that you're a big shot politician," The soft voice alerted Alec Athas as he was preparing to leave the youth centre for the day. He didn't have to look up to know it was Milie, a 14-year-old Southeast Asian girl who first wandered into his office a month earlier with tears in her eyes after a bullying incident at her school. He glanced up and smiled.

"Millie, I told you that I'm not a big shot anything," He gently corrected her and the two shared a smile as he continued to pack his laptop bag. "I'm just a youth counselor that's trying to make a difference. We'll see if the people believe in me on election day."

"Yeah, but don't you have to…campaign and stuff," She grew serious and timidly entered the office. Barely inside the doorway, her face turned a faint shade of pink. "I mean, you can still work here too?"

"Limited hours but I'm trying to do what I can," Alec replied as he zipped up his laptop bag and grabbed his phone. He stopped and carefully analyzed her face. "Is everything ok?"

"Yeah," She replied in her soft voice as she began to play with her hair. "You know, the usual."

"Did anything happen at school today?" Alec asked and continued to check her reaction. Millie attempted to hide her feelings but was rarely successful. She was shy and for that reason, ended up being powerless to those who sensed her weakness. As it turns out, everyone had a Jorge Hernandez in their lives.

"No, just the normal stuff," She said with a shrug.

"Good," Alec said and picked up his laptop bag and started toward the door. She scurried out and waited for him on the other side. He worried about Millie. She grew up in a troubled home and although things had calmed since her childhood, it was clear that the residual effects hadn't quite worn off.

"Mr. Bannister gave us a surprise test today. You know, it was kind of a shitty thing to do."

Alec laughed as he walked toward the exit, glancing into the activities room where a group of teens surrounded a laptop, laughing at a YouTube video. Beside him, Millie continued to talk.

"I wasn't prepared but I hate history," She commented with a shrug. "Why do we need to know that anyway? Who cares what happened long ago?"

"Well, Millie, sometimes it's important to learn from our history so we don't make the same mistakes again," He replied as they reached the door. Stopping for a moment, he looked into the young girl's eyes. "We have an appointment next week, don't we?"

She nodded enthusiastically.

"Will you be fine till then or do you need one sooner?" Alec lowered his voice, even though no one was close.

"No, I'm fine," She assured him. "I just wanted to say hi."

"Ok, well, I got to head out for a meeting," He pointed toward the door. "You have a good day, Millie."

"Good luck with your campaign stuff," She spoke sheepishly before turning to walk away. He watched the tiny, young woman saunter off into the activity room and took a deep breath. He had learned long ago that it was important to let everything go when you walked out the door, otherwise, the things you heard during office hours could gnaw at your brain long after you leave. He had nightmares when he started out. He still did sometimes.

The heat hit him as soon as he stepped on the sidewalk and headed for his car. Alec drove an older sedan, nothing fancy but it got him around the city. He had never felt the need to impress people with possessions, feeling that it was a trap that only sunk you a little lower until you got lost forever. There were many people in Toronto that fell into that trap and then wondered why they weren't happy. He knew why. It was something he researched in college and even now, often read papers on the topic. It was fascinating.

His interest in psychology sprang from his curiosity about what made people tick. A part of him wanted to understand everyone, to dig deep into their complex world and to simplify it. In many ways, his interest in politics gave him more opportunity to unravel some of the most complex minds he had ever met. As it turns out, the similarities between those involved in the political world and Jorge Hernandez were almost astonishing. The only difference was that Hernandez got right to the truth and didn't feel the need to sugar coat it but when it came to the overall, psychological makeup, there was no difference. Either way, he was often dealing with psychopaths. It was vastly different from the world he came from.

Alec Athas grew up in a traditional Greek household. His parents had immigrated to Canada over 40 years ago with hopes and dreams; many of which didn't come to fruition but this didn't steal their enthusiasm. They never grew frustrated with Canada but instead thankful for what it provided; free medical care when they were sick and welfare when their family needed it back in the 80s. They saw social programs as a wonderful safety net but believed it was up to each person to give back to their country.

Although Alec shared these values, he also worked with people who taught him that things were usually more complex than he believed growing up. He saw poverty, abuse, neglect, addiction; the darkest side of society walked through his door and yet, Alec stayed optimistic.

Until, one day, he wasn't.

After more government funding had been ripped away, resources drained, he grew weary of what little he had to work with in what was an already a difficult situation. He watched as politicians talked about how great the country was doing and he wanted to scream. They had no idea. That's what inspired him to get into politics. He wanted to make a difference.

As he drove to *Princesa Maria*, an upscale club named after Jorge Hernandez's daughter, he briefly wondered what his parents would think of him working for one of Mexico's most notorious criminals. Not that it mattered. Not only was Jorge Hernandez legendary, he was also untouchable. He had never been arrested in Mexico or Canada because he owned everyone from top government officials to police. He was almost like someone in a movie. Except, of course, on the big screen, there was a clear 'good' and 'bad' guy and everyone knew who won in the end. Real life was different.

Arriving at the club, he parked the car, noting that Silva and Jacobs were already there. Alec needed a moment to breathe before dealing with Hernandez. This was quickly shattered when his phone beeped. It was Paige.

Did you guys figure out the date and time for the party? Should we keep the event more upscale?

He bit his lip and thought for a moment.

No because my campaign is about reaching the average person so we can't have an uppity rich event.

Things were getting out of hand. Sometimes Alec felt like he wasn't running his own campaign. He wondered if other politicians felt this way? Was this the unspoken truth of politics? He had a feeling it was.

Good point. I will give it some thought.

He smiled. Alec sometimes could see the Paige he used to know, the woman he'd fallen for so many years ago.

His smile faded.

Thank you, Paige.

Sending a quick text to Chase, he slid the phone into his laptop bag and got out of the car. Hitting the button to lock it, he was almost at the door when the young, indigenous man swung the door open and gave him a friendly nod.

Alec returned the smile as he walked inside, where he immediately noticed Diego Silva behind the bar, pouring them all a cup of coffee. The Colombian attempted to show a tough exterior but when caught off guard, his fragility couldn't be more obvious. As soon as he realized Alec was in the room, he stood taller, sticking his chest out and made a face, almost like a mask that he hid behind to play Jorge Hernandez's game. They all were his puppets.

"So, we gonna sort out the details for this party?" Diego asked and twisted his lips as Alec arrived at the bar and sat on one of the stools.

"That's the plan," He replied and reached for his coffee.

"So Paige just messaged me that we need to keep this simple, low-key but Jorge, he wants a big, fancy affair," Diego challenged him with his eyes. "So how's that gonna work?"

"Diego, just have two parties," Chase insisted as he went behind the bar. "A fancy, one and another, more casual get together where people can pop in, meet Alec, have some free food, that kind of thing."

"I guess," Diego replied, his attitude softening after Chase spoke. "That makes sense."

"We can't have the casual one here though," Chase insisted as he pointed toward the bar. "It has to be family friendly and this place, it's not."

"Where do we have it then?"

"I dunno, Diego," Chase said with a shrug. "What do you think, Alec? What about where you work? The youth centre?"

Alec considered the idea.

"That might work."

"So we need some dates," Diego seemed to gather some of his original arrogance.

"I think we need the rich one first," Chase commented. "Then the family one closer to the election."

Diego scrunched his lips again. "Makes sense."

Alec didn't say anything. He had inadvertently been sucked into their twisted world and there was no getting out.

The door suddenly swung open. Alec didn't have to turn around to know it was Hernandez entering the club. He felt the power of his step, his intimidating stare from behind, as he walked up to the bar.

"Diego, you got me addicted to this fucking bakery," Jorge's loud voice boomed through the club. Alec turned and made eye contact with the Mexican as he bit into a French pastry from a popular downtown shop. "I'm going to get fucking fat."

"Hey, I told you, you don't got to inhale them every day," Diego was quick to point out. "Don't blame me if you get fat."

"That's all I need to be, another middle-aged, fat fuck with heart problems," Jorge commented, abruptly dropping the box on the bar and gestured toward it, his eyes softening as they met with Alec's. "Want one? You're skinny as fuck, have one."

Alec grinned and reached for a pastry while Diego rushed to pour a cup of coffee for Hernandez. Chase glanced at the box with interest, eventually taking one too.

"So you got all this party shit sorted out," Jorge asked.

"Two parties," Diego replied. "One for the rich assholes and the other for the regular people. We give them free food, you know, stuff like that…"

"Ah," Jorge nodded as he reached for his cup of coffee and nodded. "Makes sense."

"Do you mind if there's two?" Alec asked with some hesitation.

"Whatever," Jorge took a drink of his coffee. "You can have a fucking party every day, *amigo*, I do not care."

"Unfortunately, we have to be careful to make it look like we are doing everything according to election rules," Alec reminded him.

"We are," Jorge insisted and Diego let out a short laugh.

"As much as this guy ever fucking does."

"Diego, don't you got some parties to plan or *something* to do?"

"He's...you're going to plan the parties?" Alec slowly asked.

"He loves this shit," Jorge insisted. "Unless you wanna do it?"

Alec was quick to shake his head. "I don't have time, to be honest. I'm still doing counseling too."

"Me and Paige, we'll do it," Diego said as he nodded, shoving both hands in his pockets.

"Great, I do not see my wife now, she's always helping this guy," Jorge gestured toward Alec. "Now, you too?"

"Hey, now that she knows the social media," Alec quickly cut in before Diego could speak. "She can work from home if she wants."

Jorge appeared tired and shrugged. "No, do what you gotta do. That's it?"

"Have you found out any more about that teenager?" Alec quietly asked.

"The fucked up one that wanted to take over for that nutcase, Johnson, you mean?" Jorge abruptly asked. "Police knew about him all along and did nothing."

"He needs help," Alec offered.

"Don't we all?" Jorge asked.

"*You* definitely do," Diego teased and laughed at his own joke.

Jorge glared at him and turned his attention to Alec. "You work with kids, right? I got a daughter, I do not know what to do with her. She's 11 going on 35. Very strong-willed and thinks she's a teenager. Wants a boyfriend who's 14. Can you believe that? What am I to do with this?"

"Sounds like she's trying to get your attention," Alec calmly explained. "She's testing you, see how far she can push you."

"I will be dead of a heart attack if she keeps pushing me," Jorge replied. "That is how the test is working. She does not think there are any consequences to her actions. She seems to have no fear to do whatever strikes her."

Alec found himself making eye contact with Diego who twisted his lips into a grin suggesting that he wasn't the only one who saw the irony.

"I don't think you need a counselor to tell you that Maria is her father's daughter," Diego shot out rapidly, causing Alec to jump slightly. He was glad it was Diego pointing out the obvious, rather than himself.

"Ok, yes, I see what you mean," Jorge replied and turned his attention toward Alec again while nearby, Chase suppressed a grin. "But, there must be something I can do to change this before my daughter, she drives me over the edge."

"Talk to her," Alec calmly responded. "I mean, *really* talk to her. Don't lecture her but sit down, talk to her. Find out what's going on. Be blunt with her like you are with everyone else. Trust me, I work with kids who started getting into trouble when they were 11."

"Oh, did they outgrow this behavior?" Jorge asked with hope in his eyes.

Alec shook his head then quietly said, "May I ask what you were like at her age?"

Jorge seemed to shrink in his seat and look away. Unlike the larger than life man who walked into the bar earlier, he suddenly seemed quite small. And that was the first time Alec Athas realized that Jorge Hernandez had a soul.

CHAPTER

23

•••• **W**as found dead in his cell today. Police arrested Johnson earlier this month after learning he was planning to attack an all-girls school....

Jorge exchanged a look with his wife as they sat around the kitchen table. She was expressionless but gave a slight nod while an oblivious Maria stared at the television. Jorge briefly wondered if maybe they shouldn't have it on in the morning for his daughter to see but then again, he wanted Maria informed and intelligent. She had to know what was going on in the world around her. When people tried to protect their children, they inadvertently made them powerless.

"*Papa*," Maria turned her attention back to him. "Does that mean that we are safe again?"

"We should always be cautious," Paige smoothly answered for him and Jorge merely nodded.

"Why did he want to hurt kids?" Maria asked a question that had come up before as if she simply didn't trust the answers given in the past. "What did we ever do to him?"

"Because he was a crazy man, Maria," Jorge answered abruptly and gestured toward her food. "Now, eat your yogurt."

His daughter looked crestfallen but fortunately, Paige knew exactly what to say.

"Maria, there are some very unhappy people in the world and for that reason, they do some terrible things," She gently replied. "It's sad but fortunately, the schools will now be forced to be more vigilant."

"The principal said we would have a new plan if anything bad happens," Maria replied. "We are not to use our phones during class, but must have them on us all the time in case of an emergency."

"That is good," Jorge replied. "I am glad they are thinking ahead."

"But they also said it's difficult to get into our school with a weapon," Maria commented and Jorge felt his heart drop at the fact that this conversation was even necessary. "So, we should feel safe. We also have security people at the school and cameras everywhere."

"This is good!" Jorge spoke enthusiastically. "You should appreciate that you are able to go to such a school."

Jorge felt his phone vibrate in his pocket. Reaching for it, he saw it was Jesús and quickly answered.

"Did you see the news, sir?" He spoke in his usual, slow style.

"Yes," Jorge replied. "Are you still in the east, Jesús?"

"Yes sir," He replied. "I have run into some difficulty. I may need some help. Would Diego be available?"

"Yes," Jorge replied and got up to walk away from the table. "He has Sylvana in place now and Jolene at the warehouse, so it frees up some time. Right now, he is helping Athas plan some parties. I trust you can handle whatever is wrong?"

"Yes, I do believe so," Jesús spoke with reassurance in his voice. "Sometimes it is just a matter of negotiating the details."

Jorge grinned and didn't reply.

"Is Marco, is he still doing the research for us?" Jesús asked.

"Yes, but no details as of yet."

"I understand, sir."

"I got a meeting with Andrew shortly," Jorge continued. "I think he has something for me."

"Very good, sir."

"We'll talk again in a few days?"

"I should be back in town soon," Jesús replied. "I will give Diego a call."

"Perfect."

After ending the call, Jorge gave both his wife and daughter a quick kiss before heading out the door.

Thirty minutes later, he was at the same coffee shop where he previously met Andrew. The scrawny kid scarfed down a breakfast as

Jorge approached and sat across from him. He looked up and attempted a smile while chewing food.

"So, you got something for me?" Jorge asked as he set his coffee on the table. "About Harley, I assume?"

Andrew nodded as he continued to chew and eventually swallowed his food.

"I was at my uncle's yesterday," He gestured toward the window before leaning forward. "He was talking about *Toronto AM* a lot and complaining about Athas? You know, how he was a hero after the school threats and stuff?"

Jorge nodded and took a drink of his coffee.

"Anyway, he was plenty pissed about that," Andrew continued. "He was going on about how he was changing districts and would push Athas out and one of his boys asked what he planned to do and he said 'disqualify him', whatever the fuck that means?"

"Did you ask?"

"Nah, I didn't want to seem like I was even paying attention," Andrew replied and started to pick at his food again. "I pretended to be checking my phone. He didn't really say how but I thought you should know."

Jorge nodded and sent a quick text.

"There's something else," Andrew continued and Jorge looked up from his phone. "I think he either has someone watching the editor at *Toronto AM* or…something cause he talked as if he knew what they were planning ahead of time. Like the interview with Athas, he seemed to know that he was purposely going to slant things for his party…."

Jorge thought for a moment and nodded. He sent another text.

"That's it," Andrew answered. "Other than that, he was just talking about finding volunteers to help out."

Jorge grinned, nodded and sent a third text.

"What are you doing by the way?" Andrew asked. "Who are you texting?"

"Don't worry about it," Jorge replied and slid the phone back into his pocket and pulled out a wallet. Tossing some bills at him, he pushed his chair out. "Here's for your help."

Andrew's eyes lit up when he saw the cash sitting on the table and quickly scrambled to gather it.

"Now," Jorge continued as he stood up. "I gotta run but we will talk again soon."

"Ok," Andrew said as his face softened. "Thank you…if I hear anything else…"

Jorge nodded and grinned before turning to walk away.

His next stop was at the *Toronto AM* offices, where he found Clara waiting in the parking lot.

"*Buenos días. Tengo un trabajo para ti.*"

The older, Latina nodded in understanding before they entered the building. Makerson had already agreed to meet them in the lobby. The young editor spotted Jorge right away.

"Good morning Mr. Hernandez," He spoke while approaching them, his eyes glancing at Clara. "Why did you want to meet here?"

"Makerson," Jorge replied as he ushered him to a quiet corner. "I suspect someone might have a listening device in your office and we gotta check it out. Clara here will assist."

"Listening device," Makerson appeared humored and relaxed. "No, I don't think so. Maybe to you guys, that's normal but that's not going to happen in a place of business. We only have employees upstairs."

"Trust me on this," Jorge insisted. "You either got a device or you got a talker cause Harley is getting info back."

The smile fell from Makerson's lips as his eyes grew pensive, before giving them both a nod and pointed toward the elevator. "Ok, if she can check it out?"

"Yes," Jorge replied and briefly considered introducing them but knew that this would not sit well with Clara. "Trust me, if there is anything, she will find it."

For the next twenty minutes, Jorge silently checked his phone while Makerson hesitantly did some work on his laptop, occasionally glancing at Clara as she moved through the office, carefully checking for devices. It wasn't until she was at his desk that she pulled out a small object and silently showed it to a stunned Makerson. He merely nodded and pushed his chair back as she continued to search. Fifteen minutes later, she approached Hernandez with two small devices in her hand before pointing toward the door. Jorge nodded and watched her leave.

"What the fuck was that?" Makerson spoke when they were alone. "How long were those here? Who put them there? What the fuck!"

Jorge shrugged. "It is hard to say. I had a feeling."

"Fuck!" Makerson's face grew red. "I feel violated. Whoever put those here, they heard everything, even my own private conversations. Fuck!"

"At our office, we check regularly and before each meeting," Jorge informed him. "We do not find anything most times but it happens."

"Shit!" Tom said and appeared to calm down. "So this was Harley, right?"

"I think so," Jorge replied and tilted his head back. "It could be, also, your competition. Maybe Harley works with them. I would recommend that you do not leave your office unattended and maybe that pretty little secretary out there, watch her carefully."

"She's my assistant so…." He thought for a moment. "Yeah, ok, I will keep it locked up. I saw what your….associate found, so at least I can be vigilant too."

"Of course and if you suspect again, we can check," Jorge replied. "In the meantime, be careful whom you speak to and where. That is my suggestion."

Makerson merely nodded with concern in his eyes.

Jorge left shortly after, glancing at his phone on the way out. He was meeting Paige for lunch at their favorite Mexican restaurant in the city. The food was just like home, something he was missing in recent months. Although his life was in Canada, he sometimes grew homesick for Mexico; the weather, the food, the people, everything was so different from Canada. He loved both countries but being away from traditions made him appreciate them and fear his daughter would lose her culture.

Paige was already at the restaurant and studying the menu when Jorge arrived. She was wearing a red, sleeveless sundress that was elegant and classy and to him, quite arousing. Perhaps it was the way it flowed over her body, the material thin and soft, that captivated him. His attention was quickly diverted when a young Mexican waitress approached to offer him something to drink as he reached the table.

"*Si!*" He glanced over to see what his wife was drinking. "I will have a Corona also, *Gracias.*"

As the waitress rushed away, Jorge leaned in to kiss his wife, his hand grabbing her thigh under the table. "I do think, this afternoon, you and I need to spend some quality time together."

"Sounds good to me," She replied as the waitress returned with his beer. Paige was ready to order so he agreed to have the same, his desires becoming more prevalent than his hunger for food, he just wanted to eat and leave.

"*Mi amor*, you know, we could always get this food to go," Jorge suggested as his hand traveled up her arm. "Maybe it would taste better a little later this afternoon, no?"

Her eyes flared and she was about to answer when both their phones beeped.

With some hesitation, Jorge reached for his while Paige already had hers in hand. She groaned.

"What? What is this?" Jorge suddenly felt torn from his sensual thoughts to return to the stark reality of his life. "This here, this cannot be true. They text this kind of thing rather than call parents?"

Paige shook her head while Jorge caught the waitresses' attention.

"*Disculpe,* we must take this food to go."

"Should we just cancel the order?" Paige quietly asked after the waitress left.

"No, you know what?" Jorge pointed toward his beer. "Maria, she has ruined my afternoon. She is not ruining my lunch too. Let her wait in that principal's office and think about what she has done. Me, I am going to enjoy my beer until the food is ready, then we will pick her up."

Paige considered his words and nodded. "We have to do something…"

"Believe me, this I know," Jorge said and took a deep breath. "My daughter, she is out of control. I spoke to Athas about this since he works with children. He pointed out that some of the troubled teens he deals with started off like Maria so we must do something."

"But what?"

"*Mi amor*, we must scare her," Jorge replied. "I have some thoughts on this but Athas said that it is important to talk openly. Me and her, we are about to have a *very* open discussion."

Paige reached over and squeezed his hand.

CHAPTER

24

"So, Diego, you will be joining Jesús later today?" Jorge spoke abruptly into his phone as he and Paige drove to the school to pick up Maria. Although he was misdirecting his frustrations, the anger that boiled inside of him was too much and he feared his reaction when coming face to face with Maria. "He said he spoke to you?"

"Yes, got my bag packed, my flight booked," Diego confirmed. "Everything is set on my end. I'm heading out in a few hours."

"So, Diego, tell me something," Jorge continued, ignoring everything he had just said, his mind already on to something else. "How much do you think Jolene would be helpful for us right now if I need her for something...*Necesito ayuda con un proyecto serio.*"

"Ah...." Diego hesitated on the other end of the line and loudly sucked in air before continuing. "I dunno. It might be a little soon. She's doing great at the warehouse but to take on anything dicey, I am not sure."

"What about....what about Sylvana?" Jorge wondered out loud. "I need a woman who can become a volunteer at Harley's office. Someone with an aggressive personality but he will not connect with us."

"I'm sure he's got a lot of volunteers there so he won't be doing background checks," Diego guessed. "I dunno, you would have to ask Athas about that one, but he might be tipped off if a Colombian goes to his office, you know?"

"Ah, yes!" Jorge said as he shook his head and sigh loudly. "This is true besides, he's a racist prick so he may not warm up to Jolene."

"Actually, I find even the most racist assholes tend to push their rules aside for a beautiful woman," Diego insisted and on the passenger side, Paige let out a laugh. "She got the curves, you know and men…well, straight men, that's what they like, right?"

Jorge decided to not answer that question and instead moved on to the heart of the matter. "Diego, I may talk to Sylvana about this matter."

"You need someone to warm up to Harley?" Diego asked.

"Yes, really *warm* up to him," Jorge clarified.

"Yes and Paige, she won't work because she got that evil last name, Hernandez," Diego teased, laughing at his own joke just as Jorge approached his daughter's school. "Plus she's known to been working on Alec's campaign."

"Are you kidding me?" Jorge snapped as he scanned his card to get into the parking lot. "I'm not letting my wife anywhere near that fucking idiot."

"Let?" Paige gently asked.

Diego laughed. "Hey look, Hernandez, your mouth got you in trouble again."

"Come on," Jorge glanced at his wife and shook his head. "You both know what I mean. He's a fucking dirtbag. I will see if I can get Sylvana to help with this and if so, once you return to town, Diego, I will need you to pick up some of her work while she is at the office 'volunteering' for him."

"Got it," Diego agreed. "But first we gotta make sure she will do it."

"She'll do it," Jorge insisted as he found a parking space. "My cousin, she is no saint."

"*Perfecto.*"

"I gotta go," Jorge said and took a deep breath. "We are at the school cause Maria got herself in trouble again. I am at the end of my rope with her."

"Remember what Athas said the other day," Diego remind him.

"I've thought about nothing since," Jorge exaggerated. "My daughter, she is too much like her mother."

"Yeah….like her mother," Diego spoke sarcastically while Paige laughed.

"*Adios*, Diego," He said before ending the call and turning to his wife.

"We'll get through this," She said with a faint smile on her lips. "You're going to have to be really tough this time."

"I thought I was tough before," Jorge replied with uncertainty in his voice. "I do not know what to do anymore."

"You will," Paige assured him. "Take away things from her. Her drama, the voice lessons she wanted....I don't know, but I do think you need to be stricter."

Jorge opened his mouth to say something but changed his mind.

The two of them got out of the SUV and upon meeting, he reached out for her hand, squeezing it as they walked toward the school. Scanning his card again, they walked inside, through the metal detector and finally made their way down the hallway. Security for the school was tighter than the previous year and to Jorge, that this was necessary was unthinkable. What kind of world did they live in? Unfortunately, he knew the answer to that question. He was part of it.

In silence, they walked toward the reception area where a secretary politely alerted the principal in the next room. A young, white woman walked out and introduced herself as Mrs. Rabin and after shaking both their hands, asked them to step into her office. Once there, Jorge immediately saw his daughter slumped over in a chair close to the desk. Noting that she was crying, Maria glanced at him and Paige for a brief second before shamefully looking away.

"So, we had a little incident earlier today with Maria," Mrs. Rabin said as she closed the door and headed toward her desk, gesturing for them to sit down and she did the same. "I'm not sure if you're aware but we have cameras throughout school property and earlier today, Maria and another girl were caught smoking. We originally thought it was a cigarette until one of the teachers approached and quickly realized it was marijuana."

Jorge merely nodded as he bit back his anger. He felt relief when Paige reached out to touch his arm and immediately jumped in.

"We are both shocked and saddened to learn this," Paige's voice broke halfway through the sentence. "We've never had an issue like this before."

"Unfortunately, I must suspend Maria from school," Mrs. Rabin continued and pointed toward a file on her desk. "It will be on her permanent record as well. The only positive for Maria is that the other girl admitted to bringing the marijuana to school."

Jorge continued to feel his body tense up as he nodded. This news didn't give him much reassurance.

"This is obviously very serious," Mrs. Rabin continued. "Maria will need to stay home for a week and also, I want her to write a report explaining what she learned from this experience. We will also need both her and the other girl to do some volunteer work around the school after they return. This will mainly be after classes so they will have to opt out of some of the more enjoyable programs like drama, music, and sports, for some time."

"Oh, there will be no more drama!" Jorge spoke aggressively toward his daughter who immediately started to cry harder. "No, no, I wish to have Maria do all the volunteer work you need from her for as long as you want. That is not a problem."

"But *Papa*! I cannot leave my drama! I'm in the new play," Maria cried dramatically.

"Maria, you can forget about that," Jorge's voice rose in anger and he felt Paige squeezing his arm and managed to calm, if only slightly. "You will do volunteer work for Mrs. Rabin, whatever she decides. Perhaps this will make you learn."

"*Papa*, I just tried it," Maria spoke angrily. "It's not like I killed someone!"

"*Maria!*" Jorge snapped. "Enough!"

"Ok, let's calm down," Mrs. Rabin was assertive while raising her hand in the air. "Unfortunately, Maria, you will have to take this punishment. We have strict rules about smoking, drinking and, drugs at this school. Technically, this is grounds for permanent expulsion from the school. The only reason why we are letting you off this easily is that this is the first time we've had any issue with you."

Jorge gave her a warning look.

Appearing to realize how much trouble she was in, Maria fell silent and slumped over and remained quiet for the rest of the meeting.

After apologizing to the principal once again, Jorge and Paige signed some forms and the three of them headed out of the school. Maria carried out a heavy backpack of books, which she struggled with until Jorge reached for it and she gave him a sad smile.

They drove home in silence. Jorge found himself calming slightly as he exchanged a few concerned looks with Paige. He could tell she was as upset as he was, but what could he do? It was time to get strict with his daughter. He had no choice.

Upon walking into the house, Maria started toward the stairs but Jorge immediately stopped her.

"We must talk," He spoke calmly and pointed toward the couch and she silently sat down, grabbing a pillow, she hugged it tightly to her chest.

"Maria, what you did today, was completely unacceptable," Jorge commented as he sat beside her and Paige across from them both. "You could've been kicked out of that school permanently and why, why would you even try marijuana?"

"Because the other girl, she had some and I was curious," Maria avoided his eyes. "It's not a big deal."

"You're 11, it *is* a big deal."

"The school could've called social services," Paige gently commented and although Jorge wasn't sure if that was true, he nodded in agreement. "Especially where your father owns stores that sell pot. If they thought you got it from home, that we allowed you access to it, we could've been investigated."

Her comment was more directed at Jorge this time.

"What would they do?" Maria asked as she sat up straighter, fear in her eyes, she looked back and forth between the two of them. "Is this true, *Papa*? Could you be in trouble too?"

"I do not know, Maria, I am not sure of the rules in Canada," Jorge spoke honestly. "But I do believe Paige would know more than us. If this is what she tells us, it is true. Maria, this is very serious. I do not think you understand."

"I do, *Papa*, I'm sorry," Maria said and began to cry again. "You are taking my drama away! That is my life!"

"Maria, please do not exaggerate!" Jorge yelled at his daughter. "*Enough!* I have had enough of this *mierda* with you! No more. If you must continue to smoke weed, to kiss older boys, to do whatever you want when you want, I will send you back to Mexico with my mother and to a religious school."

Maria's mouth fell open, her face full of stunned disbelief as if she was suddenly unable to talk.

"Now, this here is going to stop," Jorge insisted. "No more!"

"Maria," Paige calmly cut in while giving Jorge a look. "You know, your father is worried about you, as am I. We're sort of wondering why you are doing these things. Is there something wrong?"

"I want you to start treating me like I'm an adult," Maria said and then in a rushed voice added. "Please, *Papa*! Do not send me back to Mexico. I have to *stay* in Canada."

With this, a loud sob came from the back of her throat as she began to cry hysterically.

"Maria," Jorge spoke with a defeated voice. "You are acting very dramatically. Please, you are still a child. I know you do not wish to be seen this way but you're 11. That is still a child."

"I am not a child," She sobbed and continued to hug the pillow. "I need to be an adult."

Paige exchanged looks with Jorge and stood up and moved to the couch. Sitting on the other side of Maria, she put her arm around the child who quickly curled up to her step-mother as she continued to cry hysterically.

Jorge felt himself grow emotional and had to look away. He didn't want to see his daughter like this – she was acting so erratically and out of control – what if she suffered from mental health issues? She was only 11!

"Maria," Paige spoke calmly. "You are safe with us. You need to tell us why you feel like you have to be an adult. Why do you feel such a rush to grow up? Is it because of your interest in acting?"

"No, you wouldn't understand," Maria continued to sob as she wrapped her arms around Paige, who remained composed even though Jorge was having difficulty doing the same. His eyes were burning while his heart began to race. He feared what she was going to say.

"You would be surprised what we can understand," Paige corrected her. "You need to be honest. It will make you feel better. Please, just tell us. Did someone do something to you? Did someone hurt you?"

"No," Maria answered, much to Jorge's relief.

"Ok," Paige gently replied in her soothing voice. "Then, why do you feel like you have to grow up fast."

"Because I'm in love with an older man and if I don't grow up fast, he will fall in love and marry someone else," Maria blurted out so fast that it took Jorge a moment to process her words.

"What?" He snapped. "Maria, you…"

"Ah, Jorge," Paige gave him a warning look. "Please.."

"See, I knew you wouldn't understand," Maria sniffed and reached for a nearby box of Kleenex. "You treat me like a baby and you never want me to grow up."

"That is not true Maria," Jorge insisted and took a deep breath. "But you are not in love. You have a crush on someone, that is…normal."

"No! I'm in *love*," Maria insisted dramatically. "Stop talking to me like I don't know how I feel!"

"Ok, Maria," Paige spoke up as she gently pulled her back toward her. "So, you're in love with a man and you fear that if you don't grow up fast, he won't notice you?"

"And he will fall in love and marry someone else," Maria replied. "But he must marry me!"

Jorge was stunned. He couldn't believe what he was hearing. Who was *this* child?

"Maria, you know you can't control what other people do," Paige commented. "Even if you were his age, you still couldn't make him fall in love with you and make him marry you. It doesn't work that way."

"*Papa* made you fall in love with him."

"Maria! That is not how it happened," Jorge quickly corrected her. "It was mutual. If she did not feel the same way, it wouldn't have happened. And yes, I would've been upset, heartbroken but it would not be my choice."

"But *Papa*, you always get what you want," Maria began to speak enthusiastically. "I see it all the time. You would've made her love you."

"No, Maria," Jorge laughed. "No, this is not true. I may have pursued her, sent her flowers, asked her out again but in the end, Maria, you cannot make someone love you."

"I think he would fall in love with me if we were the same age, we really connect," Maria insisted and Jorge suddenly clued in to whom was the object of her affection. He decided to play dumb though in order to not embarrass her.

"Maria," He paused for a moment and forced himself to calm down. "I do appreciate your honesty with us and I know that these feelings, to you, they seem very real but you are so young. These feelings, they will change as you grow up. This man may always be a special person to you but you must let go of this situation. It is not healthy for you."

Maria burst into tears again and he instinctively leaned forward and gave her a kiss on the forehead. Much to his surprise, she let go of Paige and quickly locked her arms around him. He felt his heart melt as his little girl sobbed against his chest. Unsure of what to say, Jorge pulled her close and remained silent. The tears, they were for so much more than either of them realized.

CHAPTER

25

"Paige, am I a bad father?" Jorge asked in the still of the night, long after they went to bed. Although silent beside him, he could tell she was awake; when his wife was asleep, her breath was soft, gentle, almost unnoticeable but on a rare night when Paige struggled to sleep, her body appeared tense and stiff. "*Por favor*, be honest with me."

At first, she didn't reply, with her back to him, he could see her slowly turning around. Her movements were so graceful and beautiful, as her eyelashes flickered open and she stared deeply into his eyes. He quickly leaned in and pulled her close.

"Why would you say that?" She finally asked. "You handled today perfectly. Maria opened up to you."

"Yes, but that was only after she reached out to you," His voice was full of vulnerability. "I was not her first choice."

"It's because she knew you were angry," Paige gently reminded him as she touched his arm. "Maria knew she disappointed you."

"But why does she do this at all?" Jorge asked as his heart began to race. "I do not understand what possesses an 11-year-old child to smoke pot or be obsessed with an adult man. Should we have her talk to a psychiatrist? Then again, is it because I'm a bad father figure? Is there something wrong with our relationship that causes her to do this? I do not understand."

"I think," Paige started off strongly then seemed to hesitate. "I think, maybe you need to form a stronger relationship with her by spending time together. Not just conversations over breakfast. Plus you were away a lot when she was younger and I'm not saying that to be critical of you, I just wonder if maybe that's why she got so attached to Chase."

"You think its Chase too?"

"I definitely think its Chase," Paige muttered. "She's always had a crush on him."

"Should we not have her spend time with him anymore?"

"No, I wouldn't go that far," Paige said and thought for a moment. "Look, I will talk to her maybe tomorrow. We'll see where we're at then."

Jorge felt his heart filling with relief. Paige always knew exactly what to do when it came to Maria because he wasn't sure.

Fortunately, after the incident at school, Maria appeared to calm down. Rather than challenging Jorge in every conversation, she was more relaxed, less intense and generally showed more respect toward him. He would come home each day to find his wife and daughter sitting together in the living room; Maria doing homework while Paige worked on the social media for Alec's campaign. It filled his heart to see the change in his daughter. He, of course, gave all the credit to Paige.

"I owe you," He admitted a few days later over breakfast while upstairs, Maria sang in the shower. "You are un ángel."

"Hardly," Paige replied with a laugh as he moved in to give her a quick kiss. "I taught her some meditation stuff, breathing exercises and it seems to have relaxed her. She's high-strung. Wonder where she gets that?"

Jorge grinned, knowing his wife was teasing him.

"At any rate, you might soon have to do me a favor," She continued, her tone becoming serious as she reached for her coffee. "I have this family thing coming up. You might have to come with me."

"Oh yes, I finally meet your family?" He teased and winked at her as he grabbed another piece of bacon. "Your secret husband, hidden away."

"You know it's not like that," Paige corrected him as they exchanged smiles. "This is going to be painful for me. I try to avoid my family as much as possible."

"I do not understand why."

"You will," Paige insisted. "And we also have that big shindig for Alec coming up too, soon."

"Ah! The party at the club," Jorge nodded and yawned. "I had forgotten about that. I must meet with Alec sometime soon. I have been busy working with Marco at the office."

"Anything new on Harley?" Paige asked as she finished her coffee. "You haven't said much lately."

"I have not had much lately, this is why," Jorge replied and shook his head. "That man, he is very secretive but I recently spoke with Sylvana about volunteering at his office. She has already looked into it and she will start as soon as Diego returns."

"How did things go in the east?" Paige asked as she stood up and walked into the kitchen toward the coffee pot. "Did they have any success taking over the pot stores?"

"It was a challenge," Jorge replied as his wife returned with the coffee pot, filling both their cups. "Thank you, my love."

"I imagine they were successful though?" Paige gently asked and raised an eyebrow.

"You, as usual, are right," Jorge replied as his eyes scanned over her body as she walked back into the kitchen. "You know, this house is quite large, we should look into getting someone to clean and cook, to free your time."

"Its fine," Page said with a shrug as she returned. "Also, I'm getting Maria to do a lot of stuff around the house now that she's home more."

"Ah!" Jorge perked up and sat up a bit straighter in his chair. "What a wonderful idea! This is good."

"If she wants to be an adult," Paige quietly replied as the shower stopped upstairs. "She's got to learn that it's not just the fun stuff."

Jorge nodded and began to laugh. "*Perfecto, mi amor.*"

After saying a quick goodbye to his daughter when she came downstairs for breakfast, Jorge rushed out to meet with Diego and Jesús in the office. When he arrived, Jorge found them both engrossed in a conversation with Marco

"Did you find anything?" Jorge asked as soon as he walked into the conference room as the door closed behind him. "Marco?"

"No, sir," He shook his head and made a face. "These men, they are hiding things well. I cannot find anything online."

"We're going to remedy that," Jorge insisted as he sat in his usual place at the table. "Soon, Fulton Harley will have a new volunteer at his office."

Everyone around the table grinned. They all knew the plan with Sylvana. Jorge's cousin was intelligent and assertive, leaving little doubt that she would find whatever they needed to know about the campaign.

"So what is the plan, exactly, sir," Jesús asked in his usual, slow drawl. "To spy on his offices?"

"I have a few plans," Jorge replied. "This is only one of them. I am hoping to maybe put a listening device in his office as well, it has also crossed my mind that Sylvana can somehow instigate him having to drop out of the race but first, we must learn what is going on with his campaign."

"My guess is he's keeping away from the white supremacists so he keeps his nose clean," Diego insisted from the end of the table. "That's probably why everything is quiet now. He don't want anyone to see the connection especially in a city like Toronto. That's not going to fly here."

"I wish I had your confidence," Jorge replied and shook his head. "But me, I do not know. I have noticed that a lot of white people feel the same way. It is an unfortunate poison in our times."

No one replied.

"At any rate," Jorge continued. "We will get Sylvana in there and see what she can find out, what her feeling is about everything and take it from there."

"Good idea, sir," Jesús said while nodding his head. "That one, I know can handle anything."

"My cousin, she is half Italian, half Latina," Jorge reminded them. "Fulton Harley, he has met his match because I am confident, she will destroy him. He won't even see it coming."

"Yeah? Well, we could've used her the past few days," Diego spoke up. "We had a few battles of our own but we got what we wanted."

"The shops? They will be ours?" Jorge asked as he glanced between Jesús and Diego.

"Yes, sir," Jesús replied while Diego nodded with a smug expression on his face. "We made sure of that….there was a mutual understanding. Our lawyers will be taking it on from here."

Jorge didn't ask. It wasn't necessary. Where they started off as smooth, polite businessmen attempting to negotiate a deal, they sometimes had to change their tactics along the way to ensure getting what they wanted. Everyone knew that Jorge's goal was to take over the Canadian pot industry and even though some political fat cats had recently been murmuring to the press that perhaps this was a reason to be alarmed, Jorge had people in his pockets that quickly countered that it wasn't exactly as if no other large companies had the monopoly in Canadian business. Profits rose after Hernandez-Silva Inc took over, as did the taxes brought in from their stores. In the end, wasn't that what everyone wanted?

"Very good," He finally found his voice, after considering what this latest accomplishment meant to the company's overall goal. His own associate back in Mexico would be pleased with this news. Although on paper, everything looked clean, in the end, it was the cartel's money that helped finance these businesses but then again, it wasn't as if this was the first time criminals financed a business in Canada. Fortunately, Jorge had noted that Canadians were often ignorant of such facts. Let them live in their fairytale land, let them believe what they needed to believe; idealistic thinking never changed the facts.

"We are doing well," Jesús said as he opened his laptop and turned it on. "But we still have some work to do."

"Then let's roll up our sleeves and do it," Jorge replied. "Is there anything else?"

"I have been talking to Athas about the event," Diego jumped in. "Next weekend?"

"That's when?" Jorge asked.

"I'm asking you," Diego asked abruptly. "Come on, you're paying for it?"

"Technically, it's donations paying for it," Jesús reminded them. "Is that not true?"

"Yes, we must be careful to account for everything to make the government happy," Jorge said as he rolled his eyes before sharing a grin with Marco. "There is always a way to work around these things. Plus, it is my bar that is donating the place to throw this big party and also, the liquor and whatever else makes people happy."

Jesús grinned. "Me, I do not think we should tell Athas about the prostitutes we will have there to flirt with the rich men…."

"It is, as they say, the way we do business," Jorge said and began to laugh. "Do not tell me that other politicians have not done the same or worse. Alec, he does not have to know about our…party favors."

Everyone laughed but Marco appeared surprised.

"Speaking of which," Jorge directed his comment at Jesús. "That is for the guests, do not play with the toys that are meant for others."

"Hey, do not worry about me," Jesús replied loudly but with a grin on his face. "I can find my own *señoritas*."

"It will be a beautiful night," Jorge replied as he stared into space. "Maybe I can have one of the hired help seduce Athas. Perhaps he deserves a treat right about now."

"Make sure it's discrete," Diego sternly reminded him. "We don't need a scandal."

"They all will be, Diego, I assure you," Jorge commented as he leaned forward on the table.

"And you, you keep away from them too," Diego abruptly commanded.

"Diego, I have never cheated on my wife and I am not about to start with a *puta*," Jorge curtly replied. "This is not me."

"I'm just making sure."

"You do not need to worry about me," Jorge replied as he stood up. "Now, is that all for today? I must meet someone else."

A half hour later, he was sitting in the usual coffee shop with Andrew. This time, the *gringo* was scarfing down a huge, greasy bacon and egg sandwich.

"Do you only eat once a week?" Jorge couldn't help but ask him. "You eat with such passion, my friend, it is as if it were your last meal."

"With Fulton as my uncle, it could be," Andrew spoke nervously. "If he ever finds out what I told you…"

"Be assured, he will not," Jorge was insistent. "Your tip, by the way, was helpful. We found listening devices in the editor's office at *Toronto AM*. This was something I had never even considered, so I do thank you."

Andrew appeared satisfied with himself.

"So, you got something more for me?" Jorge asked as he reached for his coffee.

"I need you to help me unlock my money," Andrew got right to the point. "I can't live like this anymore. I got to go beg him every time I need something."

"This, my friend, I can help you with," Jorge replied. "Just not yet. We must first do a few things to put this man in a vulnerable position before we strike. Trust me, I know these things."

"When will that be?" Andrew asked with concern in his eyes

"We got someone on the job," Jorge replied, feeling no need to give more details. "And once your uncle hits rock bottom and believe, he will, you will get your money. I will personally take care of it myself."

"Really?" Andrew asked as he hesitated with his sandwich midair. "I mean, you will do that for me?"

"Yes, however, until then," Jorge spoke sternly. "You work for me and you do what I say and I pay you."

It wasn't a question or a suggestion.

CHAPTER

26

"So, you got nothing?" Jorge asked Sylvana a few days later at the boardroom table, along with Diego and Alec. His cousin seemed unconcerned with the fact that they were putting her under a microscope, in hopes the new volunteer at Fulton Harley's office would have some helpful information. Unfortunately, it wasn't going as planned. "You weren't able to find anything? Hear anything? Place the listening device in his office? Nothing?"

"He's got the volunteers doing stupid shit like badgering people at home, preparing flyers, menial, mindless crap," Sylvana shrugged dismissively and made a face as she leaned back, pushing her breast out, her dark eyes ignoring them all. "His volunteers are like a bunch of idealistic morons who believe the drivel he feeds them. It's absolutely pathetic."

"And you can't get in his office?" Jorge inquired as he noted the frustration on Diego's face. "Or close to him?"

"Are you nuts? He's got his bulldog wife there," Sylvana replied and took a drink of her coffee, giving Alec a downward gaze. "So this is the guy he's up against?"

"I'm Alec Athas," He reached out to shake her hand, which she reluctantly took and returned her attention to Jorge.

"I'm wasting my time at his office," She spoke boldly and shook her head. "He won't let me near anything."

"Ok, so we wait a few more days and if nothing changes then you find a reason to quit," Jorge said as he quickly racked his brain. "I guess we cannot do much if there are so many eyes in the office."

"Actually, he has a bunch of speaking dates coming up," Alec spoke up. "I know for a fact that he will take his wife with him and probably half that office to show support."

"You know this how?" Jorge asked curiously.

"He has his schedule listed on his website," Alec replied innocently. "And he'll take his wife. Trust me."

"And he will bring his staff as his fan club," Diego said and began to laugh. "To build enthusiasm, am I right?"

"Pretty much," Alec nodded. "It's the typical politician thing to do."

"And you, you will not be doing the same," Jorge automatically insisted. "You must be better than him, more relatable. Not everyone is married. Politicians make the mistake of trying to cater to the middle class, to the married, to the people they think are most likely to go out and vote for them. You, my friend, will focus on everyone; rich people, poor people, old people while reminding the middle-class parents how you saved a school. You're a hero, Athas, not some random, fake politician. This is how you must see yourself."

"You saved a school?" Sylvana showed some interest. "What do you mean? Was one closing?"

"No no," Jorge cut in to answer. "The school that had the threat recently. It came to our attention and we shuffled the information around so that he could call it into the police and take some credit."

"It just happened to come to your attention?" Sylvana asked skeptically with a grin on her face. "I can imagine."

"We were looking for something else and Marco found it," Jorge quickly replied. "It does not matter, the point is that we didn't want to get involved with the police, so he said it was an anonymous tip. It worked out in the end."

Sylvana glanced at Alec, then Jorge before starting to laugh. "You always have a way of working things to your advantage, don't you?"

"You know I do," Jorge replied with a grin.

"So, we will see what happens during these events," Jorge picked up where he left off. "Make sure you are in the office. Once you have the listening device planted, we will take you out of there."

"Plant it carefully," Diego insisted. "Make sure it's somewhere no one will see it."

"Yes, like when his wife is under the desk giving him head, make sure it's not at her eye level," Jorge quipped and everyone laughed. He noted that Alec seemed less amused.

"Have you seen his wife?" Sylvana asked as she reached for her coffee. "I would be surprised if she's ever *been* under a desk"

"Oh, Sylvana, you would be surprised."

"More likely his whore on the side," Diego sniffed. "And don't sound like she's going to be near that office if his wife is hanging around."

"Originally, Sylvana, I was hoping to have you become flirtatious with him and then threaten to go to the media saying he sexually harassed you but now, I'm not sure," Jorge said and leaned back in his chair. "We need a scandal to get him out."

"There must be another angle?" Sylvana asked.

"There is…white supremacy but unfortunately, we are having difficulty tying him to it," Jorge replied and he watched Sylvana raise her eyebrows.

"Are you fucking kidding me?" She asked.

"I am not fucking kidding you," Jorge replied and nodded. "We know he's with them but we need proof."

"How do you know?"

"Someone told us."

"Have that person…"

"He's dead," Jorge commented and glanced toward Athas, who quickly looked away.

"What?" Sylvana glanced across the table at Alec. "You killed him?"

"No!" Alec was quick to reply, his eyes bulging out. "I never killed anyone."

"Ah, relax Athas," Jorge replied and turned his attention to Sylvana. "We had some incidents and turns out this Harley guy was behind them, like the time one of the shops burned down."

"How come the police can't figure out this stuff?" Sylvana complained. "Remember, they said there were no clues but yet, you knew?"

"I got people who confess to me, you know?" Jorge replied and raised his eyebrows. "The cops? Come on Sylvana! You're part Italian and part Mexican. Do you seriously believe in the police? What? Are you adopted?"

She grinned and didn't reply.

"At any rate, this is where we are now," Jorge commented. "We know what we know but proving it is another thing."

"Fulton Harley's father was a politician too," Alec added, his comment directed at Sylvana. "I heard that he was a dirty player but he was also smooth, so that might explain a few things."

"It actually explains a lot," Jorge replied. "So, we will see how the next few days go. If all we can do is get the listening device in his office, then this is all we can do."

"Well, maybe the bulldog will leave 'big daddy' alone for five minutes so I can sneak in and slip the device somewhere," Sylvana said as Jorge pushed his chair back and stood up. Her comment caused a hesitation throughout the room.

"Big daddy?" Jorge asked and began to laugh. "Is this your pet name for Harley?"

"Actually, that's what some of the young women at the office call him," Sylvana replied as she stood up from her chair, smoothing her skirt. "He seems to like it."

"That's fucking creepy."

"Hey, I said I couldn't get anything on him," Sylvana replied and shook her head. "I never said he wasn't fucking creepy."

When the meeting ended, Jorge headed toward Marco's office to see if he discovered anything helpful.

"No sir," Marco shook his head and pushed his laptop aside. "I hacked the website and emails of this Harley man and nothing. He is clearly careful in his work."

"That doesn't surprise me," Jorge replied as he stood in the doorway. "Fuck! How am I going to get this guy? Sylvana is at his campaign office and she's finding nothing. His nephew has been somewhat helpful but he can only do so much."

"You know, sir, I am thinking that this man, he is probably going to be more careful in the beginning and then relax more as the campaign moves forward," Marco commented. "But, I don't know where to find more information. Everything online, it is squeaky clean."

"His personal emails?"

"Hmm...I will see what I can learn."

Satisfied that everyone was doing what they could, Jorge left the office and headed home.

"Paige?" he called out as soon as he entered the house a half hour later.

"I'm in the bedroom," She sang out and he quickly rushed upstairs to find her in their room, staring at a pile of clothes on the bed.

"Are you moving out, what is going on here?" Jorge teased as he walked over and gave her a kiss. "What is with the clothes everywhere? I heard you say you were in the bedroom, I was hoping it was an invitation."

"Unfortunately, no," Paige said as he laughed and grabbed her ass before kissing her again. "I'm trying to find something to wear for tonight?"

"Tonight? Is this the party for Athas already?"

"No, we're invited to dinner at my sister's place," Paige hesitantly reminded him. "Remember?"

"Oh yes, that is right," Jorge nodded as he found an empty spot on the bed and laid down. "I had forgotten. Why all this effort though? You always look great, Paige. Just pick whatever."

"I feel awkward going there," Paige replied and shook her head. "I'm not close to my family."

"Well, there must be a reason you want to now."

"Honestly, its cause she keeps calling to update me on my father's condition," Paige replied with a shrug and sat beside him. "That's the only reason we're talking at all. So when she invited me to dinner, I felt like I had to say yes, but I dread it."

"Oh, *mi amor*," Jorge commented as he reached out to touch her arm. "You have nothing to worry about. You sit through dinner, stay a bit after and then say we have to go home and help Maria with her homework or some shit like that."

"Is Maria coming with us or is she volunteering tonight?" Paige asked as she turned toward him and their eyes met. He stared at her for a moment before replying.

"I believe her volunteering, it ends before dinner," Jorge replied. "Was she not talking about bringing a change of clothing with her today? Is that why?"

"Oh yes," Paige said with a loud sigh. "I was in such a rush this morning, I was thinking that she meant to change before doing volunteer work."

"No," Jorge replied as his eyes staring at her intently. "She may be good to have there. Your sister, she will be on her best behavior with a child present."

"I hope so," Paige commented. "I don't want to argue with her. I just want to get in, get it over with and leave."

"Ah! My love, do not overthink this," Jorge said and slid his hand over her thigh, his voice lowering to a seductive tone. "I do think we should take a long, hot shower though before we go, you know, to be extra clean…"

"Do you think so?" She spoke smoothly, as he sat up and leaned in close to her. His breath became labored as his lips touched hers, softly at first but quickly pressed roughly as his desires grew. His hands quickly darting underneath her shirt to touch her smooth skin as a soft moan rose from the back of her throat. Her hand ran up the side of his face, barely touching his skin, gently teasing him.

Letting go of her lips, he looked deeply into her eyes.

"Shower?"

She didn't reply, simply nodded as he led her into their bathroom. The clothing on the bed no longer seemed relevant.

CHAPTER

27

"Please come in!" The perky, little blonde lady ushered the three of them into the house. Jorge scanned the woman's face but failed to see any resemblance to his wife; other than that they both had blonde hair and blue eyes, there was literally none. She wore a knee-length skirt and a white blouse. Jorge was glad that they had all dressed up to match; Paige and Maria both wore dresses while he still had the same shirt and tie from earlier in the day. "Paige, it's about time you introduced us to your new family!"

Standing beside Jorge, his wife looked as if she wasn't sure how to respond but quickly found her voice.

"It's been a busy year," Paige attempted to explain just as a tall, white man wearing sweatpants and a T-shirt approached them. Scanning all three of them suspiciously, he appeared to force a smile on his lips. "Umm… Jorge, this is Lacey and her husband, Peter," She then turned to her husband. "This is Jorge and Maria."

Awkward handshakes followed. Not that Jorge wanted to hug these people and he certainly didn't want his daughter to either; she appeared uncomfortable even shaking hands with both Lacey and Peter. He would later consider how insightful children could be in these situations.

"Jorge?" Peter spoke up and seemed to stand a little taller. "Don't they pronounce it *Horhey* down there in Mexico?"

Jorge cringed and faked a smile. "Yes, well, I prefer the English pronunciation."

"I suppose," Peter said as he gestured toward the next room and they started to move away from the door. "Once you come to Canada, you people probably try to blend in."

You people.

Jorge clamped his mouth shut and grabbed his daughter's hand and gave it a squeeze, hoping she didn't make a comment either.

Following the others into the dining room, Jorge thought it was unusual to not sit in the living room rather than jumping right into the meal, however, he was hopeful of getting through this ordeal as quickly as possible. He was already counting down the minutes.

"Sit anywhere," Lacey gestured toward the table and they followed her instructions as she continued to rattle on. "I wasn't sure what to cook. I considered making Mexican food but I'd be embarrassed if it didn't turn out."

"That is fine," Jorge said while forcing his smile that tended to win people over. "I am sure whatever you cook, it will be beautiful."

Paige gave him a look from across the table; perhaps because he was thickening his accent, as he often did when he suspected it made others uncomfortable. Then again, had they done some research? Had they read the article from the former editor of *Toronto AM* wrote, insinuating that he was a criminal?

"Lacey is the best cook," Peter insisted as the two of them went into the kitchen. Jorge exchanged looks with his wife and then smiled at his daughter.

"I have wine," Peter announced as he returned and started to pour it. "It's from here in Ontario."

"I'm sure it will be great," Paige commented as she reached for her glass as Peter made his way around the table. He hesitated and started to pour a glass for Maria.

"No no!" Jorge automatically spoke up and shook his head. "My daughter, she is only 11."

"Oh, I'm sorry," Peter awkwardly moved the glass aside. "I was thinking in Mexico the children drank wine with dinner."

"I think you're thinking of Europe, maybe?" Jorge commented while across the table Paige rolled her eyes behind Peter's back. "But in Mexico, we do not allow such things."

"I can drink wine," Maria spoke up and received a sharp look from Jorge before starting to giggle. "Joking! *Papa,* I'm joking!"

"Peter, I told you that it wasn't the same in Mexico," Lacey said as she returned with a plate of steaming chicken. Leaning forward, she set it on the table before rushing back into the kitchen.

"I'm sorry, I didn't know," Peter spoke awkwardly and removed the glass, rushing back into the kitchen. Jorge and Paige exchanged looks. Jorge bit back his laughter.

Lacey continued to bring in dishes of food and everyone dug in; passing bowls around the table and reaching for the chicken in the middle of the table.

"This is delicious," Jorge was quick to comment and break the awkward silence. "I do not know what spices you have used but this is very good."

"It's an old family recipe," Lacey spoke enthusiastically and glanced at her sister. "Paige must have the same recipe at home or does she still hate to cook?"

Jorge grinned and didn't reply.

"Paige cooks for us all the time," Maria spoke up as she picked at her food. "And sometimes, if we are busy, we get food from other places."

"Paige always hated to cook," Lacey commented as she continued to smile her way through dinner. "Never very domesticated. The wild child, off in Latin America, teaching English while the rest of us were getting married and having babies, settling down."

Jorge nodded, managing to keep a straight face. Across from him, he noted that his wife didn't appear to see the humor.

"So, Lacey," Paige spoke calmly, appearing to ignore her sister's comments. "What are Chad and Britney doing these days?"

"Oh, the kids are doing great," Lacey said as she put down her fork and clapped her hands together. "Chad is at Dalhousie University studying to be a dentist and Britney isn't quite sure what she will do yet, but she's first year at the University of Toronto. She's thinking about studying abroad, maybe in Europe, she's not sure yet."

Jorge grinned to himself. He had met many Britney's in his youth; women who had no focus, often party girls who studied enough to consider themselves students. It was clear that the parents were oblivious to this but one day, they would learn.

"This is good, your kids, they must be smart," Jorge commented, noting that Paige appeared awkward on the other side of the table. Glancing at his daughter, he added, "Going to university would be a terrific experience for them."

Lacey caught his side glance at Maria and jumped right in.

"Oh, Maria, what do you want to be when you grow up, sweetheart?"

"I *am* going to be an actress!" Maria spoke dramatically. "A world-famous actress."

"Wow," Peter commented in a condescending tone. "Good for you! Maybe we can watch you on television one day."

"Yes, well, we will see," Jorge added and glanced at his daughter. "She is only 11, so we will see how she feels as she gets older."

Fortunately, Maria didn't comment.

"So, Jorge, I hear you work in the pot industry," Peter said and Jorge noted that the smile seemed to slip off Lacey's lips. "That's quite the big business these days."

"It is," Jorge agreed.

"What were you involved in before that?" Peter asked. "Or is that what you came to Canada for?"

"I was in coffee, back in Mexico," Jorge replied and glanced at his wife. "I came to Canada, for Paige, of course, and because my daughter wanted to go to school here. I thought it would be good for her. Pot was something I decided to get into when I realized the health benefits as well as the potential opportunities in the future."

"I got to ask you," Peter said with a forced sigh. "Do you *really* believe that there are health benefits or do you suppose maybe this is a way to market it, to make people feel like it helps?"

"I do think there are health benefits," Jorge replied, feeling his patience wearing thin. "In fact, there have been studies that prove such."

"Yes, but you can have studies on anything and find the proof you need to move forward," Peter continued while Lacey stared down at her food. "To me, if you're high enough, of course, you're gonna think you feel better."

"Well, actually, no, this is not true," Jorge said calmly. "Cannabis used for healing does not make the patient high. It is not the same as recreational marijuana."

"I don't know. I find that hard to believe," Peter countered and looked toward Maria. "And the children, do we want our children exposed to this kind of thing? I mean, we discovered Britney had some once in high school and we immediately laid down the law. I fear if we hadn't, who knows. Maybe she would be addicted to drugs, maybe not go to university, who knows, right?"

"I do not think pot is a 'gateway' drug," Jorge commented and glanced at his wife who appeared annoyed. "Maybe this is just me but I think that it is like alcohol. If used responsibly, there should be no problems."

"I disagree," Peter spoke more forcefully this time. "Perhaps in Mexico, it is different because you're more used to the drug culture unlike here in Canada, where its pretty much limited to the poorer neighborhoods. I can't help but think that if kids get their hands on pot then they're going to want to try something a bit stronger."

Jorge bit back his anger.

"Peter, that is not true," Paige sharply cut in. "I wouldn't say there is a 'drug culture' in Mexico nor would I say that Canada's drug problems are limited to poor neighborhoods. It's not that simple."

"I disagree," Peter quickly jumped back in, his voice raised this time. "Now, I've worked in the public school system for several years and I assure you, you can tell the kids who're going to get in trouble with drugs. They come from the poor neighborhoods, where it is acceptable, where they see it every day. Now, not to say that the middle class doesn't have this problem too but where are they getting the drugs from? They're going to the Northwest side of Toronto to buy them. Why do you think we see so much crime in these areas?"

"Peter, this doesn't make for very pleasant dinner conversation," Lacey cut in and gave her husband a warning look. Across the table from Jorge, he noted Paige was sitting down her fork and giving him a look. "Can we talk about something happy? Like, how did you two meet, Paige?"

Jorge exchanged looks with his wife and waited for her to launch into the usual story; obviously, few people knew that he met his wife when she accidentally mistook him for the man she was hired to assassinate. Although, that story would've definitely shaken up this table. He finished his food and noted that his daughter was also finished. They could leave soon.

"What a lovely way to meet," Lacey gushed and suddenly switched gears. "Does anyone want dessert? Lemon meringue pie?"

"Ah...Paige?"

"I'm fine."

"I want dessert!" Maria announced and Lacey smiled at the little girl before rising from the table. "Be right back! Jorge?"

"Ah…no, thank you," He politely commented and noted the frustration on his wife's face. "After that, we must go, unfortunately, Maria has homework."

Lacey merely smiled, reaching for his plate while her husband stood up and quickly gathered the rest of the plates and followed her into the kitchen.

"*Papa*," Maria said as soon as they left. "I need to pee. Can I use their bathroom?"

"Maria, you must ask them," Jorge gestured toward the kitchen. "I'm sure it will be fine."

"I think there's one next to the kitchen," Paige commented and gave Jorge a look after Maria went into the kitchen.

"It is…it is fine, Paige," He shook his head. "Do not worry."

She seemed to relax as they shared a smile. This was quickly interrupted by Maria yelling in the kitchen.

Jorge jumped up from the table and rushed into the next room with Paige right behind him.

"*Papa!*" Maria screamed as he entered the room. "They were saying bad things about you!"

A shocked Lacey was shaking her head, while Peter appeared angry.

"Your child snuck in here…"

"I had to go to the bathroom," Maria retorted. "*Papa*, he said that Paige waited too long to get married and was *forced* to marry a *Mexican!*"

"It was a joke, I didn't mean…" Peter attempted to explain, his eyes jumping from Jorge to Paige.

"You didn't mean to suggest that I was marrying below me?" Paige snapped as she stepped forward. "Isn't it bad enough you've insulted my husband all night? Couldn't you hold your snide remarks until we at least went home?"

"The child, she misunderstood," Peter was insistent.

"I did *not* misunderstand!" Maria stood her ground.

"Maria," Jorge said as he reached for his daughter to pull her back from her confrontational mode at the same time that his wife stepped forward, slapping Peter across the face. Gasping, Lacey started to cry and rushed out of the room.

"Ok, we must go," Jorge attempted to shield Maria from this scene while reaching for his wife's arm. "Dinner was nice, thank you, we must go."

The three of them rushed from the house as if it were a burning building.

CHAPTER

28

"I knew this wasn't a good idea," Paige finally broke the silence on the way home. Up until that point, everyone was in shock after she lashed out at her brother-in-law. "I'm so sorry, I shouldn't have...."

"Paige, please do not apologize for this," Jorge immediately cut her off as they stopped at a red light. Reaching over to touch her hand, he looked into her eyes. "This is not something I haven't experienced before, you know? It did not bother me as much as you. I will admit, I did not appreciate him trying to feed my daughter wine but other than that, I cannot say I haven't heard that before."

"*Papa*, he said Paige married *below* her," Maria suddenly piped up from the back seat. "Why would he say such a terrible thing? Why doesn't he like Mexicans?"

Jorge hesitated, carefully choosing his words before finally speaking.

"Maria, some people, they think like that," Jorge insisted as he glanced in the rearview mirror. The sadness on her face broke his heart. The last thing he wanted to do was to once again explain to his child that some people were racist assholes. He could see the hurt in her eyes and it infuriated him. "They do not understand other cultures. Besides, sometimes to get the best, you must wait." He gave a sideward glance at Paige who grinned.

"*Papa*, it's not hard to understand," Maria countered with frustration in her voice. "People are people. It does not matter what color they are or where they are from, we're all people. Even a baby knows that!"

"Maria, you are much smarter than that man back there," He pointed behind him to indicate the house they had just came from, as traffic started to move again. "Unfortunately, that man, he is a racist."

"I know, *Papa,* but why? I don't understand why he doesn't like Mexican people," Maria spoke with sadness in her voice that reminded him once again that she was merely a vulnerable child. "What did we do to him?"

"Good question," Jorge muttered under his breath and out of the corner of his eye, he noticed Paige turning around in her seat.

"Maria, I wish there was a reasonable explanation but there simply isn't," Paige softly commented, her composure returned. "What he said was unacceptable."

"Paige, I liked that you slapped that man," Maria seemed to suddenly perk up. "He deserved it. I wanted to hit him too."

"Now, ladies, we do not need you both fighting for my honor," Jorge teased them and winked at his wife. "I am a lucky man to have you both wanting to beat up Paige's brother-in-law."

"Technically, Peter is both our brother-in-law," Paige quietly reminded him as she started to turn back around. "So let's share that misery if we can and Maria, I shouldn't have hit him. It wasn't ok for me to do that. I shouldn't have allowed my anger to take over."

"It's ok, Paige," Maria insisted. "I understand. I have some emotional moments too."

Jorge snickered as they drove down their street. "Look, let us not think about this anymore, Let's move on. It was a disastrous dinner and unfortunately, we've seen a less pleasant side of Paige's family but that is ok. We still love Paige even though her relatives are....you know, racists."

Paige cringed even though he was teasing her.

"*Papa,* we have bad relatives too," Maria was quick to remind him. "Just in a different way."

"Yes, Maria, you are correct," Jorge nodded as they drove into their garage and he glanced at Paige. "This is true also. We all have good and bad relatives. Unfortunately, it is starting to feel like we both have more of the latter."

Maria giggled and Paige smiled.

Once inside the house, Maria rushed upstairs to start her homework while Jorge turned to Paige as he threw his keys on the counter.

"I am truly sorry," Paige repeated her earlier comment. "I feel terrible."

"Do not, *mi amor,* as I told you, this is not my first rodeo," Jorge said as he moved closer and gave her a quick kiss. "It is fine. But hey, on the plus side, maybe Peter can tell us where and when the next white supremacist meeting takes place. He might know."

"If he knows, I somehow doubt he would be telling me," Paige muttered as Maria rushed back downstairs with her backpack.

"The truth is, Paige, people end up showing their true colors," Jorge reminded her as he turned toward his daughter. "Good people, bad people. You can only hide who you really are for so long before it comes shining through. And with men like Peter, sometimes this is a very undesirable reality."

"*Papa*, you said we wouldn't talk about it anymore," Maria reminded him as she sat her bag on the floor beside the kitchen table.

With that, the conversation ended.

The following morning, everyone met in the boardroom of Hernandez-Silva to go over details for the upcoming party for Athas and other ongoing business. Jorge was delighted to find a box of his favorite French pastries on the table, as well as a cup of coffee for each of them. He turned to his wife and raised an eyebrow.

"Ah, Diego, he thinks of everything!" Jorge spoke approvingly to an empty room. "I guess we are early, my love, let us have a pastry."

"I managed to keep you away from that bakery for, what, three days?" Paige teased as they took their usual seats and they both grabbed a pasty and started to eat, while Paige reached for the cream. They heard shuffling outside the door and looked up to see Diego.

"Of course, you start eating before anyone else arrives!" He spoke in his usual, abrupt manner before reaching for his own pastry. "I better get one before Jorge inhales them all."

"I just have one!" Jorge spoke with his mouth full and Diego laughed as he sat at the head of the table.

Everyone else seemed to arrive at once. Sylvana, followed by Chase, while Athas and Jesús walked in together, involved in a political conversation about something that had recently been in the news. Jorge was about to start the meeting when Jolene came flying into the room.

"Sorry! I am late!" She said regretfully while glancing toward Sylvana, who was sitting in her usual seat. "I was tied up in traffic."

"It's fine," Diego insisted while Jorge didn't comment. He had no idea she was even coming to the meeting but decided to go along with it.

"Ok, well this will be fast because I don't think Alec can stay long," He glanced at the politician who was reaching for a pastry while the rest either already had one or focused on their coffee. "The party, it is tomorrow night, is everything ready?"

"Yes," Diego automatically answered for Alec. "The rich, influential people will meet Alec. I'm going early to help Chase set up. Alec just gotta be there."

"I guess that's easy enough," Athas replied and shrugged as he swallowed a mouthful of pastry. "This is new to me but I'm told to just talk about my political agenda and what I will do if elected."

"*When* elected," Jorge corrected him as he reached for his coffee. "Remember, you got the rich people tomorrow night so you must persuade them to vote for you. Don't talk too much about helping the poor. They aren't into that. They want to hear how voting for you will benefit them."

"My policies are more directed at lower-income," Alec reminded him. "But I think rich people sometimes like helping others too."

Jorge laughed. "Rich people didn't get rich by being generous or giving a shit about anyone but themselves. You got a few do-gooders out there but let's face it, that's more about the tax write off. Talk about getting people off the street and not helping the homeless. That wording, it's just a bit different but it means the same thing. Getting people off the street means they don't gotta look at them and feel guilty but if you say helping homeless people, it makes them feel like they may have to invest in projects. See what I mean? It's about spinning and changing the language."

Alec nodded and smiled. "That is a good point. I'm going to have to fine-tune my speech."

"Send it to me later, I will look at it," Paige suggested. "I might be able to help."

"Ok, so that is it for the party, anything else?" Jorge glanced around the table.

"Everything is in place," Chase confirmed. "The club will be at its full capacity."

"Is everyone here going?" Jorge asked and turned toward Sylvana. "Except you, of course, you gotta be spying on that asshole, Harley. Any progress there?"

"Nope," Sylvana replied. "The guard dog is still in place."

"Ok, well, we will get there," Jorge glanced around the table. "Anyone else?"

"Sir, I will try to be there," Jesús replied. "But I may have to go back East about the shops we tried to take over. The government was willing to privatize but apparently, there have been some issues erupt with the opposition party, however, I believe that will be smoothed over."

"The government, they want to privatize," Jorge reminded him. "The provinces who wanted to oversee things in the first place, they only do that because it makes the public feel safer. They had no intention to continue but quietly bow out later, allowing my company to take over. And I hear this from the top, so you know it's true. They want fucking taxes and that is all. They do not care about anything else. Less work for them, that's how the government likes things."

"Perhaps it will take time," Jesús asked and shrugged. "But maybe we will need to have a conversation with some people on the other side, the one causing the trouble."

"You do what you gotta do," Jorge replied without expanding on the topic.

"Ok, this is where I should go," Alec cut in and moved his chair back. "Is there anything else for me?"

Jorge shook his head before glancing at Diego.

"I got nothing," Diego said and leaned forward on the table. "I will be in touch with you early tomorrow and probably be at the club most of the day setting up. Chase will be there too. So if anything comes up, just call us."

Chase nodded and glanced at Alec as he stood up from his seat.

"Ok, great, thanks," He directed his latter comment at Jorge before grabbing his laptop bag and rushing out the door.

"So this party, it will be fancy, not too fancy," Jorge confirmed with Diego, who merely nodded. "*Perfecto.*"

"Everything running fine at the warehouse, Jolene?"

"Yes, it is good, thank you," She replied with a nod. "I wish to do more if you need me to do so."

"Right now, we want you to focus on the warehouse but in the future," Jorge thought for a moment. "We may need help with other matters."

"Are we getting that other warehouses in the east?" Diego directed his comment at both Jesús and Jorge. "Remember the ones we were looking at?"

"We are working out the details, yes," Jesús answered. "We hope to finish soon, so we can start on the west, I take it, sir?"

"Yes, of course, we will one day take over the country," Jorge insisted.

"Do you mean weed wise or other wise?" Sylvana spoke up.

Jorge didn't reply but raised an eyebrow, with a smooth grin on his lips.

CHAPTER

29

The party may have been for Alec Athas but in reality, it was Jorge Hernandez who was rubbing shoulders with Toronto's elite crowd. Whether it be well-known business people or anyone else known to hold power within Ontario's largest city, he boldly approached them as if he were the guest of honor. Many were aware how the Mexican had swooped in and took over the pot industry in its infancy, managing to persuade owners to sell, government to bend and did all this while Hernandez-Silva Inc. earned record profits. To many, he was the man to watch.

Not that he lacked charm either. If there was one thing Jorge learned in his early days in the cartel, it was how to read people and win them over. The man he worked for all these years made an unprecedented decision to take on this unknown, poor kid after his only son had been murdered, giving Jorge a chance to prove his value. It was a challenge he took on with great passion and quickly showed the kingpin that he was a man of his word. He had opened up new markets, solved problems and took on competition and enemies again and again. With fire in his eyes, he forged ahead and never looked back.

Now, he walked through the group of people with an electric smile on his face, well aware that his attractiveness and dapper manner immediately made people feel more at ease, which is why he highlighted these attributes when he was on the clock. People were drawn to him and that in itself was half the battle. As he told his boss many years before, people respect a man in the expensive suit who said what they wanted to hear. Throughout the years, his theory proved true again and again.

"Jorge."

He turned to see Paige approaching him. Wearing a beautiful orange dress that brought out her eyes and the natural glow of her skin, his wife looked elegant with her hair up in a fancy style that she had thrown together before they left the house. She looked a little flustered, which made him worry that something was wrong.

"Is everything ok, *mi amor?*" He reached for her hand. "You do not seem yourself. Are you not feeling well?"

"I'm a little warm," Paige replied as she slid her free hand below her neck. "I guess there are so many people in here. Maybe the air conditioning isn't working."

"My love, I am ok and I'm wearing a suit," Jorge pointed at his outfit then glanced at her thin dress. "Maybe you need some air. Perhaps we should go outside for a moment?"

"I'm fine, maybe I need a drink," She replied and looked toward the bar. "You seem to be very sociable tonight."

"What can I say?" Jorge replied with a smooth grin on his face. "People want to meet the man who is taking over the pot business in this country. But you know me, I cannot give away all my secrets."

"Probably best not to," Paige teased as she glanced toward the bar, nodding at Diego who was standing beside it. "Although, I did overhear Alec giving you a lot of praise for your help and advisement for his campaign, so I guess that has piqued some interest too."

"Ah yes," Jorge replied as he glanced around the room briefly before looking into his wife's eyes. "My advisement definitely has been invaluable."

"So modest," She teased as she let go of his hand and started to walk away.

"You know it, baby," He discreetly reached out and grabbed her ass while his eyes continued to scan the room.

"Jorge," He heard his name being called and turned to see Jolene heading his way. Glaring at her, he shook his head.

"No drinks tonight, Jolene," He gestured toward the glass in her hand. "We are not having a replay of last time."

"This, this is just pineapple juice," She replied while holding the glass up to his nose, causing him to quickly back away and nod. "I am not drinking tonight."

"Keep it that way," He attempted to move away but she caught his arm instead but then quickly let go.

"We must talk."

"Jolene, what did I just say?" Jorge spoke more gruffly this time.

"No, this is not me trying to seduce, it is about business," She insisted. "At the meeting yesterday, you talk about Sylvana helping out?"

Jorge nodded.

"She cannot do," Jolene insisted and shook her head. "You need me to take care of…"

"Jolene, I don't think that would be a good idea," Jorge muttered. "As soon as you walk in the door, they will know who you are and why you're there."

"That may be what we need to do," She insisted. "This here, Sylvana, hanging out…waiting, for what, I ask? We need to address this situation directly. I can do."

Jorge didn't reply.

"I can take care of this, you let me do it," She continued. "We cannot pussyfoot."

"Jolene," He sighed loudly and thought about his next words. "Let's wait. I want to see what Sylvana can learn and we will take it from there."

"If she does not do," Jolene said with a confidence he hadn't heard in her voice in months. "I will do. I promise I will take care of it."

Jorge pondered her comment and finally nodded. "We will talk about this next week."

Rather than reply, she nodded before slipping into the crowd. He pushed her words aside, deciding to refocus on the party.

Alec Athas was across the room speaking with a well-known businessman, who was showing interest but at the same time, Jorge couldn't help but note that his enthusiasm seemed to wane the longer they spoke. Hopefully, Athas wasn't talking about saving the fucking world to a man who only cared about money. It was necessary to see the difference and take silent cues, turn conversations toward a favorable light when dealing with these people. Did Alec not have that skill?

Tom Makerson was approaching him with a dubious smile on his face. Standing beside Jorge, he didn't comment at first but instead scanned the room.

"You got a group of who's who here tonight," He finally commented as Jorge smiled and nodded. "I notice many of them are making a beeline to you, not Athas, which somehow seems to defeat the purpose."

"Ah, but does it?" Jorge asked. "In fact, people are curious about how I moved in on the pot business so quickly. I tell them I'm just a smart businessman, you know, I got this way…"

Makerson laughed and nodded. "That's one way to put it."

"So tell me," Jorge leaned in closer. "Any more issues in the office? Keeping your doors locked?"

"Always," Tom replied, his expression becoming serious. "Now I also know what to look for, I'm still paranoid regardless."

"One day, we will get my cleaning lady in again," Jorge suggested.

"Cleaning lady, that's what you call her?"

"That's what we call her," Jorge turned toward him.

"I still don't know who was listening in but assume it was Harley?"

"You may never know for sure but always listen to your instincts."

"My instincts wonder if maybe they've been there before I took over as editor."

Jorge nodded. "This could be the case."

"Either way, it's very unsettling."

"This life can be unsettling," Jorge insisted.

"So, Athas has another event coming up," Tom mentioned casually. "In a couple of weeks, at the centre where he works?"

"Oh yes," Jorge nodded. "His idea. He wants to meet with the people in the community. You know, juice and cookies for the kids. Coffee and tea for the adults."

"A different crowd than this one," Tom replied.

"It is nice to cover the bases," Jorge said as he continued to watch Athas across the room. "Although, I must say that I am not necessarily sure that he connects with people as I had hoped. I'm not getting that sense tonight."

"Maybe it will be different with the next event," Makerson suggested. "I think Alec is always going to relate more with the lower and middle class than he will with these people. He speaks more to those struggling than big business. Either way, be reassured that the editorial in tomorrow's paper will be favorable."

"Thank you, I do appreciate that," Jorge said with a grateful smile. "I'm concerned that after tonight, he may need help."

"Well, if this election doesn't work out as you hoped," Tom commented as he started to walk away. "Maybe we need a Hernandez on the next ballot."

The two of them laughed as the editor disappeared into the crowd.

Jorge glanced around the room to find his wife. She was now talking to both Diego and Athas, who looked oddly encouraged despite the event quickly proven as lackluster. Even the *putas* he had mixed in the crowd weren't managing to improve the mood of the room, as guests slowly began to trickle out.

His phone vibrated. He was reluctant to check it in the middle of the party but considering it was a bit of a flop, did it really matter?

It was Jesús.

"*Hola*," He answered the phone abruptly. "Jesús where are you? I thought you were coming to the party?"

"Unfortunately, sir, I got tied up at the last minute," He replied in his usual, slow manner. "Would it be possible for you to leave this event tonight and come to the warehouse?"

"Is there a problem? Jolene didn't mention anything."

"Jolene, she does not know."

"I'll be there soon."

Glancing at his wife, he pointed at the door and sent a quick text on his way out.

Can Diego drive you home?

Once outside, his phone vibrated.

Yes or Alec can.

Feeling jealousy creep up as he thought about how beautiful she looked tonight, he shook his head as he made his way to the SUV. He sent a message to Diego.

Do me a favor? Drive Paige home tonight.

I will.

Reaching his SUV, he wasted no time jumping in and pulling on the street. Jesús didn't seem too alarmed so chances were that whatever it was would be manageable.

However, arriving at the warehouse to see a cop car didn't exactly calm him.

"Fuck!" He muttered before getting out of the SUV and rushing to the side door. Once inside, he made his way to Jolene's office, where, he discovered Jesús, a black police officer, and some skinny kid, probably no older than 25 sitting around.

"What the fuck is going on here?" He immediately asked as his mask of charm from earlier quickly dropped.

"We got someone trying to break into the building," Jesús pointed toward the officer. He looked familiar but he couldn't figure out why.

"I was patrolling the area when I noticed this man trying to break in the back door," The officer immediately stood up and approached Jorge.

"So what happens next?" Jorge asked suspiciously. He wondered why everything felt so casual? Why hadn't the cop dragged the kid away yet?

"That's up to you," The man replied in a lower voice as he boldly stared into Jorge's eyes. "You want me to take him to the station or do you want to deal with this yourself."

"You're actually gonna let me deal with this?" Jorge asked suspiciously. "I thought the police, you took people to the station, fingerprint, you know…..all that fun cop stuff."

"I don't gotta," The cop lowered his voice. "Look, I know who you are and that you can deal with this kid better than me. I'm going to drag his filthy ass to the station, spend a lot of fucking time on paperwork that I don't want to do, only for his parents to come bail him out in the morning and hire a fancy lawyer to get him off on all charges."

"That is probably correct," Jorge nodded. "This is our legal system, unfortunately."

"You want him, you got him," The cop glanced over his shoulder.

Jorge considered his words for a moment.

"We must talk, outside," He gestured toward the door and the cop nodded.

"Jesús, can you babysit?" Jorge pointed toward the kid. "We're going to have a conversation."

"Yes sir," Jesús said and glanced across the room. "I got it covered."

The two men stepped outside and Jorge didn't waste any time getting to the heart of the matter.

"So you expect me to believe you're going to leave this kid here for me to take care of," Jorge replied. "Like you aren't setting me up."

"I'm not setting you up," The cop insisted. "I *know* who you are and if I did set you up, you'd be arrested and let out the same night. You wouldn't spend about an hour in a cell. All charges would be dropped, I would be in shit for entrapment and that's probably nothing compared to what you'd do to me after the fact."

Jorge grinned. "This, this is true. Everything you say, it is true."

"Look, I don't know if you remember me but I was at your fire a few months ago," He seemed to relax slightly.

"Ah yes and the police, they never did find the culprit," Jorge commented with a mocking tone. "What a surprise."

"They were told to drop it," The cop insisted and Jorge nodded. "It wasn't a priority."

"I see," Jorge said with interest. "And why was that?"

"Cause you're with the cartel and no one wants to get in the middle," He informed Jorge. "It's not a priority."

"This is not a surprise," Jorge spoke honestly. "Also, it does not tie up the police when they could be solving more important crimes. You know, like an old lady having her purse stolen."

The officer grinned. "So, I take it that you'll be handling this," He gestured toward the office.

"And you're just going to go?"

"I'm just going to go."

"And this will not be spoken of again."

"Not even if I find this kid bruised and battered later."

"Oh, I assure you, you won't find a thing," Jorge replied.

"That's good," The officer started toward the door. "Because I won't be looking either."

"May I ask your name, for future reference?" Jorge said as the officer reached the door.

Without saying a word, he fished in his pocket, pulled out a card and walked back and handed it to him.

"Have a pleasant night, Mr. Hernandez."

With that, he was out the door and Jorge glanced at the card.

Michael Perkins.

CHAPTER

30

Despite Jorge's impression that Alec Athas fell short at the party, Makerson wrote a glowing editorial in the morning paper. He talked about the nominee in a balanced report stating what he proposed doing for both the rich and poor in his district, slanting the article in such a way that it was favorable toward Athas and his party. Pleased, Jorge made a note to invest more in *Toronto AM*. It was good to have the media on your side. People tended to believe anything that was spoon-fed to them because they didn't have the time, energy or interest in investigating important issues.

"Good news this morning?" Paige asked as she arrived in the kitchen wearing a pair of yoga pants, a hoodie with her hair in a bun. Despite the makeup she wore, she appeared exhausted as she made her way toward the coffee pot. "Are the reviews in on the party?"

"Yes, *mi amor,* all is well but what about you," He replied as he closed his laptop and watched Paige pour a coffee. "You were out like a light when I arrived home last night but you still…*estás enfermo?*"

"I'm fine," Paige replied as she made her way to the fridge. "I'm just tired."

"Paige, maybe helping Athas with his campaign, perhaps it is too much," Jorge suggested in the most balanced voice he could manage but his wife still gave him a suspicious grin. "I will not have that man exhaust my wife with extra work. You are already so busy with Maria."

"Most women have multiple children and work full-time," Paige pointed out as she reached for the cream and made her way back to her cup of coffee. "So that's hardly an excuse besides, I don't do that much work on his campaign."

"Still, it would be better to be safe than sorry," Jorge commented as he reached for his coffee. "Hey Paige, do you think you could be pregnant?"

"I am not pregnant," She insisted flatly and put the cream back in the fridge before walking toward the table with her coffee in hand. "I'm just…a little tired."

Jorge wasn't convinced but didn't want to push the topic.

"So, where were you last night after you left the party?" Paige asked casually. "What happened?"

"We had an issue at the warehouse," Jorge replied and shook his head, glancing over his shoulder. "Maria? Where is she?"

"Still in bed," Paige replied. "No school today, remember?"

"Ah, yes, very good," Jorge replied. "We had someone attempt to break in the warehouse. Jesús and I had to take care of him."

"Take care…"

"Well, not in that way," Jorge said and shrugged. "We scared the shit out of him but the interesting thing was that a policeman caught him and gave us the option to do as we wished."

"Really?" Paige asked and perked up. "That sounds strange. Are you sure it's not a trap of some kind?"

"I had him checked out," Jorge replied. "He's a cop that tends to get in a lot of trouble from within. He's been suspended for attacking a man he arrested, this kind of things suggests that he doesn't exactly toe the line, as you would say."

"Oh…" Paige said and pursed her lips "I would still be careful."

"Do not worry," Jorge replied. "Of all the police I already have on my payroll, this would just be one more and unlike the others, this one might be helpful. As a black man, I am sure he might even be more inclined to help us out if he knows about the white supremacists. I am thinking of meeting him to discuss this and see what he knows."

Paige nodded slowly and suddenly changed the topic. "I'm a little concerned about Diego."

"Why?" Jorge asked with interest. "This takes me a little off guard. He seems fine, no?"

"That's the thing," Paige replied. "He had a couple of drinks last night and he admitted to me that he's been depressed. I'm a little worried."

"He is?" Jorge asked, surprised to learn this information. "Are you sure? Maybe that was last night? A little alcohol perhaps made him sad?"

"I get the impression it might be more serious than that," Paige replied. "I told him that maybe he should stay with us for a while."

"With us? What?" Jorge said and laughed. "What in the guest room?"

"In the basement," Paige commented. "Clara's old apartment is free. He could stay there once in a while. We aren't doing anything with it."

Jorge thought for a moment. "Paige, how serious is this depression that you suggest such a thing?"

"I'm concerned," She replied flatly. "He's having some physical symptoms too."

"Ok, well if that is what you think."

"He may not, you know, I just put it out there."

"I would guess no or he would already be on our doorstep," Jorge spoke dramatically. "We are talking Diego but tell me, is it still over Chase? Why does everyone fall in love with Chase?"

Paige laughed. "It does seem to happen a lot, doesn't it? I think cause he's a nice guy, sincere, a good person."

"Handsome, young, in shape…."

"Yes," Paige said with a grin. "And I don't think it's just that. I think it's a lot of things going on with him now. He's reevaluating his life and he's not completely happy."

"Ok, whatever you think," Jorge replied and reached for his laptop bag. "I must go and meet with Sylvana. I am going to tell her that the project is off and she can return to work."

"Really?" Paige seemed surprised.

"It is not working," Jorge remarked as he picked up his Mac and put it inside the bag. "So Jolene, she approached me at the party last night and she is determined to fix this situation. She claims Sylvana cannot do it but she can."

"Really?" Paige appeared interested. "As if she will go under the radar at Harley's office."

"I think she has something else in mind," Jorge replied and thought for a moment. "And she might be right."

Fortunately, when he broke the news to Sylvana, she appeared relieved to return to her normal duties. Rather than meeting her in public, he stopped by her apartment. It was small and so cramped that he couldn't help but comment.

"This here, this shoebox you live in," Jorge gestured around the room. "Do I not pay you enough to at least…I don't know, move into a larger shoe box?"

"I haven't had time or patience to look elsewhere," Sylvana insisted as she sat down at her table, which barely fit in her super small kitchen. "Looking for apartments in Toronto is sheer hell."

"Yes, looking for a house is the same," Jorge replied as he sat across from her. "What? You don't offer me coffee? Something to drink? Sylvana, did your mother not bring you up better?"

"You want a coffee? There's a shop across the street," She smoothly gestured toward the window.

Jorge laughed. "Ah! So you do not mind if I send you back to your job on Monday?"

She shook her head. "I will just say I no longer have time."

"If they ask why not?"

"None of their fucking business why not, that's what," Sylvana commented. "So tell me something, how come I never travel with Jesús? I want to go with him when he's in the East fighting to take over."

"Are you sure about this," Jorge asked. "It can get pretty…dicey sometimes."

"I like dicey," Sylvana insisted. "I want all in with you guys. I know how you play, Jorge, it's no secret in the family. I want to be more involved."

"Forgive me, Sylvana, but you just had an assignment you could not pull off," Jorge spoke bluntly. "Why would I give you something more dicey?"

"That assignment had more to do with being sneaky," Sylvana replied. "Inconspicuous, which I'm not great at but I am bold and I'm not afraid to talk to people."

Jorge thought about it for a moment. "I will speak to Jesús and get back to you."

"Fair enough," She nodded. "I think there's an advantage to having a woman in the room during these negotiations."

"It may be dangerous."

"I can handle danger."

Jorge didn't reply but somehow expected that she could. Her mother grew up in a tough neighborhood in Mexico and her father, was anything but a saint. However, when he brought it up to Jesús that evening when him, Diego and Paige met at the club for drinks, there was some hesitation.

"Sir, I do not know about bringing her to these meetings," Jesús spoke bluntly. The four of them were sitting in the VIP room to have a private discussion. The room had already been checked for listening devices and locked until the time of their get together. "I have given it thought and am not sure that she will not say too much. Your cousin, she can talk, you know."

Jorge laughed. "Yes, this is a good point, Jesús, perhaps she will go overboard."

"There is a certain balance that is necessary to get what you want," Jesús continued to make his point. "I would not say that she cannot do such but I would rather be certain than lose a deal."

"What if we allow her in the meetings if she promises to not say anything," Paige suggested. "Just listen at first, see how you do things?"

"This, this could work," Jesús spoke evenly. "We will see."

"We'll have a meeting next week."

"But sir, we are, I would say, about 60% toward our goal in the East. We are about to officially take over Nova Scotia, Prince Edward Island and I'm currently working on New Brunswick and Newfoundland," He hesitated for a moment. "That was an interesting place to visit. The alcohol they gave me, it was quite strong."

Paige laughed and took a sip of her drink while beside her, Diego seemed expressionless, Jorge noted.

"So, let us not talk more business," Jorge replied. "But needless to say, Jesús there is a big bonus coming your way for a job well done. You know me, I recognize loyalty and hard work above all."

"Thank you, sir," Jesús said with a nod. "I do appreciate this."

"I assume if we don't get all these places," Diego finally spoke up. "Heads will roll? Literally, I mean?"

"We may not be that barbaric," Jorge replied. "This is Canada, after all."

"I remember being in Mexico once, years ago and hearing about a head rolling into a bar one day," Paige said with a grin on her face. "It's very...dramatic."

"Ah! Yes, we Mexicans, that is our thing," Jorge replied as he reached out and touched his wife's bare shoulder. She wore a black top that had a strange slit down the arm. He didn't understand women's clothing but certainly appreciated anything that showed this much bare skin. "We invented this expression."

"Nah nah!" Diego piped up with his big eyes bulging out. "We, Colombians, we started that."

"No no no!" Jorge argued. "This here, it has Mexico written all over it. This is what *we* do."

"I'm not fully certain it comes from either place," Paige cut in. "I think it might be some medieval thing."

Jorge and Diego both shook their heads.

"Nah nah, that's Latino, right there," Jorge insisted. "I am sure of it."

Paige grinned and looked into her drink.

CHAPTER

31

"**S**o, you got anything for me?" Jorge bluntly asked the scrawny white kid sitting across from him. Andrew Collin was slumped over with a coffee in hand almost as if he could barely keep awake for the conversation. "Any news? Got anything about your uncle?"

"Nah," Andrew shook his head, he stared into his coffee. "I've had other stuff going on."

"Oh yeah?" Jorge leaned back in his chair with a little interest. "What's a *gringo* like you got going on?"

"I was seeing this girl and she dumped me last night," Andrew said and made a face. For a moment, Jorge thought he was going to cry and although his first instinct was to roll his eyes, Paige always encouraged him to show compassion. She was right, of course, this was a way to warm them up and create loyalties.

"Sorry to hear that," Jorge fished his brain for the right words, finally settling on something Paige would probably say in this circumstances. "Is that why you aren't shoveling food in your face today like you usually do?"

"Yeah, not too hungry today," He replied and leaned his head to the side, almost as if he could barely hold it together. "Just kind of….blah…"

Jorge nodded and thought for a moment.

"So your racist uncle, you hear anything about this white supremacy group he's part of lately?" Jorge dug a little further, hoping that the sympathy that he offered was enough. "You know, any secret meetings?"

"Nah, he is pretty tied up in this campaign," Andrew said and hesitated, wrinkling his nose, he glanced toward the waitress passing them with a plate of food. "You know, doing the political thing."

"You, you sure you don't want to eat?" Jorge asked and gestured toward the waitress. "I'll buy you breakfast."

He almost regretted this offer when the kid looked at him with tears in his eyes. "You would do that for me?"

"Hey, it's just fucking breakfast," Jorge spoke sternly while gesturing for the waitress to return to their table. "I'm not putting you in my Will."

Andrew smiled for the first time since sitting down.

After he ordered what sounded like an elephant's portion of food, Jorge jumped right back into the conversation.

"So, your uncle, he's just fucking around with the campaign?" Jorge attempted to light a fire under him. "Nothing new? Nothing about us? Anything?"

"He hasn't been around much," Andrew quietly replied. "I tried to talk to him again the other day about my money but he won't budge. I got a job, so it's not like I'm being lazy but he said it's not enough. Are you still going to help me with that?"

"Yup, as soon as the timing is right," Jorge insisted. "We tried something but it didn't work so I'm looking at another approach."

"Oh really?" Andrew showed a mild interest. "He wants your Athas guy out. He's got it in for him. Tells people he's too inexperienced, spineless, a pretty boy."

"That it?"

"Yeah."

"He hasn't asked you to try to break into my warehouse again?"

"Nope."

"I had someone else try to break in on the weekend."

"Really?" Andrew appeared crestfallen with this news. "You mean, he sent someone else over?"

"Nah, you don't got to have your feelings hurt," Jorge said as he studied his face. "It was some random kid."

"Be careful, sometimes the cops set that up to get on your property."

"I was kind of thinking that too," Jorge commented. "This cop showed up. Told me to do whatever I wanted with the intruder cause it was a waste of his time."

"He said that?"

"Basically."

"Is he a black guy?"

"Yes," Jorge replied. "Perkins?"

"I think I know that guy," Andrew said and thought for a moment. "When I had the coffee shop, I had a break-in and I think he was the guy who showed up. That name sounds familiar."

"I doubt he was hanging around your uncle's place," Jorge said with a snicker.

"A black guy? Highly unlikely," Andrew joined him in laughter. "The only cops I've seen him talk to are old, fat, white guys."

"No doubt."

"Exactly," Andrew replied as his breakfast arrived; a massive platter of every kind of breakfast food possible.

"Oh, my fuck!" Jorge said as the waitress set it down. "Are you trying to have a heart attack this morning? Cause me, I got no CPR."

The waitress laughed and asked if she could get them anything else before disappearing.

"Want some?" Andrew pointed toward the food as he picked up his fork.

"I might," Jorge leaned in and took a slice of bacon and popped it in his mouth. "You're seriously gonna eat all that?"

"Yup," The kid replied as he began to shovel it in.

"Anyway, so this cop, I'm having him looked into, see if you can find out anything," Jorge requested. "I got a feeling he's a dirty cop but I always make sure before I have anything to do with them."

"Are there many?" Andrew asked as he chewed.

"Yes, but usually more the guys at the top," Jorge answered and leaned back in his seat. "Not the bottom guys, most think they're making a difference in the world. They gotta believe it. The guys at the top, they don't care. They just want to retire on a nice, fat pension and do as little as possible until that time."

"Yeah, sounds about right," Andrew continued to dig into his food with gusto. "The cops, it's a power trip."

Jorge didn't reply but reached for another slice of bacon. Popping it into his mouth, he had a thought.

"Andrew, you say you think that's the cop that helped you when your place was broken into?" Jorge asked.

"I said he was there, I didn't say he helped," Andrew corrected him. "He didn't seem to give a fuck, that's why I thought it was the same guy. Tried to suggest that I didn't have the doors locked properly. I'm sure I did but he wrote in the report that I wasn't sure."

"And you signed off on that?" Jorge asked as he reached for his coffee.

"I had to," Andrew said with a shrug. "He wasn't going to file the report if I didn't. In the end, he did nothing anyway."

Jorge didn't reply

With a busy day ahead, he pushed the topic out of his mind until that evening, when he met Paige and Diego for dinner. They were already seated when he arrived at the restaurant, the inviting smell of chicken filled the air as Jorge made his way through the crowd to find his wife and best friend at a back table. Diego was having a glass of wine while Paige was sipping on water.

"*Mi amor*, you still not feeling well?" Jorge asked as he leaned across the table and gave her a kiss before sitting down. "You look pale."

"I'm always pale," She grinned and shrugged. "I'm fine."

Jorge paused and glanced at Diego who was giving him a wide-eyed look.

"What is going on here?" Jorge immediately sensed something was up. "You're pregnant, aren't you?"

"No!" Paige protested. "I told you that already, I'm not pregnant. I'm just not feeling great lately. I'm probably missing some vitamins."

Jorge tilted his head down, his eyes suddenly illuminating as he looked at them both. "There is something."

"We were talking about how we should've invited Chase and Jolene," Diego spoke quietly.

Paige nodded, her blue eyes widening as she did.

"And Jesús is off with Sylvana," Diego said casually as he leaned back in his chair. "They got PEI and Nova Scotia where they want them, so we will officially take over sometime next month. Now, we got to get the rest of the Atlantic region and we got Ontario, so it's just Quebec and the West after that."

Jorge nodded but his thoughts were still back to his original comment.

"Paige, you are pregnant, this I know," He insisted with fire in his eyes. "I can see it."

"I'm not," She blinked rapidly. "I wish you would stop saying that."

"I know you think it is not possible," Jorge continued. "But I know your body and I am sure…."

"You know her body better than she does?" Diego mocked. "Oh, give me a break."

"I do, I do think I know her body very well," Jorge insisted as the waitress appeared. "We must get champagne to celebrate!"

"No no!" Paige protested, her hand reaching across the table. "No, please, can we…I'm not, ok, I'm sure, please."

Jorge grinned and shrugged. "Ok, whatever you say."

Paige looked upset and so, he dropped it.

"I will have a Corona," He said to the waitress. "Could I also see a menu, please?"

After she left, he turned his attention back to Paige. "I don't know, I can see it the more I look."

"I'm certain," Paige assured him. "Please, can we talk about something else?"

"Ok," Jorge replied as he sat up a bit straighter, pushing his chest forward. She wasn't ready to admit it yet…but he knew.

The waitress returned with their drinks and menus. He scanned it quickly, checked to see what his wife and Diego were ordering and finally decided on chicken and rice. Excitement built up in him but he felt the need to throw water on that fire, he changed the subject to please his wife.

"So, Athas was happy with the party?" Jorge asked as he reached for his beer. "The next one, it is the poor one, next weekend?"

"We can't call it the 'poor one'," Diego said discreetly as he leaned forward on the table and Jorge merely grinned. "The 'family' party."

"Ah! Yes, of course," Jorge said with an amused grin while checking his wife's face again. She wasn't giving anything away. He was almost too excited to focus. "That is what I mean. The cookies and juice party. It will be fun. I think Athas will be in his element there."

"But the problem is that Harley seems to gather more confidence with people because he's older, more experienced," Paige added. "I'm a little nervous. People like Alec but I'm not sure if they think he's ready yet."

"Ah! I see, well then we must show them he is," Jorge replied. "I will meet with him this week."

Jorge continued to sense something was going on. Diego and Paige weren't their usual selves and it concerned him. He studied both their faces in silence and finally asked.

"Ok, guys, what is it?" His attention jumped between the two. "Why are you acting so strangely? Please, you must tell me."

Neither said a word.

"Paige, what is it, are you sick?" Jorge felt his original excitement crash and burn before his eyes. Perhaps she was ill and didn't want to tell him. "Please, tell me, what is wrong?"

"It's not her," Diego cut in and hesitated for a moment. "It's me."

CHAPTER

32

"Why did you not tell me this?" Jorge asked Paige as they drove home later that evening. A chill in the air was a mild introduction to fall as a few drops of rain hit the windshield. Beside him, Jorge could see the regret in his wife's eyes and yet, he couldn't stop talking. "We do not keep secrets, Paige. I know he is your friend but why hide this from me?"

"He didn't want to tell you until he knew more," Paige replied gently and reached out to touch his arm as he stopped at the light. They exchanged looks and he nodded. "And it wasn't like he had a diagnosis yet so he wanted to wait."

"Yes, but it is not about that," Jorge insisted as the cars ahead of him started to move again. "It is about him being family. You do not have secrets from family."

"He barely told me," Paige said as her hand slid off his arm as they continued to move through traffic. "I had to pry it out of him. I thought he was just depressed but he finally admitted that he was going for tests."

"It could be nothing," Jorge stated with some doubt in his voice. "This here, it could be nothing?"

"Yes," Paige confirmed as they got closer to home. "I hope so and honestly, it probably is but you know Diego."

"So, what do you think?" Jorge asked in a calmer voice as sadness moved in. "Do you think it is serious?"

"I think it's stress and coffee," Paige spoke with an assertion in her voice. "He's scared he has stomach cancer."

Jorge didn't reply but bit his lip.

"It could actually be a lot of things," Paige continued. "I've been worried and wanted to tell you but he wanted to keep it a secret."

"I guess...I guess that's fair," Jorge spoke with some reluctance. "I do not agree but I understand."

"That's why I haven't been feeling well," Paige continued "I have been worried about him. I guess I went into overthinking mode."

"So you aren't pregnant?" Jorge asked. "I thought for sure you were."

"No," She replied flatly.

"I mean, I do not know..." Jorge paused for a moment. "It is not that I necessarily wanted it to happen but if it had, I feel it would be good news."

"I'm not pregnant," Her reply was emotionless. "But I get the impression you were hoping I was."

"It was not that Paige," Jorge decided to clear this matter up right away before the conversation got out of hand. In the past, her fears of not being able to conceive had caused misunderstandings that quickly erupted between them. "I thought, at first, you were sick. So, when it occurred to me that you might be pregnant, I was relieved. I would rather see you have a baby than an illness."

Paige didn't reply and he glanced at her.

"But this is not something I would miss either," Jorge continued, choosing his words carefully. "I do not miss being 45 years old father to a baby, you know? Even with Maria, I feel it is a lot. It is not easy, being a parent."

Paige remained silent.

"But, of course, what you want is what I want," Jorge continued. "Can you please speak. I do not want to fight about this."

"We aren't fighting," Paige finally reassured him. "I don't even know what I want sometimes."

"Well, this is something you must sit on your meditation pillow with," He teased her. "This is completely up to you. I am there regardless, you know this."

They shared a smile.

The following morning, Jorge called Diego while Paige was in the shower.

"My friend, my brother, I wish you had told me this sooner," Jorge spoke bluntly into the phone. "You know, I am here to help."

"There isn't much you can do unless you're a doctor," Diego spoke quietly on the other end of the line. "Until the tests come back, we won't know."

"Well, I recommend a second opinion," Jorge insisted. "Regardless, I will find a doctor that is better and we will deal with whatever it is."

"*Gracias*," Diego replied and seemed to hesitate. "I just…I gotta keep busy so I don't think about it, you know?"

"I do," Jorge replied. "Come with me today. I have a meeting later this morning. We will keep you busy and preoccupied."

"Can *Paige* come?" He asked and momentarily reminded Jorge of a schoolboy asking about his crush. "We could all go for lunch afterward?"

"Nah, she is meeting with Athas after she drops Maria at school," Jorge replied. "They are doing social media for this here party coming up. This weekend? The poor people party."

"Ah! Yes! We were working on the details the other day," Diego confirmed. "And once again, you probably shouldn't refer to it as the 'poor people' party."

Jorge laughed and ended the call.

Forty-five minutes later, he and Diego arrived at a small coffee shop that wasn't known for either the food or coffee, simply because it was conveniently located. The two sat at the back of the room watching the door.

"He's black, you said?" Diego confirmed. "This cop?"

"Yes," Jorge replied. "He is."

"And we can trust him?"

"My sources say he is barely hanging on by a thread," Jorge replied as Michael Perkins walked in the coffee shop. Dressed in civilian clothing, he quickly saw them at the back of the room and gave a nod. "His mouth and tactics have been known to get him in trouble."

"If anyone would know about that, it's you," Diego sniffed and twisted his mouth in the usual, arrogant manner. "You got a mouth."

"Last time I checked, so did you," Jorge smirked and glanced at Perkins, as he purchased a coffee and made his way to their table.

"Hernandez," Michael nodded and glanced at Diego before extending his hand. "Michael Perkins and you are?"

"Diego Silva," He replied and sat up a bit straighter as he shook hands with the officer before he joined them at the table.

"So, Perkins," Jorge started right away. "I hear you get yourself in a lot of trouble."

"You hear that?" Michael appeared humored. "You did a check on me or something?"

"You better fucking believe it," Jorge said with a sly grin. "You don't get where I am in life by being stupid. So, you get in a lot of trouble?"

"A few time."

"Doing what?" Diego spoke up. "Not ironing your uniform or something?"

Michael laughed. "Nah, that's more when in the police academy but these days, I sometimes get a little rough with the trash I deal with."

"Ah, and suddenly, the police have an issue with this?" Jorge asked as he leaned back in his seat. "Last I heard, this was not a problem unless it was recorded."

"There are always exceptions to that rule," Michael said as he reached for his coffee and took a drink. "If you leave bruises and broken bones, sometimes this is considered an issue."

"But not always?"

Michael shook his head no. "You would be interested in seeing what I see at work. I saw a homeless guy get pissed on by one of our men a few nights ago. You tell me there aren't different rules for different people?"

"So, this is why you have no issue doing your own thing?" Diego asked. "Cause you don't like seeing someone pissed on."

"Well, it ain't right," Michael replied.

"But what you do is ok?" Jorge asked.

"No, but there's a logic to it," Perkins replied. "Pissing on a defenceless homeless guy is fucking sick. Beating the shit out of a guy who punched his Mother or wife in the face, that's a whole other thing. Where I come from, we call it justice. You see, that's what I used to believe in until I was part of the system and quickly saw, it wasn't true. There is no justice. There's only what the public has to know but what goes on behind closed doors, is another thing."

"So when you saw the guy trying to break into our warehouse?" Jorge asked and noted that Diego was watching him carefully.

"I knew he would get away with it,' Michael replied and shook his head. "They usually do. These kids, they got rich daddies bailing them out. It's just the way it is. I knew who you were and I figured he would get a more… impactful lesson from you. That's all."

"So you want money?" Jorge cut to the chase.

"No," Michael quickly answered. "I figure we can help each other. Sometimes, I have a situation I need taken care of and my hands are tied. Sometimes, you might need information or something."

Jorge thought for a moment and nodded.

"Ok, so if this is true," Jorge finally spoke. "We need information."

"What you want?"

"There is a white supremacy group that Fulton Harley is involved in," Jorge replied and leaned forward on the table "I gotta know how involved he is and when they meet."

"See, the thing with that," Michael said and slowly tilted his head back and forth. "There's a lot of them. There are a couple primary ones here in Toronto but these guys, they travel. If he's part of one group, there's nothing stopping him from dipping his toes into another group too. They're insidious. Our hands are tied unless they do something or, at least, that's the official word."

"And unofficially?" Jorge pushed.

"You don't want to know what I would do to these people if I found them gathered in a group," Michael spoke bluntly. "Cause I have seen the damage they've done first hand."

"Unfortunately, so have I on a few occasions," Jorge replied and glanced at Diego who appeared enthralled by what Perkins had to say.

"Yeah yeah, your shop that was burned," Michael replied. "The one we were told to 'leave be'? Oh yeah, these guys got friends at the top too. Not just politics."

Beside him, Diego let out a groan.

"What? This is news to you, Diego?" Jorge teased. "That is how the world works. Here in Canada, they try to put on a friendly face but they have a lot of shit going on behind the scenes but when I say this, no one believes me."

"You're right," Michael confirmed. "You wouldn't believe the stuff that never makes it on the news. Don't think that isn't controlled either."

Jorge nodded. "So, you got nothing then?"

"I wouldn't say nothing," Michael said and hesitated for a moment. "You're not going to get a politician tied to this group during election time, it's not going to happen but that doesn't mean I can't find them for you. Harley's involved but he's not the head of this machine. I can get you the guy who is."

Jorge felt a smile cross his face, a darkness crept into his thoughts and he merely nodded.

"How big is this guy?" Diego asked.

"The top," Michael insisted. "He's a fat cat, rich asshole. He runs the show behind the scenes while to see him around town, he's a nice, family man who goes to church every Sunday but he's the head of probably the biggest white supremacist group in Canada."

"You know, Diego," Jorge spoke in a quiet tone. "You've been feeling kind of stressed lately. I may have an idea of a way to help relieve some of that stress. Have you had the baseball bat out lately?"

"I have not."

"Well, it will not be collecting dust much longer," Jorge replied. "Its time to get your swinging arm ready my friend, cause you're about to get back into the game."

Michael glanced at Diego and back at Jorge. He didn't reply but his eyes said it all.

CHAPTER

33

"So this here, it is not serious?" Jorge asked, confused by the sudden flux of information after Diego rushed into the house, hurriedly talking about his doctor's appointment. Paige was hugging Diego before he even finished speaking, relief on her face as Jorge stood back and attempted to grasp what was going on. "This Celiac? This is a disease that isn't bad? I do not understand.

"It's just a gluten allergy," Diego spoke excitedly, his eyes grew in size as he slowly let go of Paige and approached Jorge with the same gusto, pulling him into a strong embrace. "I'm not going to die."

"Well, I hate to be the one to tell you," Jorge replied as he hugged Diego back as cologne filled the air. "But we are all going to die at some point, *amigo*."

"Yes, but I don't have cancer," Diego continued to speak with excitement in his voice as he let go of Jorge, his comment directed more at Paige. "This, I can handle with diet."

"Yes and Diego, there are so many restaurants and companies that make gluten-free food," Paige calmly reminded him. "In fact, it's almost better to not have it in our diets, with or without the condition."

"So you cannot eat what?" Jorge said as they walked toward the living room. "Certain foods, they are bad?"

"No bread, wheat, that kind of thing," Diego replied as he sat on the couch, with Paige plunking down right beside him. Jorge gingerly sat across from them in a nearby chair. "It's going to be a hassle to get used to but it's doable. At least it's nothing I can't fix. I mean, I was so sick, I was sure it was cancer."

"Well, this is good, we must celebrate," Jorge offered as he exchanged looks with Paige. "Maybe we have a dinner...you know, somewhere you can eat, perhaps this weekend?"

"Sure," Diego replied as he smiled at Paige and then turned his attention back to Jorge. "This here, it has given me a new lease on life."

"Oh, and once you change your diet," Paige jumped in. "You'll see, you'll feel so much better."

"You know, I think you're right," Diego said as he crossed his legs, nodding with enthusiasm, his full attention on Paige. "I think this was making me sick for so long, I don't know what its like to feel good."

"You will, very soon, you will," Paige insisted affectionately. Jorge nodded but felt more like an outsider looking into their conversation.

"So, anything new with you guys," Diego finally turned his attention to Jorge. "Hey, did you find out about that white supremacy guy, the one Perkins told us about?"

"I did," Jorge replied then shifted attention to his wife. "Or I should say, Michael did. We found out that his name is Don Stumples. Sounds like an evil villain in an old-school nursery."

"He kind of is," Paige replied while beside her, Diego got serious. "He's the head of one the largest white supremacy groups here in Canada."

"At least so far," Jorge cut in. "New ones seem to crop up all the time. Somewhere along the line, this has suddenly become 'acceptable' so they are barely hiding it."

"Except for this guy," Paige said and nodded. "He's been hiding it for years. He works behind the scenes to change laws that make it more difficult for immigrants to get into this country and harder for them to work here in their trained profession. He's fought against refugees and helps create a backlash when we've had an influx of them into the country. These are a few examples. I mean, the guy is anti-immigrant, hates that this country is built on multiculturalism."

"Sounds like an asshole," Diego injected and made a face.

"That's the tip of the iceberg," Jorge insisted and leaned back in his chair, tapping his fingers against the side. "This man here, he does not get his hands dirty but he's got his followers to do things like burning my shop down, that kind of thing."

"Yes, he finds angry white men and tells that them their problems are because of immigrants," Paige added. "They're making housing prices unaffordable, they're taking the jobs, they're…taking over the marijuana industry." She pointed toward Jorge and Diego slowly nodded. "Really, he can turn it around regardless of the situation."

"Ah, so if say, his girlfriend dumps him," Diego joined in with a devious grin on his face. "It's a brown man's fault? He stole her away?"

"Well, that there," Jorge jumped in. "That could be true."

Paige laughed and Diego quickly joined in.

"But our friend," Jorge spoke sarcastically. "He causes a lot of trouble in this city. But he does enjoy having a few drinks with some of his fat cat friends once a week. Last night, he met up with friends and on his way to the car later, he apparently passed out. Must've had too much to drink."

"Really?" Diego asked as he nodded and twisted his lips.

"Yes, well he woke up in a dark, dreary warehouse in an unpleasant way," Jorge continued. "It seems that someone was branding the fucker. A swastika, right on the forehead."

"We figured that it was only right that people learn what he's really about," Paige calmly remarked. "He can't hide it any longer."

"No, he cannot," Jorge agreed. "And unfortunately, his wife, she is gone on a holiday with friends so no one is likely missing him. I do not think we will kill him. But I do think it would be nice to….punish him more, you know, as a way to make up for all he's done to people like us, Diego. Karma, as they say, can bite you on the ass."

"What you got in mind?" Diego's eyes lit up as he leaned forward on the couch.

"Do you still have your baseball bat in your car?"

"Yes."

"I think, Diego, we should go for a little drive."

"You don't have to," Paige said to her friend. "It's merely a suggestion. He's probably suffered a lot already."

"Oh no," Diego spoke abruptly. "I want to be part of this."

"Ok," Paige said as the two men stood up and she quickly did the same. "I have to go figure out the last-minute details with Alec for the weekend."

"The poor people party," Jorge asked.

"You have to stop calling it that," Diego reminded him. "You were poor once too."

"I was not saying it in a bad way," Jorge insisted. "I call it that because it is the opposite of the last one, which to me, was the rich man's party."

Paige laughed as the three of them headed toward the door.

On the drive out of town and to the warehouse where Don Stumples was located, Diego talked non-stop, his mood greatly improved from the previous weeks. It made Jorge wonder how long this worry had weighed on his friend's mind. He was like a whole new man.

"Diego, I cannot remember the last time I saw you like this," Jorge commented as they drew closer to the place where they were to meet his associates and the white supremacist leader. "You're joyful and excited, I hope this does continue."

"It will," Diego insisted as he leaned forward and turned up the radio allowing a Christina Aguilera song to pour through the car.

"Oh, turn that down," Jorge commented and shook his head. "Maria was playing around with the radio channel. I had it on a classic rock station."

"Christina is a Latina!" Diego insisted. "We have to support her."

"Yes, because us listening to this one song will make or break her career," Jorge commented sarcastically as he reached to turn the radio down. "I believe, Diego, she is doing fine without us."

"I'm just saying," He said. "We gotta support our own."

"Ok, yes, well.."

"I once had a big argument," Diego cut him off. "With this guy, I was dating. He was more of a Britney guy and I was on team Christina."

"Oh yes, Diego, this is the *team* you are on," Jorge teased.

"It is!" Diego was insistent. "I just said, you know, I can't deal with no Britney guy."

"You dumped a man because he was more of a Britney Spears fan?" Jorge asked with laughter in his voice. "Are you insane? Does this matter?"

"It was a deal breaker," Diego spoke abruptly as if it were the most normal thing.

"Diego, you really dislike Britney Spears this bad?"

"I love Britney Spears," Diego insisted. "I happen to love Christina more and yes, this was a deal breaker for me. It said something about the kind of person he was."

"Diego, because I am wearing sunglasses now," Jorge said. "You cannot tell but I am rolling my eyes at you. You are truly insane."

"Hey, aren't there deal breakers with you?" Diego asked.

"I do not care what kind of music Paige listens to," Jorge said as they turned on the road where the warehouse was located. "And you, you shouldn't care about these things either."

"Music is my life," Diego insisted.

"I also love music," Jorge said as he checked the address and pulled into a parking lot of an abandoned warehouse. "You know this."

"Yeah but you love old school music," Diego reminded him. "You don't like the music of today."

"To me," Jorge said as he stopped the SUV and pulled off his sunglasses. "Music, it ended in 1997. After grunge and all this pop garbage came out, it was over for me and it has not been good since."

"Nothing?"

"Some but for the most part," Jorge hesitated. "No, it has not been good. The first time I saw The Spice Girls on TV, I said, music, it has died."

"You don't like The Spice Girls?" Diego looked stunned.

"I do not," Jorge confirmed. "Now can we go inside and do this thing?"

"But you blame them for the downfall of music?"

"I do not blame them, no," Jorge replied as he reached in the back for some ski masks and gloves. "What I mean is that when this music came along, it was a sign to me that it was over. Music was going downhill. Now…can we please end this conversation and actually go see this twisted fuck in the warehouse."

"Ok," Diego agreed as Jorge handed him a ski mask. "I'll grab my bat."

As they made their way toward the warehouse, Diego suddenly broke his silence again. "You know, Paige is a big Doors fan."

"Ah yes," Jorge laughed as he pulled on his mask. "Jim Morrison, that crazy fuck. How can you not love his music?"

"It's dark."

"We're dark, Diego."

Pulling on gloves, he reached for the door and pulled it open. Once inside, he attempted to not breathe in the pungent air as they walked toward the back, where three men waited, all wearing masks. Lying on the ground was a fat, white man with his hands and legs tied, a huge swastika branded on his forehead. His mouth covered with duct tape but it didn't prevent him from attempting to speak.

"Look at that," Diego used his baseball bat to point toward the man's head. "Finally, the world can see his true self."

"This is good," Jorge joined in the conversation. "It is so freeing when you allow your real self to shine through, do you not think so?"

"Ah yes!" Diego replied. "One must always be their true self. Unfortunately, with this comes consequences."

Without any warning, he lifted the baseball bat in the air and with great fury, it came hurling down toward the man's legs. Even with his mouth covered, his muffled screams could be heard through the duct tape, as Diego continued to beat the man savagely, with no hesitation. Jorge watched as he brought the bat down on both his legs, his arms and finally held it over his head but then stopped.

"I do think, he is in enough pain," Jorge commented airily. "Perhaps he has learned his lesson."

"Perhaps," Diego slowly lowered the bat, moving away from the man who appeared relieved, as tears ran down his face. Then with one sudden move, Diego hit the man again; this time on the ass.

"Ah see, no one likes a racist," Jorge casually commented as he exchanged looks with Diego, who merely nodded and gestured toward the door.

Without saying anything more, the two men headed back toward the door, leaving the others behind. Once outside, both removed their masks just as the door opened and another man walked out to meet them. Taking off his ski mask, they could see the face of Michael Perkins and Jorge merely grinned.

"We'll drop him off somewhere...fun, later," Perkins remarked and glanced toward the warehouse. "I will be in touch."

With that, he pulled the mask back on and returned to the building.

34

" **W** ow, lots of people," Jorge commented as he reached for Paige's hand and the two of them walked through the crowded youth centre. Unlike the first political event, Alec was a rock star here. Groups of people crowded around him, taking selfies as excitement filled the room. It was a positive indication however, Jorge had to wonder if these same people would show as much enthusiasm when voting as they did when posting pictures on social media.

"It's a great sign," Paige commented and squeezed his hand. "Everything is falling nicely into place."

"We will see," Jorge spoke in a monotone voice. "But I somehow doubt that those kids getting their picture taken with him are of voting age."

"But their parents are," Paige leaned in and whispered. "You never know what can change someone's mind."

"*Papa*," Maria came rushing up to them carrying a small paper plate filled with cookies and chips. "I heard that a rock band is coming to play later, is this true?"

"I do not know about a rock band Maria, but yes, some musicians will be performing," Jorge replied and ushered her closer to them. "Come here, *niñita,* we do not want to lose you in the crowd."

"How about me and Maria go for a walk around," Paige gently suggested as she glanced toward the entrance. "I see Diego over there."

"Oh yes! I must talk to him!" Jorge commented and turned his attention back to Maria. "You ladies go for a walk, see if you can find out more about this rock band. I believe there are other activities taking place as well."

"Awesome!" Maria spoke excitedly and rushed ahead while Paige followed.

Turning toward the door, Jorge made eye contact with Diego as he approached him. "I see you have made it to the poor…"

"Don't call it that!" Diego cut him off before he could even finish the sentence. Glancing around suspiciously, he made a face and shook his head. "How many times have I told you, it's a different *kind* of party."

"In truth, people here, they do not look poor," Jorge muttered as he glanced around. "Just normal, I guess. Paige, she told me to make sure I didn't wear a shirt and tie today. I guess she didn't tell you the same?"

"You have two modes, don't you," Diego started, ignoring Jorge's question. "Expensive suit or jeans with a Beatles t-shirt."

"I have other shirts too," Jorge corrected him. "I'm a businessman so I must wear a suit and tie most of the time. Also, for your information, I have three modes. I also enjoy being naked."

"That does not surprise me," Diego said and made a face. "What we got?

Jorge gestured for them to walk away from the crowd and into a quiet corner. "So Jesús and Sylvana are on the way home. PEI and Nova Scotia are complete and details will soon be finalized. He's now working on Newfoundland. When he goes to New Brunswick, Paige may go since she speaks French. That's what they like there."

Diego nodded.

"No problems, though," Jorge continued. "For all the talk when we enter a province, most, they end up seeing it our way. It benefits them more to join than to run away, you know? This is good. We will soon have the Atlantic and we are also well into Quebec. My goal is by Christmas to have the majority in this country."

"So what are you going to when we are finished?" Diego grinned. "What big project comes next."

"Oh Diego, you will see," Jorge spoke mysteriously. "I think many will be surprised by my next decision."

"Going back to Mexico?" Diego joked.

"Hey, there are days I wish I could," Jorge spoke honestly. "I miss it a lot."

"Yes, I can understand that," Diego agreed. "But regardless of what you might think, you, Paige, Maria, you're much safer in Canada."

"I know but I wish to leave Toronto," Jorge admitted. "Somewhere quieter. Maybe once this is complete, I can do that. I need to step back. I would prefer more time to enjoy my family."

"Like retire? Is that even an option for you?" Diego asked as he leaned in. "The boss in Mexico?"

"He's making a lot of money now," Jorge pointed out. "The return is higher than we originally thought. The best part is it's legal. He can run his…less than legal money through it. Trust me, this here is working to his benefit too much to care what I do. We are getting richer and as long as we are vigilant and pay off the right people, everything will continue to move smoothly."

"You always make it work," Diego shook his head. "When you first told me you wanted to get away from cocaine, I didn't think it would happen. It's the cartel, you don't get out of these kinds of things."

"It's the cartel," Jorge corrected him. "They do not care as long as they are making money. This here is the easiest money we ever made. Other than investing, he does not have to lift a finger and it's legal, so there are no risks to him. He's an old man. This appeals to him as well, you know?"

"Fair enough," Diego said as he watched the crowd. "Athas, you think he's gonna make it?"

"He better fucking make it after the money I spent," Jorge replied. "I plan to soon have Harley out of the game. Once that happens, the other candidates, they cannot hold up to Athas. This I am sure."

"So, I was talking to Michael Perkins," Diego suddenly changed the subject. "I guess they dropped off the Nazi near a hospital?"

"Near," Jorge nodded. "He had a few broken bones."

"He can't confirm anything," Diego continued. "Michael said that in the police report, Stumples said he woke up in a warehouse, didn't know where he was, didn't know who had him, everyone had a mask. Get this, the fucker tried to say he thought it was Muslims!"

"Of course, that is the racist's favorite target these days, is it not?" Jorge shook his head. "It does not matter. He has nothing. And if he ever points his finger our way, he will have more than a few bones broken."

"It didn't go nowhere," Diego confirmed. "He also asked that they keep it out of the media. Keep it quiet."

"Oh yeah?" Jorge asked.

"Should we call Makerson?"

"Fucking right, we should," Jorge said as his lips curved into a grin. "In fact, he is here, today. We must ask him to get a picture of the Nazi with his new...*tattoo.*"

Both men laughed.

"So Michael, he talks to you before me?" Jorge asked. "I did not speak to him yet."

"Well, you know, we were chatting the other day," Diego shrugged. "Online."

"Diego, I hope you did not discuss any of this online," Jorge quickly grew concerned. "I know we feel we can trust him but I would not go so far as having anything in written form."

"Of course not!" Diego said and shook his head. "We actually talked about this in person over dinner yesterday. He did the talking. We can trust him."

"You had dinner with him last night?" Jorge asked suspiciously and suddenly had a bad feeling in his stomach. "Oh Diego, why must you always chase these men who are straight?"

"He is gay," Diego immediately corrected him.

"He is not gay," Jorge said as he shook his head. "You want to think he is but, I do not see it."

"Trust me," Diego corrected him. "He *is* gay."

Jorge automatically backed up a bit. "Really?"

"Yes, trust me," Diego said and paused for a moment. "He is, I can promise you this."

"Ok, you know what?" Jorge put a hand in the air. "I do not need details, please. I just, I did not realize this about him."

"He's a very nice man," Diego added. "You know, with my health scare, I got a new lease on life. I see things so differently and suddenly this man comes into my life, it was like synchronicity, you know?"

"Wow, that is....great, Diego," Jorge hesitated. "I am happy for you if you are sure?"

"That he's gay, oh yeah, he.."

"No no," Jorge replied with a grin on his face, his hand in the air. "I mean, that he is trustworthy. I am pretty sure but not 100%, you know? I would be careful. Plus, do you want to shit where you eat?"

"Its fine, I promise," Diego replied. "We don't even talk about any of this much. He just mentioned dropping the white supremacist off near the hospital. We laughed about it and that was about it. We connected."

"That is good," Jorge reluctantly agreed. "I would be careful. Still, I had no idea he was gay."

"You don't got the gaydar," Diego said and twisted his lips. "You wouldn't."

"That I do not," Jorge replied airily just as he spotted Tom Makerson in the crowd. Catching his eye, the editor approached them both in the corner. "I see you have made it."

"Yes, I was talking to Alec and some of the people in the crowd," He gestured toward the group. "A lot of people here today, that's a good sign."

"Is it, though?" Jorge was skeptical. "They are here but will they vote?"

"It looks good," Makerson confirmed. "In politics, it's often more about appearances."

"Ain't that the truth," Diego sniffed.

"This one here, he wants to make changes," Jorge pointed toward Alec as he made his way toward the stage. "People see that in him."

"People see what they want," Diego corrected.

"I got another story for you," Jorge cut him off and leaned toward Makerson. "We will talk about it outside."

Tom nodded and the three of them headed toward the door.

"There was recently a situation that didn't make it to the press," Jorge commented. "That I feel your readers will…"

Suddenly, his words halted when a group of police came rushing through the door. Exchanging looks with Diego, he silently cursed his friend, assuming he had said too much in an intimate moment with Michael Perkins and now their world was about to cave in. His heart pounded. Fear caused his mouth to go dry. His breathing became shallow as he watched the police rush the building but it only took a moment to see them hurrying past and not toward him. His mind racing, Jorge completely missed the words being screamed throughout the room, as everyone rushed frantically toward the door. Diego grabbed his arm and pulled him forward.

His body felt limp, weightless as Diego pulled him along as if he were as light as a feather, while he saw Makerson holding up his phone as he followed them. It wasn't until they were outside and a few raindrops fell on his head that Jorge came back to life. Blinking rapidly, he looked around as the police continued to encourage everyone to move away from the building and across the street to a nearby park. He felt his phone vibrating and managed to come out of his haze and grab it as he rushed ahead amidst the crowd.

It was Paige.

Meet you at the park.

"What the hell is going on?" Jorge finally found his voice. "I do not understand. What is happening?"

"Bomb threat," Tom Makerson replied, already on his phone tweeting the news.

Sirens could be heard roaring through the streets, followed by a slew of police cars and other emergency vehicles. Turning toward Diego, he saw fear in his eyes. It was at that moment that he saw Maria pushing her way through the crowd with tears running down her face.

"*Papa!* I'm so scared," She rushed toward him and he immediately reached down and pulled her in a hug, just as Paige caught up with concern on her face. They shared a look and he noticed she was holding back her tears, as she tapped on the phone.

"Alec, is he…"

"He was taken away by the police," Paige quietly replied as Tom Makerson stopped tweeting and gave her his full attention. "He was the target."

It was as if the world stopped.

This meant war.

35

.....candidate Alec Athas said that this incident will not discourage him as he continues to seek a win in district....

J orge turned away from the television to look at his family. He attempted a smile but it barely touched his lips. The last thing he wanted was for his daughter to live in fear however, he couldn't lie to her. How could they carry on as if it were just another day? Alec Athas now needed security with him during public events and although he persisted in front of the cameras, behind the scenes he considered dropping out. Jorge knew he needed some reassurance but the truth was that the episode lodged fear in him that went deep into his soul.

"The Prime Minister released a statement last night," Paige commented in an even tone while Maria slumped over her cereal. "He said that we will have zero tolerance for these threats. The mayor of Toronto also weighed in and said that there will be an increased police presence at political events until the election."

"But it wasn't a political event when that crazy man threatened the school," Maria piped up anxiously. "Why do people do these things, *Papa?*"

"Maria, I do not understand," Jorge calmly replied. "We live in a very complicated world but we cannot live in fear."

"I don't like living here anymore," Maria continued to complain. "*Papa,* I thought Canada was a safe place. My friend Lisa, from school, she said it's just Toronto because all the crazies come here. Do you think that's true?"

Paige snickered and Jorge followed suit. "Ah! Maria! We moved here, we are not crazies, are we?" He teased. "This is not true. There are good and bad people everywhere. Whoever did this wanted attention."

"Didn't they catch the guy?" Paige asked even though she knew the answer. The couple shared a look.

"Yes! Paige, they did catch the man," Jorge spoke with enthusiasm. "It is not in the news yet but I spoke to my friend at the police department and they got him last night."

"How come it's not in the news?" Maria asked suspiciously.

"Hmm...how come, indeed," Jorge muttered. "This is interesting. How much does not get on the news? The media, they have everyone scared that this man is running around town but it's a secret that he was found. I do not understand."

Paige shook her head and made a face.

"Why did he do it?" Maria asked him, her brown eyes full of such innocence that it broke his heart.

"*Bebita,* I do not know," Jorge admitted. "Perhaps because he is a crazy man."

"The news said there was something on the property," Maria continued. "So he wanted to kill us all."

"Maria, please, we cannot think that way," Jorge insisted. "We can only think about how lucky we are to be safe."

He said the words but they felt hollow. Sometimes it was impossible to know what to tell your child. He didn't want to scare Maria but on the other hand, he wanted her vigilant and ready for anything. How did you find the right balance?

"Perhaps today, you and Paige, you can do some shopping or something fun?" Jorge suggested anxiously. "I have a meeting a little later here...."

"Chase is taking me to the mall," Maria spoke up with excitement in her voice, a vast contradiction to the child moments earlier. "I texted him last night and told him about the horrible thing that happened to me and he offered to take me to the mall to cheer me up. Isn't that nice?"

Although Jorge had mixed feeling, knowing that his daughter had a strange fascination with Chase, he also wanted Maria to enjoy her day and not worry. He nodded and glanced at Paige who widened her eyes.

"That does sound nice," Jorge agreed. "I have a few meetings this afternoon but maybe tonight, we can go out to dinner or something?"

"Awesome!" Maria jumped up and took her plate to the dishwasher. Jorge noted that she barely ate a thing. He glanced at his wife who appeared concerned. However, they wouldn't speak of this until after Chase dropped by to pick up Maria.

"I do not know what to tell her," Jorge confided in Paige. "I have so many fears for my daughter. I fear for her safety. I fear that she is not eating enough. I fear her fixation with Chase and yet, today, I would've done anything to make her happy so I could not say no to her spending time with him."

"I kind of let Chase know about her...fascination with him," Paige leaned in and touched his arm. Her quiet voice immediately calmed him. "Just so he's aware and can gently let her know where he stands."

"It is strange," Jorge shook his head. "But I do trust Chase. I believe spending time with Maria makes him feel better since his own children are so far away."

"And he hardly sees them," Paige added. "He's busy here. When was the last time he went on vacation?"

"When was the last time any of us went on a vacation?" Jorge replied and gave her a quick kiss just as the doorbell rang.

Diego was on the other side. He wore a casual shirt and jeans; an unusual wardrobe choice for him.

"Come in," Jorge said as he stood aside.

"Michael is parking the car," Diego hurriedly rushed in and Jorge looked outside to see the Lexus carefully being parallel parked on the street.

"You allow this new man you barely know to drive your car?" Jorge asked with laughter in his voice. "Wow! I never thought I would see the day. Your precious *Lexus*!"

"I have control issues," Diego commented and twisted his lips together, his eyebrows wrinkling up as he made a face. "I realize that. I'm working on it."

"This here, it is huge," Jorge commented as Michael started up the walkway. Wearing jeans, a t-shirt, and leather jacket, it suddenly became clear why Diego was also dressed casually.

Diego made a face and headed for the kitchen, where he immediately began to make coffee. Paige quickly rushed over and gave him a hug, changing Diego's whole demeanor. Jorge turned to see Michael walk through the door, his eyes glancing toward the kitchen.

"Those two are close," He commented with a grin on his face as Jorge closed the door.

"Ah yes, you must meet my wife," Jorge commented as they headed toward the kitchen. Introductions were barely made when his phone beeped. It was Alec Athas.

"Ah, the politician is on his way," Jorge commented.

"He must be pretty shaken up today," Michael commented while Diego shook his head with a somber face.

"We're all shaken up today," Jorge insisted. "However, he was the target and this clearly scared him."

"You know it's from Stumples, I assume?" Michael asked casually as if they were talking about the weather. "I mean, there's no proof but come on…the guy's got an ax to grind."

"Yes, well, so do we," Jorge replied and shoved his phone back into his pocket. "Makerson is writing a revealing article today that tells how Stumples is a racist and about his new..tattoo, shall we call it?"

"Gotta love freedom of the press," Michael grinned and glanced at Diego who nodded. "People got a right to know."

"Obviously yesterday was a way of trying to intimidate us," Paige gently commented. "He picked the wrong people this time around."

"Yes, my guess is he intimidates people to get what he wants," Jorge remarked just as the coffee finished brewing and Diego reached for some cups. "But we do not work that way."

"Athas, he got security now," Diego commented. "Someone who volunteered?"

"Yes, volunteered," Jorge replied with sarcasm in his voice. "That guy is costing me but I did not trust the person the police wanted to send."

"Chances are, he's safe now," Michael said as he glanced at Diego who was pouring coffee for everyone. "But its better safe than sorry."

"If anyone tries to attack him again," Jorge replied as he glanced at his phone again. "They will be sorry."

"Do we know the person's name?" Paige asked.

A knock at the door interrupted them.

"Some fucking kid," Michael replied, "Probably 20, 21 years old. One of Stumples' puppets."

Paige nodded as Jorge headed toward the door to let Athas in. With bags under his eyes, it was clear that the previous day had taken a toll on him.

"Alec, do come in," Jorge commented as the politician walked through the door and he gave a knowing nod to the man waiting outside. "We have much to talk about."

"I don't know if I have much to add," Alec commented and headed toward the kitchen where everyone was preparing their coffee or standing around. Jorge quickly introduced him to Michael without revealing that he was a dirty cop.

"We can go in the living room or wherever you wish to talk?" He suggested but everyone seemed content where they were, so he continued. "Ok, well, I wanted to talk about yesterday. Of course, we know that Makerson will be writing a story on Stumples, this is why yesterday happened, we are quite certain."

"So, who is this Stumples guy, again?" Alec cut in and shook his head. "Remind me."

"He, my friend, is a white supremacist," Jorge replied. "He is, you might say, the head guy of one of the largest groups in the city. Big business guy who sits on many boards, that kind of thing."

"A fat cat," Diego abruptly commented. "An asshole."

"He had…ah….an incident recently where someone branded a swastika on his forehead," Jorge said with an impish grin on his face. "Maybe a few broken bones, I hear…at any rate, he was hoping to keep it low-key so he could rush out and try to get plastic surgery or laser…something to remove this branding before the public sees it."

Diego let out a loud laugh.

"However, the public has a right to know," Jorge continued. "We must make sure the story hits the paper tomorrow."

Alec nodded and looked concerned.

"So that guy was the one who sent the threat?"

"We think…he might be connected with Harley," Jorge replied even though, he wasn't certain. Relieved that Alec appeared to accept this news, he continued. "And that was perhaps a way to scare you and to retaliate against us at the same time. It is hard to say. Michael, do you know?"

"Its pretty hush hush around the station," He replied casually as he reached for his coffee. "Only certain people are privy to that information.

I'm not one of them. We heard it was some kid and they're hiding it from the media."

"The station?" Alec looked confused.

"I'm a cop."

"But we can trust him," Diego piped up.

Michael nodded and took a drink of his coffee.

"I feel like a lot has been going on behind the scenes," Alec commented and glanced at their faces. "Is there anything else I should know?"

"No, this about covers it," Jorge replied. "But you, you must know something about this since you were the target."

"No," Alec admitted. "This is the first time I heard the cops had anyone in custody. They told me it was an 'ongoing investigation'."

Michael snickered and rolled his eyes. "The kid, he's probably gonna walk. They are hiding this for a reason. If it gets out, the kid will have to be charged."

"We got ways to make sure it gets out," Jorge reached for his phone and tapped a message to Makerson. "We are not fucking around. Maybe this will publicly connect Harley to this shit and expose him."

"I doubt it," Alec shook his head. "He's covered. He's got a lot of people looking after him."

"And you, my friend, have a lot of people looking after you," Jorge reminded him as he sent the message to Makerson. "I casually asked him if he heard someone was arrested for the bomb threat."

"Why would they want to let this kid go?" Alec wondered. "He could've killed all of us."

"Notice the threat was called in long before it was to go off," Michael pointed out. "It was carefully planned. This one 20-year-old kid, you think he could orchestrate this alone? He's got someone behind him. I've seen it before. Lots of people get brought through the doors as a 'person of interest' and shuffled out again. You have no idea."

"I do," Jorge countered. "I got no faith in the cops….you know, no offense."

"None took," Michael commented. "I don't either. It's political. It's all about perception. It's not about looking after people it's about looking out for the right people. Trust me, it's a shitshow right from the top."

"And we know what happens to shit from the top," Diego grunted.

"You gotta keep your mouth shut or have no job, your reputations pulled through the mud," Michael replied and took another drink of the coffee. "People have no idea."

"They don't want to," Paige commented. "Being blissfully ignorant becomes a choice after so much time."

No one replied. They didn't have to.

36

"Ah! I do love this front page," Jorge said with a grin as he stared at the online version of *Toronto AM*. Large black letters boldly asked the question, *Is White Supremacy Taking over Toronto?* The article included a blurred image of Don Stumples wearing a trucker hat pulled down to almost his eyebrows, while beside it was a close-up image of him wearing the Nazi symbol on his forehead. "The police, they had to release this picture after Makerson went after them. *Perfecto.*"

Paige leaned over the back of his chair and scanned the article. A smirk touched her lips as they shared a look. She leaned in and kissed him on the forehead without saying a word.

"*Mi amor,*" Jorge whispered in a seductive voice. "We always win and this case will be no different. This article reminds Stumples, Harley, everyone how powerful we are and this story along with the reveal that police hid that they caught the man responsible for the bomb threat, we win this round."

"The fact that the police were trying to hide it," Paige whispered. "It's unsettling to the public."

"As it should be," Jorge agreed with a nod. "It now makes them wonder how many other things are hidden. Makerson got them on the spot. There's a press conference this afternoon. Just enough time for them to spin their lies, I suspect."

"I think you're right," Paige replied.

"And you will be at the campaign office today?" Jorge asked as she began to walk toward the living room. "Athas will be swamped with reporters, perhaps he needs his own press conference too?"

"I had suggested it but he doesn't want to bring more attention to the attempt," Paige said as she stopped and turned back. "Alec has back to back interviews today. I'm going to attempt to listen in while taking care of social media. Twitter and Facebook lit up since this took place on the weekend. He had to report a few threats that popped up on social media last night. It's getting out of control."

"And they say that I am the crazy one," Jorge said with a shrug as he closed his laptop. "Whoever thought Jorge Hernandez would be the voice of reason?"

Paige began to laugh and shook her head. "Whoever thought?" She replied with an uplift in her voice, as she turned around and headed toward the staircase. "Maria! Let's go!"

Jorge decided to meet Diego and Jesús at the bar just before the press conference took place, to discuss business. When they weren't there when he arrived, it gave Jorge a few minutes to talk to Chase.

"So you take my daughter to the mall yesterday?" Jorge spoke up as he entered the club, after spotting Chase behind the bar with an iPad in hand. "Thank you, my friend."

"No problem," He replied as Jorge walked through the empty club. He noted that the indigenous man appeared ill at ease. "I can't believe there was a bomb threat. I was just reading that article you sent me. What the hell is going on in this city?"

"My friend, the crazies, this is nothing new," Jorge said and sat on a stool. Chase gestured toward the coffee pot and Jorge nodded. "These people were always there but the difference is now, we have shown a light on them. So, in a way, this is good. At least now we know who they are, no?"

"True," Chase replied as he poured a cup of coffee and sat it in front of Jorge. Reaching under the bar, he pulled out the cream and set it down. "I guess I grew up ignorant. A small-town boy and although I was different from everyone in Hennessey, I wasn't treated differently so I never thought about racism until I moved to Calgary. That was when I noticed people looking at me differently for the first time. Here in Toronto, I didn't think this was an issue since there are so many ethnicities in this city."

"Sometimes that makes it more of an issue," Jorge pointed out as he poured cream into his coffee. "This is, again, not something new. It's our reality. We live in a world where people see our differences and not how we are alike. It's unfortunate and how do you explain that to a child?"

"I don't know," Chase admitted and glanced down at the bar for a second before continuing. "Maria did talk a lot about the bomb threat yesterday. I tried to tell her it was only meant to scare people that she shouldn't worry because everything was fine, but you know, I wasn't sure if I believe that myself. I keep hearing stories about this kind of thing, especially in Toronto."

"Chase, this here, it could happen anywhere," Jorge reminded him. "It does not matter if it's Toronto or a small town in the middle of nowhere. We never know when someone is going to be crazy. Wait, was Clara in today?"

"Just before you," Chase nodded and leaned against the bar. "We're good."

"I mean, me, I am hardly a saint," Jorge said and raised an eyebrow as he reached for his coffee. "I do not, however, threaten groups of innocent people to make a point or whatever the hell these fuckers are doing. Me, if I want a political opponent out, I am going to deal with that person one on one. Only a pussy like Harley would do something like this."

"Think he's behind it?"

"Either him or this Stumples guy in the article," Jorge replied as the door opened and Diego flew in with Jesús sauntering behind him. "Well, look who showed up!"

"Boss, we got here as quickly as we could," Jesús said while Diego made a face and jumped on the bar stool beside Jorge. "It is a crazy day with traffic."

"The news conference, did it start yet?" Diego asked as Chase poured coffee for both men. Jesús joined them at the bar, wiping sweat from his forehead.

"Nah, not for ten minutes and you know how these guys are," Jorge shrugged. "They will probably be late."

"It's gonna be bullshit anyway," Diego insisted as he grabbed his coffee and poured cream into it. "All that 'we care about the public's safety' bullshit and some crap excuses why they didn't reveal everything from the beginning."

"Ongoing investigation," Jesús said and let out a laugh as he reached for his own cup of coffee. "It is predictable."

"Hey, so we almost got it wrapped up in the east?" Jorge asked, feeling the need to change the topic. Beside him, Diego took a sip of coffee and made a face. "With the Atlantic provinces?"

"Very close," Jesús confirmed. "They are much easier to negotiate with than I originally thought and Sylvana was surprisingly helpful."

"She was?" Jorge asked and nodded.

"She is persuasive, I must admit," Jesús confirmed. "I would not want to have to argue with her about anything."

"You, have *no* idea," Diego confirmed with his usual dramatics. "That woman is relentless."

Chase nodded. "She's tough."

"This is good," Jorge replied as he took another drink of his coffee. "That is what we need."

"We should have the Atlantic region wrapped up by next week," Jesús continued and took a sip of his coffee. "I have already made some efforts in Quebec so I think we will have an easy time."

"What about the biker gangs?" Diego asked. "That might be tricky. They don't fuck around."

"They do not care," Jesús insisted. "We are legal and they are not. We travel in different circles. They will not be a problem."

"Good," Jorge replied. "Cause we don't need more problems."

"I did see the article you sent today," Jesús commented as he leaned against the bar and glanced toward Jorge. "The police, they like to hide a lot, I see."

"Yes, they certainly do," Jorge replied. "In the interest of public knowledge, I made sure the truth came out."

"Makerson must be the hero of the media world about now," Diego sniffed. "He's got these stories before the others."

"Actually, I spoke to Makerson this morning," Jorge replied. "He has received some threats from anonymous sources due to his work. I have offered to help him but he seems to have little concern. He has instead reported it to the police and plans to make it public in order to send a message to those who are threatening him."

"Its empty threats," Diego insisted. "Michael says that most people threatened won't be attacked because if someone really wanted to hurt them, they just would."

"Diego! I could've told you that," Jorge said with a burst of laughter. "You act like this is news. Where have you been for the last few years? This here is our life."

Everyone laughed.

"See it is when you are in love with this *hombre,* that suddenly everything he says is like the words from God's lips," Jorge spoke dramatically and began to laugh while beside him, Diego gave him a dirty look. "That is how it is."

"That is *not* how it is," Diego complained. "We don't necessarily play by the same rules."

"Well, this here, this is true," Jorge agreed and glanced toward Chase, noting that he looked uncomfortable. "We are our own kind of animal."

"That we are," Diego agreed.

"What is this about?" Jesús asked. "Is that not the police officer that was at the warehouse recently? That found that *gringo* trying to break in?"

"Yes, same guy," Jorge replied. "It appears him and Diego are….what? Lovers? Boyfriends?"

"Ok, you know what?" Diego shot him a dirty look. "You're being an asshole."

"I am teasing you," Jorge said with an innocent shrug. "I did not know the man was gay let alone….you know, caught up in your web."

"He wanted to be in my web," Diego replied defensively. "For your information."

"Oh Diego, you know I just like to tease you," Jorge said and slapped him on the back. "I tease Jesús about his Asian whores…"

"Hey, I said that was only once," Jesús said with laughter in his voice. "You never let a man forget!"

"And Chase….what do I tease you about?" Jorge thought for a moment. "Oh yes, the sadist you were dating? Remember her? The man could barely walk for a week. This here is funny to me."

"No one ever teases you about Paige," Diego noted.

"That is because we are frightened by her, sir," Jesús said with wide eyes. "One of the best assassins in the world, you do not piss this *señora* off."

"Hey, my wife, she has not killed anyone…." Jorge thought for a moment. "Oh yes, well, I guess she has killed recently. At any rate, is this press conference on yet? I need a good laugh."

"I'm watching here on my iPad," Chase commented. "It's on the news channel but they are still waiting to start."

"Imbeciles," Jorge shook his head just as his phone rang. It was Paige.

"Hello, *mi amor*, you should join us at the bar," Jorge spoke into the phone. "We are just about to watch the press conference."

"Actually, I have something to talk to you about," Paige commented evenly. "I scheduled a meeting with Makerson. He was planning to interview Athas but we have to talk to him. Clara is coming over just before and….Jorge it's important."

'Ok….sure," He replied and nodded. "Do you need the others."

"Not necessarily," She replied. "We need to talk to Makerson though. It's urgent."

"Is he there now?"

"He's on his way," She said and hesitated for a moment. "I hope."

37

"There's some 19-year-old kid caught for the bomb threat but they aren't giving anything more," Makerson announced as soon as the door to Alec's office closed. The editor continued to speak with excitement in his eyes. "Can you believe that? Someone sent him but of course, they won't release the name and say it's still part of an *ongoing investigation*."

"You may as well forget about it," Jorge quickly jumped in and noted a look of concern in Alec's eyes. "They aren't going to do a thing. They'll let the kid take the shit for it and hope you stop asking questions."

"Yeah, well, that's not going to happen," Tom sharply replied and pointed toward the door. "If they think I'm going to go away quietly, they have another thing coming to them."

"Actually, that's why we're here," Paige spoke up, capturing the three men's attention. "That's what they're trying to do."

"Oh, you mean the threats?" Tom shook his head and shrugged. "They've threatened me before, it's nothing. I go to the police, they look into it and I carry on. The media, politicians, anyone in the public eye always deal with this kind of thing. It's an attempt to intimidate us."

"Except when it's not," Paige spoke evenly, her eyes glanced at Jorge. "Look, I have some powerful connections that tell me that the threats against you are serious. You're getting your nose into places that are usually cut off for reporters. You're digging a little too deep and someone out there wants to stop you."

"How do you.."

"I can't talk about that," Paige gave Jorge another look and he nodded while Alec looked away. "Trust me. These aren't hollow threats this time."

Tom Makerson's face turned white and he slumped over as he walked across the floor and sat down.

"Clara?" Jorge softly asked.

"Yes, she was in," Paige replied and moved across the room to sit beside Tom while Jorge sat on her other side and Alec nervously moved behind his desk.

"Someone wants me dead? Over *this*?" Makerson quietly asked. "Are you sure?"

"I am, yes," Paige replied. "I have some connections that I check with regularly. I was actually checking for Alec after the bomb threat on the weekend and that's when your name popped up."

"So, what do I do? I already called the cops," Tom asked with vulnerability in his voice. "I'm a walking target for telling the truth. Just for exposing Stumples and now this information the police were hiding from the public?"

"I thought about it," Paige gently replied in her usual, soothing voice. "You can stay at our house. We have an empty apartment in the basement. You will be safe."

Paige had briefly discussed this with Jorge upon his arrival so he knew it was coming but across the desk, Alec looked as horrified as Makerson.

"But, I…"

"You'll be safe," Paige insisted. "Trust me."

Alec was nodding vigorously. "Trust me, you will."

"Oh wow," Tom slowly replied while glancing at Jorge. "I….I can't believe this is even happening. It's like something out of a movie. Why would they threaten me? What the hell is out there that they think I will discover?"

"I believe you have already started," Jorge replied while glancing at his wife, who appeared calm despite the nervous energy in the room. "And some powerful people are involved, which means money is also involved. People, they do not wish to separate themselves from two things; power and money. Once you have either, you will fight for your life to keep them."

"So I move in with you guys and what? Hide in your basement?" Tom asked in stunned disbelief. "Forever?"

"No," Paige quickly assured him. "I'm on top of this. Once we find out who's threatening you, we will take care of it."

"Do I want to know what you mean by that?" Tom quietly asked.

"It is better you do not ask," Jorge spoke up. "And of course, you do not report this. We are here to protect you. Throw us under the bus, you throw yourself into the line of the fire."

"I won't be reporting on this," Tom shook his head and swallowed. "I reported that I received threats in a general sense but I won't elaborate."

"Good," Paige said with a nod. "Now, what we will do is have you stay in our house and we'll have someone with you until we sort this out."

"What about work?"

"Can you not work remotely for a few days?" Jorge asked.

"Kind of hard with everything going on now," Tom replied with some hesitation. "But yeah, I guess. For how long?"

"I don't anticipate it will be that long," Paige replied. "I'm waiting to hear back from my sources and when I do, we'll take care of it."

Her expression was blank but Jorge saw the fire in her eyes.

"*Amigo*, you are fine at our place and Paige," Jorge said with a short hesitation as he looked at his wife. "She will do as she says."

Makerson continued to seem unsure.

"This is insane," Alec suddenly spoke up. "This entire situation. Bombs, death threats, white supremacists, what the fuck is going on?"

"It is the world we live in," Jorge quickly replied, slightly annoyed by Alec's rose-colored glasses. "Is this new to you?"

"In Canadian politics? Yes, it's new to me," Alec quickly answered as his eyes grew in size. "This doesn't happen here."

"Ah, *mi amigo*, it *does* happen here," Jorge corrected him. "In Canada, you smugly believe yourself to be a bit above other countries when it comes to such things as greed and hate, but you are not above anything. It's a secret that pops up at the most inconvenient times. I am new to this country and yet, I saw it right away."

"You're saying this is about money and power?" Tom asked, reminding Jorge of a child who was attempting to understand why his dog died. "The threats, the intimidation....all over money."

"Money *and* power," Jorge corrected him. "Money is nothing without power. These people, they have kept everything in line for a long time and you, my friend, have shaken up the system and a lot of dust has come out and settled. They do not like this."

"But you pushed me to do this," Tom suddenly grew angry. "*You* wanted me to write the Nazi story, to dig a little deeper at the police station.."

"Right and that is your job," Jorge quickly countered. "And you jumped in with both feet."

"Ok, we need to calm down," Paige spoke up and put her hand in the air. "This story had to get out. No one should've been threatened but you were Tom and now, we'll resolve it."

Makerson nodded and looked away while Alec shook his head.

"This is fucking insanity," Alec commented. "All of this. Are you sure your sources are right, Paige?"

She nodded but didn't offer an explanation.

"And me…."

"There's nothing … as serious," Paige replied. "However, you will continue to have someone with you until we sort it out. I believe everything is connected."

Jorge observed both of their reactions. They were like a couple of whiny teenagers asked to clean their room. Frustrated, he decided to take hold of the situation. Jumping out of his seat, he rose his hand in the air.

"Enough! My wife, she has made efforts to protect both of you, so I suggest you show her some fucking appreciation. Would you rather we feed you to the wolves? This is all we can do for now. Stop being a couple of fucking pussies and do your jobs and we will do ours."

Paige opened her mouth to say something but instead, stood up and calmly glanced at the two men.

"Yes, thank you," Alec slowly replied and turned his attention to Tom. "Trust me, if anyone can help us here, it is Paige and Jorge. I've seen them….in action."

"Let us not go there," Jorge sent him a warning glance before turning his gaze on Makerson. "We must have Clara check out your apartment as well."

Tom nodded.

"She will meet us when you wish to go there."

"Now is fine," Tom answered as he slowly stood up, his body language demonstrated defeat.

"Very well," Jorge said as he grabbed his phone and sent a cryptic message to the 'cleaning lady'. "Let's go."

Later that afternoon, when Clara confirmed there was nothing of concern in his apartment, Tom seemed a little relieved but he continued to appear agitated.

"Your place, it's a shoebox," Jorge repeated the same comment he made weeks earlier, upon first meeting Tom Makerson. "It is like, how do you breathe in this small space?"

"This is Toronto," Paige quickly cut in. "Remember my old apartment?"

"Yes, but I think you had a few more things in *your* shoebox," Jorge reminded her and she grinned.

"I'm a minimalist," Tom explained to Paige. "I believe possessions weigh you down."

"I can't deny that," She replied and then added. "You must have an interesting outlook considering the enemies you've made are most likely the complete opposite in their beliefs."

"It blows my mind sometimes," Tom shrugged as he sat on his couch. "How much people fight to get ahead, to make more money, to buy more stuff and for what?"

"It's a good point," Paige replied. "It's ridiculous when you think about it."

"But people, they need money to live." Jorge reminded him.

"I'm not disputing that," Tom replied. "After all, I wanted to move up at my work but for me, it was about being able to get a condo. Not to fill it with expensive things."

"But vacations, you do not wish to go on vacations too?" Jorge asked as he sat beside him while Paige continued to hover.

"Yes, I mean, that's about the experience though," Tom replied and seemed to relax. "That's what I work for….to experience life, not to just buy, buy, buy."

"That is something I can respect," Jorge admitted. "Me and Paige, you will see, we have stuff but not really. Just the basic comforts, I would say. Although, more than you."

Tom laughed as Paige's phone rang.

"Hello," She calmly answered.

Jorge and Tom both watched her in silence.

"Your grandmother is in town?" Paige commented enthusiastically. "How lovely for you."

Jorge didn't comment but Tom looked discouraged.

"Right, ok then, I can pick her up at the airport."

She ended the call and Jorge raised an eyebrow.

"One can never be too careful when they're on the phone," Paige commented and glanced between the two men. "That call was confirming a discussion I had earlier today."

"Sounded like you're picking up someone at the airport," Tom raised an eyebrow. "Or is that some kind of code?"

"Some kind," Paige replied and Jorge nodded. His wife often got, what appeared to be, very innocent messages or phone calls: they weren't.

"Was that about me?" Makerson asked nervously.

"That call was from one of my sources," Paige sat down on a small chair nearby. "I know who is threatening you."

"Stumples? Harley? Someone higher up?" Jorge began to rattle off possibilities, already knowing that it was most likely the least expected person. This time was no different.

"Louise Stumples," Paige replied. "Don's mother."

"What the fuck?" Tom looked outraged. "I have a hit on me by some old lady? Just because I wrote the story about her son?"

"Not just *any* old lady," Paige corrected him. "She is the powerhouse behind his family's fortune. This family has a lot of money and they've been controlling things in this province for years. She's as twisted as they come."

Jorge nodded without replying. This was not a surprise to him.

"So, what are you going to do?" Tom asked, his emotions clearly hurling toward erratic. "Threaten an old lady? Kill an old lady?"

"*Amigo*, she was going to kill you," Jorge reminded him. "Did you not understand this part?"

"She requested a hit, yes," Paige confirmed. "And she's willing to pay a lot so clearly, you're snooping around some sensitive areas."

"Can we connect this to Harley? The threats on Alec?" Jorge asked.

"Not officially but they're connected," Paige replied. "Louise is also highly invested in Big Pharma and the proven health benefits of pot are stealing their customers. In fact, shares are already dipping. People are tired of overpriced drugs that are making them sicker. Athas has a pot warehouse in his district, which Harley can do something about if he gets voted in. Even better, he will be able to establish connections at the top to start reversing pot laws behind the scenes."

"I guess propaganda can only do so much," Tom replied. "But why me? Why not Athas for running in the district or Jorge, for that matter, since it's his pot empire."

"Hey, do not think I have not had threats myself," Jorge boldly commented. "You do not know what I've been through the past year."

"You're the public voice," Paige attempted to answer. "You are telling the world the truth. Chances are you were on the verge of finding out something more and they wanted to put a stop to you before you did."

"But what?" Tom shook his head. "What was I about to find out?"

"Good question," Paige said as she looked at Jorge. "I wonder who's name this guy spilled to the police that they are so carefully hiding?"

"The younger they are, the easier they are to scare."

"All this for power and money?" Tom said in disgust. "Unbelievable."

"Yes, it is," Jorge said with a grin on his face. "This is no surprise. Guaranteed if we can get the kid to talk, we will learn that he was paid to do this by the same old bitch."

"I'm working on it," Paige insisted.

38

"The fucking kid is dead," Alec blurted out as he rushed into the house. Before Jorge could reply, Alec dramatically swung around. "From the bomb threat? He committed suicide. So the police said, 'well that was your threat so you're safe now and we can close this investigation'. As if there wasn't anyone behind this fucking guy. Can you believe it?"

For a moment, Jorge stood in stunned disbelief. He had never seen Alec Athas so vocal, so passionate about anything; if only he used the same passion when he talked politics but unfortunately, Canadians seemed to think they should be calm, balanced, yet upbeat when on a podium as if it somehow translated to a better leader. He didn't share this belief.

"*Amigo*, you do not have to sell me on the shortcomings of the police," Jorge pointed toward his office while closing the door. "The fucking police, they are useless, is that not what I always say?"

"I thought that was because you come from Mexico and...you know, the police are sometimes considered corrupt there," Alec spoke diplomatically as they made their way toward the office. "No offense, not that..."

"I understand," Jorge cut him off as they arrived at the office door. "Believe me, I am not offended by that statement but I will say, your police here, not necessarily better, no?"

Alec didn't reply but his face was full of words that would never be spoken. They joined the others, who were chatting among themselves.

"We got the whole gang here today," Jorge gestured toward the small group as they turned to look at Alec. Paige had compassion in her face, while Diego merely looked at him with interest and Michael swung his arm over the back of the chair casually, glancing at Chase. Jesús didn't even look up from the chocolate donut he was eating.

"I can't believe you brought donuts knowing I can't have them!" Diego shifted his attention to Jesús and returned to an earlier complaint. "Did they not have anything gluten-free there?"

"I am sorry," Jesús attempted to explain. "I just heard of this food sensitivity the other day and did not think of it when I picked these up."

"Diego, what you want him to do?" Jorge complained as he walked behind the desk and Alec grabbed a donut before taking a seat. "Go out and look for something gluten-free for you? Is this all we're going to fucking hear about now? If this is a problem, we got apples in the kitchen."

Michael grinned and shared a look with Paige while Diego glared at Jorge before continuing.

"I could *die* if I don't get this sorted out," He spoke dramatically. "Like you, I now have to watch what I eat because of health reasons. *Very* serious health reason and this is not just a sensitivity," He directed his last remark at Jesús. "It's a food allergy and I get sick if I consume gluten. It's serious."

"Can we move on to something a *little* more serious," Jorge immediately cut him off, "Like, you know, death threats on Makerson."

"Should we close the door?" Alec asked. "Isn't Makerson still staying here?"

"He's in the basement, working," Paige replied with a shrug. "We have to wait for Jolene to come back from the bathroom."

Jorge rolled his eyes. The last thing he wanted was to have her join them but unfortunately, it was necessary.

"This place," Her voice suddenly boomed from the doorway. "It is nice. I really like!"

"Thank you," Paige replied as Jolene entered the room, closing the door behind her. "We're about ready to start."

"Yes and let us try to keep our attention on the matters at hand," Jorge commented. "Not Diego's new diet or whatever else is going on in our lives."

"I got some information," Michael immediately jumped in ignoring the scowl on Diego's face. "I did some digging at work. Don Stumples' mother was never arrested but there have been suspicious activities around her. Such as, information about competing drug companies getting hacked, maybe someone who has a lawsuit against the company she invests in has a sudden change of heart…or an accident…"

"So she keeps her hands clean?" Chase asked and Michael nodded.

"The woman is known as a viper in business," He continued. "People are scared to cross her or she'll eat them alive."

No one commented.

"So, I would think that putting a hit on someone, it is probably not such a stretch," Jorge commented and turned his attention to Paige.

"It's not the first time," She replied and glanced toward Michael. "I found out that she's had a few, all successful, I might add."

"So, me, Makerson?" Alec turned to Paige.

"There isn't a hit on you," She assured him. "As I said before, there's only one and it's on Makerson."

"So we get to her first," Diego abruptly commented, his eyes bulging in defiance.

"Actually, we need to get her to call it off," Paige replied. "Nothing has gone in motion yet but once it does and money has exchanged hands, it's too late. We got to find her tonight."

"Then kill the bitch," Diego finished her sentence.

"I want to do it," Michael spoke up. "Hey, I can get in saying I'm the police…."

"I think Paige, she will be best," Jorge cut him off and noted the surprised look on Michael's face. "This is her…area of expertise."

"Oh yes, this her area of expertise," Jesús spoke up in his usual slow manner as he reached for another donut. "She is good."

"Well, technically, we're all good at what we do," Diego spoke arrogantly. "You know but Paige, she's the pro."

"Oh?" Michael gave her a sideward glance.

"No, do not say why!" Jolene spoke up abruptly. "Why do we trust this man? He is the police? Jorge, you hate the police. You say, never trust."

"He has proven himself to me," Jorge insisted and sat back in his chair. "Ok, how are we going to get to this old bitch? She's probably got people around her all day, looking after her…."

"She actually doesn't," Paige cut in. "I have been looking into it. She ah….actually lives alone."

"Security system?" Jesús asked.

"Easy to hack into," Paige replied smoothly and shared a look with Jorge. "We got people for that."

"Ah!" Michael nodded. "Impressive but I'm surprised she doesn't have someone live with her."

"No, apparently, she's quite eccentric," Paige replied as she turned toward Michael. "She doesn't trust anyone in her home except the cleaning lady that comes in twice a week."

"What's her name? She got a name?" Chase asked with a smooth grin and Jolene began to laugh.

"Louise," Paige and Michael replied at the same time.

"Ah...yes," Jorge noted that Diego's face lit up. Sensing the conversation was about to go off track, he cut in. "Ok, so we do not have to fight over who takes care of this situation but we must do it right away."

"I want to do it," Michael jumped in. "Let me do it. Look, it's like Jolene said, I'm the cop here so you have no reason to trust me. Let me do it or at least, be part of this. I want to prove my loyalty."

Jorge considered the idea for a moment and nodded. "Ok, well, this will be fine. You and me, we will do it."

Glancing at Diego, he noticed he appeared crestfallen.

"Diego, you too, you can come as well," Jorge said and noted his face lit up again. "Jesús, you need a day off, you've been working like crazy. Chase, the three of us, we were at the bar with you if anyone asks and Paige....*mi amor*, you can simply check back with your contacts to make sure when the hit is off. I suspect if she is out of the picture, her followers will fall apart. This woman's strength held them together so if she is no longer there, they may dismantle."

"Perhaps," Paige spoke up. "However, wouldn't it be better if we made it look like a suicide."

"You can do that?" Michael asked with interest and nodded. "That takes some skill."

"My wife, she has skill," Jorge quickly replied. "However, I do think that a bloody murder scene might also send a message. A suicide may encourage the others to 'man up' and become more powerful. A really messy murder has a way of instilling fear in people, especially when it is a woman who was greatly admired for her strength."

"So, we make sure she makes the call first," Michael confirmed. "Once the hit is off on Makerson,..."

"I will send a text to let you know that it went through to the top," Paige jumped in. "Then you guys....can do *whatever* you want to her."

"You know, this is a *lot* more than I should know," Alec spoke up.

"Well, you do," Jorge spoke abruptly. "This here, it is not your first rodeo, need I remind you?"

Alec looked away.

"Now, we must get moving….I don't got all night."

"What time?" Michael asked.

"I have the security cameras set to go off at 7:30," Paige commented. "So anytime after that point should work."

"So 8?" Michael asked.

"Perfecto." Jorge commented. "Anything else?"

"So is this the same lady, sir, she was behind the bomb threat?" Jesús asked with interest.

"We believe so," Jorge replied. "It all lines up. She's Big Pharma, Athas is working with us, we're as anti-Big Pharma as you can fucking get. Plus she's far-right, she wants her white supremacist voted in, not Athas. Us, we are her nightmare."

"Tonight around 8," Michael commented. "We're going to be her biggest motherfucking nightmare yet. You tell me what to bring and I'll be there."

"A gun, of course, not your work gun either," Jorge replied. "We will meet here first but I gotta ask you guys something…"

Diego and Michael both watched him with interest.

"This is a really old lady," Jorge said with a little laugh. "You got a problem killing grandma, cause if you do, this will not be good for you."

"I got no problem," Diego spoke up, his eyes bulging out as he shook his head.

"A racist old bitch?" Michael shook his head. "I don't think so."

"Hey, in case you did not notice," Jorge gestured around the room. "You don't got a lot of white faces here. We all feel the same way… as she will soon know."

Michael grinned and nodded.

CHAPTER

39

"You know, she's an old lady," Michael whispered after they got into Louise Stumples' house. Not that it was a difficult task since her security system had been completely dismantled; it always surprised Jorge how quick people were to upgrade to the latest and most convenient technology without first considering the downside. Old lady Stumples had a system which was easy to manage through her phone but it was also easy to hack. The rest was gravy.

"So?" Jorge said with a casual shrug as he glanced around the dark room with a faint interest. For being a rich, old bag, she certainly didn't have the finest in furnishings. This room itself looked like it hadn't been aired out, let alone changed, since the 70s. "What's your point?"

"Her days, may be numbered already?" Michael continued with a shrug. "She's in her 90s. Maybe we just scare her, slap her around a bit…."

"And have her report a black and a brown guy broke into her house," Jorge finished his sentence. "Then go on doing exactly what she's been doing for her entire life. You do realize that this woman here has done everything she can to keep immigrants out of the country and thrives on others misery, right?"

"I know but…"

"Trust me," Jorge continued as he led the way to the door. "I fucking guarantee you will change your mind."

Michael didn't respond. Jorge started to regret bringing him and wondered if maybe he couldn't trust Diego's new boyfriend. He was glad that they left the Colombian in the car to keep a watch on things rather than have him inside with his new boyfriend putting doubt in his mind.

"I hear the television," Jorge commented as he eased the door open to glance around an equally dark hallway. Michael didn't respond but followed him. When Jorge heard Archie Bunker's voice fill the house, he simply glanced at Michael, who raised an eyebrow. Neither said a thing as they moved forward, finally making their way into the living room, where the old lady was sleeping on the couch.

"She looks peaceful," Michael muttered with some reluctance, his eyes watched her.

"Not as fucking peaceful as she's about to look," Jorge replied and rushed ahead, his voice suddenly booming while he pulled out a gun. "Rise and shine grandma!"

Louise Stumples was suddenly wide awake. However, her original vulnerability quickly disappeared.

"What? What's going on?" She said and reached for her glasses. Her eyes immediately bulged out as she put them on. "How did you get in here? What do you want? Is it drug money? Are you crackheads?"

"Lady, I probably got more fucking money than you," Jorge snapped at her as he watched her sitting up, pulling a blanket close as if it were a shield. "We need you to make a call."

"You? *You* have more money than me?" She snapped, suddenly fully alert. "How would a *spic* get money unless he was a drug dealer?" Her eyes moved on to Michael. "Who's this ni…"

"Lady, I don't got time for your racist shit today," Jorge cut her off, sensing that Michael's original apprehension was slipping away. "You got to make a phone call to cancel a hit on Makerson."

"What?" She appeared stunned.

"Don't play fucking dumb," Jorge snapped. "I don't got all day. I'm gonna call a number and you're going to tell that person that the hit is off or I'm going to blow your fucking head off."

She looked stunned.

"Hello?" Jorge continued to grow impatient as she turned white as a ghost. "Now, I'm gonna call and you're going to speak."

"But…how do you know.."

"I know everything," Jorge snapped and glanced at Michael's gun before sitting his own on a nearby table and reaching for his phone.

Removing one glove, he started to hit the number that would automatically take them to a secret world that few knew existed.

Placing the phone on speaker, the old lady appeared stunned when a dignified voice answered, apparently familiar to the woman.

"I...yes, this is Louise Stumples," The old lady spoke nervously. "I would like to cancel our previous arrangement ….. Thomas Makerson who works at *Toronto AM*. It's off."

The call went on with confirmations followed by an abrupt end. At which time, Louise stared at the two men. Once he received confirmation from Paige, he slid the phone back into his pocket, put on his glove, and reached for his gun.

"I have done what you asked," She remarked over Archie Bunker's voice. "Now, take the money, whatever you wish and leave me be."

"I told you before, I don't need your money," Jorge commented and glanced around the room. "I got my own."

"You aren't going to rape me, are you?" She pulled the blanket a little higher and Jorge laughed, while beside him Michael appeared repulsed.

"Lady, I got no interest in seeing you naked," Jorge shot back and shook his head. "We are going to have a little conversation about you and your connection to Fulton Harley."

"Fulton Harley is a fine man," She sat up a bit straighter and made a face. "I have known him and his family for years. I will support him in any way I can."

"Like that bomb scare at the Alec Athas' event last weekend," Jorge asked. "That your way of weeding out the competition? Violence?"

"You're a Mexican," She snapped back. "That's how you people work down there. Such a beautiful country, unfortunately, its full of savages."

"Savages?" Jorge repeated and glanced at Michael. "As opposed to you and your outstanding friends, the white supremacists who kill people, create propaganda and do all you can to keep immigrants out of this country."

"You people can do whatever you wish," Louise continued as she removed the blanket and set it aside. "You can all kill one another for all I care, just stay in your own goddamn country. We don't need you here. We have our own people to look after. This country was found by white Europeans and it should've stayed that way but as soon as people from shithole countries hear about all our social programs and think they're getting something free, they rush here to grab everything they can."

"What the fuck?" Michael suddenly snapped. "Are you fucking kidding me?"

Jorge was surprised when Perkins suddenly broke his silence.

"You people brought violence on our streets, the drugs, the crime, the break-ins," She gestured toward her door. "You two broke into my home tonight, that just proves what I mean. You're like animals, you rape innocent white women and ruin them with your half-breed babies, it's repulsive."

Although Jorge laughed at the woman's ignorance, clearly Michael Perkins was deeply offended because a shot was suddenly fired. The old woman was immediately silenced, her blouse turning red as the blood flowed from her. She was struggling to breathe and that's when Michael shot her again. As if in a daze, he continued to do so until there were no bullets left in his gun.

Unfazed by the woman's lifeless body slumped on the couch, Jorge glanced around the room. Splattered blood was everywhere but the couch absorbed most of it while some began to drip on the floor A vulgar smell filled the air and that's when he turned to Michael and shook his head.

"We gotta get out of here," He spoke hurriedly. Noting that Michael appeared stunned, Jorge grabbed his arm to pull him back to earth.

"Come on, *amigo*, we gotta go," Jorge repeated and Michael stared at the old lady.

"Yeah, yeah…let's go," He nodded as they made their way through the house and toward the room where they had first come in. Archie Bunker's voice continued to fill the house with a racist comment; the dark irony didn't escape Jorge as they headed for the door.

It wasn't until they were back in Diego's Lexus that they spoke again.

"So the old lady," Diego asked as they started to drive away. "She dead or what the hell happened? You guys weren't as long as I thought you would be."

"She did what we asked right away," Jorge replied with a shrug and glanced toward the backseat. "Then your boyfriend shot her. Like a 100 times. The police might have some questions about that…"

"It's a gun I got off the street and it wasn't that many times," Michael quickly corrected him. "It was a few…."

"If you had 100 bullets, it would've been a 100 times," Jorge confirmed. "Trust me, you were on a mission."

"I can't explain it," Michael spoke mechanically. "I started and for some reason, I just couldn't stop."

"In honesty, the woman, she was deplorable," Jorge said with a casual shrug. "I'm hungry, is anyone else hungry."

"You just saw a woman murdered and you're…hungry," Michael asked in disbelief.

"Hungry and horny, but right now, I wanna eat," Jorge commented with a shrug. "What can I say, death brings out my most primal needs."

Diego laughed and shook his head.

"Unbelievable," Michael spoke up from the backseat.

"What?" Jorge asked with a grin. "You never kill anyone before? Even Diego isn't this uptight when he kills someone."

"I just want a drink after I kill someone but it depends on the time of day," Diego calmly replied. "A nice shot of Tequila would be nice."

"Hey it wasn't too bad either because we didn't get any blood on us," Jorge continued casually as he started to play with the radio to look for a classic rock station. "So we can go out like normal."

"It's all about how you do it and positioning," Diego continued. "You two must've been far enough away."

"We did good," Jorge glanced in the backseat at Michael who looked ill. "Hey, you don't look so well."

"I don't feel so well," He answered. "Diego, can you pull over?"

Without replying, he eased the car to the curb and within seconds, Michael pushed the door opened and started to gag. Jorge made a face and turned toward Diego, who appeared alarmed. When Michael finished vomiting, he slouched back into his seat and closed the door.

"You ah…you ok?" Diego asked hesitantly.

"Yeah," Michael quietly replied as Jorge glanced over his shoulder as the smell of vomit filled the car.

"Was this your first time?" He boldly asked. "You never shot anyone before, did you?"

Diego appeared more alarmed by the question than Michael, as he eased back on the street. "Of course not, he's a cop. They shoot people all the time."

"Not really," Michael gently replied. "It actually was the first time I *killed* someone."

"Wow," Jorge replied and shrugged. "I guess that is possible."

"It's not exactly like what we do is normal," Diego quickly reasoned. "We're not in Mexico anymore, Hernandez."

"Now you sound like the old lady back there," Jorge tilted his head toward the window. "You should've heard her talk…"

"Can we…not talk about this anymore," Michael gently suggested from the backseat and Jorge nodded.

"You'll get over it," He insisted. "It gets easier."

"Obviously," Michael said with surprise in his voice. "You're talking about getting food and getting laid."

"You know, I'm not so hungry anymore," Jorge commented and made a face. "Diego, drop me home. I gotta find my wife."

CHAPTER

40

Jorge was hit with loud, pop music immediately when he walked into the house. Maria's voice could be heard singing loudly along to the music but after looking through the house, he was unable to find Paige. Walking from room to room, he finally texted his wife to ask her where she was and what kind of demon had taken over their home.

I'm sitting on the back step.

It was pathetic. In Mexico, he had a beautiful home with a pool and all the luxuries money could buy. However, in Canada, he had to show modesty so they instead had a *nice,* boring home that didn't expose their joint wealth. Fortunately, as he continued to take over the marijuana business, he would eventually be able to have the kind of home that reflected the real Jorge Hernandez. Not that he lived in a shack but it was not to his standards. There wasn't even a place to sit outside. What kind of monster built this kind of house?

"*Mi amor,*" Jorge said as he opened the back door to find Paige sitting on the cement step. "This is terrible. We must build a nice place for you to sit outside and enjoy these beautiful evenings."

"It wasn't so much the evening I was out here to enjoy," Paige replied as she looked up, her blue eyes shining when met with a nearby light. "I had to escape for a few minutes."

"*Si,* yes, I hear the music," Jorge sat down beside her and gave her a quick kiss. "My daughter, does she now want to be a rock star?"

Paige nodded.

"What? Just now, I was teasing," Jorge said with a seductive grin on his face as he felt his desires churn, his thoughts far from the topic at hand. "Is this true? She wants to be a singer"

"Makes you miss the days when she only wanted to be an actress, doesn't it?" Paige quietly asked as their eyes met and he eased in, answering her question with a kiss that quickly grew very passionate despite the obnoxious music pulsating inside the house. He reached out and pulled her close, his hand eased up her leg as his breath grew labored. Paige suddenly stopped him and moved away.

"We have to go inside," She whispered.

"Do we?" He challenged her and moved forward. "There is a fence around our house, no one can see."

"I would feel better inside," She quietly replied.

"Me, I don't care, *mi amor*," He teased and moved forward to kiss her again before glancing at the cold cement beneath them. "But yes, it is not exactly comfortable here."

Standing, he reached for her hand. Helping Paige to her feet, their eyes met but neither said a word as he led her inside the house. Locking the door behind them, Jorge ignored the music and quickly led her into his office, where he pulled her inside and abruptly pushed the door shut. Their lips met instantly, his hands wasted no time exploring underneath her clothes while her fingertips ran past the waistband of his pants to find the zipper. He gasped in pleasure as she reached inside while Jorge abruptly pulled down her pants, which she quickly stepped out of as her breathing seemed to grow heavier.

Feeling as though he was on the edge as his fingers slid inside her thong and began to work quickly, anticipating that the music would soon stop and his daughter would be looking for them. Paige wiggled beneath his hand as soft moans flowed from the back of her throat. Jorge quickly pulled the thong down and his wife walked out of it before he gently pushed her against the wall. Pleasure rang through his body as he slid inside of her, grasping her hips to lift her up, she tightly wrapped her legs around him, her fingers digging into his back. Her gasp became louder as he pushed deeper and deeper inside of her, as she continued to ferociously cling to him until she started to let out animals like sounds as her hot breath touched the side of his face. Waves of pleasure flowed through his body which quickly felt like jelly as he slowly, gently let go as her feet touched the ground.

Within minutes they both slid to the floor, backs against the door, his arm pulling her close, Jorge kissed her on the cheek. "That was beautiful, *mi amor* but I'm afraid we will soon have to leave our world of pleasure to tell Maria to turn that fucking music off."

Paige snickered and didn't reply.

"The music, it is loud," Jorge added. "We do not want neighbors to complain."

"You can barely hear it outside," Paige replied. "But it is getting late."

"It is," He pulled her close to kiss her forehead.

"How did it go tonight," Paige suddenly turned to him, her eyes huge. "The old lady?"

"She made friends with the Grim Reaper," Jorge whispered in a seductive voice. "Courtesy of our new friend, Michael."

"So, he is clearly trustworthy," Paige commented. "Diego is smitten."

"Diego, he often is smitten but at least this guy is gay," Jorge commented as his fingers played with the strap on her top. "I do not know how things are with them but it is better to not get involved. I hope that if they break up it doesn't affect us all. Although, I cannot see this man turning against us. I saw him repeatedly shoot an old lady tonight."

Paige looked into his eyes and nodded.

"Not to say, she did not deserve it," Jorge continued. "Very racist and an indirect, but a cold-blooded killer. It only seems appropriate that she died at the hands of someone she spent a lifetime hating."

"I can't believe that racism is so prevalent in this day and age," Paige commented and shook her head.

"This, it should not be a surprise," Jorge replied as he started to move away from her and the two of them stood up. "People, they are racist. It does not matter the year or the government. It just matters that they feel free to speak and there will always be sheep that follow and not think for themselves. That is our world. It is nothing new."

"I know," Paige spoke sadly as she pulled on her thong followed by her pants. "But why? This is Canada. We are a multicultural country."

"*Mi amor*, it does not matter," Jorge replied as he pulled on his underwear and pants. "You do not see that people are people, regardless. There is a need, an emptiness that they must fill and for some, that is love and for others, that is hate. Hate, unfortunately, is easier. People like what is easy."

"I'm shameful of white people who think that way," Paige spoke with a touch of sadness in her voice. "That certainly doesn't represent most of us."

"No, my love, it does not represent *you* but there are many where this is an issue," Jorge reminded her and they stood in silence until he reached out and gently kissed her lips. "The world, it has told white people for so long that they are the superior race and they believed it. Our history is never so far away that we risk repeating."

Paige nodded as they walked out of the office.

"Makerson?"

"He was packed and out the door shortly after I relaid the message to him," Paige replied. "He said thanks and he'd speak to you in the morning. I think he had a story he was chasing."

"Right," Jorge nodded and reached for his beeping phone. "Jesús is looking for me."

"I'll go talk to Maria about the music," Paige commented. "Meet you upstairs?"

"*Mi amor*, I will be there shortly," Jorge replied as she walked away. He quickly hit a few buttons on his phone.

"Jesús, hello," Jorge spoke into the phone. "I hope you are enjoying your night off."

"Sir, I am so tired, I think I slept most of this evening," Jesús replied. "And you, did you do well this evening?"

"We did well," Jorge replied.

"I am back in Quebec tomorrow," Jesús continued and hesitated. "There may be some trouble but nothing I cannot handle."

"Do you need me? Diego?"

"I think Sylvana will be fine," Jesús replied. "As I have said, she is proving very helpful. I believe she could even work her way up some more."

Jorge suspected his cousin had a dangerous side. *Perfecto.* If there was something Jorge appreciated, it was a strong woman.

"This is good, I must keep it in mind," Jorge replied as the music in Maria's room suddenly stopped. "Do keep me informed."

Ending the conversation, he noticed a message from Jolene.

Do you need my help soon?

Soon, Jolene. I will discuss this with you in a few days.

Tonight? Did it go well?

Perfecto.

Buenas noche.

Jorge slid the phone back into his pocket. Walking into the kitchen, he started to turn off the lights as he moved upstairs. His primary goal was to take a hot shower and go to bed. Instead, he met his daughter in the hallway.

"*Papa*, I want to be a pop star," She commented while behind her, Paige shook her head and walked into their bedroom. "Then, I will become an actress later."

"Oh, Maria, can we not talk about this tonight," Jorge shook his head. "*Papa*, he has had a long day. I am very tired."

"Can I take voice lessons?" She pushed as he turned toward his bedroom. "Remember we were talking about it before and my punishment, it's coming to an end soon."

"Maria, we will talk about this later," Jorge spoke sternly. "It is too late. You must get some sleep, there is school tomorrow."

She looked crestfallen.

"*Papa*, we must not waste time. Ariana Grande and Selena Gomez and many others started as kids and they became huge stars."

"Maria, why do you want to be a star?" Jorge bluntly asked her. "Why does being famous mean so much to you?"

"Because I'm meant to be a star," She replied dramatically and Jorge found himself growing impatient. "*Papa*, it is like you being a...."

Jorge gave her a stern look before she could finish her sentence. "Maria!"

"What I mean, is that we all have a path in life and this is mine," She replied bluntly. "I am meant to be famous. You have to believe me."

"Again, Maria, we will talk in the morning," Jorge spoke sternly. "I am tired, I had a long, long day, I must sleep. This is not the time to discuss this topic."

"Ok," She finally relented. "I will make you see."

"I am sure you will," He replied and noted that she seemed satisfied. "Good night, *niñita.*"

Rushing forward, they embraced and he gave her a quick kiss on the forehead before she ran to her room. Frustrated and exhausted, he went into the bedroom, where Paige was reading under the covers.

"That daughter of mine," Jorge started as he closed the door. "She will be the death of me."

Paige laughed.

"Pop star?" He shook his head. "Not exactly a step up from movie star."

"Maybe she'll eventually work to a doctor," Paige suggested as he began to remove his clothes and throw them on a chair.

"We can only hope," Jorge gestured toward the bathroom. "I am going to take a shower then, I will be back to have a passionate night with my wife."

He winked and walked into the next room.

It was later that night when the phone woke him with the difficult news.

CHAPTER

41

"I should have gone," Jorge quietly said to Paige as he sunk his head into both hands. The sound of Maria bouncing down the stairs only filled him with more dread. He took a long, sorrowful breath before lifting his head – which suddenly felt as though it was double in weight – his body exhausted after being awake most of the night. Glancing at his daughter, he saw her go pale, as fear collected in her huge, brown eyes.

"*Papa?*" Maria muttered as she hesitated at the end of the staircase. Her usual enthusiasm instantly disappeared replaced by reluctance and fear. She glanced from Paige to her father and slowly moved forward. "What is wrong?"

"Maria, please, come sit," Jorge gently placed his hand beside him on the couch. On the other side, Paige squeezed his shoulder and moved closer to him. His daughter showed apprehension as she approached and finally sat down. "We had an unexpected call last night."

She nodded and sat up a bit straighter, as if in preparation for the news.

"You know, *niñita*, when we lived in Mexico how I would warn you to be careful because it was common for people to kidnap?" He awkwardly asked, unsure of how else to broach the subject. Her reaction was slow, nervous and although he wasn't sure how to say the words, Jorge continued. "Last night, I received a call that your *abuela* was kidnapped."

Maria's eyes automatically doubled in size but the immediate shock quickly turned to sorrow as tears spilled down her face. It was not uncommon for kidnappings to take place in Mexico and in fact, it has happened to one of her friends at a very young age. Not that it was only children. Many kidnappings took place when a family member was wealthy such as Jorge and some for revenge. In this case, Jorge suspected it could've been both. He had certainly made many enemies throughout the years.

"Oh, *Papa*!" Maria immediately wrapped her arms around him as she sobbed, causing his heart to break a bit more; how many times had he delivered bad news to his daughter? He pulled Maria close and kissed the top of her head. "Is she going to be ok? Do you have to give them money? Did you call the police?"

Jorge merely grunted at the last question. *La policía!* They were probably behind the kidnapping! He felt Paige squeeze his shoulder a little tighter and after taking a deep breath, he finally spoke.

"We are handling it, Maria," Jorge said and had to take a moment to continue. "Jesús, he has gone to Mexico and he will take care of everything."

"Oh no!" Maria let go of him and terror filled her eyes. "Will he be ok? What if the kidnappers, they hurt him?"

"No, the kidnappers, they want money," Jorge replied and took a deep breath as he pulled her closer and kissed the top of her head. "They will not get money if *anyone* is hurt, do you understand?"

She nodded and collapsed in tears again.

"Maria, you can stay home today," Paige spoke up in her usual, gentle voice which reminded Jorge of an angel at that moment. "I will call the school."

"No," Maria said as she pulled back and shook her head. "I must go today. I have a test and I must be strong."

"Maria, it is ok if you want to stay home," Jorge reassured her. "This here, this is a lot. It would not be a good day to take a test."

"No, *Papa*, I must go," She insisted and then lowered her head slightly. "Unless you need me here?"

It amazed him how his child, a little girl of 11, could be so strong and mature especially considering the many terrible situations she had dealt with already in her life. Most children might lose a grandparent to illness or perhaps suffer some minor tragedy such as losing a pet but his daughter, she had lost so much; a mother, all but one of her grandparents and now her last one, was in danger.

"Maria, you do not have to be strong," Jorge commented even though he was secretly proud of her. "No one expects you to soldier on."

"But look at you *Papa*," She responded in a quiet voice. "You are strong. I wish to be like you."

"I was not so strong last night," Jorge spoke honestly and shook his head. "This is news I have had hours to deal with. You have just learned it now."

"I will be fine," Maria insisted and stood up, leaving Jorge in stunned silence as she walked toward the kitchen. "*Papa*, it is important that I continue to get good marks in school and not miss time."

Jorge couldn't speak. He merely glanced at Paige.

"Maria, are you sure?" She asked with some hesitation. "You do realize that your grandmother is in a dangerous place? It might be good if you stay home with your family today.."

"She will be fine," Maria spoke confidently. "*Papa*, he always fixes everything."

"Oh Maria, I would not necessarily say that," Jorge spoke with a break in his voice and he leaned back on the couch. Glancing down, he wore the same bathrobe he had put on shortly after the call. "I do my best but I cannot fix everything. This situation, it will most likely be resolved but please, do not make me out as a superhero."

"But *Papa,* you are," Maria commented as she opened the fridge door. "You always make everything better."

He couldn't reply but sat in stunned silence.

With much reluctance, Paige took Maria to school. Jorge stayed home, his heart and mind preoccupied with the unexpected fear surrounding his mother's kidnapping. The two had been estranged because of his anger surrounding what happened during his childhood. It was 30 years since his brother's death but it still caused a deep hurt in their relationship. Now there was a chance she could be brutally murdered by some monster in Mexico. The irony of this was that he was as much a savage as the men who held his mother hostage. The truth roared through his veins like a poison that was slowly killing him with every second that he waited for his phone to ring.

Paige returned home to find him sitting in the same spot as when she left. A full glass of water in front of him, along with a cup of cold coffee and a piece of toast. He barely looked up at her when she crossed the room to sit beside him.

"Jorge, you have to eat or drink something," She spoke gently but with a forcefulness in her voice. "This isn't healthy. You need to keep up your strength."

"*Mi amor*, I cannot."

She stared into his eyes before pulling him into a hug.

"I cannot move, not until I hear from Jesús," Jorge replied with no emotion in his voice. His body feeling weak, his stomach turning as he said the words. "I must wait."

"You should take a shower," Paige suggested. "You'll feel better."

"No," He shook his head.

"I can get the phone…."

"No, I must wait."

He turned and stared into her eyes and that's when his mask of strength began to crumble.

"Paige, I did not think something like this would upset me so much," Jorge spoke as she leaned against him. "For all the years, all the anger I held in my heart. I did not consider that someone would kidnap her and that if they did, I would be so frightened."

"It's your mother, Jorge."

"It is my mother but our relationship, it has been bad since childhood," Jorge reminded her, his voice barely a whisper. "Since Miguel, since that terrible accident that took him away."

"It wasn't your fault," Paige insisted as she pulled him closer. "You were a kid."

"I was 12, I should've known better," Jorge replied. "I carry that with me every day of my life."

"You shouldn't," She spoke sternly, her blue eyes blazing. "You were a kid. You made a mistake."

"I killed my brother," Jorge said as he shook his head. "He would be alive now. If I had not insisted he get on that dirt bike with me, he would've lived."

"Jorge," Paige spoke more sternly this time and moved away from him. "You have to stop blaming yourself for this…it was a mistake. You would *never* hold anyone else to these unreasonable standards. Plus how your parents treated you afterwards was unacceptable."

"It is not the same," Jorge corrected her. "I held my mother to high standards when she allowed my father to beat me. I blamed her and because of it, we did not speak…"

"Jorge, don't you think it is time you let this go," Paige said as she looked into his eyes. "I'm not saying what happened was right but, doesn't this kidnapping bring everything into perspective?"

"You are right, *mi amor*, you are always right," Jorge said as he reached for her hand. "It is time."

Paige finally persuaded him to take a shower and eat, however, his movements were slow and mechanical. Although Jesús was now in Mexico and ready to meet with the kidnapper, the entire ordeal seemed to take forever, despite the fact that he would pay the obscene amount of money required to recover his mother. It was just money and he had so much of it.

It was when the subdued family sat down to dinner that his phone rang. Fear stabbed his heart as he reached for it. Across from him, Paige offered him a compassionate smile while his daughter's eyes filled with tears. He quickly answered it, as he stood up and rushed out of the room. This was a conversation he wanted to have alone.

It was after he pulled his office door closed that Jesús delivered the news.

"*La tenemos*!!" Jesús hurriedly yelled into the phone. "Sir, she is fine! I exchanged the money and she is fine."

"Oh my God," Jorge felt his body sink to the floor as relief filled his heart. His hand reached out to touch the wall as if it would somehow hold him together. "*Gracias*!! Oh my God! She is ok, everything is fine?"

"Yes, sir, she is good," Jesús spoke with assurance in his voice. "Would you like to speak to her."

"*Si!*"

"Jorge," Her voice was suddenly on the other end of the line and he was unable to speak as tears filled his eyes. "¡*Estaba tan asustado! Esos hombres malvados. ¡Me sacaron de mi casa!*"

"I know, Mama," He managed to pull himself together. "I am so sorry they did this to you. Did they hurt you? Are you ok?"

"I am…I am fine," Her voice shook and another wave of tears overtook Jorge as his heart raced. "I am scared. Will they take me again?"

"*No, mamá, vienes aquí!*" He felt his heart race. "You are not to go back to that home."

"But I cannot leave!" She began to sob. "My life, it is in Mexico."

"No, Mama, you cannot stay," Jorge sniffed. "It is not safe for you in Mexico. Jesús, he will help you but you cannot stay. It is dangerous."

"I am scared they will take me again," His mother cried. "I was in my home and they got in and took me, told me I would die if my son did not pay the money. They wanted to torture me."

"*Mama,* this is over," Jorge insisted. "You must come here. We have room. It is better. You will be safe in Canada."

"But they will not allow *señora mayor* like me to go to Canada," She spoke weakly. "I have nothing to offer."

"They will, I will make sure of it," Jorge spoke sternly. "Just pack your bags. Jesús, he will take care of you."

"*Si,*" She sniffed on the phone. "I will, *gracias* Jorge. This is so much."

"It is fine," He said and wiped his face. "*Mamá, te amo. Estarás a salvo aquí.*"

She started to sob again and this time something inside of Jorge began to shift.

42

"It's not that I think she hates me," Paige spoke with defiance in her voice. Jorge quickly placed his phone on the coffee table and sat back on the couch, turning toward his wife. "It's that she's not made an effort to talk to me and now she'll be living in our basement?"

"Ok, in our basement, not with us," Jorge spoke abruptly but immediately regretted it. His mother hadn't even stepped on Canadian soil yet and was already causing a conflict between him and his wife. "This is, I don't know, perhaps temporary? Paige, I could not allow her to stay there. This would only happen again, do you understand?"

"Of course I understand," Paige raised her voice slightly. "It's not like I don't know how these things work but what I'm saying, is that your mother barely acknowledges my existence. Not to mention that she barely acknowledges you either. So it's difficult to have her in the same house."

"In the basement," Jorge corrected her and shook his head. "*Mi amor,* come on, do you think I want her here…in our house, wandering around? I love my mother and yes, I'm relieved she is alive but do not misunderstand, it is better if she stays in her apartment."

"And you're going to tell her that?" Paige asked, her body appearing tense. Jorge didn't know what to say. "I can't believe you didn't talk to me about this."

"I did not talk to you about Clara and it was fine," Jorge reminded her. "She lived here for months and you were happy."

"Yes, with *Clara,*" Paige reminded him. "I like Clara and she likes me. She minded her own business and vice versa."

"My mother, she will do the same," Jorge insisted even though he wasn't completely convinced. "We have a lock on the door that connects us. It *will* be locked, *mi amor*, I assure you of this because I also like my privacy."

"That's all I ask," Paige insisted. "I don't want a relationship with your mother."

"Paige, come on," Jorge said in stunned disbelief. "This here, it cannot be true. I thought you would be the first person to insist I heal the relationship with my mother."

"*You* can," Paige shook her head. "*I'm* not. I saw how she treated you and Maria."

"I do see what you mean," Jorge commented and touched her hand. "My love, I do understand and I appreciate that you are so protective but this is something I must do. Maybe it will be good for Maria. I mean, for me, I suppose as well."

"I'm trying to understand how involved she will be in our lives," Paige countered. "I don't want a mother-in-law hovering over me."

"Paige," Jorge spoke with humor in his voice. "*Mi amor*, this will not affect you and me. I do not necessarily know what this means or how it will look, but I assure you, she will be staying in her apartment and all I ask is you be civil."

"I'm not driving her around or helping her with anything," Paige was insistent. "I'm not."

"Ok, this is fine," Jorge attempted to wrap his brain around everything. "Paige, please, be calm, ok? She is my mother but my first commitment is to you and Maria, you are my family. Just relax."

Paige eventually went upstairs to meditate while in the basement, Maria was inspecting everything to make sure it was in acceptable condition for her *abuela* when she arrived. Jorge was left by himself in the living room, wondering why his wife had such a strong reaction to his mother moving in. Not that his mother seemed happy with the arrangement either.

It was late in the evening when Jesús brought *madre* Hernandez to the door. Still angry, Paige had gone out with Diego for coffee, which left him and Maria home to greet her. Although he originally expected their reunion to somehow be much more profound and beautiful, in the end, her coldness could be felt as she hugged and kissed him.

"I am sorry this has happened to you," Jorge commented as he led her to the couch while Maria bounced along excitedly and Jesús quietly followed. "This must've been so frightening for you, *Mama*."

"It was, I thought this man, he was going to kill me," She spoke dramatically as tears formed in her eyes. Maria grabbed a box of tissue as they all sat down, passing it to her grandmother who muttered "*Gracias*" before continuing. "This has always been my fear, being kidnapped."

"Yes, unfortunately, this is very common in Mexico," Jesús spoke up and nodded, sharing looks with Jorge, before glancing at Maria. "But everything is ok now."

"But for years, this was my fear," She wiped her eyes. "With *Jorge* involved in…"

"*Mama*, please," Jorge gently cut her off, suspecting how this sentence was about to end. Noting the look of concern in his daughter's eyes, he quickly shifted gears. "I have told you that I use the English pronunciation of my name now, not the Mexican."

"Yes, of course," She nodded in understanding as she glanced at his daughter. "I do understand."

"Maria, why don't you and Jesús take Mama's luggage into the basement?" He asked and exchanged looks with his associate. "I must talk to my mother for a moment."

"Ok," Maria popped up from the couch and rushed toward the door while Jesús grinned as he stood up.

"Slow down, I'm an old man," He teased Maria.

Jorge merely grinned until the two were out of earshot.

"Mama, there are some rules to my house," Jorge spoke sternly, suddenly feeling his original apprehensions return. "You do not talk about anything I do especially to or in front of my daughter. You do this once, I will send you back to Mexico."

She shook her head. "But you say I cannot go back."

"Then you do not talk," Jorge continued. "The door between your apartment and this house will be locked but you have your own separate entrance. You are not to come here unless invited or you knock. My family, we enjoy our privacy. My wife, you will respect."

"Of course, I was never disrespectful toward her," His mother began to cry. "It is her, that is why you are so unkind to me. She does not want me in this house. It is *her* that wants me hidden away in this basement."

"No," Jorge quickly corrected her. "This here was my idea. My wife, she does not even know you. It is true that I do love you and want you safe but *Mama*, it does not take away the many years our relationship was difficult."

"It was your father…"

"No, *Mama*, it was you," Jorge replied and shook his head. "I do not want to talk about this now. I'm exhausted. Perhaps you should go downstairs and rest?"

"Yes, I am tired," His mother meekly replied and they both stood up. "And your wife? Where is she now?"

"She's out with a friend," Jorge replied as they started toward the apartment door.

"She did not even want to see me when I arrive?" His mother appeared insulted. "If this was a *Latina*, she would not disrespect me like this."

"*Mama*, do not go there," Jorge instructed sternly. "I made the decision to have you move in without discussing it with her. She is out with a friend."

"Why would you discuss it with her?" His mother challenged him. "This is your house, you may do as you please. I am your *Mama*, this is not for her to decide."

"We do not have a marriage like you and *Papa*," Jorge insisted as his daughter arrived back in the room. "Our marriage, it is equal, I do not *control* her. Marriages are partnerships. No woman is to be controlled by a man."

His last comment directed toward Maria; he noted the understanding in her eyes.

"You will find, this will not work especially with a white woman," His mother's comments were sharp.

Taking a deep, frustrated breath, Jorge turned toward his mother, still aware of his daughter's presence.

"In this house, we do not talk this way," He managed to bite back his anger.

"Paige is a good *Mama* to me," Maria spoke up, her eyes fixating on her father. "Why does she say this about white women, *Papa*?"

Jesús returned to the room and appeared uncomfortable but remained silent.

"She, that woman, she is *not* your *real* mother," Jorge's mother spoke defiantly. "Your *real* mother was a Mexican woman, not a white woman."

The timing couldn't have been worse for Paige to walk in the door with Diego behind her, the two of them laughing.

"I must go!" Jesús suddenly lurched toward the door. "We will talk tomorrow."

"Jesús, I don't even know how.." Jorge began but he was already shaking his head.

"No need."

Then he was gone. Paige stopped and shared unfriendly looks with his mother while Diego twisted his mouth in an awkward pose.

"My *real* mother was a terrible woman," Maria shot out dramatically. "I do not care that she was Mexican. *Abuela* you are a *racist!*"

Jorge wasn't sure who was more stunned. Everyone fell silent as Maria rushed toward Paige and protectively grabbed her hand. As much as the entire scene was increasingly awkward, a sense of pride filled his heart over his daughter's actions and words. Meanwhile, both Paige and Diego appeared shocked.

"I am not a racist!" His mother immediately complained. "Jorge, it is not acceptable for her to speak to me this way."

Using the Mexican pronunciation of his name once again was simply the straw the broke the camel's back, as Jorge swung around.

"That is it!" He fumed. "It has been a long day."

"But your wife is off with another man, your daughter is rude to me," She dramatically waved her hands in the air. "Do you have no control over your family, *Jorge?*"

"Ok, for the last *fucking* time, stop calling me by the Mexican pronunciation of my name," Jorge snapped, causing the room to fall silent. "As for my wife and daughter, they are *not* for me to control. Perhaps, *Papa*, he controlled you forever but in this house, it is not like that. My wife's friend, Diego, is also my friend. In fact, he is like a brother to me so yes, of course, she spends time with him."

Diego stood a little taller and nodded, continuing to make a face while Paige seemed to relax her stance as Maria continued to protectively hold hands with her.

"My daughter, I do not wish for her to grow up feeling like she is unable to speak for herself," Jorge continued. "Yes, I am strict with her and yes, I have rules but you know what, if she makes a mistake, no matter how bad, I never *ever* beat her. You may also not agree with that but this is how it is in *my* house. If you do not like it, you are free to go back to Mexico!"

Glancing around, his heart pounding, it took him a minute to realize that he was shouting. Feeling slightly embarrassed, he realized that the expressions on his family's faces was not judgment but compassion. Suddenly exhausted, he pointed toward the floor.

"Mama, you can go to your apartment and settle in," Jorge continued. "There is a set of keys on the table. You should have everything you need down there."

"*Gracias,*" She sheepishly replied and walked toward the door that led to her new home.

"*Papa,*" Maria finally let go of Paige's hand and approached him after she was gone. "I do not like her. She is mean."

"Maria, it was a long day for everyone," Jorge said as he pulled her into a hug and gave her a quick kiss. "I am very proud of you for defending Paige. That was a beautiful thing to do."

"Of course," Maria replied. "That is what we do, right, *Papa*? Be loyal to those we love?"

"Yes, niñita," He replied and gave her a second kiss and noted Diego nodding while Paige simply smiled. "This is what I have always taught you, no?"

"*Si, Papa.*"

"It is late," Jorge commented. "You should get to bed."

She nodded, shyly looking back at Paige.

"Can you come upstairs with me?" She asked. "I need to talk to you about woman business."

Paige looked a bit startled but agreed. "I will be right there."

Maria rushed away while Diego raised an eyebrow.

"Well, it's another interesting evening in the Hernandez household," He commented with a grin on his face. "You people should have a reality show."

Jorge rolled his eyes and Paige laughed.

"Well, I came in to smooth things over but ah…it looks like that train already left the station," Diego continued. "I will talk to you both tomorrow…"

"Yes, Diego, it will be business as usual," Jorge agreed and glanced at his wife. "Thank you."

He didn't reply, simply winked and slipped out the door.

CHAPTER

43

"I cannot believe that I had to have a stern conversation with my mother," Jorge whispered as he slowly climbed into bed beside Paige. His body welcomed the mattress beneath him like it never had before, as he collapsed, his eyes on the ceiling as his wife slowly turned around. It was as if the weight of the day had finally caught up with him and he was powerless against it. "I tell her to not tell anyone where she is for now. Of course, she does not want to listen or understand why it might be dangerous to share our address with the goddamn world."

"How could she not know?" Paige spoke in her usual soft, beautiful voice as she reached out and gently ran her fingers over his face. "How could a woman who lived her entire life in Mexico *not* understand the dangers? Especially when she was *just* kidnapped?"

"The kidnapping, it was for money," Jorge insisted and hesitated for a moment. "They did not plan to hurt her, it was a quick way to extort cash from me. A corrupt officer was the instigator. If I find out who, he will be dead."

"It's late," Paige spoke wearily. "Let's talk about this in the morning."

"I agree," Jorge replied as his wife moved in and gave him a kiss. "But *mi amor*, I hope you are not angry with me."

"I'm not angry with you," Paige calmly replied. "I feared that she would come between us and that she would disappoint you."

"Well, as you can see," Jorge said as he snuggled up closer to her. "You weren't completely wrong about the disappointing part but she could never come between us. My loyalty is with you, as you saw tonight. Until then, she hadn't expressed her feelings for you but I am glad she did because I now know."

"So what happens now?" Paige asked. "She lives in our basement forever?"

"No, I do not see this as long-term," Jorge commented. "Especially after tonight. I guess I had some fantasy that she would be ok and that perhaps Maria and her would bond but I was wrong."

"To be honest," Paige admitted. "I didn't see things turning out like this either. I figured she would be critical of me and point out my flaws to you."

"What flaws?" Jorge teased. "You are perfect, aren't you?"

"Hardly," Paige snuggled closer to him. "I don't cook…at least not well, I'm hardly the good, domesticated, Mexican wife."

"Ah but I don't care about that," Jorge replied as he pulled her closer. "I can be a bit of a chauvinist but I would like to think that I'm not that bad either. My mother, her ideas are old-fashioned. I do not believe she is good to have here with Maria, now that I see this side of her tonight."

"I think Maria isn't that easily swayed," Paige reminded him with humor in her voice. "In case you hadn't noticed."

A smile lit up Jorge's face. "This is true. I am so proud of my daughter. It is good to know that even though she often raises my blood pressure that some of what I teach her is working. It makes it worthwhile."

"She got her period today," Paige threw in the comment and patted his arm.

"Oh fuck! Why you tell me these things?" Jorge groaned. "In that incidence, I am old-fashioned and that is woman stuff that…I do not want to think about. She's only 11."

"I know," Paige calmly reminded him. "But she's growing up."

"I feel like she was just a baby," Jorge replied. "Then one day, she was taking over the house. How does this happen?"

"We had a lengthy conversation," Paige continued. "I think she might have told Chase."

"Oh fuck me!" Jorge moaned. "This day, please, if there is more, just shoot me in the head."

"I hope not," Paige giggled and kissed him. "You need sleep."

"How do I sleep after you tell me this?" Jorge complained. "I have to see Chase tomorrow."

As it turned out, Chase merely laughed it off when the two met the next morning.

"I am sorry, that is not appropriate of my daughter," Jorge insisted as he sat at the bar. "I had a talk with her this morning. I tell her, this was a overshare."

"It's not the first time Maria has overshared," Chase reminded him with laughter in his voice as he leaned against the bar. "Remember when she started at her school and was telling everyone about her mother dying…"

"Oh yes, do I ever," Jorge replied as he took a drink of his coffee. "So now I have both a daughter and a mother who want to tell the world everything. Did you hear about the kidnapping?"

"I heard," Chase said and cringed. "That's pretty scary. I assume she's ok?

"She is," Jorge replied. "I thank you. Unfortunately, I am not sure about having her living in my house even though it's the basement apartment."

"Your house is huge," Chase reminded him. "Even if she were…"

"Do not even say," Jorge cut him off. "Would you? Would you want your mother living with you?"

"My mother and I don't have a relationship," Chase spoke solemnly. "So no."

"My mother and I, we also don't have a relationship," Jorge said and shook his head. "Not since I was 12 and now, she is back in my life and I had to fight the urge to buy a pack of cigarettes this morning. It has been months since I quit if that tells you something."

"It does," Chase said with a compassionate smile.

"Let us not talk about this anymore," Jorge suggested and pointed behind the bar. "Could I trouble you for a shot of tequila?"

"Of course," Chase immediately grabbed the bottle and shot glass. "So the night of the election, are we having the party here?"

"I don't think it's big enough for that party," Jorge reminded him. "But maybe a more private party later that night?"

"A private function sounds good," Chase nodded as Jorge knocked back his shot. "Just tell me what I need to do."

Jorge didn't reply as the alcohol burned the back of his throat. The door behind him opened.

"I will leave this for you to figure out. Maybe even talk to Paige. This is more her thing."

"Sounds great," Chase replied as he glanced past Jorge. "Diego."

Jorge turned to look over his shoulder as the Colombian strutted in the room wearing a suit, phone in hand, he swung his other hand in the air.

"What's going on here?" He abruptly asked. "A little early for tequila, isn't it? You're not a young man anymore."

"I need it after the night I had," Jorge insisted.

"Wow!" Diego said as his eyes grew in size. "Your mother...wow..."

"You don't gotta tell me," Jorge replied as Diego sat beside him. "This is why we don't have a relationship."

"After paying that much money to her kidnappers, I hope you get some respect," Diego replied as he grabbed the tequila bottle and poured himself a shot. "You Mexicans and your kidnappings. It seems like a lazy way to make money."

"Can we not talk about this?" Jorge said with frustration in his voice. "Let us please try to get back on track."

"That old lady you and Michael took out, she's not reported yet," Diego said before knocking back his shot. "It's been what? A couple of days?"

"Yeah, so?" Jorge replied.

"What? Nobody missed her or anything?" Diego said with a shrug.

"You think anyone would miss that old cunt?" Jorge said and swung a hand in the air. "Did Michael not tell you about her? Trust me, no one will miss this woman."

"He barely talks about it," Diego replied, his voice automatically losing some of its original vigor. "I think he has PTSD."

"He's a fucking cop and you're trying to tell me, he got PTSD from shooting an old lady?" Jorge asked with a raised eyebrow. "This is the same man who *insisted* on shooting her, using every bullet from his gun and you're telling me, now he's having emotional issues about it?"

"He's a very sensitive man," Diego replied and Jorge rolled his eyes. "You can't tell by how he acts but he is. He's like me."

"Oh yes, Diego, you are so sensitive about killing people," Jorge spoke sarcastically. "Are you fucking with me?"

"I am sensitive!" Diego replied and sat up straighter. "I have my demons, like everyone else. Not everyone's a sociopath like you."

Jorge merely answered with a warning look.

"Remember that Urban guy who was going to torture and kill Paige? The one we got...." Diego trailed off and glanced around. "Clara? Has she been in?"

Chase nodded.

"I had nightmares after that," Diego quickly continued and lurched forward with his bulging eyes. "You, you probably went home and took a nap, didn't think twice about it but I had nightmares."

Jorge processed his information but merely shrugged. "I guess, me, I'm a bit desensitized."

"A bit? You think?" Diego shot back. "Really?"

"Ok, so he's not going to talk, right?" Chase cut in and stared at Diego, who immediately calmed down. "He's not feeling guilty….going to go to the police shrink? Nothing like that?"

"No, are you kidding, he'd never do that," Diego insisted with a shrug. "They don't see that part of him at work but I do."

"Diego, find a creative way to take his mind off of things and let's move on to another topic," Jorge replied as he took a deep breath. "So the old lady wasn't reported, your boyfriend is having nightmares or some shit like that, what else? What have I missed since my mother's ordeal took over my fucking life?"

"Makerson is back investigating everything," Diego replied. "He's still talking in editorials about the bomb threat and the lack of police information. He's implying a cover-up."

"There obviously is," Jorge said and shrugged. "He's good?"

"Fine."

"I might have another story for him soon," Jorge thought out loud but didn't elaborate. "I gotta talk to that Andrew kid later to see if he's learned anything new. It seems Harley is keeping pretty tight-lipped these days."

"The dead old lady, that might shake things up," Diego reminded him. "What if they retaliate?"

"They got nothing on me," Jorge insisted.

"The election is coming fast," Chase said as he grabbed a nearby calendar. "Less than 10 days. You have a plan to make sure Harley doesn't win? People are saying Athas isn't experienced enough, they think he's kinda soft…"

"He is but I got a plan to get Harley out of the picture?"

"Can I come this time?" Diego immediately jumped in. "I don't think Michael can handle another traumatic experience this soon."

"The guy's a cop," Jorge reminded him. "You're trying to tell me that he never shot anyone before? Come on! They can walk away with a clean slate for that kind of thing so why the hell hasn't he?"

"He's a *black* cop," Chase commented and raised an eyebrow.

"Yeah, this is true," Jorge nodded. "There may be some questions if he did."

"He gets in enough trouble without killing," Diego continued. "He's hardly handling these people with kid gloves when he arrests them. There's no way he would get away with shooting someone. Plus, that's not his nature."

"It was his fucking nature the other night when he shot that racist bitch repeatedly," Jorge pointed out. "Never underestimate anyone. We're all animals just waiting for a chance to escape our cages."

No one could disagree.

CHAPTER

44

….was discovered this morning when her son, Don Stumples entered her residence after not being able to reach her for a couple of days…

Jorge grinned over his coffee and sent a quick text to Diego. He kept it short and sweet.

Amigo, it's a beautiful morning!

A laughing emoticon popped up on Jorge's screen, causing him to snicker.

Not for everyone, amigo.

Placing his phone on the table, Jorge shared a look with his daughter.

"So, *Princesa,* how is school? Now that you are back in drama, you must be happy?" He asked as Paige sat down with a piece of toast layered in butter. "*Mi amor,* the butter, it is not good for your heart."

"She's stress eating since *mi abuela* moved downstairs," Maria commented, her eyes grew in size as she talked. "*Papa,* she is a terrible woman."

"She is your grandmother, you must respect her," Jorge said even though his stomach tightened with each word. Reaching for his coffee, he took a drink. "We are looking for other living arrangements, Maria, believe me, it will be fine."

"I'm glad she stays down there," Maria spoke dramatically, swinging her hands in the air. "I do not like her. Yesterday, she told me that I was speaking about something inappropriate and lectured me on being a proper lady. Who the hell does she think she is?"

"Ok, Maria," Jorge said while raising his hand in the air. "I do understand that this here is uncomfortable for us all but we must do the right thing. I have Diego on the job. He will find her another place and that will be that."

Maria shrugged.

"Back to what I asked you," He continued while glancing at Paige eating her toast. "School, it is good?"

"Yes, *Papa,* I am doing very well."

"*Perfecto,*" Jorge replied and leaned forward to give her a quick kiss.

His phone vibrated and he picked it up.

"I must go," He said while pushing his chair out. "Paige, maybe we will meet later today?"

She nodded but remained silent. He leaned forward and gave her a kiss, hesitating for a moment to look in her eyes. There was something wrong but he would ask later about it later since Maria was at the table.

Jorge felt some reluctance leaving but had a meeting with Andrew. Hopefully, that meant he had some new information about Fulton Harley. It was time to make a move on him. The election was days away and there was simply no guarantee he wouldn't win the district despite everything Alec had done to increase his popularity. It was strange how people believed empty promises and lack of ethics over sincerity. This observation should've disturbed him and yet, he carefully tucked it away to a place in the back of his mind. Another time, another day, this information could wait.

As usual, Andrew was shoveling food in his face when Jorge arrived. Ordering just a coffee, he shook his head as he looked at the scrawny kid across from him.

"You're going to fucking die if you keep eating like an animal, you do know this, right?"

Before he could reply, the waitress returned with his coffee. After leaning in and brushing her breast against him, she rushed away. Jorge glanced at her and grinned.

"She wants to fuck you bad, man," Andrew said as his eyes bulged out. "You totally should."

"I'm married."

"Obviously, you don't tell your wife."

"Obviously, if I wanted to stick my dick into anything that moved, I wouldn't be married."

"I thought you mob guys had women on the side?" Andrew asked as he shoved another forkful of food in his mouth.

"You there, you watch too much television," Jorge said as he poured cream into his coffee. "I'm not the fucking mob and I don't cheat on my wife. That waitress, what she did, was to get a better tip."

"Really?" Andrew seemed genuinely surprised. "Seriously?"

"I guarantee it," Jorge replied.

"She didn't do that to me though," Andrew attempted to prove his theory. "If that were the case, she'd done it to me too."

"You're dressed like a fucking bum," Jorge nodded toward him. "An old, jean jacket, t-shirt, you don't get tits brushing up against you wearing that."

Andrew glanced down at his clothes.

"I'm wearing a very expensive suit," Jorge continued. "Women, they can smell money."

"God," Andrew said in disgust. "I wish I had more money."

Jorge laughed and glanced at his phone.

"That's actually why I'm meeting you, I was wondering when you're going to get my money?" Andrew suddenly looked crestfallen. "Fulton's tightening the purse strings cause he's mad at me lately."

"Oh yeah, how come?" Jorge asked as he took a sip of his coffee.

"I won't do his shit for him anymore."

"Like?"

"Like he wanted me to break in Athas office," Andrew replied sadly. "Then I get caught, get arrested."

"Or even worse," Jorge added. "You gotta deal with me."

"You know I helped you put the cameras in his office," Andrew reminded him. "Now I need your help because he's being a dickass."

"Well, as it turns out, this is beautiful timing," Jorge replied. "I got a meeting shortly with the person taking care of it. She will make sure you get your fucking money."

"Wait...I thought you were taking care of this personally," Andrew said with concern in his eyes. "Who's *she*?"

"Remember the lady who kicked you..."

"Oh fuck! Her?" Andrew asked with fear in his eyes. "She was crazy."

"Me and her are going to pay Harley a visit, maybe even today," Jorge said thoughtfully, glancing at his phone again. "We got a few things we want to talk to him about and believe me, you're on the list. You're going to get your money if I have to squeeze it out of his fucking veins."

"He's going to kill me."

"Do you want your fucking money?" Jorge asked with a shrug.

"Yes, of course, but when he finds out I went to you for help…"

"I assure you, he won't fuck with you," Jorge replied and waited for a moment. "He gives you your money, you do whatever the fuck you want. But do it right. Don't piss it away on stupid things like partying or giving tips to girls who shove their tits in your face, you know?"

Andrew glanced toward the waitress as she walked by and smiled at Jorge.

"Do something fucking useful," Jorge continued. "I don't care what but don't be stupid. That's all I'm saying. I may not have made my money in the most moral way but you know what? I'm not stupid with it either."

Andrew nodded. "I want to get my life together."

"Then do it," Jorge eased toward the edge of his seat. "I will let you know when I know but don't worry about your uncle. He's going to sign your money over and then he's going to slink away if he knows what's good for him."

Andrew gave him a sincere smile as Jorge rose from his chair and tossed some cash on the table. "Enjoy your breakfast. I left enough so maybe you get a tit brushed up against you too."

Andrew was laughing as Jorge walked away. Outside, the words 'Indian summer' flowed through his mind as he rushed to his SUV. Glancing across the street at a jewelry store, he thought of his wife. Grabbing his phone, he texted Diego.

I need help finding Paige an anniversary gift. Can you help sometime?
Yes!!!

Jorge grinned as he got into his SUV and pulled onto the street.

As he drove to the warehouse to see Jolene, he thought about Paige. Something was wrong and it made him nervous. Had his mother said or done something that she was hesitant to share? Although his mother had only been a guest for a few days, already her negativity weighed down his family. While Maria was defiant toward her grandmother, Paige simply avoided her.

Arriving at the warehouse, he quickly jumped out of his SUV and headed toward the door. Using his pass card, he slipped inside and down the long hallway to find Jolene in her office, squinting over her laptop.

"Ah! I see Diego isn't the only one who needs glasses," He commented abruptly while closing the door behind him.

Appearing startled at first, she closed the laptop and moved it aside. "Do not tell! He will never let me hear the end."

"I won't say a word," Jorge said with a shrug. "So, you and me are going to visit Harley."

"Right now?" Jolene raised an eyebrow.

"You got something else to do this morning?"

"Should we go when his office is full of people?"

"I got it on good authority that they are out running his errands while he sits in the office looking at porn."

"What?" Jolene's mouth fell open. "You tease me, right? He is not really doing this?"

"I got Andrew to put in some cameras one night," Jorge grinned. "The entire office is empty after a morning meeting. I also got Marco to hack his computer. For a white supremacist, he sure got a thing for big black women and Latinas cause he watches a hell of a lot of porn with both."

"Hey, I am not…" Jolene started with defiance.

"Hey hey, I am not suggesting that," Jorge said and began to laugh. "No, we will do what we talked about already. But the fact that he gets aroused by such women might help when you come walking in the door." He raised an eyebrow. "Come on Jolene, you know how to make this work. I don't gotta tell you that we both can threaten him but you got something that I don't got."

Jolene smiled and nodded. "This is true. Men, you are so easy at times."

"*Perfecto*, you know what to do," Jorge continued as he moved to the edge of his chair and tapped on his phone before handing it to Jolene. "This is their outside office now. You can see its empty and he's with his wife in his office…and in walks this stunning Latino lady, like the ones he likes to watch on his computer. You immediately will have him off guard. You women, you got a power that is worth a hundred bullets."

"How come me, not Paige?" She quietly asked. "Cause this man, he is into Latinas?"

"Because you asked for another chance," Jorge spoke bluntly. "You got it. This is your one and only chance, Jolene. So you gotta get him to step down and you gotta get this Andrew guy his money. If you can do that and possibly entertain me in the process, you have secured your original position with our little family."

"And you will trust me again?"

"As much as I trust anyone."

"You will forgive, everything…."

"It is the past Jolene and although you did do some stupid things," Jorge considered for a moment. "You also paid in more ways than one."

She looked away for a moment, attempting to hide the sorrow in her eyes before nodding. "I have paid dearly."

"It is your time, Jolene," Jorge continued. "Not many people get a second chance with me, this you know. It almost never happens so you must take Fulton Harley on with everything you have; every bit of anger, every bit of pain. I want you to take this man on as if he is the cause of your misery. I know you can, Jolene. But you must be strong. The strongest you have ever been in your life."

"I will," She replied in a small voice. "I will do right by you."

"Then," Jorge glanced at his phone. "Let's go."

CHAPTER

45

If there was one thing that Jolene Silva didn't do it was fade into the background. When the beautiful, Colombian strutted into Fulton Harley's office, she did so with an obnoxious confidence that could've been modeled after Jorge Hernandez himself. Her heels clicked loudly against the floor, immediately alerting the pathetic, middle-aged man in his private office, where he sat in front of his desk facing a white woman. Their discussion immediately halted upon seeing the Latina walk through the otherwise, empty room, boldly entering the small office with Jorge Hernandez sauntering along behind her.

For all the attempts Fulton Harley had previously made against Jorge, his businesses and Alec Athas, he looked as if he didn't even recognize the Mexican man when he entered the room. Exchanging confused looks with his wife, he remained silent as Jorge stood back and watched as Jolene took over.

"We must talk," She spoke slowly with repressed fury gripping at her voice. "She, this lady, she can go."

The white woman looked pissed off by Jolene's demands and sat a little taller as tension-filled her face.

Fulton Harley opened his mouth as if he wasn't sure whether to laugh or speak, which apparently infuriated Jolene because her demand became louder.

"Does this lady, here, does she not speak *English*?" Jolene snapped. "I tell her to leave so I can speak to you, so why she still here?"

"I'm sorry but you can't come in demanding my wife leave," Fulton spoke sheepishly as he glanced at Jorge Hernandez and back at Jolene. "If you and your husband would like to make an appointment…"

"He is *not* my husband," Jolene cut him off and leaned toward Harley. "He is my business associate now tell your fucking wife to leave because we must speak."

"Hey now," Fulton said and began to laugh. "You got to calm down ma'am. I'm sure that whatever is wrong, we can resolve. How about we discuss this once the election is over since I will have more power then, but today, we're busy. The campaign is well underway and we have some important matters to discuss."

Jorge continued to stand back in silence. This *was* Jolene's circus and these *were* her monkeys, so it was up to her to put them in line. Her tactics were somewhat predictable and bordered on soft, so it was obvious why she wasn't being taken seriously. Fulton clearly viewed her as a hysterical woman and no real threat, while his wife was probably concerned with him speaking to a curvy Colombian that resembled the women in his favorite porn. Still, it was intriguing to watch it all play out.

"I am here now," Jolene insisted with fire in her eyes. "We will talk now."

Fulton scratched his face while continuing to grin, he raised an eyebrow and finally nodded toward his wife. "It's okay, Susan, I got this. I will meet up with you later."

After shooting Jolene a glare, Fulton Harley's wife stood up, grabbed her purse and walked toward the door. Her eyes observed Jorge with interest but she didn't speak as she left the office, slamming the door behind her.

"Now, you got my full attention," Harley grinned with a condescending look in his eyes as Jolene continued to stand over him with fury in her eyes. "What can I help you with today, Miss…"

"My name is not important," Jolene continued to stumble for footing in this conversation. "We are not here to makes friends."

"Oh, I see," Fulton said with a lingering smirk which he attempted to hide but the humor continued to shine in his eyes. "And so, your associate, does he also not wish to reveal his name?"

"Oh, quite the contrary," Jorge spoke up with an abruptness that seemed to send a bolt of lightning through Harley. "I think our introduction is, in fact, long overdue."

Jolene crossed her arms over her breasts. Her eyes narrowed on Fulton as Jorge walked a few steps closer.

"I am Jorge Hernandez. I think you might have heard of me."

Although he spoke in a much gentler tone than Jolene, it was clear that his words had an intense effect on the man who had targeted Jorge both directly and indirectly for months. In fact, Fulton Harley seemed to shrink in his chair and where his eyes had been full of glib interest and amusement, they faded as if he were a scolded child. While this didn't surprise Jorge, he played the role of intimidator for many years, it was clear that Jolene was struggling with the fact that her own presence was barely an afterthought in comparison.

Fulton cringed as if suddenly realizing that Jolene Silva wasn't just an emotional, high-strung beauty that wandered into his office but perhaps a dangerous adversary. He attempted to jump out of the chair, only to have Jolene shove him back down.

"You, you do not move!" Her voice grew in strength and continued to do so with each word as she moved closer to Harley. "I am here to talk to you and you, are going to listen."

"Kind of makes you wish you had listened to her in the beginning, don't it?" Jorge grabbed a chair and pulled it away from them both and sat down. Making himself comfortable, he leaned on the side and watched with interest. "She ain't fucking around Harley."

"What are....what's going on here?" Fulton Harley began to stutter as his confidence drained away. "What do you want?"

"Ah! See, we have a few....I would not call them wants, so much as demands," Jorge replied with a shrug and took a deep breath. "However, I will allow my associate to take it from here. I'm just here for the show."

Fulton's second attempt to spring from the chair was a clear sign of his fear. Again, it was to no avail. Jolene was quick, like a wildcat watching its prey, she used even more force to shove Harley back into the chair for the second time.

"I tell you to sit!" She became louder, her voice booming through the room. "And you listen!"

She hissed these last words like a wild snake that was about to bite its victim and Jorge couldn't help but grin. She sat in the seat facing the pathetic politician, grabbing the arms on both sides of his chair, trapping him, Jolene leaned forward in an intimidating manner.

"You are going to do two things for me," She instructed with a confidence that made a brazen return. "The first is you will call your lawyer and release your nephew, Andrew's inheritance. You will not give him any trouble. You will not speak to him. You will look the other way."

"The kid is an idiot, he'll piss all the money away," Fulton attempted to explain but she quickly cut him off.

"This is not your problem," Jolene snapped back and continued. "The second thing you will do is remove yourself from this election."

"What?" Fulton Harley said with a nervous laugh. "You want me to step down? The election is days away and you want me to walk away? Are you kidding me?"

"Do I, do I look like I am joking?" Jolene countered as she moved in closer and although she was attempting to intimidate, it was probably turning on the middle-aged man since she practically had her breasts in his face. "I tell you to quit and I mean it."

"Why would I do that?" Fulton shook his head. "You can't just walk in here and tell me to release my nephew's money, quit the election just because of.....what...." He turned his attention toward Jorge. "Because your boss, this supposedly tough Mexican narco needs a *woman* to do his dirty work."

Jorge knew Fulton Harley was attempting to provoke him. The implications and disregard for the woman in front of him might've seemed clever as the words smoothly slipped from his lips. However, by the time he recognized his mistake, it was too late. The sudden realization appeared to hit him when Jolene pulled a gun from her purse and pointed it at him.

"My English, it is not so good," Jolene calmly replied as her eyes continued to blaze. "I hope I misunderstood what you say."

Fulton Harley froze at the sight of the gun pointed at him. Jolene pushed her chair back and continued to watch him with interest.

"From here, it sounded like he was suggesting that I was a pussy because I had a woman helping me out," Jorge calmly replied with a shrug. "I assume that is because he sees you as weak."

Jolene's normally beautiful face quickly tightened up, her eyes darted toward the man and for a split second, Jorge was certain he saw a resemblance to Diego cross her face as she jumped up from the chair and backhanded Fulton Harley with such a powerful force that an involuntary whimper came from the back of his throat.

"I am weak, am I?" Jolene shot back as the man reached for his face as Jolene pointed the gun directly at his head. "How would your pretty little wife feel if she came back here to find your brains splattered all over the wall behind you? Hmm? Do you think that a *weak* person does such things? And the blood, it would be *everywhere*."

"No..I..." He began to stutter and Jolene quickly cut him off.

"You seem to have a lot to say," Jolene stalled for a moment before continuing. "But I am from Colombia. In my country, respect means something and disrespect, sometimes, it means even more. You cannot say many more offensive things to me if you do not have a tongue."

"It is not a pleasant way to go," Jorge offered in a manner that suggested he was being helpful while he continued to grin. "But the Colombians, they have their ideas. See in Mexico, we cut off your whole fucking head."

Leaning against his hand, Jorge's eyes widened in excitement as he watched Fulton Harley struggle to keep it together. It was rewarding to see the weasel suffer especially at the hands of a woman.

"No, please....if you do this, my wife, she knows you're here," Fulton attempted to throw some logic on the situation. "She...she will tell the police."

"Actually, we got someone who has diverted her attention outside," Jorge offered with a sniff. "She won't be calling anyone."

Fear encompassed Fulton Harley's face as he glanced from Jolene to Jorge and back again.

"How do I know that you won't kill me anyway?" He finally asked.

"Because we would have already," Jorge offered. "Last time I checked, a dead man cannot run in an election. Also, I believe that if you are to die, Andrew would automatically get all his money."

"So, it better to kill him," Jolene spoke abruptly as she focused on her victim with more intensity. "This is good. Let us just do that."

"No!" Fulton started to shake his head. "No, please, I will do whatever you want."

"You will call and release Andrew, his money for him, no?" Jolene asked and made a face.

"Yes, I will do it now!" Fulton swung a hand in the air as he began to gasp for air but rather than faint, he began to cry. "Please! This isn't worth it! He can have his fucking money and party it away, I don't care"

"And the election?"

"I will drop out!" Fulton rushed to reply. "Just don't kill me or my wife!"

"Of course, he is a good politician," Jorge offered with a shrug. "That is how democracy works, is this right? Two out of three people in the room want him to quit."

"It is good, no?" Jolene said with a raised eyebrow. "We all are in agreement, then?"

"Whatever you want," Fulton replied as he continued to cry. "Just please, don't kill me. Don't kill my wife. We have a family. We have kids. Please!"

"Canada, I love this country," Jorge commented as he stood up from his chair. "The people, they are always so accommodating."

A grin spread across Jolene's face as she continued to fixate her gaze on Fulton Harley, glancing briefly at Jorge. "And the devil, he will laugh."

CHAPTER

46

…..in a surprising announcement today, Fulton Harley of district….

"Just like that," Paige quietly commented as they both watched the news through an app on his phone. "He's done. He's completely out of the picture."

"Just like that, *mi amor*, just like that," Jorge repeated as he stopped the video feed and placed his phone on the nightstand. "It was easier than expected. We didn't even have his wife. But he fell for it and did everything we asked."

"I wonder if he would've beat Alec?" Paige suggested as she snuggled up closer to him.

"I do not know," Jorge confessed as he looked into her eyes. "Elections are funny. You may think for certain they will go one way and they instead go the other. Polls aren't always accurate and if you ask me, sometimes these are fixed. However, with Harley out of the picture, it seems unlikely that Athas has any real competition."

"They will most likely replace him," Paige reminded him.

"But with who?" Jorge asked as he pulled his wife closer and kissed her on the forehead. "They already have their best players on the field. It does seem unlikely they will pull someone from the ashes at this point. Let the fuckers spin."

"Alec will make a speech in the morning," Paige spoke quietly. "Since Harley stated it was family issues taking him away, he will wish him well with his upcoming challenges and pretend that he enjoyed going up against him in this election."

"Ah! Yes, of course," Jorge said with a grin. "It has been one exciting adventure for us all, hasn't it?"

Paige laughed but didn't reply.

"So Athas, he got this one," Jorge continued. "He has quickly become one of the most prominent members in this election. Him warning the authorities about one potential threat while managing to avoid his own, this has put him on the political map of the country. Ironically, our enemies have managed to help make Athas a star. He's been on the national news a few times. Now, if the party is voted in, this means he is almost assured a Minister position. This is good for us. The higher up he is the more powerful."

"It's really going to happen," Paige spoke with some emotion in her voice. "The work we have done will pay off. His party is in the lead and in part, probably because of him."

"You sound surprised by this," Jorge said before leaning in to kiss the top of her head again. "Did you not think we could do it?"

"It felt dicey," Paige replied. "At times, I wasn't so sure."

"Ah! But you must have faith that in the end," Jorge said as his lips moved closer to her ear. "We always win."

Paige didn't reply but simply gave him a look that said it all. Although their night was beautiful, full of pleasure and love, he felt his original concerns reignited the following morning as he watched his wife rushing about the room. There was something in her face, her eyes that suggested that she was anxious, concerned and yet, why wasn't she telling him these fears? It was unlike Paige to hide anything from him. Was it his mother causing these strained emotions?

"So, *mi amor*," Jorge slowly began to speak as he got out of bed. Still naked from the night before, he started toward the bathroom, grabbing his robe on the way. "How are things with *Mama*? Is she giving you any issues? Please tell me if she is."

"What? Ah, no, I actually didn't even see her yesterday," Paige spoke hurriedly as she pulled clothes out of the closet. "I was out until I picked up Maria from school. I guess I should've checked in on her?"

"No no," Jorge commented as he reached the bathroom. "This is not for you to worry about. I was concerned she might be upsetting you again."

"No," Paige replied a bit too quickly. "I'm fine."

But she wasn't fine. Jorge was certain of this fact. He knew his wife. She had been on edge for the last few days, if not weeks. Perhaps it was Athas. The man was much like a child in his naïvety. For an adult man, he needed a lot of hand-holding and though this made him easier to control, his lack of confidence had drawbacks. Of course, in fairness, there had been many dragons to slay in their short time together. Although Paige thrived on the adventure as he did, Jorge also recognized that sometimes one needed a break from being on constant high-alert.

They would go on vacation to celebrate their anniversary! They both needed time away from the insanity. She was tired and really, wasn't he too? It was during those quiet moments when he stopped to look back at the previous year that he recognized everything that had taken place. Their lives were anything but boring.

After Paige left to take Maria to school followed by a day of dealing with Athas, Jorge poured himself a second cup of coffee and looked up vacation destinations online. A knock on his door interrupted him. It was his mother coming from the basement.

"*Buenos dias*," She said as she walked up the last two steps to Jorge's portion of the house. "I need a drive to the grocery store."

"Fine," Jorge replied and quickly turned off his laptop. "I have a meeting so I will drop you off on my way."

"And how will I get home?" She asked defiantly. "Do you wish for me to walk?"

"I can pick you up" Jorge offered with no emotion in his voice.

"I do not want to stay here," She spoke defiantly. "I want to return to Mexico."

"*Mama,* it is not safe."

"I will move in with my sister."

"That won't be safe either."

"Jorge, it is better this way," She insisted. "The kidnappers, they have your money. It is finished."

He didn't reply as he took his cup to the sink and rinsed it out.

"*Mama,* have you spoke to Paige since arriving?"

"No, she is never here," His mother replied. "Gone all day, the three of you, do you not spend time together as a family?"

"It is a busy time, *Mama,*" Jorge replied as he walked back across the room and grabbed his laptop and keys. "We do the best we can."

"In Canada, everything, it is rushing," She pointed out as they headed toward his door. "Always rushing. I can see this right away."

"That's life in general," He replied as he joined her at the door and they both headed outside. "We are all busy."

"Not I," she replied as they walked to the SUV. "This is why I must go back to Mexico to stay with my sister. We do many things every day but here, I do nothing. My own granddaughter does not want to see me."

"*Mama*, this is because of you," Jorge commented as they both climbed into the SUV. "You cannot speak to my family with no respect and expect them to, in turn, respect you."

"I speak honestly," She insisted as she fastened her seatbelt. "Your wife, she does not look after her family. That is her role."

"This here is old-fashioned," Jorge quickly pointed out. "Women are independent. This is what I like."

"But too independent is not good," His mother insisted as they drove down his street. "When people get a taste of independence, they push the boundaries again and again until they do not want their families anymore. They want their freedom."

"*Mama*, this is not true," Jorge explained as he felt his stomach tighten. "You have made many negative and unfair assumptions about my wife. She loves me and Maria very much, that is all I wish for."

"If she loves you both so much, why is she never home," His mother pushed a little harder and Jorge felt his anger increase. "Where is she all day?"

"She's helping a politician that is in our election next week," Jorge replied with an edge in his voice. "This is something we both agreed would be a good idea."

"Oh, I *see*," She replied and fell silent.

Although Jorge caught her insinuation, he refused to comment. This was her game and he wasn't willing to play.

When they arrived at the grocery store, Jorge dropped her off with some cash and told her the time he would return to pick her up. He pointed out that this gave her an opportunity to not only look around but to also have a snack, a cup of coffee, whatever she wished. Not that she appreciated this gesture.

Driving away, he wanted to scream. The doubts she had planted in his mind were to create a wedge between him and Paige. What kind of mother did such a thing to their child? She was poison.

Although it hadn't been his intention, it was within minutes of meeting Diego at a nearby restaurant that Jorge poured out the entire story. Knowing that he was close to Paige, it only made sense that his friend would have some words of reassurance for him. Instead, he appeared surprised by these comments.

"Well, first," Diego insisted as he leaned forward on the table. "I can guarantee that there's nothing going on with Athas or anyone else if that's what your mother is suggesting. She hasn't talked to me about anything being wrong either."

"It's probably nothing," Jorge attempted to shrug it off although he did feel some relief from Diego's comments. "I worry over nothing."

"Your mother, she is trouble," Diego quickly pointed out. "Send her back to Mexico."

"But *amigo*, that could be dangerous," Jorge attempted to reason even though, he had considered the same thing himself. "What if the kidnappers return?"

"You know what," Diego replied while making a face, just as the waitress approached them. "Let's cross that bridge when we come to it."

After both ordered coffee and a simple breakfast, Jorge finally replied. "Diego, I think you're right. Perhaps I had assumed that since I did so much for her that our relationship could be strong but it is not possible. This is something I must face."

"Trust me," Diego said as he quickly checked his phone and set it aside. "This is something I know. I have also attempted to reconnect with my *Mama* but as you know this did not work out for me either. So, I do understand why you wish to do so but sometimes, it is not possible."

Jorge nodded.

"Put her on a plane and wish for the best," Diego suggested. "That is what I say."

The waitress returned with their coffee. After thanking her, Diego watched him, as if to see what he would say next.

"That is what I must do," Jorge agreed. "Perhaps after that, I will see a difference with Paige. Maybe having her mother-in-law in the same house is too much."

"Would you want her mother living in your basement?"

"Yes, well, this is a good point too," Jorge replied. "I have so far only met her sister and that was a disaster."

"Oh! Paige told me," Diego leaned forward again before reaching for the cream for his coffee. "You gotta do what you gotta do."

"So, Jolene," Jorge decided to change the topic. "She was impressive yesterday."

"Clearly, if Harley stepped down," Diego's eyes grew in size. "Perhaps, there is hope for her yet."

"Perhaps," Jorge commented as he reached for the other cream container. "I was not sure but she got the job done. Harley has slunk away, no problem. This is good."

"So, she's won back your trust?" Diego asked as he lifted the cup to his lips.

"As much as she ever could," Jorge muttered. "It was good. Everything was sorted out. The election takes place next week and perhaps all will calm"

"And we got all the pot shops in the Atlantic region, Quebec is almost done and Ontario, it was tough but it's taken over too."

"Now the west," Jorge commented.

"But now that we own the east," Diego pointed out. "The west, they will be easier. By next year this country, it will be ours."

"*Perfecto.*" Jorge replied. "I'm already thinking of having a huge pot festival in Toronto next year. We will pick a time and plan it. Bands, food….lots of weed. It will be fun, everyone will want to come and eventually, this will be across the country."

"Jorge Hernandez, you never stop thinking," Diego said with a smug grin on his face.

"This has been my life," Jorge reminded him. "The power, it is an addiction."

"So after you have it all when you take over the Canadian pot industry and get more power in politics," Diego asked as he swung his arms in the air. "What is next?

Jorge gave him a smooth grin and his eyes narrowed.

"My friend, I'm just starting," He replied. "One must always have a huge, monstrous goal in site. This is what I live for, *mi amigo.* This here is just the beginning. I will not stop until I die."

CHAPTER

47

"**W**hat do you mean you can't find her?" Paige sounded confused on the other end of the line. Jorge paced outside the grocery store where he dropped off his mother over an hour earlier. Watching the crowd rushing by, his brain scanned through the possible explanations but came up with nothing.

"I do not know. *Ella desapareció.*"

"She *disappeared?*" Paige repeated with some frustration in her voice. "Well, where would she go? I don't understand. Were you late getting back?"

"No, in fact, I was early," Jorge explained. "I had the lady page her through the store but she did not show."

"And you looked around?"

"I looked around."

"Did you ask if there were any medical emergencies?"

"Yes, I ask everything," Jorge replied. "The lady at the store, she did not seem concerned but she paged her a couple of times. I do not know."

"Maybe she got a cab and went home?" Paige suggested. "It's the only thing that makes sense."

"I suppose."

"She doesn't want a cell phone," Paige stated. "There isn't a phone in her apartment. We might have to look into that."

"Yes, if we find her."

"We *will* find her," Paige agreed. "Do you want me to...I don't know... check with hospitals or go check the house?"

"No, *mi amor*, I think I will go back to the house now," Jorge replied. "I've been through this store a few times but it is so huge that it would be easy to miss someone. What if someone…"

"Let's not assume the worst yet," Paige immediately cut him off. "Chances are good that she's fine and there's a reasonable explanation. I mean, if she just took off, it would be very inconsiderate of her."

"There are other businesses nearby but I cannot see her wandering," Jorge commented. "I will go home and look."

"I will be home soon," Paige insisted. "I'm helping Alec now but it's nothing urgent."

"If you wish, *mi amor*," Jorge shook his head. "I am not sure what to do."

"Maybe call Marco, see if he can find anything," Paige suggested. "Maybe she went to the airport? She kept talking about returning to Mexico."

"Yes, this is true."

Immediately after ending the call, he phoned Marco and repeated the entire story.

"Perhaps she decided to go to another store?" Marco suggested. "That store you have mentioned, it is quite large, perhaps it was overwhelming."

"I cannot see this," Jorge said after some consideration. "She is too nervous. I will go home and see if she is there."

"Very good sir," Marco replied. "And I will check flights leaving Toronto."

Jorge ended the call and headed for his SUV. While a part of him was angry, assuming she took off with no consideration, another part of him feared the worst; what if she had been kidnapped again? It seemed unlikely in the middle of a crowded grocery store in Canada. It's not as if she would go quietly.

Back at home, he rushed inside and to the downstairs apartment.

"*Mama? ¿Estás aquí?*"

There was no answer. His heart began to race. Going through each room, he reached for his gun. Moving quietly, slowly, his eyes attempting to find proof, any sign that she had returned or perhaps that anyone else had been in the apartment. His movements were careful until he had inspected everything and yet, he found nothing.

Sitting down on the bed, he placed the gun beside him and reached for his phone to text Paige.

She's not in the apartment.

Any sign she returned?

No.

Is her passport there?

She probably kept it in her purse. Why you think she leave?

Maybe?

No, she would make a dramatic production if she did.

His phone rang. It was Maria. She rarely called from school. His heart raced.

"Maria!" He quickly answered. "Are you not at school?"

"Yes," She replied. "Father, we have been removed from the school for a fire alarm."

Even as she said it, he could hear the roaring in the background. Other students must've been around for her to call him 'father', she usually only did so in attempts to fit in.

"Ah, I see, are you ok?" He couldn't help but ask.

"Of course," She quickly answered. "I am a strong, independent woman."

"Yes," Jorge said with a grin on his face. "It is just that you never call from school."

"Did *mi abuela* leave yet?" She replied.

"What?" Jorge asked in stunned disbelief but immediately grew annoyed. "Did she tell you she was leaving?"

"She said, yes, she was," Maria replied. "She called me."

"Today?"

"Yes, she left a message on my phone," She replied. "But she does not have a phone, so I didn't know if you were taking her to the airport."

Jorge decided it was best to be upfront with his daughter.

"Maria, I do not know what you're talking about," Jorge spoke quietly into the phone. "I dropped your grandmother off at the grocery store this morning. She told me she wanted to purchase some things and I could pick her up later. I went back and couldn't find her. I am now at the house, I thought maybe she found her way home."

"Maybe, *Papa*, she was leaving town and didn't want to say goodbye," Maria replied in a very adult-like voice. "I do not know. Her message was brief. I wonder where she called from because it was an unfamiliar number."

"Maria, do not erase that message," Jorge immediately demanded.

"I won't," Maria replied. "But we are going back to the school now so I must hang up."

"*Gracias*, Maria, I think this information will be helpful."

"Ok. Kisses!"

He wasted no time calling Paige. After explaining the situation, there was a pause on the other end of the line.

"Is her luggage gone?" She asked.

Glancing around the bedroom, Jorge spotted her suitcase.

"No."

"This doesn't make sense," Paige continued and sighed loudly. "Maybe she's playing a fucked up game."

"*Mi amor*, I do not know," Jorge confessed. "I do not understand. She is not one to take off like this, you know?"

"But do you know?" Paige asked. "She was talking about going back to Mexico however, it seems unusual she wouldn't take her stuff."

"What if…" He didn't finish the sentence.

"But what are the chances they would know to come here or the grocery store?" Paige reminded him. "Too crowded. Too many people. I don't know. This isn't making sense. I'm on my way home now."

"Ok, *mi amor*, I will see you soon."

Jorge continued to look around the apartment but found nothing. His mother wasn't on the Internet, she didn't have a cell phone so it seemed unlikely that she contacted anyone in Mexico. It wasn't that he had held any of that back from her but simply that she had no interest.

However, she had called Maria so maybe she had also called her sister in Mexico.

Finding her number in his phone, Jorge quickly called it. Glancing at the clock, he realized it would still be relatively early in Mexico but his aunt would be awake.

"*Hola*."

"*Es Jorge. ¿Sabes dónde está mi madre?*"

"Jorge?" She spoke sternly. "*Tu madre desapareció hace días. Escuché que fue secuestrada.*"

Of course, no one had been in contact with his aunt for days, so she wasn't aware that his mother was safe. With some regret for not reaching out sooner, Jorge attempted to explain the situation, even though his aunt cut in many times with comments and questions. After a lot of back and forth, he finally learned the information he had sought in the first place;

she knew nothing about his mother returning to Mexico. In fact, she hadn't heard from her since before the kidnapping.

After chastising him for not letting 'his people' in Mexico know what was going on, he hung up with no new information. He bit his tongue many times during their conversation, wishing to tell her that he paid a substantial amount of money to protect his mother's life with no thanks in return. His aunt had his number and for all her claimed concerned, she never once called him to check.

Standing up, Jorge glanced around the room one last time but could see nothing that indicated that his mother had plans to return to Mexico. Perhaps she went somewhere else? Heading upstairs, he sent a quick message to both Diego and Jesús. Maybe they would have some thoughts on where he could look.

Jesús called.

"Sir, do you think there is reason for concern?" He asked. "I've been thinking about this a lot and sir, this kidnapping felt strange. It was almost too easy to make the payment and to find your mother, unharmed."

Jesús was more familiar with kidnappings than Jorge. In fact, he was usually on the other side of kidnapping.

"Do you think this here, it was a scam?" Jorge wondered as he walked back upstairs. "Do you think she might be involved?"

"Sir, I don't like to say," Jesús spoke gently in the phone. "But it is a possibility."

Jorge didn't reply.

"I say possibility but that does not mean I am right."

"Is there any way you can find out?"

"I will look into it, sir."

Their call ended as Paige walked into the house. With concern in her eyes, she approached him in silence and they embraced.

"I know you're worried," She whispered.

"I am conflicted," Jorge admitted as he slowly let her go. "Jesús and I were discussing how maybe this kidnapping….it was too easy. What if it was a scam?"

"Seriously?" Paige seemed stunned by the idea. "To extort money from you?"

"I do not know," Jorge spoke honestly as they walked toward the kitchen. "But also, why call Maria?"

"I don't understand. Why would she even bother going to the grocery store? Nothing makes sense."

"No."

"Passport? It's not down there?"

"No," Jorge replied. "It would be in her purse and she had it with her."

"Maybe we should check the grocery store again?" Paige suggested. "Maybe have Diego look?"

"Good idea," Jorge commented as he reached for his phone. "Paige, I have tried to put this together and it doesn't make sense."

"I know, I don't get it," She replied. "Maybe she thought you wouldn't let her go and that's why she wouldn't tell you but why the grocery store? I don't understand."

"Unless she was involved in the kidnapping," Jorge reminded her. "She might make plans to leave town suddenly and never be found again."

Paige stared into his eyes but didn't reply.

"I know, Paige, it is…it is bad but," Jorge shook his head. "It is possible."

Texting Diego, he then sent another one to check in with Marco. Before either replied, the doorbell rang.

"Maybe that is her," Jorge commented and set his phone down on the counter.

Paige quickly nodded as he made his way toward the entrance. Pulling the door opened, he found the police on the other side.

48

Had he been a man with a conscience, the sight of the police at the door would've instigated fear; perhaps the game was over and he had lost? However, when you're Jorge Hernandez, it brings out the dragon who has no intentions of going down without a fight. He had worked too hard and for too long to get where he was in this world to have anyone fuck with it.

However this time his defenses melted away when he saw the look on the officer's face.

Forgetting momentarily of his mother, he immediately felt his heart pounding furiously when he thought of his daughter. Was it Maria? Had something happened at the school? Had the fire alarm been a farce to get her outside? A way to lure out the students and kidnap her much in the same way they had done with his mother in Mexico? What if someone had attacked the school?

There was a split second when fear made him unable to breathe until an even louder roar from deep inside rose up, screaming through his veins. Jorge slowly made eye contact with the officer and asked if he could help him.

Unfortunately, the news he was about to receive wasn't any easier.

Hours passed and he was still in stunned disbelief. Sitting on the edge of his bed, he asked Paige for some time alone. It was too much to process. She would look in once in a while with a concerned expression on her face until finally, Paige broke her silence.

"I'm going to pick up Maria," She spoke evenly as she walked toward him and gently placed her hand on his shoulder. "I'm not sure...how do you want me to do this?"

"I...I do not know, *mi amor*," Jorge shook his head as she sat beside him and reached for his hand. "I cannot understand. How do I explain it to my daughter?"

"I will do it," Paige insisted.

"No, please, I must," Jorge spoke frankly. "This is for me to do."

"You're still in shock," Paige calmly reminded him. "I can do it."

"But I'm her father..."

"It doesn't matter," Paige said as she shook her head while squeezing his hand.

"Do we tell her...everything?" He stumbled on the last word.

"It might be on the news," Paige quietly reminded him. "Makerson said she is being referred to as a Mexican tourist, no connection to you."

"Ok," Jorge replied. "So Maria will know it wasn't an accident."

Paige didn't reply but nodded and squeezed his hand.

"I feel like I'm coming back to this world," Jorge commented as he looked around. "The fog of earlier, it is going away."

Paige didn't reply. She had been by his side for every second of it. He had immediately been in denial but that only lasted a few minutes before the shock hit him hard. Jorge had broken down in a way that he had never expected to in this circumstance. His body shook in uncontrollable tremors while his heart raced and tears poured from his eyes. It had been unlike anything he ever experienced in his adult life. The last time he felt such intense sorrow was when Miguel died. Of course, his time to grieve had been ripped away with the many lashes from his father's leather belt. That thought alone had pulled him out of the land of sorrow to a bitter, dark place in between.

"It's still pretty fresh," Paige reminded him as she leaned closer and Jorge instinctively put his arm around her.

"I know, *mi amor*, it is *too* fresh," Jorge's voice caught with the words. Clearing his throat he continued, "I do not know how this could happen."

"We may never know," Paige gently replied.

"Have you told the others?" He suddenly found himself thinking like the captain of his ship once again. "Diego? Jesús?"

"Yes," Paige replied. "Also, I told Chase and Jolene."

Having no words, he simply nodded.

"I have to go to the school now," Paige said as she stood up gently letting go of his hand. "I hope it was the right decision to leave Maria there for the day."

"*Mi amor,* I am sure it was," Jorge immediately replied. "I do not think it was necessary to take her out. There is nothing she can do. It is…it is better she come home now."

"Ok," Paige replied before leaning in to kiss him gently on the lips before walking out of the room.

After Jorge heard the front door close, he mindlessly stood up and wandered downstairs and into the basement apartment. His mother had brought almost nothing with her, just some clothes and few personal items. Picking up her suitcase, he discovered an unexpected calamity when touching her possessions. Searching through the bag in hopes of finding something that gave him an explanation, instead, he found nothing. No journal, no agenda but instead leaving him even more confused. He sat on the edge of the bed and stared at her opened suitcase.

Time went by and eventually, he heard Paige and Maria return home. His body felt heavy as he climbed the stairs to find his wife and daughter in the kitchen. Suddenly frozen on the spot, he looked at Maria's smiling face and wondered how could he tell her such terrible news?

"*Papa,* what is wrong?" She immediately rushed toward him and reached out to give him a hug. Behind her, Paige shot him a compassionate look as Jorge gave his daughter a kiss on the top of the head.

"Maria, let us sit down," He suggested as she let go of him and studied his face with curiosity.

"Is something wrong with *abuela?*" She immediately asked as Jorge led her toward the couch in the living room. "Did something happen with her flight? Did she leave cause she is angry with us?"

"Maria, I have some very disturbing news to share with you," Jorge spoke honestly, as they sat down. Paige crept into the room, joining them on the couch, sitting on the other side of the child. "Your *abuela,* she has died."

Maria opened her mouth to reply but no words come out. He immediately put his arm around her.

"There was an accident….." He began than exchanged looks with Paige who shook her head. "No, I have not said this right. This is not what happened."

Paige looked down, tears forming in her eyes.

"There wasn't an accident?" Maria looked up with her big, brown eyes, as tears leaked out the corners and slid down her face. "Was it her health? A heart attack or something?"

"No," He replied honestly and thought for a moment about how to choose his words. "She went to the subway. Maria, I do not know how to tell you this but your *abuela*.... she...she jumped in front of the train."

A look of stunned disbelief filled Maria's face and for a moment, Jorge feared how she would react. Suddenly, she crumpled, falling into his arms, Maria began to cry. Paige was visibly upset too but she quickly looked away. At that moment, there was something about watching his family distressed that made him feel protective. A strength rose within him as he took a deep breath and sat up straighter. This was what his *Mama* was doing to his family. In her death, she continued to hurt people. She had a choice, a decision and rather than come back to the house or return to Mexico, she instead decided to take her own life.

"Maria, it will be ok," Jorge attempted to console his daughter, pulling her tiny body into his arms for a powerful hug, He kissed her on top of the head. "I am so sorry to have to share such disturbing news with you."

"But why?" Maria moaned as she leaned against his chest. "Why would she do this? I do not understand."

"Maria, I wish I knew what to tell you," Jorge spoke honestly as she moved away and looked into his eyes. "But I do not know either. I am as confused as you now."

"But, what if it was an accident?" Maria immediately asked. "Maybe she fell? Maybe someone ran into her and pushed her?"

"No, Maria, these are things I asked the police," Jorge responded honestly. "But they say there were a number of witnesses who watched her sit her purse on the ground and jump. One man, he rushed to grab her but it was too late. They could not help."

Maria stopped crying and looked down at her hands.

"Again, It is difficult to share this terrible news with you," Jorge confessed. "But I must be honest. If I tell you that it is anything but a suicide it would be a lie. I do not lie to you, Maria. You know this."

She nodded as she wiped her eyes.

"I don't understand why she would do this," She replied in barely a whisper.

Jorge shook his head and bit back the anger growing inside of him. How could his mother put his family through such a terrible ordeal? It suddenly infuriated him. Why should he be explaining something as dark as suicide to his daughter at her tender age of 11? It seemed he was always breaking the bad news to his Maria. What effect would this have on his little girl? Would she carry all the tragic deaths with her as he carried Miguel's for all these years? Jorge did not want that for his daughter.

"Maria," Paige suddenly spoke and cleared her throat. "We can only guess why she decided to do this...I wish we had better explanations but we're as confused as you. No one knows what she was thinking."

"We do not know," Jorge repeated and shook his head, continuing to hold back his anger.

"Mental illness is a huge problem," Paige spoke frankly.

"Why didn't she talk to someone?" Maria asked as she slowly turned toward Paige, who shook her head.

"Maria, suicide, it is a very selfish thing to do," Jorge suddenly felt his strength regain and Paige shot him a look. "I am sorry, that is not a nice thing to say but it is true. It leaves us trying to understand why and never having the answers."

"Maybe she left a note," Maria commented as if she hadn't noticed the anger in his voice.

"Not unless it's in her purse," Paige commented. "And the police have it"

"They went through it," Jorge continued. "I do not think there was anything. They only knew she was with us because our address was in her purse."

Maria didn't reply. In fact, she was quiet for the rest of the day, eventually going to bed early.

It wasn't until they were alone in their bedroom later that night, that Jorge finally opened up with the anger he had brewing since breaking the news to his daughter.

"I spend over a million dollars to save her from kidnappers only to have her jump in front of a fucking train," Jorge snapped as he removed his clothes and placed them on a chair. "She tortures me as much in death as her life."

"Jorge, I'm sure that deep down," Paige approached him and looked into his eyes. "That this is part of the mourning process. You were really upset when you found out earlier today."

"Earlier today, yes," Jorge agreed as he looked into her blue eyes. "But now, after seeing you crying for a woman who showed you absolutely no respect, after having to break the news to my daughter, my compassion is no longer there. It was like I say to Maria earlier, she committed a selfish act."

"She clearly wasn't well," Paige attempted to explain. "Maybe that's why she was always so miserable."

"Well, this could be true," Jorge agreed and nodded. "Yes, but that doesn't mean she had to do something so…horrendous to this family."

"But suicidal people,' Paige calmly tried to remind him. "They usually think that they are an inconvenience to their family. That they will be better off without them. Maybe that's what she thought."

Suddenly exhausted, Jorge ran a hand over his face.

"Did you get in touch with your aunt?" She cautiously asked.

Jorge let out a disgruntled laugh. "Oh yes, that went so well! She says it is my fault, of course, that I probably hired someone to push her. I tell her to call the fucking police herself if she does not believe."

"Jesus, that's harsh," Paige said with anger in her eyes. "So, what are your plans…are you planning the funeral?"

"No, she is," Jorge seemed to calm with this reply and leaned in to kiss her. "I will go to Mexico soon and bring Maria. You can come but I believe they may need you here, the election is days away."

"No!" Paige shook her head. "Jorge I will be with my family."

"Whatever you wish," He reached out for her hand. "But *mi amor,* I will certainly understand if you do no wish to join us. She was always so unkind to you."

"It's not her I'm going to be there for," Paige reminded him as she leaned in to kiss him.

CHAPTER

49

"The trip, it was too much for you, *mi amor*," Jorge announced shortly after they returned home from Mexico. Their flight had been early in the day allowing Jorge to find his footing again. "Why don't you take a nap?"

"I should go to the office to see if I can help Alec with anything," Paige commented but didn't budge from the bed. She had collapsed on it the moment they returned home. The trip to Mexico had been brutal. They agreed on the plane to not discuss the terrible ordeal upon arriving home but focus on the positive. "The election is tomorrow."

"I cannot believe it is finally here," Jorge commented as he sat on the side of the bed. "We have been talking about this election and Alec getting voted in for months. Now that it is time, I don't know, I guess I feel sort of apathetic. Is that the correct word?"

He turned to see Paige nodding. She looked as if she could barely keep her eyes opened.

Loud music suddenly blared from Maria's room and she began to sing along to a pop song with a questionable topic.

"Does she know what those terrible lyrics mean?" Jorge pointed toward the door as his forehead wrinkled. "I will tell her to turn it down so you can rest."

"No, I'm fine," Paige slowly sat up and yawned. "And if it were any other 11-year-old girl, I would say no, she has no idea what those lyrics mean but since it is Maria, she probably does."

"I do not like this thing where she grows up fast," Jorge complained.

"I believe that puts you in the same category as..probably most parents," Paige calmly replied with a grin. He couldn't help but to lean forward and kiss her. It was so instinctual.

"I like to think I'm cooler than most parents," Jorge replied. "I'm about to take over the Canadian pot industry, baby! I may not be a celebrity or prestigious doctor or lawyer, but I know how to put my mind to anything and make it mine."

"I can't argue that point," Paige commented and he began to laugh.

"I got eastern Canada, I got Ontario and later in the week, Jesús is heading west," Jorge commented as he looked into her eyes. "But he's already made some connections and it seems like this part will be easy."

"You already own so much," Paige whispered and reached out to touch his hand. "They know who they're dealing with."

"Yes, and me, I give them an offer they cannot refuse," Jorge insisted. "I'm not trying to fuck them over. I am fair. There have been some rumblings about me having the monopoly and that is fine. The government does not care. I create a lot of jobs, I pay fair rates, this is more than many industries in this country can say. Also, I would like to create opportunities for new Canadians looking for work, a special program, I think that would be good."

"I think that would be great," Paige lit up as she replied.

"It is only right, Paige," He replied. "There's a lot of people who are willing to work hard that need that chance."

Paige merely smiled and nodded. Her eyes were still tired and this worried him.

"I'm an immigrant too," Jorge reminded her. "I just happen to come here with a lot of money in my pocket. Not all are lucky. When I hear someone like Marco talk about his start in this city. It is hard for many."

"Now you're sounding like the politician," Paige teased.

"Is that a bad thing?" He asked while running a hand up her arm. "Do you think it would be awful if I were out there, doing what Alec is doing?"

"I can't picture you being as accommodating as him," Paige said and immediately laughed. "You're not exactly a 'Yes, ma'am, No, ma'am kind of person."

"Ah, but Paige, people do not want that," Jorge replied. "They want someone a forceful, powerful person, who will take charge. They want someone as passionate and fiery as me. Think about it. On election day, they are not voting for the king or queen of the prom, they want the pussycat who's actually a lion inside. But it must be those two things in equal balance. People want a gentleman who's obnoxious when it suits them."

"Or a *gentlewoman*," Paige corrected him.

"Yes, but unfortunately *mi amor,* that doesn't seem to be very common," Jorge reminded her.

"Well, look at how women are treated when they're in politics," Paige reminded him as she leaned closer. "Death threats, personal attacks, you name it."

"This is true," He said and watched her stretch and tilted his head. "Are you feeling better, *mi amor*? Perhaps you should stay home today and rest."

"Yes, I'm fine," Paige replied with her eyes watching him carefully as she opened her mouth to continue, only to hesitate as a tension filled the room. "I have something to tell you."

"Ok," Jorge moved closer to her, sensing a nervous energy between them. "Paige, you can tell me anything."

"I...I think I might be pregnant," Paige quietly said as tears formed in her eyes and Jorge felt his heart lift.

"Paige!" Jorge said as he grabbed her hand but suddenly couldn't speak.

"I'm not sure," She continued with a mixture of worry and sadness in her eyes. "I was always told that I couldn't conceive and if I did, the baby would never make it to term. I wasn't even sure I should tell you because...I'm not exactly 25 either."

"Paige, that does not matter," Jorge spoke nervously, briefly looking away and back into her eyes. "This is fabulous news, *mi amor!* Did I *not* tell you that you were pregnant?"

"I didn't think I was," Paige replied and shook her head in disbelief. "I was actually worried that something serious was wrong with me."

"You're scared," Jorge decided to calm down even though he was quite excited. "This here, it will be fine. Whatever happens, either way, it will be fine."

"I don't know how I feel," She admitted in a whisper. "I guess, either way, I'm terrified. I don't know if I can handle it if I am, and...I don't know..."

"Paige, do not worry," Jorge insisted and moved closer to her. "You must remember, this baby is a Hernandez and we are strong. The fact that the doctor says you could never conceive and yet, here you are maybe pregnant, this is proof."

She didn't reply her eyes were full of fear and uncertainty.

"I recently told Jolene that women are stronger than 100 bullets," Jorge continued and squeezed her hand. "But they must believe this and many, they do not."

Paige gave him an apprehensive smile.

"You must believe this Paige," Jorge said and hoped he had picked the right words as she slowly nodded. "This here is possibly a miracle and if not, well, then it is not meant to be. We can only accept what happens, does that make sense?"

She quietly nodded.

"But Paige, I will not lie," Jorge said as a grin lit up his face. "I am very excited with this news. Another Hernandez to carry on my name."

"You already have one in the next room," Paige reminded him as a smile lit up her face. "The pop star in the making."

"Nah nah…I mean a boy to carry the Hernandez name," Jorge commented sheepishly. "Because, I assure you, this child, it is a boy."

"We don't even know if I'm pregnant yet," Paige reminded him. "Let alone that it's a boy."

"You are, I told you this weeks ago," Jorge said and winked. "You will take a test to know for sure and it will be a boy."

"Your psychic powers tell you so?" Paige said as a smile released some of the stress from her face.

"*Mi amor,* I know," He said and pointed toward his chest as he sat up a bit straighter. "I am right."

"We'll see," Paige laughed as her eyes widened.

"Real men make boys," Jorge said while Paige rolled her eyes.

"And Maria?"

"I was drunk and high that night, *mi amor,*" Jorge reminded her as he leaned in to kiss her. "So it's different."

Paige laughed.

"Thank you for this beautiful anniversary gift," He whispered and kissed her again.

"We don't know yet," She whispered. "So please, don't tell anyone."

"It will be our secret, *mi amor.*"

Paige left for the drug store shortly after while Jorge thought about the news. It was like an electrical charge flowing through his body, sending little shocks to his heart for the rest of the day. It reminded him of when he first met Paige, a year earlier, those first days of uncertainty, when love put him on an unexplainable high that was unlike anything he had ever experienced.

In truth, he was as nervous as Paige but it was necessary that he never show her this side. She needed him to be the lion now, not the pussycat.

While she was gone, he received a call from Diego that he and Michael were on their way over with some news. It would be hard to focus on anything but Jorge knew he had no choice. For now, no one could know this secret.

Maria continued to sing upstairs, having no breaks since returning home. Jorge decided to make some coffee, even though that would be the last thing he needed with conflicting feelings of excitement and fear. What if Paige wasn't pregnant, would she be disappointed? Then again, if she was, would she be worried? *Should* she be worried? Were they too old for a new baby?

Diego and Michael arrived shortly after their call. He sensed things were good between them, although he had some doubts about Diego getting involved with a cop; no matter how dirty. Once again, it was something he would simply monitor. At this point, it was clear that Michael was aware of what would happen if he were to go up against them.

Although the two gave their condolences, it wasn't long before they switched gears and started to talk business.

"Michael, he got news," Diego spoke dramatically, his arms swinging in the air. Everyone seemed to be ignoring the loud, booming voice of Maria as she continued to sing upstairs. "Wait till you hear this."

"Remember how you wanted to find out when the white supremacy meeting was taking place?" Michael asked and it was clear there was a different look in his eyes than when they first met. Had the shooting changed him? Was he being reborn into a stronger man?

"Yes, I thought it was pushed aside because of the election?" Jorge replied. "Why? You got something?"

"He got the place, time, everything!" Diego abruptly answered for him, leaving Michael to grin.

"I got all the info," Michael continued. "They were waiting till after the election. It's because even though we got Harley out, they still seem confident that they'll get a few of their own people in. This will be a victory meeting along with making plans for what's next."

Jorge simply nodded and listened.

"It's going to be all the top guys," Diego continued.

"The top guys for *this* particular group," Michael reminded him and Diego shrugged. "There are more than one but this one, it is the most powerful in this province, if not the country."

"And they meet?

"Oddly enough it's going to be the day after the election," Michael said as his eyes widened. "They want to get their game plan together immediately except they call it a 'family reunion'"

Jorge nodded.

"We gotta do something," Diego jumped in again. "They're getting together."

"Do not worry," Jorge said and nodded. "We *will* be doing something. We gotta get the rest over here for a meeting."

"Even Jolene?" Diego raised an eyebrow.

"Jolene, Chase, Jesús…"

"He's flying back right now," Diego checked his phone and began to tap the screen. "Or he should be. I will make sure he knows."

"We will meet tonight to go over the details," Jorge said. "Where is the *family reunion* to take place?"

"It's out of the city, in a cottage area," Michael replied. "Away from everyone."

"Perfecto," Jorge replied with a grin. "I know what we must do."

CHAPTER

50

We need passion in our lives. It's what gives us butterflies while sending a sense of excitement to our soul. It's anticipation on fire. We can easily be lost in our world, tied down with the problems and negativity and fears that surround us but underneath it all, passion is always there. It sits and it waits with a patience that many of us can never fully understand. However, without it, we are merely compliant machines waiting to die.

The thing about passion is that once you've gone so far, you can never go back. It is like going from a fast food meal to a fine dining experience; once your palate has experienced sheer perfection, how can you return to greasy fries and a substandard burger without a sense of disappointment? For Jorge Hernandez, this was the theme of his life. Having always lived on the edge, it was difficult to ever return to the center. A desire that surges through your body can never be satisfied by the simple life. The key is to get close to the fire without going up in flames.

One of the most beautiful experiences is when you find friends who share your values and passions. Some would refer to them as your *tribe*. Although not necessarily related by blood, a family was something you found along the way. These were the people by your side when you needed them as you would be by their side when they needed you. Jorge Hernandez was lucky to have found his tribe and together they were unstoppable.

"I gotta hand it to you," Diego announced at the private victory party after the election. "You were right about Athas. The people, they love him! I don't even think it would've mattered if Harley was still in the race."

"*Si, amigo,*" Jorge agreed with a slow nod. "But for me, I not only wanted to see him humiliated but degraded. It is important that a man knows where he fits in the food chain and now, Fulton Harley will be surrounded by bottom feeders."

Diego twisted his lips into an evil grin.

"This is only one of many steps I plan to make in the political world," Jorge gestured toward Alec Athas. "That man, I own him now and unlike other politicians that I have…influence over, this one, he will take orders from me. He won't be able to piss without my permission."

"So what's in it for him?" Diego asked.

"He got a great job," Jorge said and began to nod. "A nice pension down the line and some influence and status. He can still push for his dreams but it will be my dreams he will live."

"Ah yes," Diego replied and shook his head. "A puppet."

"We are all puppets to someone," Jorge reminded him. "You just must choose carefully who's pulling your strings."

Turning his head, Jorge saw Paige approaching and the two shared a powerful look. Wearing a simple, black dress, she still stood out in the room. He quickly swooped her into his arms and gave her a kiss.

"What's that about?" Diego asked suspiciously.

"Love, Diego! Love,"Jorge glanced at him with a grin on his face. "Like your new boyfriend and by the way, he going to be ok tomorrow night?"

Paige leaned in as if to hear his reply.

"Yeah, he'll be fine," Diego assured them both. "He was a little freaked about that old lady."

"You mean the one that no one gave a fuck about?" Jorge bluntly asked and Paige began to laugh. "She was fucking dead for days, no one even noticed her gone. What does that tell you?"

"Rumor has it that her son collected a lot of money after she died," Paige gently added. "Maybe you did him a favor."

Jorge didn't reply but merely raised an eyebrow with a smirk on his face.

Don Stumples wouldn't enter his mind again until the following evening when he arrived at the place near where the white supremacists were to meet. It was a secluded area in rural Ontario that had seen a consistent population decline over the years and now, was mainly a popular cottage area for those wanting to escape the city. It would be a great place to carry on an affair, fall off the grid or if you were a 'white nationalist' group, to conduct a meeting.

"So, this here, is where these nazis fucks gather to speak of hatred?" Jorge commented on the chilly, fall evening after getting out of his SUV. Paige was quickly by his side, while on the other side of him, Michael and Diego got out of a Lexus. Chase and Jolene got a drive with Jesús who parked on the other side. "I guess it makes sense, in the middle of fucking nowhere."

"They don't tend to like too much attention," Paige quietly commented and Jorge gave her one last pleading look; they had a long dispute on whether she was to take part. However, before he could say anything, it was Diego that spoke up.

"The way we're fucking dressed," He said referring to their casual appearance as the group gathered together. "You'd think we were about to start a campfire and roast marshmallows."

"Something is gonna be roasting tonight," Jorge insisted as he glanced around, noting the kind of gun each had brought. Chase was the only one without one. "But it will not be fucking marshmallows."

Beside him, Jesús laughed and took over the conversation.

"Everything is in place, sir," He commented and glanced northward. "They are in the cabin."

"No time like the present," Jorge commented.

"How many are there?" Chase asked while beside him, Jolene seemed quite subdued.

"Not many," Michael answered. "It is only the cream of the crop tonight."

"Ten? Maybe fifteen?" Jorge asked.

Michael nodded. "They got to figure out their plan."

"Chase," Jorge turned in his direction. "Gasoline is spread?"

"All around the cabin," Chase replied. "But we gotta get out of here fast cause when it starts, it's going to move fast."

"*We* will move faster," Jorge insisted. "They may run but they won't get far. Then the fire, it will take care of the rest."

No one replied.

"The fire index, it is quite high sir," Jesús reminded him. "People are being warned."

"But people, they don't listen," Jorge commented and shared a look with his longtime associate. "They do as they please. At least, that is how it will look in the news later. Fortunately, these things, they are never traced. The fire, it will destroy everything but in this town, there isn't much to destroy."

"Are we beginning soon?" Jolene spoke nervously. "It is getting dark now."

Jorge nodded and everyone trudged ahead, eventually moving into place.

It started with a match; so simple and yet, it began a fire that would burn a group that thrived on hate. The elders of the movement, they helped keep racism alive and while others would continue, the strongest gathered to find a way to incite anger toward minorities in the country. It was a way to draw in the weak, the gullible and the angry into their extremist world, creating the illusion that immigrants were what threatened their way of life. It was ridiculous to most but to those who fell for it, did so with mislead passion that drove them to meet in the middle of nowhere to discuss their twisted ideology.

The ring of fire tightly surrounded the cabin starting gently but quickly grew in both size and force, causing a parade of white men to rush outside. The initial shock created a vulnerability that made them easy targets as a shower of bullets met the panicked group. Some fell quickly while others took longer but whether or not the shots killed them didn't matter; in the end, it was the fire that would be the insurance policy for Jorge Hernandez. Those who died from their bullets were lucky. Burning to death would be the most excruciating way to perish.

Jolene and Paige were perhaps the most ambitious, both capable of making the 'perfect' shot, they worked together with a pristine timing and accuracy to shoot several of the men despite the increasing smoke. However, it was when that fat fuck Stumples waddled out behind the others that Jorge found personal satisfaction in pulling the trigger and watching him going down like a fucking farm animal and if he could have, he would have slaughtered him like a butchered pig.

"We gotta go!" Chase could be heard yelling over the bullets, as the smoke became thicker. No one else was leaving the cabin. Even if anyone stayed inside, they would never make it out alive. The fire was moving in to absorb the bodies that lay on the ground.

"Let's go!" Jorge yelled and glanced back at the fire. The heat from the flames could be felt on his face, the smell of death began to fill his lungs. The smoke was heavy as they all rushed toward their vehicles, some were coughing and Jorge pulled his jacket up over his face to avoid breathing in any smoke. He grabbed Paige's hand and pulled her forward, his eyes burning now, he felt relief when they both got into the SUV. The other two vehicles had started and already were racing down the road, while he wasted no time hitting the ignition and shifting into drive.

His heart racing, Jorge was finally able to catch his breath as they flew down the rough, country road, the fire behind him yet the smoke continued to follow. His focus on keeping up with the others, he finally felt some relief when they made it to the highway. Reassured when met with some traffic, he reached out to touch Paige.

"Oh, *mi amor,* for a moment, I was not sure we were going to get away fast enough," Jorge commented and it wasn't until he heard her whimper in reply that he turned to look at his wife. She was crying. At first, he didn't understand what was going on until he saw the blood.

Immediately pulling over to the side of the road, the others almost out of view, he abruptly put the SUV into park while his brain grasped what was happening. Paige was bleeding. His wife had been shot. He felt his heart pounding in fear as he touched the scarlet stain on her jacket. He could barely breathe. The original satisfaction he felt upon leaving the monstrous scene was slipping away as fear filled his soul.

"Oh my God! Paige," He started to panic and quickly scanned her body. "Is there anywhere else."

"No, just my arm," She cried, her eyes full of panic.

"Ok," Jorge managed to calm himself enough to think straight. "We must find something to tie..oh my God, I knew you shouldn't have come with us..."

Pulling off his leather jacket, he quickly threw it aside and pulled off his shirt to wrap around Paige's arm but the blood quickly soaked the material causing him to panic. His heart raced while tears filled his eyes and he silently prayed. This was bad. This was really bad.

"We must get you to the hospital," Jorge said as he reached in the back seat to grab a sweater that belonged to Maria and wrapping it around and felt some relief when blood didn't fill it as quickly. Calming down, he glanced up to see Diego and Michael returning, doing a U-turn and pulling up behind him. He silently thanked God.

"No, we can't," Paige whimpered. "We can't get the police involved."

Jorge opened his mouth but no words would come out. Just then Diego pulled the door opened.

"I saw you stop and.." He suddenly halted when he saw the blood. Michael was right behind him but unlike Diego, a strength filled his face and he immediately took over.

"Jorge, take Paige in the back seat," He commanded then directed his attention to Diego. "Take my phone, look up someone under the name Trish. Call her. Tell her Michael has something for her. She'll know what I mean."

Without asking questions, both did as instructed while Michael jumped in the driver's seat.

"Diego, follow us!" He yelled out the window and barely gave him time to get back into his own car when Michael turned on the four-way flashers and accelerated at an incredible rate.

In the backseat, Jorge pulled his wife close, putting pressure on the wound, he felt her shaking and grabbed his jacket that had been tossed aside earlier to place it over her torso. He tightened his grip around her as she silently cried in pain as the SUV sped toward the city.

"Where are we going?" He finally asked, feeling vulnerable yet relieved that Michael was there to take over. "Will we be much longer?"

"I know someone," Michael replied as he sped down the near-empty highway. "She will fix this for us. We'll get there soon."

"We can't have the police find out," Paige spoke, her voice shaking. "There will be too many questions."

"Paige, I do not care," Jorge insisted. "As long as you are ok, I don't give a fuck about the police."

"She's right," Michael insisted from the front seat. "But this woman, she can handle it and keep it off the record. She's helped me out in similar situations in the past."

"Someone shot?" Jorge asked.

"Me," Michael replied and glanced in the rearview mirror.

Jorge nodded.

"When you're a cop," Michael replied. "Trust me, there are a lot of fucking questions and some of them, you don't want to answer."

Jorge nodded and Paige whimpered again.

"*Mi amor*, please be strong," Jorge said as he stared into her eyes. She nodded and he kissed her on the forehead, closing his eyes.

The drive was fast but yet, it felt like they were going in slow motion. His fears were strong and he wondered if hers were the same. Jorge opened his eyes and swore at that moment, he would never let her be in danger again. He would do anything to keep her safe.

"I saw one guy with a gun when he ran out," Michael spoke suddenly causing Jorge to come out of his trance, in time to see a string of firetrucks flying past them. "I didn't think he shot at us but with all the smoke…."

"I did not see until we were on the road," Jorge confessed, his voice much calmer than he had felt. "There was blood, it was everywhere."

"That doesn't mean anything," Michael reminded him.

"I'll be fine," Paige whispered. "I promise."

Relief filled his body when they finally arrived at their destination. It was a small building on a quiet street; it took him a moment to realize that it was a vet. Jorge cringed. They were taking his wife to a *vet*.

"Is this for real?" He asked suddenly feeling weak.

"She can do it," Michael insisted as if reading his mind. "I promise you."

They were barely parked when a young woman wearing glasses rushed out the door and toward the SUV. Everything suddenly happened very quickly. Jorge grabbed Paige and rushed her inside the building with the young woman right behind, asking questions. It wasn't until Michael's friend was examining her that Jorge could finally breathe. He stood aside in anticipation as she removed the homemade tourniquet and cut the sleeve off Paige's sweater to check the wound.

"It just grazed her arm," She replied after a few minutes of careful inspection. "She's going to be ok."

"Thank you," Jorge replied in a quiet voice that he almost didn't recognize. "Please do whatever you must do."

"I have to examine the area a little more thoroughly and make sure it's clean," She replied. "If you can give us a few minutes?"

"Ok," He looked at Paige and saw hope in her eyes and with that, he felt hope too. "I am going to tell Diego and Michael. I will be outside, *mi amor.*"

His legs felt wobbly as he made his way into the waiting room, where Michael and Diego sat. Both jumped up when they saw him, Diego quickly launching into questions.

"Is she ok? What's going on? Who…"

"She is fine," He confirmed. "The bullet just grazed her arm."

Diego's eyes filled with tears as he reached over and hugged Jorge.

"That's what I suspected," Michael awkwardly replied as Diego let go of Jorge and wiped away a tear. "I'm glad she's going to be ok."

"I thank you, my friend," Jorge reached out and shook his hand. "Without you, I do not know what I would do."

"No, I…I just brought her here," Micheal insisted.

"Still, you were there when I needed your help," Jorge continued to grasp his hand. "If you ever need *anything,* I will be there for you too."

Michael nodded as Jorge let go of his hand and turned toward Diego. "How did you know to come back? On the highway?"

Diego shook his head. "I just knew."

Jorge nodded and glanced toward the bathroom. "I want to throw some water on my face."

It wasn't until he was in the bathroom with the door closed that he could smell it. The smoke from the fire infused his hair and filled his lungs. He leaned against the sink and closed his eyes for a moment, only to suddenly open them again and look into the mirror. He saw a man with dried blood on his naked torso, face and neck but with a special light in his eyes. It was at that moment that a grin eased across his lips as Jorge Hernandez realized that he had won again.

The angels may sing in heaven but here on earth, the devil will laugh.

Can't get enough of the Hernandez series? Don't forget to check out We're All Animals, Always be a Wolf, The Devil is Smooth Like Honey and A Devil Named Hernandez. Go to www.mimaonfire. com and sign up for the newsletter to keep up to date on the next book in this series!

Love the book? Write a review.

Thank you,

Mima
xoxo

Printed in the United States
By Bookmasters